# GAUL IN CÆSAR'S TIME

Miles

| 0 | 50 | 100 | 200 | 250 |

Kilometers

| 0 | 50 | 100 | 200 | 300 | 400 |

ENUS (R. Meuse)

SABINI (Sabinus' Camp)

RONES

RONIS (Cicero's Camp)

ENNA (Ardennes)

TREVERI

Meuse

VOSEGUS M. (Vosges)

JURA M.

RHENUS (R. Rhine)

SUEBI

DANUVIUS (R. Danube)

GERMANY

VESONTIO (Besançon)

ANI

HELVETII

ES

BROGES

CISALPINE

L. BENACUS (Lago di Garda)

BRIXIA (Brescia)

VERONA

MEDIOLANUM (Milan)

GAUL

PADUS (R. Po)

RAVENNA

GENOA

ARIMINUM (Rimini)

LUCCA

RUBICON R.

GAUL

NICAEA (Nice)

ASSILIA (Marseilles)

ROMA (Rome)

# THE SCARLET MANTLE

*Maisie Wheatley*

# THE
# SCARLET MANTLE
### A NOVEL OF JULIUS CAESAR

## BY W.G. HARDY

MACMILLAN OF CANADA
TORONTO

**Canadian Cataloguing in Publication Data**

Hardy, William George, 1895–
The scarlet mantle

ISBN 0-7705-1567-3

I. Title.

PS8515.A67S33     C813′.5′2     C77-001311-2
PR9199.3.H37S33

Printed in Canada for
The Macmillan Company of Canada
70 Bond Street, Toronto
M5B 1X3

TO
HELEN, GEORGE, AND MARGARET
MY CHILDREN
SO LOVED

# ACKNOWLEDGEMENTS

My special thanks to Margaret Coleman Johnson, my assistant editor, whose intuitive intelligence and perceptive eye have left their imprint upon these pages; and to my secretary, Kay M. Baert, who typed this manuscript with hands and head and heart. Also my warm appreciation to Douglas M. Gibson, editorial director, for his fine-handed editing, to George W. Gilmour, president of Macmillan of Canada, for his unswerving support, and also to Bob Stuart, Bella Pomer, Rick Miller, and other members of George Gilmour's staff. Finally, my gratitude to Hugh P. Kane, former president of Macmillan of Canada, whose vision and enthusiasm inspired me to complete this novel.

W. G. H.
*Edmonton*
November 1977

## ACKNOWLEDGEMENTS

# AUTHOR'S NOTE

The primary sources of *The Scarlet Mantle* are Caesar's *Gallic Wars* and *Civil War*. Secondary sources are Suetonius, *The Twelve Caesars,* Plutarch's *Parallel Lives,* and Appian's *History of Rome*. For interpretations of the people and events of the period, a number of authorities have been consulted, including Ferrero's *Life of Caesar* and Mommsen's *History of Rome* (both in translation), as well as the works of more recent historians. The author has been fortunate enough to have travelled in France, Italy, and Greece, and to have visited many of the sites and places described in the book. It should be emphasized, however, that *The Scarlet Mantle* is not a history, but a novel.   W.G.H.

# PRINCIPAL CHARACTERS

## ROMANS

Gaius Julius **Caesar**, b. 102 B.C., patrician but leader of the "Populists" (Populares — People's Party). In 60 B.C. organized the "First Triumvirate" of Crassus, Pompey, and himself. Consul 59 B.C., Proconsul of the three Gauls and Illyricum, 58-49 B.C.

Marcus Licinius **Crassus**, b. ca. 116 B.C. In 71 B.C. defeated Spartacus and his slave army. Wealthiest of the Romans. A leader of the Populists but influential with financiers (the "knights") and the Senate. Killed by the Parthians in 53 B.C. after his defeat at Carrhae.

Gnaeus Pompeius Magnus (**Pompey**), b. 106 B.C. In 67 B.C. cleared pirates from Mediterranean; in 66-62 B.C. subjugated Asia Minor and Syria. Murdered in Egypt in 48 B.C. after his defeat at Pharsalus.

Marcus Tullius **Cicero**, b. 106 B.C. Foremost Roman orator and spokesman for Italy's middle class. Consul in 63 B.C. when he crushed Catilinarian conspiracy. Exiled by Clodius in 58 B.C. Brother, Quintus, a legate in Caesar's army.

Publius **Clodius** Pulcher, a Claudian who in 59-58 B.C. organized citizens of Rome into electoral guilds and controlled the streets of Rome. Killed by Milo, a rival gangster, in 52 B.C.

**Fulvia**, wife of Clodius, then of Gaius Scribonius Curio (killed in Africa in 49 B.C.), and finally of Marcus Antonius.

Marcus Antonius (**Antony**), b. ca. 83 B.C. Led Roman cavalry when Romans restored Ptolemy the Flute-Player to Egyptian throne. Joined Caesar in Gaul and became his principal legate.

Titus **Labienus**, Caesar's second-in-command, who defected to the Conservatives in 49 B.C.

Marcus Porcius **Cato**, Marcus Calpurnius **Bibulus** (married to Porcia, Cato's daughter), Lucius Domitius **Ahenobarbus** (married to Cato's sister) — three principal leaders of the "Irreconcilables" of the Conservative nobles who opposed and hated Caesar.

**Servilia** — Caesar's mistress. Half-sister to Cato. Married to Marcus Junius Brutus, a Populist noble put to death treacherously by Pompey in 78 B.C., then to Decimus Junius Silanus (consul, 63 B.C., and a Populist). Through her salon, she achieved political influence in Rome.

### GAULS (names Latinized)

**Dumnorix**—Aeduan prince who from 58 B.C. opposed Caesar.

**Ambiorix** — Co-king of the Eburones, a tribe in northeastern Gaul. Chief leader of Gallic revolt in winter of 54-53 B.C. Massacred a legion and a half. Is thought to have escaped into Germany.

**Acco** — Prince of the Senones. Flogged to death by Caesar, autumn 53 B.C., at Durocortum (Reims).

**Commius** — Made king of the Atrebates by Caesar. Joined Vercingetorix' revolt in 52 B.C. Escaped to Germany. Finally crossed to Britain to become king of those Atrebates who had migrated thither.

**Indutiomarus** — Claimant to throne of the Treverans, a tribe along the Rhine, but rejected by Caesar, so joined in revolt of 54-53 B.C. Killed by Labienus.

**Vercingetorix**—Arvernian prince, 52 B.C. Led the great Gallic revolt which almost expelled Caesar. Taken prisoner at Alesia, confined in Rome, strangled during Caesar's triumph in 46 B.C.

### OTHERS

**Antipater**—Chief minister of the Jews and ally of Cleopatra.

**Cleopatra** — Co-heir with her younger brother-husband of Ptolemy the Flute Player. Expelled from Egypt by Pothinus, but joined Caesar as his mistress. Desire for power her ruling passion.

**Pothinus** — Eunuch chief minister of Ptolemy the Flute-Player. When Ptolemy died, president of the Regency Council during minority of the young Ptolemy.

PART ONE
## 54-49 BC

# THE FAILURE
# OF SUCCESS

# CHAPTER I

I T WAS A MID-MORNING OF EARLY JULY in the seven-hundredth year of Rome. From a cloudless sky the sun stared down at the blue Mediterranean and the lands and cities that rimmed it. In Alexandria, at the northwesternmost mouth of the Nile, the throngs in the broad avenues were sweltering in the heat. But in the palace of the Ptolemies, sprawled along the eastern horn of the Great Harbour, a cooling breeze from the north flowed through the main courtyard into the pillared throne-room. There the princess Cleopatra, slim and rounded, her vivid face scornful, stood among a gaggle of courtiers and watched her father, the Ptolemy, waddle like a perambulating bowl of jelly toward the dais at the farther end.

Purple robes swathed him. Bands of gold, inset with rubies, circled his flabby arms. The double crown of Egypt wobbled on his head as, laboriously, he mounted the steps of the dais and swung his belly around to seat himself on his golden throne. Behind him two slave-girls, naked to the waist, were swaying ostrich-feather fans rhythmically. The Ptolemy wiped sweat from his forehead. With a pudgy, beringed finger he beckoned his eunuch minister, Pothinus, to stand beside him. Then his eyes, shrewd prunes almost hidden in pouches of fat, surveyed the room.

Cleopatra glanced this way and that at the giggling, gossiping men and women. Then, eyes downcast, she composed her face into a mask. The Alexandrians, in derision at her father's harem of curly-headed boys, called this Ptolemy "the Flute-Player". Five years back they had vomited him forth, and Cleopatra's elder sister, Berenice, had taken the throne. But when, a little over a year ago, a Roman army under Gabinius had brought back her father, he had had Berenice strangled. No, Cleopatra told

1

herself, one should never underestimate this Ptolemy. At fifteen, she had already learned to walk as if on peahens' eggs.

And then, she heard what they had all been awaiting, the tramp of hobnailed boots in the courtyard. The room fell silent. Cleopatra's eyes, everybody's eyes, turned toward the entrance. Out in the courtyard there was a barked command and a single thud as if one gigantic foot had halted. Another command, a thump of boots and spear-butts, then in they marched, the real masters of Egypt—Gabinius, a solid hogshead of a man, and, a half-step behind and to his right, the brilliant leader of his cavalry, Marcus Antonius, usually, as Cleopatra knew, called Antony.

Herculean, Cleopatra thought, staring at Antony as the two Romans, without a glance to right or left, strode down the long room. A head taller than Gabinius. Broad brow, aquiline nose, full lips, chin firm, limbs like tree trunks. Herculean in his appetites, too, the Alexandrians said. Huge dishes of fish, fowl, and meat. Tankard on tankard of wine. And women, one, two or three at a time, they said. Big-breasted and wanton, or pert, coy, and lissome, it was all one to him. She wished that she had met him, just once. Men! She could manage them.

The Romans had reached the throne-dais. They halted in one precise motion. They saluted negligently, almost contemptuously.

And her father! Last night at the banquet, soaked in wine, he had boasted that, this time, when these Romans came to make their farewells, he would not stir from his throne. Let them bow to him. Was he not the Ptolemy?

But now, look at him! On his feet, stumbling down the steps of the dais, arms outstretched. Babbling. Bobbing his head. And the two Romans—standing there carelessly, almost sneeringly, as if the Ptolemy of ancient Egypt were a nothing.

Power! Cleopatra thought, clenching her hands. To have power such as that! Sometime, somehow, she'd have power. It would have to be through a Roman. Rome ruled the world. That Antony, for instance, standing there, looking down at her father as if the Ptolemy were a beetle or, rather, a gibbering monkey.

2

Though Antony or even Gabinius, she remembered, were of no importance compared to the three men who held Rome in the folds of their togas — Pompey the Great, Crassus the billionaire and the new governor of Syria, and Julius Caesar, the general who had conquered the Gauls. Now, if sometime she could meet one of them —

She became aware that her father's voice had risen and that the courtiers were listening. Unclenching her fists, she listened, too.

"More legionaries," her father was demanding shrilly in his heavily accented Latin. "I must have more legionaries."

"We're leaving you a legion — ten full cohorts," Gabinius pointed out.

"If Rabirius raises the taxes again, there'll be riots," Pothinus put in, pretending anxiety.

Cleopatra knew, everyone knew, that the financier Rabirius had come from Rome to take control of the Egyptian economy so that he could collect the enormous sums — thousands on thousands of gold talents — that he had loaned the Ptolemy, wherewith to bribe the Romans to set him back on his throne. She watched her father gesticulate wildly.

"Riots! Send me another legion — half a legion anyway," he begged. "Five more cohorts."

"One Roman," Antony cut in, "can slash the guts out of a thousand Egyptians."

"You'll have to make do," Gabinius decided. "One legion is enough."

Cleopatra saw her father and Pothinus exchange a quick glance even as they continued to expostulate. Didn't these Romans realize what every courtier in the throne-room knew — that the Ptolemy was preparing an excuse to expel Rabirius before he collected the money?

Probably they did, she conceded. After all, Gabinius had got his money. Antony, too.

As she thought this, Gabinius interrupted her father.

"Enough," he said abruptly. "It's decided, Ptolemaios Neos Dionysos. Our ship to Antioch waits. Hail and farewell, Ptolemaios."

He saluted. Antony saluted. Turning, the Romans marched back to the entrance, the light glinting on their armour, leaving the Ptolemy staring after them. Power, Cleopatra thought again fiercely. She'd need Egypt with which to bargain, if and when her father died. She herself was a possible heir, though there was that sickly brother of hers — only nine years old now — and if there were some way to get rid of him —

She realized suddenly that her father had turned to scan the room once more. If he — or Pothinus — had any idea of what she was thinking she would be dragged to a dungeon. Hurriedly she turned to the man next to her, her Greek tutor, Apollodorus.

"Talk to me," she said. "Anything. Just talk."

Out in the courtyard, Gabinius paused. "So you've decided not to join Crassus."

Antony nodded.

"A big army. Wish I had it. There'll be pickings once he's through the Parthians to India."

Antony shrugged his shoulders. "I'm a cavalryman. Crassus has his son Publius in command of the Gallic horse Caesar sent. No real chance for me."

"So after Antioch, what?"

"Back to Rome, with you. Then — well, I've a letter from Caesar. He's a cousin, after all."

"Think you'll like Gaul? After Syria and Alexandria?" Gabinius glanced at him sideways. "Gallic women won't be, shall we say, so expert."

"Might be fun to have to wrestle." Antony glanced at the sun. "Well, shall we go?"

"Right." Gabinius turned to the centurion. "March us to the ship, Rufus."


## 2


As the centurion saluted and turned to his men, across the eastern Mediterranean, in Apamea in the Parthian sector of Upper Mesopotamia, Publius Crassus came into the house his father

4

had commandeered. There was a frown on the young man's face. They had captured the town at daybreak. His father had immediately sent a couple of cohorts to seize the temple treasures and to dump them here. Now, at an hour already past mid-morning, instead of looking after his troops as Caesar would have done, he was pacing about the main room, watching half a dozen secretaries sort and make lists of the loot. Publius cleared his throat.

"I've posted sentries and guards," he said.

"Good, good," his father answered. He picked up a golden goblet, beautifully inset with emeralds and sapphires. "Look at that, lad. Worth a fortune."

Publius took a step forward. "You'll have to come out and take charge, father. The troops are getting out of hand. Looting. Raping."

"Be careful," his father shouted to a secretary, putting down the goblet hurriedly, "that's fragile."

The secretary cautiously set down an ostrich egg banded with gold.

"Father. The troops."

"See to it, there's a good lad." His father, scanty white hair plastered to his head, hurried over to a pile of brocades. "Look at these, lad. Stitched with gold thread, every one of them."

Not like Caesar, young Publius thought unwillingly. To Caesar money was merely something to use. Yet Marcus Licinius Crassus, triumvir, had been a good general in his time, the man called on by a terrified Senate to crush Spartacus and his slave-army.

That was years ago. Now, here he was, gloating over this treasure. Babbling last night, every night, about the riches of India. What he ought to be doing was to prepare for the Parthian reaction to his incursion into their territory.

A secretary had emptied a sack of gold coins onto a table. His father sat down to count them, mumbling to himself and putting them into glittering piles.

"Millions here," he gloated. "Millions, lad."

Turning on his heel, Publius stamped from the house. Outside, a brassy sun beat down on the white-baked houses and the pavement of the narrow street. Publius paused to stare at his troop of yellow-haired Gauls, a horse champing at its bit there, another tossing its head, still another pawing at the pavement. Until he had led them to join his father's army, they and he had served under Caesar; and at that instant he felt a sudden wrenching nostalgia for Gaul, its misty rains, its deep forests, rolling plains, abrupt heights, rushing torrents, and broad, placid rivers. Why was he here in this land of sun-smitten sand and white-plastered, almost treeless towns?

Publius knew why. At the Conference of Lucca in North Italy, two springs ago, where the Roman world had been split up between its three masters, Caesar had got for himself five more years of supreme command in Gaul. To win that much he had had to concede to his sulky and restive son-in-law, Pompey the Great, the two Spains and the five legions there, as well as the right to stay in Italy and control it. To reconcile Crassus to the arrangement, he had been given Syria and an army, also for five years. It was common knowledge that Pompey and Crassus disliked each other.

"Pompey's always flirting with the Conservatives," Caesar had pointed out to Publius. "Cato, Domitius, Bibulus—they'd like to have my head, and every now and then Pompey considers joining them. He'd like to be respectable and constitutional—with himself at the head of the Republic, naturally. This way I have him in a nutcracker between my Gallic legions and your father's army in Syria."

Clever, it had seemed. Yet, perhaps, not so clever if Caesar were to see his fellow-triumvir at this moment. Caesar, face like an eagle, quick, decisive . . .

There was a fresh burst of yelling from the northeastern part of the town. Smoke pouring up, too. Publius leaped onto his horse. With a wave to his men to follow, he galloped down the street.

6

# 3

As Publius rode toward the looting and the burning, far to the west in Italy, on a hill near Arpinum, Marcus Cicero, famous orator and leader of Italy's middle class, walked down the steps of the sunken rock-garden of his villa. Along the upper terraces, interlaced branches of plane-trees and elms shut out the sun. On the lower stages, amid the arbutus and the honeysuckle, beds of chrysanthemums, marigolds, and white and red roses bloomed. In the centre as he reached the bottom of the steps, a cupid eternally poured cascading water into a limpid pool.

The orator sniffed the cool, fragrant air. He settled himself on a stone bench. Then he broke the seal and unrolled the letter one of Caesar's couriers had just brought. It was from his younger brother, Quintus, now a general on Caesar's staff but really there as a hostage for his, Marcus', good behaviour. Apart from the usual greetings, the letter gave instructions about the villa which Quintus was having built from the loot he had already amassed in Gaul. At the end was a note that he would shortly be sailing with Caesar to Britain.

Britain! Cicero went back to the date of the letter. It had been written twenty-six days ago from Portus Itius on the northwestern coast of Gaul. Britain! That misty, far-off island, a place of mystery and danger.

The orator let the letter drop to his lap, his sensitive face furrowed with thought. If anything happened to Quintus . . .

Yet after Lucca — all his hopes of an alliance between Pompey and the Conservative nobles smashed — he had had to agree to Quintus joining Caesar's staff. In modern Rome words were peashooters against swords.

Cicero picked up the letter, rose, and went around the cupid to the steps, reflecting that, since that time, Caesar had courted him. He had, for example, lent him money, and had constantly praised his orations and his books.

Halfway up the steps he paused. Quintus and he, he remembered suddenly, playing as youngsters in that dark but friendly house in Arpinum. Now, Quintus sailing to Britain and he, at fifty-two, the most important politician in Rome, retired, his only function to write. What unlooked-for paths life or destiny traced out for one!

He went on up the steps, head down.

# 4

As Cicero walked up the steps of his garden, to the south, on a pergola of his villa near Naples, Pompey the Great was reclining on a sofa, his gouty leg stretched out to rest on a bench. Across from him, his wife, Julia, Caesar's daughter, sat on a richly ornamented stool. She was heavy with child, and her fingers were busy with her knitting. Beside her, on a table of citron-wood, was her father's latest letter.

The pergola projected outward from the villa, purple clematis and climbing roses entwining its sides and open-timbered roof, and a cooling breeze from the Tyrrhenian Sea drifting through it. A puff of air threatened to roll Caesar's letter from the table. Julia reached out to put a bronze statuette of Venus Anadyomene on it.

"Dear father," she thought. "He always takes time to write, no matter how busy he is."

She glanced across at her husband. His eyes were closed and he was snoring.

"I must make him cut down on his food," she told herself. "But he loves it so much, poor dear."

A tender smile curved her lips, as she resumed her knitting, a tiny wool helmet for the child. Her marriage five years ago had been a political one, she at that time a girl of nineteen and Pompey forty-nine. She had heard, too, all the scandal about her father and Pompey's previous wife, Mucia. In fact, her husband had divorced Mucia because of her father. But men were like that and, in any case, her marriage had turned out well. Pompey was kind and considerate and very much in love while she — well, she'd known how to keep the peace between the two men who mattered to her, her father and her husband.

8

The child kicked within her. She stopped her knitting, shifted her body to get comfortable, and looked down over Naples. The city was rose and russet as it dropped down its hill to meet the blue curve of the bay. Her eyes followed the curve to the fronting cliffs of Sorrentum. In between was the tall cone of Vesuvius — an extinct volcano, they said — with crops and vineyards tumbling down its slopes in a green torrent to the blue water. On the gulf, coloured sails, scarlet and russet, orange and purple, floated like exotic butterflies.

The boats made her think of her father. Julia turned to her husband.

"Gnaeus," she said. "Gnaeus, darling."

Pompey stopped snoring. His eyes opened.

"Gnaeus. Wake up. I want to ask you something. Is this invasion of Britain dangerous?"

"Eh? What's that?"

"My father's sailing to Britain. How dangerous is it?"

Pompey struggled to a half-sitting position. He rubbed his eyes open.

"I went much farther in Asia," he said, somewhat sulkily.

Julia remembered quickly that her husband had resented the twenty days' thanksgiving voted to her father last fall for his incursion into Germany and his expedition that same year to Britain. There had been those shouts, too, of "Caesar, our only general!"

"I know, dear," she said. "But my father hasn't had your experience. And you said yourself that he was lucky to get back safely."

"Which is what those fools in Rome realize now," Pompey said, mollified. He rubbed his double chin thoughtfully. "This time, however — five legions, he says. I'd say he ought to be all right."

"Thanks, darling. I only wish you were with him." She started to rise. "Luncheon, dear?"

"Don't get up," Pompey told her. "Call the maid. Let's have it here." He smiled at her. "We want to be extra careful of *him*, don't we?"

9

He *was* a dear, Julia thought, reaching for the bronze gong. What a lucky woman she was, Pompey her husband and Julius Caesar her father.

# CHAPTER II

AT THAT MOMENT, in northwestern Gaul, Gaius Julius
Caesar, proconsul of the three Gauls and Illyricum, stood in
bright sunlight on a cliff overlooking the estuary at Portus Itius.
Around him was a group of generals and two Gauls whom he
trusted, Commius, whom he had made king of the Atrebates,
and Vercingetorix, the handsome young Arvernian prince. Behind him, on a rising slope almost a half a mile inland, rose the
ramparts, palisades, and towers of the Roman camp. Below him
rocked the almost nine hundred ships of his armada — the six
hundred barges his legionaries had built during the winter added
to last year's fleet, along with twenty-five warships and vessels
owned by merchants.

Caesar stared down at the tangled mass of shipping. Then he
glanced to his right. Beyond the waves of the channel, a shimmering, indistinct line marked the cliffs of Britain.

He had intended to land on that island two months ago. But a
threat of revolt among the Treverans had forced him to lead four
legions all the way to the Rhenus. By the time he had reached
Portus Itius a strong wind from the northwest had prevented
him from setting out. For twenty-five consecutive days that
wind had kept blowing.

"I suppose we can't risk it?" he asked Mamurra, a jolly,
lecherous man who was his efficient Chief of Engineers.

"In the teeth of that wind?" Mamurra answered. "Your barges
would never make it."

"Midsummer," Titus Labienus, Caesar's crusty second-in-
command, pointed out. "Half the campaigning season gone.
Better call the whole thing off, Julius."

Caesar glanced toward Britain again. Last year, he had seen
only the southeastern corner of the island. He wanted to know

11

more. The desire to know, he thought, was one of the highest human attributes. No use, though, to use that for an argument with Labienus. He turned to him.

"Last year," he answered, "it was only luck that got me back safely. The Britons know that. So do the Gauls. That's something we must rub out. Romans always win. That's our legend and our strength."

What he really meant was that Caesar must always seem to win, so as to impress the Senate and the Roman mob, Labienus thought sourly. He hawked and spat.

"Look, Julius," he said, "I've said it before and I'll say it again. We've conquered Transalpine Gaul from the Rhenus to the Pyrenees. That's enough to manage."

"And I repeat, we must teach those Britons a lesson. They sent ships to help the Venetans against us. Any Gaul who flees to them is made welcome. You talk of unrest in Gaul. The Britons are part of the cause."

Labienus' square and somewhat brutal face was stubborn. "You're taking five legions and half the cavalry," he pointed out. "I'm left with only three legions and two thousand horsemen. Suppose a revolt does break out?"

Labienus was an excellent general but unimaginative. Caesar turned from the cliff. He looked up at his camp. In and out of the two gates visible to him, patrols, foraging parties, and carts, wagons, and mule trains bringing in supplies or returning for new loads were moving in a constant stream of traffic. Between him and the camp, legionaries were at weapon drill.

His legionaries, Caesar thought with a surge of pride. Men who could and would do anything for him. Like marching fifteen to twenty miles a day carrying a hundred pounds of arms, armour, and equipment, winning a battle at the end of it, and then building a camp for the night. Like building those six hundred barges down there — or bridging the Rhenus last year. He began to stroll toward the camp. Labienus fell into step beside him. In front and on the flanks of the group, the bodyguard, a score of trained veterans, took up their positions.

"There's another thing," Labienus pointed out, "the drought.

That means shortage of supplies. Worse still, empty bellies for the Gauls. Empty bellies breed trouble."

"I agree with Labienus," a voice said.

That was Quintus Cicero. Quintus was a somewhat beefy man, given to composing third-rate tragedies based on Greek models. Yet he was a good general, thanks to five hard years as governor in the Roman province of Asia. Caesar halted.

"Look, Titus and you, Quintus. You know that if this wind changes and I do sail I'm taking the trouble-makers, actual and potential, with me—Indutiomarus of the Treverans, Acco of the Senones, Dumnorix of the Aeduans, Ambiorix of the Eburones, and the rest. That takes care of revolt in Gaul, doesn't it?" He looked at the two men, then laughed. "Besides, if this wind keeps up another week, I won't be going."

He was about to start on again when he saw a group of Gallic cavalry, lances high, trotting down the slope toward him. His bodyguard waited. Caesar waited. Trained legionaries could always defeat horsemen who had only knees, thighs, and legs to hold them in their seats.

Fine-looking beasts, he thought as the group came closer. And fine-looking men, these Gauls, in their tartan trousers and cloaks, shields and outlandish helmets glittering. Yet only semi-civilized. In battle, brave as panthers one moment, running like rabbits the next. Except for a few such as Commius and Vercingetorix, one could not trust them.

The group pulled up, a short javelin's cast away. Caesar frowned as he recognized the leader. It was Dumnorix, prince of the Aeduans — Dumnorix, who from the day four years back when Caesar's legions had first marched into the Aeduan country to repel the Helvetian migration had never stopped plotting against the Romans. He was still busy with intrigues. So, what now? He watched as Dumnorix dismounted, walked forward, and, making a show of it, laid his helmet, sword, spear, and shield on the ground and straightened up.

"A conference, Imperator," he called in Latin.

"Let him through, Ceretus," Caesar told the centurion in command of his bodyguard.

13

"Between you and me, Imperator. By ourselves."

"Take your men to the left and right," Caesar ordered Ceretus. "Watch carefully." He turned to his officers. "Move back a little."

"He has a dagger," Quintus Cicero warned.

Caesar smiled grimly. "So have I."

Dumnorix strode forward. They faced each other, the Roman five feet eleven, deceptively slender but powerfully muscled, the Gaul half a head taller and appearing even taller because of the long hair put up in a topknot. Dumnorix fiddled with his moustachio an instant, his blue eyes fixed on a point past Caesar's left ear.

"My oath," he said. "I come to you again, Imperator, about my oath. My oath to sacrifice to Lugh under the sacred oak at Bibracte in my own country. I must leave at once."

"And I tell you, as I've told you before," Caesar said coldly, "that your oath must wait until we return from Britain."

The blue eyes focused to stare at Caesar. "You won't be sailing now. Not with that wind."

"The wind will change. We'll sail."

Could this demon have power over the winds, too, Dumnorix wondered.

"But my oath," he began.

It was time for Caesar to show his teeth. "Shall I tell you of the oaths you've been demanding of the chieftains?" he interrupted. "For them not to sail!"

Dumnorix glanced to where Commius and Vercingetorix waited. "Those dogs," he grated. He spat toward them. Caesar took a step forward.

"And shall I tell you of the lie you've been spreading among the chieftains, that I'm taking them to Britain to murder them there because I'm afraid to kill them here?"

Dumnorix' eyes came back to Caesar. "It's true."

"It's a lie."

The Gaul's hand went to the hilt of his dagger. He glanced to the right and then to the left at the bodyguard. Not now, then, but when the chance came.

14

"I'm prince of the Aeduans," he stormed at Caesar. "Free allies of Rome, you keep saying. So I'm a free man from a free country. Sail or not sail to Britain, I don't care. I'm not going. By Lugh and by Cromm, I swear it."

"By Mars and by Jupiter, you will," Caesar told him, "even if I have to drag you on board by ropes."

"You wouldn't dare."

"Try me."

The Gaul's mouth was working under his moustache, his eyes and face almost insane with fury. Caesar watched him closely. Over to his left Ceretus took a couple of steps closer, javelin poised. Dumnorix saw the movement. With a curse he turned, strode back to pick up his armour and weapons, ran to his horse, leaped onto its back, swung it around, and, with a wave to his escort to follow, galloped recklessly back toward the camp.

Caesar looked after him. Dangerous, that man, he was thinking. As his officers came over to join him, he glanced at Vercingetorix, the Arvernian prince. He was recalling that when Vercingetorix' father had been for a year or two king of most of Gaul it had been the Aeduans who had led the movement to depose him and to burn him alive. He motioned to the young man to come closer.

"Would you keep an eye on Dumnorix?" he asked.

Vercingetorix looked at him, a frank, open look. "Willingly, Imperator."

Caesar put an affectionate hand on the young man's shoulder and with the smile and manner that could charm hawks out of the sky added, "Have dinner with me tonight, will you?"

Vercingetorix' eyes flashed. "Gladly, Imperator."

Caesar turned to the others.

"And now, gentlemen, on our way." He smiled again, ruefully this time. "All those reports and letters on my table—every one of them needing an answer. Sometimes," he glanced at the weapon-training groups, "I wish I were a legionary. Just a legionary."

15

# 2

As Caesar, accompanied by his staff, moved toward the camp, on a strip of ground not far from the front gate, the centurion Thermus growled to his squad, "Take a breather."

The men had been in two ranks, armour on, drilling in pairs with shields and wooden swords that were weighted with lead to give them the heft and balance of the real weapon. Stinking with sweat, the legionaries relaxed. All were veterans, except for a replacement who had come in with a squad from the Verona camp two days ago. He was a big man, this Fadius, and the centurion, who was also his maternal uncle, had recruited him the previous winter from a farm near Brixia. At this moment, sitting on the baked ground, Fadius wiped away the sweat and glanced at the camp. It was much bigger than the Verona camp in which he'd been trained. He felt Rullus, with whom he'd been duelling, seat himself beside him.

"You're good with that sword," Rullus said. "For a recruit."

Fadius glanced at him. Rullus was a short but stocky Italian and the only one of the veterans who had made any gesture of friendliness.

"It's my reach," he told him.

"No, you're quick on your feet. A few tricks you've got to learn yet."

"That backhanded swipe you use," Fadius commented, "the one where you check and drive the point up for the throat. I hadn't run into that."

"I'll drill you on that." Rullus glanced at Thermus. "Makes us sweat, the bugger, doesn't he?"

"I'm off a farm."

Rullus chuckled. "Know what you mean. I'm off a farm, too. Sabine hills. Little patches of ground. Stones mostly. Work from before first light until after dark."

"Same way with me. Only our fields are bigger. And flat. Hundred acres in our farm."

"Why'd you leave?"

Fadius shrugged his shoulders. "Four brothers. All older."

"On your feet," they heard Thermus roar. "Two ranks. Face

16

outward, damn you. At attention. Don't move an eyeball."

It was Caesar and his staff approaching. As the proconsul came opposite, Thermus brought up his sword in salute. Caesar stopped, glanced at him, and came over.

"How goes it, Thermus?"

"Well enough, Imperator."

"Like to put them through it for a moment?"

Thermus turned, snapped orders. The men fell into two ranks, facing each other. They attacked and retreated, each pair fighting furiously. Caesar watched them critically, the savage, controlled slashes, the swift, deadly lunges with the two-foot-long wooden swords. They could really bruise, Caesar knew; except that these men knew how to use their man-covering rectangular shields.

"Who's the big fellow?" he asked.

"Replacement, Imperator. Cisalpine Gaul. Fadius." He paused, then said somewhat reluctantly, "My sister's son."

Caesar watched for a moment. "Light on his feet," he commented. "Alert, too. He'll make a soldier. Well, stand them easy."

Thermus stood them easy and saluted. Caesar strolled back to his officers. The centurion turned to his squad.

"Called me by name," he said. "Did you hear? Eight legions. Sixty centurions to a legion. Yet he called me by name."

He glanced at his men. All of them were staring after Caesar. Everyone's face was admiring. Except one. Thermus pounced.

"Wipe that grin off your face," he roared, bringing his vine stick viciously across his nephew's shins. "Stand at attention, damn you." He cut his stick across Fadius' shoulders. "Not as big as you, eh? That grandmother of yours—big cow of a Gaul." He thwacked Fadius again. "More brains in his toenails than in your big, stupid cabbage of a head. What d'you think of that, you bastard?"

Fadius already knew better than to answer or to stir a muscle.

"Think you're a swordsman, eh? Caesar'd chop you to pieces before you could get that shield halfway up, you stupid ass."

Fadius had learned that in the army a centurion was Jupiter and Pluto, too. He stared straight ahead.

"That man," Thermus growled, "can outfight, outride, out-

17

swim, outscrew any of us. That means you, too, Fadius." He stared at his nephew, challenging him. Fadius stood as if he were a rock on a beach. Thermus walked back to his post. "To work, you buggers," he barked. "Move, damn you. Put some guts into it."

A couple of hours later Fadius and Rullus walked through the forty-foot-wide front entrance of the camp, guarded at this point by a tower on each side from which scorpions, the two-man steel bows, could fire their bolts. Ahead was a two-hundred-foot-wide space that ran right around the camp within the ramp so that at the trumpet blast the legions could form up rapidly. The two men crossed it to enter the crowded Via Praetoria.

"Rough on you, your uncle, eh?" Rullus mentioned.

Fadius shrugged his shoulders. "Had worse from my dad." He glanced without curiosity at the neat rows of hide tents on either side. By this time he knew that every Roman camp was always laid out in exactly the same design, with four main gates and with each unit assigned to its exact spot. In front of them, as the broad Via Principalis crossed the Via Praetoria, ending it, stood the altars, the eagles, and the tribunal. Behind them, in the centre, were the quarters of Caesar and his staff.

Fadius and Rullus turned right and then left again. The tent that they shared with six others was halfway down between the Via Principalis and the next broad cross-street, the Via Quintana. Behind it, again in the centre, as both of them knew, were the quarters for the sick bay, for hostages, and for the heavy baggage and the loot of each legionary.

They had reached the entrance to their tent. Inside it was hot, even though the flaps were drawn back. The two men stripped off their armour and arranged it neatly. In a ten-foot-square space, each legionary had to stick to his exact space. Fadius picked up his helmet and began to polish it. But Rullus stretched and said,

"How about a woman?"

Fadius thought of the three or four girls he'd had in Verona and then, suddenly, of his first time in a copse on the farm with

Staphyle, the slave-woman, smelling, he remembered, of wool and cheese.

"How much?" he asked cautiously.

Rullus laughed. "A penny or so. Swarms of them outside the Porta Decumana at the back. Good value, too, these Gallic wenches."

"There's supper to cook."

"Lots of time for that." Rullus clapped him on the shoulder. "Come on, lad. Do you good."

He wanted Rullus for a friend. Fadius put down the helmet.

"Let's go," he said.

# CHAPTER III

THAT NIGHT, in the palace of the Ptolemies, unable to sleep, Cleopatra sat up in bed, reached for a silk robe to fling around her, and tinkled a bell for her maid.

"Get Apollodorus," she ordered.

The Greek came in, rubbing the sleep from his eyes. During the previous year Cleopatra had selected him for her personal exploration of sex—not that there was any mystery about it in the court of the Ptolemies—and at first Apollodorus hoped that this was what was in the Princess's mind now.

"No," she said, waving him back. "Not now. Later, perhaps." She settled herself comfortably, pillows at her back. "All about Rome," she commanded. "How it's governed. Its masters —Pompey, Crassus, Julius Caesar, and this Clodius you mentioned, the man who controls the mob that votes and who jumps from one side to another like a flea whenever it suits him, even though he is supposed to be Caesar's man. Also the leaders of those nobles who hate Caesar and why they do. Don't miss a thing."

As Apollodorus began to speak, in Apamea, Crassus mumbled in his bed, dreaming of the riches of India; while his son, accompanied by Crassus' quaestor, Quintus Cassius, a gaunt, bitter-faced man, checked the guards throughout the town. In his villa in Arpinum, Marcus Cicero, a candelabrum behind him, was bent over his desk, rearranging carefully the sequence of words in a sentence of the book he was writing. South of him, in Pompey's villa, Julia stirred in bed and cried out.

"There, there," her childhood nurse said, coming over. "It'll be all right, sweet. All right."

Julia turned over and drifted into sleep again. Many leagues away, in Caesar's camp, Prince Dumnorix, slumped on a couch

20

in his luxurious tent, roared to a slave to bring him another goblet of Rhodian wine. Earlier he had visited his intimates among the Gallic nobles, striving to persuade them to join with him in leading their cavalry home and starting a revolt. No success.

"If the wind changes—which it won't," Acco of the Senones had said, "it will be time enough to talk. Why stir a sleeping bear?"

"Lugh and damnation," Dumnorix had exploded. "That demon made it clear today. Free Gauls? We're not free Gauls. We're hostages."

"All the same," Ambiorix, king of the Eburones, had begun.

"Look," Dumnorix had interrupted, "I've told you before. I tell you again what I said to my brother, damn him. 'Give a Roman a toe in the door and he walks in and takes over the whole house.' My brother's dead now, and I rule the Aeduans. I'll start the fire, if you'll join. Come on. It's not too late to drive out the Romans, if we act as one."

"Wait till winter," Ambiorix had said. "Wait till that demon's gone back to Cisalpine Gaul."

"Suppose the wind does change? Drag me on board with ropes, that Caesar said. Me, prince of the Aeduans."

"It won't change," Acco had repeated. "He'll never get to Britain. Not this year."

All that effort for nothing, Dumnorix thought. He took a gulp of the wine the slave had brought. He wouldn't be stopped, he told himself. He'd smash that insolent bastard of a Roman somehow. Dragging him on board with ropes—that's what he'd said—him, prince of the Aeduans.

He finished his drink. "Boy!" he shouted.

The slave scuttled in, carrying another goblet of wine. Dumnorix knocked it out of his hand.

"Ass!" he bellowed. "A woman—that's what I want. Bring me the one with the big tits."

A half-hour later he rolled off her and, at that moment, two-score yards away in the headquarters tent, Julius Caesar came awake. That evening, after answering dozens of reports and

21

letters, he had had his secretary bring to his inner tent Fiammar, the green-eyed princess of the Senones, the best in bed among all the Gallic women he'd had. So now he was aware of her breast warm against his arm and of one of her hands clasped loosely around him as she slept.

It wasn't she who had awakened him. He let his thoughts range — Julia, how was she? — Pompey — Crassus — Cato — Dumnorix, that savage, ambitious troublemaker. Then, for some reason, Servilia, his mistress, flitted into his mind. There was a tender smile on his lips as he recalled their first coming together, away back during the hot blood of youth. Curious, he thought, remembering how in Rome he had once overheard that troublemaker, Clodius, talking.

"Caesar, the bee," Clodius had quipped, "sipping from every flower but always back to the same cold, white lily."

Cold! He could visualize Servilia now — broad brow, grey-blue candid eyes, slim waist, firm breasts, desirable to any man but with such a quiet, dignified manner that it gave not a hint to the world of the volcano in private. Here he was, forty-eighth birthday upon him, and still that merging of body, mind, and spirit with Servilia. When he got back from Britain — Britain! Abruptly, he knew what had brought him awake. The wind no longer gusted down from the palisade to slap at the northwestern side of his tent.

Carefully, he drew his arm from under Fiammar and disengaged her hand. As she muttered something, then turned over, he slipped from the couch, threw a robe around himself, and went into the outer tent. His secretary, Faberius, stirred. Caesar told him not to worry, stepped outside, waved an impatient hand at the centurions on guard to stay where they were, and moved out half a dozen paces.

Changed! The wind had changed. Coming now in little gusts from the southwest! Caesar swept back into the outer tent.

"Up, Faberius," he said, his voice vibrant. "Up, man. Get your lists. Britain! We're sailing to Britain. Tomorrow. No, today!"

## 2

The sun was climbing the sky. At the crest of the slope outside the western gate of the camp, Dumnorix, his groom holding his horse near by, was watching the embarkation. The Cretan archers, the Balearic slingers, and the other light-armed auxiliaries were already on board. Now the legions, maniple by maniple, were on the move, an endless snake from the front gate of the camp to the cliffs and down over them to the boats. At one side stood a group which would be Caesar and his officers.

Caesar! Dumnorix glanced at his fellow chieftains. They, too, their grooms and horses near them, were watching. In spite of the change in the wind and the movement of troops on board, Acco, Indutiomar, and Ambiorix had refused to ride off with him. He looked back to where, behind them, the Gallic cavalry in tribal contingents, also dismounted, were waiting. Even his own Aeduan chieftains had not seemed perturbed.

Fear of Caesar—that was the difficulty. Dumnorix gnawed at his moustache. What was he to do? Go on board, a castrated ram? He saw Acco of the Senones glance at the sun and then at the marching legions.

"Mid-afternoon for us, I'd guess," he said.

"If we go," Dumnorix said. He took a step toward the chieftains. "I've told you and told you. Our one chance is to ride off now. All of us."

Ambiorix of the Eburones, a stocky, swarthy man, glanced at him sideways. "And if Caesar comes after us?"

"The legions are off to Britain." Dumnorix waved an arm toward the long column. "Caesar won't stop now."

"Suppose he does?" Ambiorix persisted. "Suppose he attacks me and my Eburones? Will you come to help me, Dumnorix? With Vercingetorix and the Arvernians ready to pounce on your Aeduans? Or you, Acco? Or you, Indutiomar?" He looked around the group. He knew what they were thinking. Not only tribe against tribe, but factions within each tribe. Noble at enmity with noble. The merchants pro-Roman and opposed to the nobles; the Druids jealous of the nobles and the merchants, of

23

anyone, in fact, who might threaten their rank and their power. "Well, Acco of the Senones?" he repeated.

Acco looked at the ground. "There's Comm and his Atrebatians," he muttered. "Before I could march I'd have to be sure he didn't attack."

"So the Romans chop us up one by one—as always," Ambiorix said. He spat. "Sooner than take that sort of chance I'll go with Caesar."

"We'll take oaths," Dumnorix cried in desperation. "Right now. To each other. For once, to fight as one. We're free men, aren't we? We're the best fighters in the world, aren't we? Or so we boast. Is it only a boast?"

He stared at the chieftains. Not one would meet his eyes. He looked away to where Caesar and his officers stood. He could imagine him, careless, confident, contemptuous. Abruptly, it was too much. Take him on board in ropes, would he, that demon? No, by the arrow of the Shining One!

He strode over to his horse, took the reins from the groom, and vaulted onto its back. He stared down at the chieftains.

"I'm going. If you're free Gauls, follow." He waited. No one moved. "Kiss Caesar's ass, then," he roared, turning his horse and jerking it to a gallop.

His groom trotted after him. Acco took a half-step forward and halted, frowning. Ambiorix looked at him and turned to watch Dumnorix shout and wave to his Aeduans. As they began to mount, Ambiorix went over to his horse. His groom bent and cupped his hands to give his master a leg up.

"Where are you off to?" Acco demanded.

Ambiorix grinned, gathered the reins, and urged his horse down toward the cliff. "To tell Caesar!" The realization came to the chiefs simultaneously. "Credit with Caesar!" There was a wild scramble to mount and follow.

On the cliff-edge Caesar and his officers were watching the legions flow over the cliff and down into the waiting boats.

"Smooth," Mamurra, the embarkation officer was exulting. "Eh, Julius? Smooth as the skin on a woman's ass."

24

Caesar's face was alight, eager. Tomorrow, Britain! he was thinking. Then Vercingetorix spoke:

"Imperator! Look! Back there!"

Caesar swung round. Near at hand were the Gallic chieftains, flogging their horses. Behind them, half a mile away, there were horsemen moving toward the woods behind the camp. Even as the chieftains dismounted and rushed toward him, shouting, he knew.

"Dumnorix!" they were yelling. "He's gone. Back to his own country. Gone."

For the space of ten seconds Caesar stood immobile, seemingly not hearing. In those few seconds he had made his appraisal and his decisions. He looked at the chieftains. He even managed a smile.

"You will be rewarded," he said. "Now, ride back. Take your men. Follow him. Bring him back." Then, as the chieftains mounted, he turned to Vercingetorix. "Join them with your Arvernians," he ordered and added softly, "I depend on you, Vercingetorix. Keep them loyal."

The young man saluted, eyes flashing. He swung away to his horse.

Caesar said to his trumpeter, "Signal the German horse to get ready — fast." He turned to Quintus Cicero.

"Order the Roman horse to watch the rest of the Gauls. You take Commius and his Atrebatian cavalry and the German horsemen, too. There's four hundred of them. Good men. Well-paid. Loyal. Now, do you remember how, inland, the river bends to the left before one comes to the ford?"

"Yes, Imperator."

"Dumnorix will ride inland, around the bend, the other Gauls on his tail. You'll go just beyond the neck of the estuary, then swim your cavalry over and cut straight across country to the ford. You'll get there first. You'll stop him. You'll bring him back. Understood?"

"What if he won't come?"

"You heard me say bring him back." Quintus nodded. "And

Quintus, make no mistake. Get to that ford first, no matter what."

Quintus and Commius were already running to their horses. Caesar turned to Mamurra.

"Stop the embarkation."

"What!"

Caesar took time to explain. "Those Gauls — we don't know what they'll do. Vercingetorix is loyal. The rest — at the last moment they could join Dumnorix. We could have all Gaul in flames. So give the order. At once."

The trumpeter blew the signal. The column stopped moving. Mamurra asked, "So now what do we do?"

Caesar's lips set in a firm line. "We wait."

Three-quarters of the way toward the cliff, Thermus stopped his century. He glanced at where the cavalry was in motion. Something gone wrong, he told himself. To his men, he growled,

"All right. Put down your packs. At ease."

Fadius stuck the butt end of his eleven-pound javelin in the ground. Then he lifted from his left shoulder the long forked pole on top of which was packed his cloak, six days' rations, his cooking pot, his trenching spade, his wicker basket for carrying earth and other odds and ends. Next he unslung and laid down thankfully his twenty-pound shield, loosened the thongs by which his helmet, pickaxe, sickle, and hatchet were tied to him, and sat down. Rullus was beside him.

"What's up, d'you think?" Fadius asked.

"Don't know," Rullus answered. "Don't care. Rest while you can, soldier." He lay back on the ground. "Nice sky up there," he observed. "Look at the puffs of clouds. Like sheep's fleeces."


# 3


Dumnorix glanced back at his pursuers. Their van was cresting the ridge a half-mile behind him. His own Aeduans were already riding to the summit of the gentle rise which, on the other side, sloped down to the ford. Once across that ford, they could scatter into small groups and make for home.

"Hurry up there," he shouted to his rearmost chief, Coltan. "Keep your men moving."

He turned to ride back to his van, heard shouts, and saw the men pulling up their horses.

"Sons of pigs," he cursed, driving his steed forward. Then he, too, stopped. The river and the ford were only a couple of hundred yards down the incline. But the farther bank was lined with cavalry, and the sun glinted on their spear points.

How could that demon have got them there, he thought wildly. They must be phantoms — or devils. He looked around him desperately — the copses, the sward green in the sun, but down there, indisputably, rank on rank, pennants steady, the German cavalry and the Atrebatian horse. Behind, he remembered, and coming on fast, the pursuit. Trapped!

He would not be trapped! Never!

"Come on," he shouted to his Aeduans, levelling his spear. "Charge!"

"No," a voice called.

He wheeled his horse. It was Coltan. Two other chieftains were with him.

"No chance!" they shouted. "We haven't got a chance."

Dumnorix exploded. "It's our only chance," he yelled. "Can't you see? It's downhill. We break through. Then, we're away. Free."

"They'd catch us in midstream," Coltan cried out. "Smash us. No use, Dumnorix. No use, I tell you."

It was too late now, in any event. The pursuit had caught up. Dumnorix, in a torrent of obscenities, got his Aeduans arranged in a defensive formation at the top of the rise. The pursuers did not attack. Instead, they swung around them, Vercingetorix' horsemen blocking the Aeduans from the rear, Acco, Ambiorix, and Indutiomar bringing their men to Dumnorix' right. The Aeduan prince chewed at his moustache. If he could start a mêlée, he and a few of his retainers might break through somewhere. Or else, even at this hour, he might persuade Acco or

27

Ambiorix or Indutiomar or all three. He glanced at the cavalry guarding the ford, hating them and the man who had sent them.

At this moment, Quintus Cicero, hot and sweaty in his armour, was saying, "We'll move in now. Take the bugger."

"Let me try something first," Commius said.

"What for?"

"If there's a battle, who knows what might happen? You can't trust Acco or Ambiorix or Indutiomar. Vercingetorix — yes. Not the other three."

"What's your plan?"

"Let me parley. The Aeduans can't be too happy. Maybe they'll surrender."

Quintus shifted in his saddle. "A quarter of an hour," he decided, glancing at the sun. "I'll give you that much."

An instant later Dumnorix saw Comm's horse splashing through the ford. Comm's lance was laid crossways on his steed's neck. A half-dozen of his retainers were following him. One of them held a green branch aloft. So it was a parley. Why not?

The Aeduan prince gestured to a group of his retainers to accompany him and rode forward slowly, his own spear held crossways. The two parties halted in the middle of the peaceful glade. The leaders faced each other, the Aeduan's wolf's-head helmet glittering in the sun, Comm's helmet, a boar's head, facing him.

"Well?" Dumnorix demanded.

"The net's flung over you," Comm said quietly. "Give up, Dumnorix. Come back with us."

"Never!" From the corner of his eye Dumnorix saw Acco, Ambiorix, and Indutiomar, each with an escort, riding toward them. They were fearful, he realized, of missing some deal or other. Now was his chance. Dumnorix raised his voice.

"I'm a free man," he shouted. "We're all free men, we Gauls. If we choose to be. Ride with me, Acco. You, too, Ambiorix. You, most of all, Indutiomar. Cut through the ford. All of us!"

Comm saw the chieftains pause to look at one another. He,

too, raised his voice, bawling it out to make sure that even the Aeduans could hear.

"Caesar is clement. No penalty. Caesar has promised it. Ride back, Aeduans. No penalty."

With a curse Dumnorix levelled his spear and rode at him. Comm swerved his body just in time. As his horse and that of Dumnorix bumped together, the spear went through the man carrying the green branch and stuck there. Dumnorix, yelling, drew his sword and slashed. Comm caught the blow on his shield and thrust with his lance. The point glanced off Dumnorix' shield and caught his shoulder just enough to tumble him from his horse. The Aeduan was on his feet in a second, sword flashing. His retainers and those of Comm were in a wild mêlée.

"To me, Aeduans," Dumnorix was yelling. "To me."

"Acco! Ambiorix! Indutiomar!" Comm shouted. His stallion rose on its hind feet and, whinnying, lashed out with its front hooves. One hoof caught Dumnorix and sent him sprawling. As he got to his knees, still shouting, Acco and Ambiorix and their men rode in. A spear went through Dumnorix. Yet, though he staggered, he still slashed with his sword.

"Free," he was shouting, as another spear caught him in the throat. He fell back, dying. Comm turned his horse quickly. He rode toward the Aeduans. Some of them were starting to move forward. Comm stopped.

"Dumnorix is dead!" Comm shouted. "Dead! Make up your minds. Ride back. Or die. Now."

The Aeduans halted. Behind Comm the mêlée was over. Coltan, after a quick consultation, raised his hand, palm outward.

"We return," he called.

Comm raised his own hand in acknowledgment. He turned and signalled to Quintus Cicero. The Roman led the cavalry through the ford and took charge.

"Back to camp," he ordered. "In troops. Acco, Ambiorix, Indutiomar, take the van. Then Vercingetorix. Next, the Aeduans. I'll bring up the rear."

29

"Dumnorix?" Comm asked, looking down at the dead prince, sprawled on his back, sightless eyes staring at the sun.

"Across his horse's back," Quintus decided.

He turned his horse away. A couple of Comm's retainers dismounted to carry out the order.

"Just a moment," Ambiorix said briskly, sliding from his horse and drawing his sword.


## 4


The legionaries had been sitting or sleeping while the sutlers from the back of the camp moved along the column offering coarse red wine and sweetmeats for sale. Rullus and Fadius had bought a jar.

"Another drink?" Rullus asked.

Fadius held out his cup. "What's that up there?" he asked, pointing to the woods at the back of the camp. Rullus paused.

"Looks like horsemen coming," he said.

Caesar, too, saw the movement. He took a step forward, shading his eyes with hand on brow. The Gallic cavalry was emerging, tribe by tribe. And there was Acco, along with Indutiomar, Ambiorix, and Vercingetorix, riding toward him. His face relaxed. Acco and Indutiomar dismounted and came up to him.

"Your bidding has been done, Imperator," Acco said; "the Aeduans are back."

"Dumnorix?" Caesar asked.

"Among the shades," Ambiorix called out. He urged his horse forward. "See?"

Caesar looked. Between the forelegs of Ambiorix' horse, severed head hanging by its topknot, the face of Dumnorix stared at him, eyes open, lips drawn back from the teeth in the grimace of the death-throe. For a second there was a horrifying feeling that those eyes, those lips, were putting a curse on him.

He controlled himself, noting that the other principal Gallic chiefs had gathered. His voice rang out, clear, confident.

"Gaius Julius Caesar, proconsul, gives thanks to you, noble chieftains," he said. "More than thanks." He turned to Faberius, his secretary. "Take these princes to the treasure in the camp. Let each select a token from me, Gaius Julius Caesar, whatever he wants, as much as he wants."

This time they saluted, then turned to follow Faberius. Caesar watched them for a moment. Men like Acco and Indutiomar were easy to assess. Never trust them for an instant. Ambiorix, however, was more complex. He had been effusive in his thanks when Caesar had released his people, the Eburones, from the overlordship of the Atuatucans and had restored to Ambiorix his son and nephew, held as Atuatucan hostages. Yet there was a certain slyness in the man's eyes and sometimes almost the hint of a sneer, as if he understood thoroughly that he was being bought.

I'll watch him, Caesar told himself. He turned to Mamurra.

"Embark," he ordered.

# CHAPTER IV

CAESAR STOOD ON THE FOREDECK of his flagship. Gathered around him in a circle of light from a horn lantern were the shipmaster, a half-Greek, half-Spaniard from Massilia; the admiral, Quintus Atrius; Volusenus, a dark, intense young man who had scouted the coast of Britain before last year's expedition; and Commius. On the outskirts of the circle were Quintus Cicero and Trebonius, Caesar's second-in-command for the British campaign, both of them turning away every now and then to run to the rail and retch.

"So where are we now?" Caesar asked.

Volusenus pointed to the chart the shipmaster held. "About here, I'd say."

"Here" was well past the southeast corner of Britain. Thanks to Dumnorix, Caesar reflected, the armada hadn't left Portus Itius until sunset. At first, it had been fair sailing. But as they reached that southeast corner, they had suddenly run into a different weather pattern—clouds, and spits of rain. In addition, a tidal current had seized the fleet, carrying it north-by-northeast.

Caesar glanced to right and left. It was past midnight and as dark as the inside of a man's gut. On either side the lanterns of the huge armada dipped and rose, winking like fireflies.

"It's too dark to turn in," he said. "So what do we do about this tidal current? It's carrying us well past the landing-place, isn't it?"

Volusenus cleared his throat. "Let it carry us until the tide changes, Imperator. Then, turn and row back."

"How long before it changes?"

"Three to four hours," the shipmaster answered.

Caesar glanced again at the winking lights of the fleet. "I'm

32

going to catch some sleep," he told the others. "I'd advise you gentlemen to do the same." He paused. "As soon as the tide changes, wake me."

Pulling over a coil of rope for his head and wrapping his cloak around him, he lay down on the deck. In an instant he was asleep, breathing quietly.

"That's Caesar for you," Volusenus commented in a hushed voice.

On a barge in the armada, astern and to port of the flagship, Fadius, too, was asleep. At first the excitement of the voyage had kept him interested and alert. He had watched, too, while of the one hundred and fifty legionaries on board, man after man had become violently seasick, including Sporus, the senior man in the tent Rullus and he occupied. That had been a satisfaction, since he himself, for some reason, didn't suffer so much as a qualm, and Sporus had been riding him, a recruit, mercilessly. Even his uncle, Thermus, he had noted, kept hovering near the side of the barge.

When it became dark and there was nothing to see, Fadius began to yawn. Finally, when the word was passed from barge to barge that there was to be nothing to do until the tidal current changed, he had found a corner free of vomit and let himself drop into slumber. Hours later he was in the middle of a dream about the farm near Brixia — pigs grunting as they fed on the acorns, then himself on his back staring at a blue sky that clouded over suddenly, and just as suddenly his father was roaring at him.

It was Rullus shaking him.

"What's up?" he asked, sitting up and smelling the stink of vomit all around.

"We're turning. Quick, help me get the sweep out."

Fadius stumbled to his feet, noting that a hint of false dawn was breaking the darkness, but that the lights of the ships were winking signals and the horns were braying and the bugles shrilling.

There were two men to a sweep and the legionaries, sick or not sick, had to man them.

"Port oars, pull," Thermus bellowed.

33

They came about. "All oars, pull," Thermus shouted. "Put your backs into it, you stinking sons of bitches."

Fadius and Rullus put their backs into it. As they pulled, Caesar watched from the flagship. He was thinking with pride that though some nine hundred vessels were carrying men, horses, and equipment, somehow the whole fleet had come about with no more than a dozen minor scrapes. And look at his legionaries row! His men!

He walked up and down the deck. As daylight began to come, he observed British forces on the shore, keeping pace with the fleet. Last year the landing had been a near thing, his legionaries waist-deep in water and blue-dyed Britons on the beach hurling darts and spears. But the eagle-bearer of the Tenth — what was his name? — Baculus, that was it — had jumped into the water and, forging ahead with the eagle, had put fire into the legionaries. This year, he recalled with satisfaction, the barges had been built wider in the beam and to draw less water so that they could move in closer.

And then he noticed that the Britons were withdrawing inland. The sight of the host of vessels, he guessed immediately, had aborted any plan of resisting the landing. Caesar stopped pacing. He decided that as soon as the troops had landed he'd send out patrols so as to find out where the British forces were. From last year he knew that four kings divided Cantium between them. If he could smash their army at once —

He smiled to himself. It was an ambition which he had confided to no one, not even to Labienus. But why not conquer Britain, or at least the southern and central parts of it? Like Gaul, the whole country was divided among warring tribes. For that matter, on board this ship he was carrying a young prince of the Trinovantes who had fled to him in Gaul for safety. The Trinovantes lived north of the river which Caesar's ears had heard as Tamesis. Recently that tribe had been conquered and the young prince's father killed by another king, whose name Caesar had noted down as Cassivellaunus. Would not the return of the prince, if backed by the Romans, inspire the Trinovantes to revolt?

34

He glanced up at the sky. Between low-lying broken clouds, high up, other clouds were scudding.

"Wind up there," Volusenus said, seeing him looking.

Caesar wasn't interested. "When do we turn in?" he asked. "To the landing-beach, I mean."

"About noon, I'd say."

Four hours from now. "Faberius," Caesar called.

The secretary, who had been curled up in an angle of the deck, got up and came over. Caesar examined him keenly.

"Better now?" he asked.

Faberius had been seasick. The sight of land seemed to have restored him. He nodded.

"Have them get you a stool and something for a table," Caesar said. "I'll dictate those reports and dispatches we didn't finish at Portus Itius."

Letters to Servilia and Julia, too, he thought. How was Julia anyway? Carrying his grandson.

As Faberius got his table and stool ready, Caesar turned to the direction in which Italy ought to be and stood very still for an instant, willing his love to cross the leagues to his daughter. Then he turned to Faberius.

As Caesar dictated, his legionaries sweated at the oars. Finally, about mid-day, the signal came to turn in to the beach. As they began to bring the barge around, Rullus snatched a quick glance at the shore.

"No Britons," he grunted. "No Britons."

"Lucky for you, recruit," Sporus sneered from the sweep behind. "You'd have pissed your legs."

"Stow the gab," Thermus shouted.

A few moments later they landed. Horses were manhandled ashore and cavalry patrols sent out. The legionaries were at once set to work to build a camp on a hill overlooking the shallow stretch of water just offshore where the fleet rode at anchor. Fadius and Rullus found themselves helping dig a section of the trench surrounding the campsite. From the earth they and their comrades of the first century threw inward, the other century of the maniple was building an eight-foot-high rampart, behind a

35

breast-high palisade of stakes carried from the barges. The rampart itself would have a platform wide enough for the soldiers to fight from, after they had climbed the steps leading up to it. Inside the half-built rampart, working parties were dumping the war-engines, the supplies, and the leather tents, each load in its exact location, which never varied from camp to camp.

"When do we eat?" Fadius asked through the side of his mouth.

"When the camp's all finished," Rullus grunted.

At last, quite late, the cooking-fires were lit. The legionaries, each group of tent-mates in a circle outside their tent, made wheaten bannocks and washed them down with sour red wine brought in sheepskin bags from Gaul. A light rain had begun to fall, and now and then a savage gust of wind beat at the palisade.

"I'll sleep like a stone tonight," Fadius remarked, wiping his eyes and stretching.

"I wouldn't count on that, recruit," Sporus said.

Fadius gaped at him. Sporus grinned. "They say our Caesar's found out where the Britons are. The rest of us know our Caesar, recruit." He poked with his toe at Fadius' thigh. "Wait till the Britons get at you, recruit. Dyed blue. And those chariots of theirs. Enough to make a man puke."

Fadius wanted to ask about the chariots. He didn't. All the rest of his tent-mates were veterans. So, best to keep his mouth shut. But wait, he thought. Wait till he, too, had killed a man — or a dozen men — in battle. Then he'd face up to Sporus.


2


It was midnight of that same day, and ground-dark. Below the camp, the armada rocked at anchor. In front of it, four legions in light marching order and all the cavalry except three hundred were drawn up. The three hundred horse, along with ten cohorts, were being left to guard the camp and the fleet. Where the rest of the army was off to, no one except Caesar and his officers and guides knew. To fight Britons, naturally.

What a day, Fadius was thinking as he stood in the fourth rank of his century, shield on his left arm, heavy javelin in his right hand. And now this! Maybe he ought to have stayed on the farm.

The signal to move came. For four hours, with cavalry in front and on the flanks, the legionaries slogged northward, a wind from the northeast mingled with occasional bursts of rain beating at their faces. To Fadius it was as if he were marching from nowhere to nowhere, up hill and down, with copses and woods dimly discerned and, apparently, no end to it all.

Suddenly the trumpets blared to signal deployment from column into line. Up front, there were shouts, yells, and the whinnying of horses. A stream with Britons lining the far bank and the cavalry going in—that was the word passed from maniple to maniple. Then came an order to advance. The Britons, it was reported, had fled to a nearby wood. Fadius found himself splashing through a stream, and marching a couple of hundred yards farther before the line was again halted. Not too far away, and at this hour merely a dark mass, was a wood. From it came the defiant shouts and barbaric yells of Britons. Breastworks along the edge of the wood was the news. The Britons would have to be winkled out.

"Our legion'll get the job," Sporus predicted sourly.

Fadius stared at the dark trees, his hand suddenly sweaty on the ash-wood shaft of his javelin. What would it be like to kill a man? Or to face a man trying to kill him, Fadius? He shifted his shield, making sure it was sitting just right on his left arm. But the Seventh legion was the one sent in. In spite of the darkness and a wind that was now gusting violently, they made short work of the Britons. Locking their shields above their heads, they threw up mounds against the breastworks, swarmed over them, and chased the enemy out. No Roman was killed, although about a score were wounded. Then, before Fadius could believe it, he was helping dig another trench around another campsite with the wind making it difficult to hear himself think.

"Legionary!" he bawled to Rullus as his shovel struck a stone. "Wish I'd stuck to the farm."

But by the next morning the gale had blown itself out. Fur-

37

thermore, Caesar, with his usual consideration for his men, had ordered a late reveille. It was getting close to noon when Fadius found himself in one of three flying columns of horse and infantry setting out on a search mission with Trebonius in overall command.

From the gate of the camp, Quintus Cicero beside him, Caesar watched the columns descend into a wooded valley. It was his intention, if Trebonius sent back word of any sizeable enemy force, to lead out his legions. Conquer all Cantium in one battle, that was his hope and objective. As he watched, a body of Romans rode around the northeastern angle of the camp. Caesar recognized the leader, young Quintus Laberius Durus, a knight who had been left behind at the coastal camp. Caesar took a couple of steps forward. Laberius slid off his horse, hurried up to him, and held out a sheet of papyrus. Caesar broke the seal.

"Fleet wrecked," he read. "Details from bearer. Quintus Atrius."

Caesar looked up. "Bad?"

"Kindling wood, Imperator," Laberius told him. "A hundred vessels smashed. Not a one that isn't damaged."

"The anchors?"

"Didn't hold, not in that roadstead."

"The storm wasn't all that bad, not up here," Quintus Cicero said.

"With us a hurricane, Legate."

Atrius, Caesar was recalling, had wanted to use rollers to put the fleet onto the beach, but he himself had been too eager to smash the Britons. It was the same mistake he'd made last year when a gale had damaged his ships in that same roadstead. To make the same mistake twice was colossal stupidity. He decided that he'd correct the error.

"Send couriers to recall Trebonius," he said to Quintus Cicero. "I'm riding to the coast. At once."

# 3

Once more, twelve days later, Fadius found himself marching in
column from the inland camp. In between, the army had put in
ten days and nights of the hardest work Fadius had ever known.
When the legions had marched back to the coast they had seen
over forty vessels smashed to pieces and the rest were damaged
hulks, either driven up on shore, or lying, listed over, in the
water. In irony the sun was shining.

From then on, it had been drive, work, drive. The vessels in
the water had been put on rollers to be dragged onto the beach.
Those on shore had been righted. Details had been set to work to
patch up the damaged barges and ships, using copper, timber,
and cordage from the forty wrecks and half a hundred other craft
adjudged useless. The rest of the army had been given the job of
building fortifications to enclose both the coastal camp and the
whole fleet.

Drive, drive, drive, that had been the ten days and nights.
Then, leaving the same garrison of three hundred horse and ten
cohorts in the coastal fortifications, Caesar had led four legions
back to the inland camp, and this morning had marched them
northwestward again.

Everyone knew, however, that during the twelve days the
military situation had changed. Setting aside their feuds, the four
kings of Cantium and the tribes beyond the Tamesis River had
combined under the king the Romans called Cassivellaunus,
though to Fadius, a quarter-Celt, his name sounded more like
Caswallon. So the army had set out that morning on the alert,
auxiliaries and cavalry on the flanks of the columns and scouting
the country in front.

Fadius was rather enjoying the march. The sun was up and the
morning air was fresh and invigorating. He looked out at the
countryside. It was greener than anything he'd seen in Gaul and
so wooded that from a distance it seemed nothing but trees. In
between he saw homesteads and fields yellow with ripe wheat.
Looks like good crops, he was thinking, when from the woods

39

on either side came the British chariotry, ponies racing at full stretch.

The column halted and on command faced outward on each flank. Fadius gaped. As the Gallic cavalry on his flank turned to meet the charge, the chariots swerved broadside. Out from them spilled yelling, blue-dyed footmen. Three to four of them would go after each cavalryman and, if they got him off his horse, in would go the spears. A few moments of this, then back to their chariots and away as a fresh swarm came galloping in.

"Get your javelin up, you half-wit," Sporus hissed at him. Fadius closed his mouth, realizing that his century was about to charge in support of the cavalry. They doubled forward. Before they could reach them the Britons were in their chariots and driving back into the woods. The column re-formed and marched on. A half-hour later the chariotry came in again.

That was the way the day went, until Caesar devised a new tactic. He waited until a swarm of chariots dashed in, then had his cavalry and light-armed troops turn tail and run. The British footmen rushed after them, yelling. But from in front of them and from behind them a cohort doubled out. The chariots and their footmen were trapped. The heavy eleven-pound javelins arced into them, pinning men and beasts, and then the swords came out. From that swarm of Britons few escaped. The attacks stopped.

That night in camp Sporus said to Fadius' tent-mates,

"Did you see our recruit? Mouth open wide enough to swallow a sparrow — or a starling even."

They all laughed. Fadius flushed. If only a chance would come to prove himself.

"Lay off, you buggers," Rullus growled. "Give the lad a chance."

Fadius looked at him gratefully.

# 4

There were no attacks the next day either. The army started at first light, marched northwest until noon towards the Tamesis and stopped to make camp. This time Fadius was lucky. He was on outpost duty with a dozen comrades, Sporus in charge. Scattered along the defence perimeter were other outposts. Behind Fadius the usual camp was being built on the usual hill sloping down to a thick wood that at this point was about two hundred yards away.

Peaceful, Fadius was thinking, as he slouched at ease. The fringes of the wood had been scouted an hour ago and no Britons had been seen. The sun was warm. There was not even a stir of a breeze. The wood and the rich sward were green. He glanced at Rullus who was about twelve feet away at the right-hand end of the outpost. Good to be lazy, he wanted to say to him, while the rest of the century sweated at the trenching back behind them.

He yawned and at that instant there was a sudden wild yelling and from the wood a cloud of chariots burst, galloping on them at full speed. Automatically, the dozen legionaries fell into formation, javelins poised.

"Cast," Sporus shouted.

The heavy javelins arced into the chariots. Fadius didn't see whether his had hit anyone or not. The chariots were on them, the British footmen spilling from them even as the ponies swerved. A spear slammed into Fadius' shield. He thrust with his sword and missed. And then he saw Rullus down and three Britons at him. There was an unthinking fury in Fadius as he leaped out and over to his friend. His sword went into the back of one man, his shield knocked over another, and then he was duelling with a third. It wasn't a long duel. Fadius sliced through the spear-shaft as the Briton thrust, put his sword into the man's guts before he could recover, turned on the one he had knocked down who was scrambling to his feet, and with a backhanded swipe almost took his head off. Next, to his surprise, there was Rullus beside him.

"I'll watch your back," Rullus shouted as four more Britons

rushed them. They put one down. The rest hesitated."Back," Rullus shouted again. "Back to Sporus."

An instant later they were back in the group. Half the Romans were done for, but the Britons were leaping back into their chariots and the chariots were charging on toward the camp. A glance told Fadius that most of the outposts on this side of the camp had been overrun.

"You okay?" he asked Rullus.

"Damned chariot-wheel," Rullus grunted. "Caught me as it swerved." He limped around in a circle. "Bugger it," he said.

"What's wrong?"

"Bruises. Those buggering spears."

"What now?"

"Look."

Two cohorts, sent by Caesar, had come running from the front gate and were forming up just as the chariots hit them.

"Venus, Jupiter, Mars, look at the buggers," Sporus swore.

It was unbelievable. The British chariotry, the men in them hurling spears, had broken right through the centre of the cohorts and charged up to the half-finished ramparts. But the legionaries had already dropped their shovels, seized sword, shield, and javelin, and lined the mound. The two-score chariots wheeled and drove back through the cohorts. They turned again. This is it, Fadius thought. This time they would be massacred.

But Roman cavalry was charging in on the flanks, and from right and left cohorts were running. With derisive yells, waving their spears, the chariotry disappeared into the woods. There was no pursuit. From the partly built tower of the front gate, whence he had seen the whole action, Caesar watched the two shattered cohorts reassemble and on the perimeter what was left of the outposts take up position again. The Gallic cavalry was riding along cautiously between them and the woods. He could hear the Britons yelling tauntingly, triumphantly.

"Admirable," Caesar said.

Quintus Cicero and Trebonius looked at him, puzzled.

"The Britons, I mean," Caesar explained. "Did you notice how they drove right through and back again and then away?

Perfect. Excellent control. Two of our men down to one of theirs." He paused. "Was that young Laberius I saw killed?"

Quintus Cicero nodded.

"Pity."

"Our outposts fought well," Trebonius suggested.

"There was a big fellow out there," Caesar said. "I saw him jump out to save a comrade. Find out who he is, Trebonius." He paused. "Let's hope, gentlemen, that this success makes the Britons try a battle."

Later, the camp built and the outposts called in, Fadius was finishing his meal when his uncle, Thermus, came up.

"You, Fadius," he said gruffly. "Get your armour on."

"Me?"

"Yes, you."

What the hell had he done wrong, Fadius wondered. He cast back in his mind as he got into his corselet and helmet. Fortunately, he'd furbished them carefully.

"No shield, no weapons," Thermus said. He wheeled. "Come along."

A public flogging? Fadius wondered. Or pack drill? Or what? Thermus led him into Caesar's tent, stopped, saluted.

"Titus Fadius Lupus, Imperator," he announced.

Caesar looked up from his desk. "Ah, yes," he said. He reached over for a gold disc, stood up, and walked over to Fadius. "I saw you from the tower," he said. "Saved a comrade. Killed three Britons. Confirmed by Sporus, senior legionary." He held out the disc. "Take this, Titus Fadius Lupus. Wear it with pride."

Fadius, head reeling, took the disc as if it were red-hot.

"Salute, soldier," Thermus barked.

Fadius hurriedly transferred the disc to his left hand and saluted. Caesar returned the salute then reached out his hand to clasp Fadius' hand.

"Keep it up, Fadius," he said, and to Thermus, "Got any more nephews like this one, Thermus?"

"Maybe," Thermus grunted.

Caesar laughed, let go of Fadius' hand, and went back to his desk. Fadius followed Thermus out of the tent, his mind in a whirl. He'd done nothing, except what had had to be done. Outside his comrades' tent, Thermus halted.

"I had nothing to do with this," he rasped. "They all know that, thanks be. No favouritism." He paused, then slapped Fadius roughly on the back. "You've done well, lad," he said and walked away.

Fadius didn't want to enter the tent. He made himself step inside, head down.

"Got yourself a clinker, eh?" Sporus boomed.

They all laughed. But it was friendly laughter.

"Come on, let's see it," Rullus said.

Half ashamedly, Fadius gave it to him. Rullus looked at it, then tossed it to Sporus.

"For valour," Sporus read laboriously. He tossed it to another soldier. "Don't get a big head, lad."

"Not likely," Fadius mumbled, taking off his helmet and undoing his corselet.

"What he needs now is a wench," someone suggested.

"None here," another retorted.

"Tell you what," Rullus said. "First British wench we grab, we'll hold her down and Fadius here can have first go."

"That blue dye on 'em," Sporus observed. "It puts me off." His comrades laughed. But Rullus clapped Fadius on the shoulder.

"Ass," he pronounced, "is ass. Right, Fadius?"

Fadius wasn't really interested. He nodded. Later that night, curled up in his cloak, there was a great warmth in him. Now, at last, he was at one with his tent-mates. He thought of Rullus showing him how to attach the medal to his corselet; then his thoughts went back to that scene in the Imperator's tent. He relived every instant of it. When it came to the handshake his throat choked up and his eyes misted. For that man, Caesar — Gaius Julius Caesar — he'd do anything — anything.

At that moment in the headquarters tent Caesar was talking to his legates.

"I have a hunch Cassivellaunus directed that attack today," he was saying. "In any case, let's hope success tempts the Britons to a pitched battle. We need wheat. So I'm sending you out, Trebonius, with cavalry, mules, drivers, slaves, and three legions to forage. Quintus Cicero and you, Commius, will command the cavalry under Trebonius. Be on the alert, all of you."

# 5

It was like old times, Fadius thought the next day as, sickle in hand, he cut wheat. His helmet hung from his belt and his corselet was hot in the sun. Every half-dozen steps forward, according to orders, he had to get his shield and javelin and bring them close to hand.

The wheat was a real crop, as good as any he'd seen on the home farm, the heads well-filled and heavy, and it was a lovely, rolling countryside, green with hedges, copses, and woods. Behind him Rullus was gathering the wheat and tying the bundles into sheaves with two twists of straw knotted together, just as they did on the farm near Brixia. The slaves and the drivers took the sheaves back to the mules and the carts. Every quarter of an hour, he and Rullus changed over. Occasionally each of them would glance to see where the standards of their century, maniple, and cohort were and would note in the distance the cavalry patrolling the perimeter.

Trumpets from the northeast alerted them. And then there were trumpet blasts from everywhere. The slaves and drivers had already run for the carts. Rullus and Fadius followed, clapping on their helmets as they dog-trotted.

Within fifteen minutes the legions were in a three-line battle-formation in a rough arc, the carts, mules, and drivers behind them. Their three eagles glinted in the sun and so did the forest of standards. From the perimeter the cavalry were withdrawing before the charges of British chariotry. Behind the chariots, advancing across the fields, was a mass of infantry.

The cavalry and the light-armed troops drew in behind the legions, while in front the British infantry took a few moments to arrange their phalanxes. Trebonius had picked his field of battle well. The Britons had to charge up a slope, facing the sun.

45

In their front ranks, standing close together, were well-armed men in outlandish helmets and leather jerkins, with long, narrow shields and spears. Most had one-edged swords at their sides. Behind was a mass of men equipped only with scythes, axes, or bill-hooks, local levies of peasants without a doubt.

The front ranks were beating their shields with their spears and shouting. Then the British war-horns blared, and with a wild yell their phalanxes surged forward, individuals stopping for a second to hurl their spears, then drawing swords to attack. The legions stood steady until at fifteen paces the signal came.

"Cast," the centurions roared.

The first and second ranks hurled the heavy javelins, pinning shields and Britons to the ground.

"Out swords," came the order; then, "Open ranks."

The odd numbers of the first rank jumped forward. Now the first rank was two ranks, each legionary with six feet of space to swing his deadly sword.

"Charge!"

With a hoarse shout the first line of the legions, eight files deep, charged. As their first rank cut into the Britons, the third and fourth files arced their javelins over the heads of their comrades into the mass behind.

It was death from the sun. It was easy, Fadius found, ridiculously easy, when after ten minutes of slaughter he and the rest of the even numbers of the first rank jumped through to take the place of the odd numbers. It was feint and stab, then slice upward at the belly or bare throat of another blue-dyed Briton.

There was no need for more than the eight files of the first line of the legions. The Britons broke. And then for Fadius and his comrades it was chase and kill, red slaughter among the trampled wheat. The cavalry took up the pursuit, spearing the fleeing infantry. The British leader, whoever he was, sent in his chariotry. The cavalry, this time, bold as wild boars, rode over them. It was a massacre.

"Well, that's taught them," Caesar said grimly when Trebonius reported.

46

# CHAPTER V

SEVEN WEEKS AFTER THE BATTLE in the wheatfields, the Roman Army was across the Tamesis River and deep into mid-Britain.

"Bloody buggering Pluto," Rullus was swearing, "I'll never be dry again." He was in the tent, unwinding the woollen strips of cloth with which the legionaries had wrapped themselves from crotch to boots. "Or warm either," he added. "Goddam this bloody buggering island."

"Rain every bleeding day," Rudex, usually called "Pimples", put in. "Don't it never stop? Wood won't burn. Armour rusts." He blew his nose, then wiped the snot on his tunic.

Fadius said nothing. Like everybody else in the tent, he had the sniffles.

"Knock it off," Sporus said hoarsely and fell into a fit of coughing. The cough came from his guts.

"March and counter-march," Rullus grumbled. "No loot. No bloody women. Swamps, woods, yelling Britons in them bloody chariots. Rain, rain, rain. This bugger of a country. Let the bloody Britons have it, I say."

"I said, 'Knock it off,'" Sporus cut in. He coughed again. "Caesar'll look after us."

At that moment Caesar was standing on the six-foot-wide platform behind the palisade on the rampart staring southwest over the breast-high stakes. In front of him, the ground sloped down to a wooded valley. There would be another accursed swamp down there and most likely a stream to splash through, and then a climb up the opposing hill with British chariotry bursting in to throw spears and darts and wheel away, yelling. They knew every trail, every pathway, of mid-Britain. Useless

47

to pursue. They could outdistance the legionaries, and it had been proved, time and again, that light-armed troops or cavalry would be lured to a spot where the Britons could turn and cut them down.

Caesar felt a tickle in his left nostril, drew out a square of cloth, and blew his nose. That rain! Always the same, day after day, week after week. It was mid-afternoon and only a light drizzle was falling, but to the east heavier clouds were bending down. Soon there'd be another of those infernal downpours.

He glanced back at Trebonius, Quintus Cicero, and Commius, standing with the escort a dozen paces away. They were awaiting his decision about the envoys Cassivellaunus had just sent, requesting a conference. Somewhat bitterly, Caesar reflected on how high his hopes had been seven weeks ago, when his legionaries, shoulder-deep in water that was studded with up-thrusting sharpened stakes, had forced a passage across the Tamesis. Then when, a few days later, the Trinovantes, who held all the eastern bulge of mid-Britain as far as the sea, had accepted his client prince as king and joined him, he had thought that he was on his way to victory. With their help, he had found and stormed Cassivellaunus' headquarters, and five more tribes, two south of the upper Tamesis, three to the west and north of Cassivellaunus' holdings in mid-Britain, had come over to him. The Britons, he had told himself exultantly, were, like the Gauls, falling to pieces. Soon he'd have the whole of the Midlands in his hands.

But Cassivellaunus was a wilier leader than any of the Gallic chieftains. He'd sent his infantry home, but had kept his trained chariotry. No more pitched battles. Instead, the cattle, swine, sheep, and people had been removed into the forests. From those same forests at any instant the chariotry would erupt for swift harassing attacks and melt away like phantoms. And the rain!

There must be a different weather system here from that in Cantium, let alone Gaul, Caesar reflected. As for the country — swamps, fens, only the occasional farmstead. Mid-Britain, he had discovered, depended on herds and flocks rather than on grain. Therefore there were no towns to plunder and not even temples or holy places to loot as in Gaul. No wonder the soldiers were grumbling. And then, three days ago, a courier from Atrius had come to tell him that the four kings of Cantium had attacked the naval camp. They had been beaten back, but Atrius warned that no more convoys of supplies could be sent. For that matter, the heads of two couriers had been flung over the rampart of yesterday's camp.

Caesar paced a half-dozen steps along the platform and paused again. In those same dispatches there had been the news of his mother's death. Caesar stared at a twig close to his right toe. You could say that she'd had a good span of life — well along in her sixties. You could remind yourself that death was inevitable for every man, woman, and child. Still, the death of his mother was a shock. It was as if a solid pillar of his life had suddenly been torn away. His father? He'd died years and years ago when he himself was just entering manhood. He had been forgotten. But his mother was still real in his mind — her stern, grave face, her unbending principles. He remembered that morning years and years ago when he'd been leaving to find out whether the Romans would elect him Chief Pontiff or not.

"Your eyes, Julius," she had said, "are much too big for your stomach."

She might be right this time. The last dispatch from Labienus had warned of serious unrest among the Gauls. He himself was now in effect cut off from the naval camp, and the equinox and its storms were approaching. So was he prepared to winter in Britain? And with Gallic unrest, did he dare? Likewise, what about his troops? Loyalty could be stretched only so far.

He would have to admit to himself that he could not conquer Britain, at least in this campaign. Yet somehow, he must be able to pretend victory for the Senate and the Roman mob. This meeting with the envoys from Cassivellaunus might present what he needed. And what other choice did he have? This bloody, buggering island, he thought, as he walked back to his officers.

"Send back the envoys," he told Commius. "Tell them I'll meet this Cassivellaunus here, in front of the camp, two days from now." He paused. "Tell them to tell Cassivellaunus that this is his one chance to sue for peace."

He went down the steps from the rampart platform, his officers following him. As he made for his headquarters tent, his mind was busy. Perhaps when he got back to the naval camp there'd be news about Julia and the grandson she was carrying.

With a wave of his hand to his officers, he entered the tent and sat down behind the table, his mind reviewing rapidly what he needed for his report to Rome. The mob? In spite of the anti-Caesar speeches that that rascal Clodius was reported to be making, he was certain that he could hold their allegiance. The Senate was a different sort of cauldron. Once it had ruled Rome and the Empire, and the old traditions died hard. In this day and age it was split into groups — a Pompey clique, a gaggle who owed money to Crassus, a Caesar faction, and other fluctuating combinations. The main difficulty was the irreconcilables, with Cato their chief spokesman.

Caesar clasped his hands behind his neck and leaned back. The irreconcilables, the die-hards, as he liked to call them, were the menace. They hated him because he, a patrician noble, was the leader of their political enemy, the Popularists, and he himself, by forming an alliance with Crassus and Pompey, had smashed their power. So the die-hards were watching for a chance to hit him back. Give them a single chance and they would pounce. So for them, somehow, he must be able to claim a victory in Britain. Unclasping his hands, he rested his elbows on the table, his chin on his cupped hands. For a moment his thoughts ranged: Crassus in Parthian territory; Rabirius in Egypt — how was he getting along collecting money from that flabby Ptolemy?

This last thought made him recall that he'd written to Antony, accepting his request to be put on his staff in Gaul. Brilliant in Gabinius' Egyptian sortie, according to reports, he remembered. That was a new aspect of Antony, a lad who in Rome had been renowned for only one thing, debauchery. Perhaps he ought to write to Labienus to expect that young man.

Sun in Gaul, he told himself, hearing the rain splash down on his tent. For that matter, sun in Italy, in Egypt, everywhere but here. He pulled a sheet of papyrus toward him.

As Caesar picked up his pen, far to the southeast the princess Cleopatra was on a pleasure-barge that floated on the lake just north of Alexandria. Awnings kept off the sun. Sweetmeats and jars of Cretan wine sat on tables. Cleopatra was chattering with her maids, she and they practically nude in robes of clinging byssus. Apollodorus watched her with misery-ridden eyes. He had tried to interest her in the intrigues that had forced Rabirius, the financier, in fear for his life, to embark for Rome.

"Oh, I know all about that," she had interrupted, with a sidelong glance at the handsome Macedonian captain of the escort who was standing in the stern of the barge. "Father was clever, really. Bribing that Roman legate and the senior centurions not to interfere with the mobs attacking Rabirius. Let's forget that. Finish your drink, Apollodorus."

He sipped at his wine, watching her.

"Who's for a swim?" she said, and slipping off her robe, naked and completely depilated even to the patch between her thighs, posed on the edge of the barge, arms outstretched, rounded body beautiful as a statue but rosy with vitality. This pose, Apollodorus knew, was for the Macedonian. He looked at him. He was staring at Cleopatra, eyes narrowed, the look of a predator in every line of him.

Cleopatra waited another instant. Then, with a light, silvery laugh, she dived. Her maids followed. There was one who was as voluptuous as the goddess of lust. The Macedonian never looked at her. He kept staring at Cleopatra.

Apollodorus drained his goblet. It was a mark of non-intelligence to be jealous, he argued to himself. He was forty, after all, and she was now sixteen. Sooner or later she was bound to take someone else, someone young, virile.

She swam to the side of the barge. She reached up an arm.

"Help me up," she ordered. Apollodorus pulled her aboard. Her maids followed her.

"Towel me," she commanded them.

Apollodorus watched as she turned this way and that, showing herself.

"When Crassus returns to Antioch," he tried.

"We're here for fun," she interrupted, "not lectures." She glanced at the Macedonian. "Captain," she called. "Come for a swim!"

"My orders, princess," the captain began.

"Orders!" Cleopatra said. She raised her chin. "I order you to swim." She walked to the edge of the barge and posed there. "Coming?"

Without a word the Macedonian, never taking his eyes from her, began to fling off his armour and clothes.

"Well built," Apollodorus thought miserably. His glance dropped lower. "Well hung, too. Oh, Zeus, Hera, all the gods and goddesses — "

"Catch me," Cleopatra called to the Macedonian. "If you can."

She dived. The Macedonian was not a second behind. One must not be jealous, Apollodorus tried to tell himself. He wouldn't look. No, he wouldn't. With a hand that trembled he seized the wine jar and filled his goblet, splashing the overflow on the deck. What was one to do? What was one?

# 3

As he asked himself this question, to the northeast Crassus was finishing the supervision of the packaging of the enormous treasure he had gathered. Tomorrow, he had ordered, they were to begin the march back to Antioch. Meanwhile, the troops were completely disorganized. They, too, had gathered loot, and each soldier had only one thing in mind—how to arrange for a spot on a cart or a camel or the back of a slave to get his plunder to Antioch.

"Can't do a thing with them," young Publius grumbled.

"Why can't you get your father to do something?" Cassius asked in his usual direct way.

Publius rubbed his forehead and lowered his voice. "All he can talk about is Jerusalem. The Jews, he says, have a huge treasure in their temple."

"In case the Parthians attack on the march, tomorrow," Cassius said, "you'd better have your Gallic horse as the rearguard, Publius."

As Publius nodded assent, in her palace on the Palatine Hill in Rome, Servilia took time to sponge her face and hands in a basin of water. Then she held up a mirror to make sure her finespun hair was correctly coiffed, and retraced an eyebrow. Like any beautiful woman, she knew that her attractiveness was one reason for the success of her salon. She turned away from the mirror. It was always a turmoil during the first few days when, after the summer in the villa in the Sabine hills, one moved back to the palace. There were the rooms to open up and clean, the hundred or so slaves to supervise and get settled, and, even more annoying, the constant calls from her daughters and from all her other friends and acquaintances. In July and August Rome was a deserted city as far as the nobles and the knights and anyone else who had money were concerned. Now, in September, it hummed again. Her husband, Silanus, a pleasant, bumbling man, was no help. At this moment, he'd be in the Senate-House listening, probably, to her half-brother, Cato, fulminating about the corruption in Rome. Julius? He was away, somewhere in Britain, that remote island on the fringe of the world. Men! And their ambitions.

Not quite knowing what to do with herself, she stepped into the garden. The flowers were still beautiful. She paused by a bed of yellow marigolds and noted that she would have to speak to the steward about the weeding. September was really one of the best months of the year, she thought, strolling along the patterned paths toward the summer-house at the back. Warm, but not too warm. Trees beginning to tint their leaves with bronze. Thunderstorms at noon and then the sun out again. What was it like in Britain?

She paused, fingering the glossy leaves of an arbutus. Had Julius by this time received her letter of condolence about his mother's death? There was Julia, too. She ought to inquire about her. She must be about due.

Julius! she thought resentfully. Why wasn't he here when she needed him — physically? So long since she'd had him. Last

53

winter, in fact, up in Cisalpine Gaul, and she wasn't like her friends to whom any man halfway respectable served when the urge took them. She'd make an excuse to get up to Cisalpine Gaul earlier than ever, she decided. That Marcus Antonius, now. He'd come to visit her yesterday. Said he was off shortly to join Caesar. Why shouldn't she send a personal note to Julius with him?

Down in the Forum Marcus Antonius, too, was thinking of Caesar. A week ago he had reached Rome. He had seen the toddler who had been born to his wife after he'd left for the East three years back, but the youngster hadn't interested him particularly.

He might as well get ready to leave for Gaul and Caesar, he was telling himself as, followed by over a dozen slaves, he shouldered his way through the crowds. Already he was getting tired of Rome. There had been changes, naturally, since he'd left. He had gone to see Pompey's new stone theatre, constructed as a shrine to Venus in order to get around a Roman law against any permanent theatre. Near by Pompey had also built an auditorium large enough to accommodate the Senate as well as fabulous colonnades and walks, all in marble. Everyone knew that Pompey was trying to win the favour of the mob of Roman voters. So was Caesar. Antony had glanced at Caesar's new voting-pens, also in marble and near Pompey's theatre. Right here in the Forum gangs of workmen were tearing down houses and shops where, in the northwest corner, Caesar was planning a new basilica for the law courts.

Must be lots of loot in Gaul, Antony told himself as he pushed through the senators, the women in sedan-chairs, the throngs of plebeian Romans intermingled with Spaniards, Syrians, Jews, Egyptians, North Africans, and what have you. The sooner I get there, the better.

Then he saw Cicero making his way toward the Senate-House and veered to the left. He had hated the orator ever since Cicero as consul had had his stepfather strangled over there in the gloomy prison above and to the left of the Senate-House.

"Wordy old bastard," he muttered to himself. "Look at him. Talking. Always talking. A diarrhoea of words, that's him."

And then he saw Curio the Elder and veered still farther left to miss him. This was the man who had made him leave Rome four years ago. What he needed, Antony decided, was a drink. Turning, he strode decisively to a tavern on the Vicus Tuscus, a narrow alley beneath the northwestern face of the Palatine. He seated himself. To the tavern-keeper he said,

"Wine. Lots of it. Some of those sausages, too." He waved carelessly toward his slaves. "Pour them drinks, too."

It was the same tavern in which he and Curio the Younger had sat the previous afternoon. There had been a certain constraint as they estimated each other. Four years ago each of them had been millions and millions of sesterces in debt. There had been boating-parties on the Tiber, wild orgies in the Subura, villas in the hills bought for mobs of strippers from the mimes, expensive courtesans from Athens and the East, prostitutes of both sexes, a fleet of barges built on Lake Nemi for an evening of nude swimming by moonlight. And always crowds of hangers-on.

The debts and the senseless spending had infuriated Curio the Elder. But when the wits of Rome began calling Antony and Curio the Younger "husband and wife", and graffiti about them were scribbled on the walls, Curio the Elder had boiled over. He had bought up the debts of the two of them. Then had come the ultimatum. If Antony got out of Rome, he'd tear up the debts. If not, both of them could take the consequences and be damned to them.

He'd done him a favour, actually, Antony had thought yesterday, staring at Curio the Younger. Curio himself had realized that time had flowed forward.

"A Hercules, I hear," he had drawled, lifting a languid hand to arrange the curls around his left ear. "Or so the matrons report."

"I've bedded a dozen," Antony had answered. "Eager, I grant you. Not as expert as the Syrian tarts."

"So you've gone that way?"

Antony had nodded. "And that young man against the wall,

55

looking knives and spears at me, that tells me something."

"A dear boy," Curio had said, glancing at the young man. "Frightfully jealous."

"He doesn't need to be," Antony had answered, underlining a point Curio already understood. "Besides, I'm for Gaul — and Caesar."

"You always were blunt." Curio had taken another look at Antony. "I'm engaged in politics now, you know." He waved a limp wrist gracefully. "So delightfully corrupt, dear boy. Did you know Cato is hauling the consuls and the candidates for next year's consulships into court?"

"What for?"

Curio giggled. "A deal. Extraordinary. The elections are late. So this year's consuls have taken bribes to help next year's candidates get elected. Fascinating, really."

"I prefer swords."

"And women. Well, tonight at Clodius' dinner, take a look at his wife. Red-headed. Best-looking bitch in Rome."

It was Clodius' wife that Antony was considering now. Hair a deep, rich red. Lower lip full, sensual. Body so voluptuous you wanted to tear her robe from her. Sleepy-lidded eyes that, by Venus, promised. She was a demanding ache in his groin. Clodius, he reflected, would be somewhere with his gangsters. Probably hunting his opponent, Milo, Pompey's man. Besides, Clodius, as he'd known him four years ago, was a man who enjoyed every form of sexual excitement. Surely he wouldn't care if someone else tore off a piece. And why not now? Fulvia would probably be alone in that enormous palace on the Palatine.

Antony got up, flung a gold piece on the table, gestured to his slaves, stepped outside, and made for the ramp that led up the Palatine Hill. It was a shock to be suddenly confronted by Clodius. Antony stopped. Clodius was a lean, dark man, half a head shorter than himself, but with that arrogant sneer that all the Claudians wore.

"I was looking for you," Clodius said. He came a step closer. "Lay off."

Antony's face flushed. "What d'you mean?"

56

"I watched you last night." Clodius lifted his chin. "To repeat, lay off. Understood?"

Antony's hand went to where his sword ought to be. No sword! He glanced around in a quick soldier's estimate. Behind Clodius was a gang of his bully-boys, hands on daggers. To Antony's rear in the Vicus Tuscus, filling it from wall to wall, another group. His own dozen slaves, unarmed, were huddled together. Antony glared down at Clodius.

"Understood," he said hoarsely, a fury in him he could scarcely contain. "Now, make way. Or, by Mars — "

He lunged forward. Clodius had already gestured to his men. They opened a path. Smiling slightly, Clodius watched Antony shoulder his way through. Later that night, Clodius walked into his wife's boudoir, an elegantly furnished circular room, the walls done in glossy black panels relieved by a diamond pattern in red. She was sitting in a gilded chair, watching in a mirror of polished silver as a maid brushed the rich auburn of her hair, which fell loosened to her waist. Under the gossamer robe her nipples had been touched with rouge, and one slender foot rested on a low stool as another maid gilded her toenails.

"Like?" she asked, without turning her head.

"Very much," he replied, leaning an elbow against a pedestal on which stood the statue of a dancing satyr, head thrown back and mouth open to catch, presumably, the wine from a jar held high by his outstretched right hand.

"I've told your latest admirer what's what," Clodius added negligently.

"Did you, then?" Fulvia let the mirror drop to her lap and gave him a sideways glance from her sleepy-lidded, sensuous eyes. "Don't you like other men to want me?"

"As long as that's as far as it goes."

His voice wasn't casual this time. She laughed and held up the mirror again. Clodius kept on watching. Initially it had been the size of her dowry which had attracted him; and he had had no idea then how totally she would fascinate him. It wasn't merely her voluptuous body, linked with a complete lack of inhibitions and a temperament that was as fiery as her impulsive rages. She also had a brain and an ambition that he had never suspected.

"There, that's enough," she said to her maids. "Away with you."

As the slaves left, she got up from her chair. Clodius straightened and took a step toward her.

"No, wait," she told him. "I've had an idea."

"Oh?"

"That Antony last night, talking about rumours of unrest in Gaul," she explained.

"Get to the point."

"When I married you, you ruled the roost in Rome. You'd sent Cicero into exile. You had Pompey locked up in his palace. Then, Pompey hired Milo. Got him elected tribune. Gave him money to collect gladiators to fight your bully-boys. That's how Cicero got back from exile. But you still were cock of the roost. Until Lucca. There Caesar ordered you to calm down."

"I said, get to the point."

"I want Milo dead. I want you master of Rome." She came closer so that the musky perfume she wore was in his nostrils. "Look, Crassus is in the East. Caesar is away in Britain."

"He'll be back in Gaul, soon."

"If the Gauls were to rise up . . . You know Verres in Massilia, don't you?"

"Yes."

"Exiled. Greedy for money. Send Sextus up there. Let him and Verres organize agents to stir up the Gauls. Then, if Caesar is kept busy, you can operate here."

Clodius knew that Sextus Clodius, a distant cousin, was completely loyal; and the idea of thumbing his nose at Caesar was appealing.

"I'll think about it," he said.

"Tomorrow. Not tonight." She dropped to her knees. "Now, let's see how *he* is."

Clodius looked down at her shining hair. A surge of passion flooded through him. Yes, she was the best. The very best.

# CHAPTER VI

AT THIS MOMENT, in his tent in Britain, Caesar blew his nose and leaned back in his chair. He had sent a courier under escort to Atrius at the coast to warn him to get ready to sail before the approaching equinox. More couriers had ridden off to the new king of the Trinovantes and to the kings of the other five tribes which had joined the Romans, ordering them to be present two days from now. Then he had toured his troops, seeing to it that they were as comfortable as possible, knowing that the rumour of the conference with Cassivellaunus would already have travelled through the camp. Now he had just finished writing in his own hand a draft of a dispatch to the Senate and the Roman people, one which claimed a success in Britain, a claim to which the conference must, somehow, give verisimilitude.

In this moment, his face was gaunt; there were deep lines in his forehead and from his nostrils to the corners of his mouth. Whatever mask one presented to others, he was thinking, one had to be honest with oneself. So, let's face it. This island—and the Britons—had defeated him. Since Dumnorix, in fact, little had gone right.

Caesar dismissed that thought. He got up to stroll around the tent. It would be good to be back in Gaul, he reflected, away from this eternal rain. Totally different problems there; the drought had continued and Labienus' dispatches had warned that most of Gaul would be short of grain and fodder.

He sat down again and put his chin between his hands. In Gaul, too, there would be news of Julia and, he hoped, of a grandson. A fond smile curved his lips. Julia, his only child. Though it was possible that Brutus, Servilia's first-born, was his son. Neither he nor Servilia could be sure because at that time her first husband was alive. Still—possible.

59

His thoughts returned to Julia. She was so sweet, so feminine in her trustfulness and acceptance that everything he did was right or could be excused. Yes, news of Julia—and then, once the legions were settled for the winter, off to Cisalpine Gaul — and Servilia.

Meanwhile, that meeting with Cassivellaunus must be carefully planned. He pulled over a sheet of papyrus and picked up his pen.

## 2

The sky was heavy with clouds. As a welcome change, it wasn't raining. Grouped around Caesar were his officers, along with the Roman-supported king of the Trinovantes. The kings of the other five tribes had sent excuses, waiting to see what came out of the conference. Behind Caesar stood his bodyguard, and a quarter of a mile back rose the rampart and palisade of the camp. With Cassivellaunus was a well-armed group of retainers. The woods behind him, Caesar was certain, would be full of Britons.

It was time. Caesar, in burnished armour but bareheaded, walked forward slowly, his officers following him. From the opposite side came Cassivellaunus, accompanied by a group of chieftains. Their tartan cloaks and leggings were in greens and reds, and they carried bronze shields, cunningly enamelled with rosettes of gold. Their swords were hanging at their sides. Except for Cassivellaunus, who, like Caesar, was bareheaded, they wore horned helmets—of bulls' and wild boars' horns. The two leaders stopped, estimating each other. Caesar saw a man as tall as himself but stockier, with a moustache and brown hair in a topknot. The face was, as usual, dyed blue. But if one looked past the externals, the features were strong and the grey-blue eyes were steady.

Not a man to panic, Caesar thought. Intelligent, too, as his tactics had proved. He waved behind him with one hand. A slave brought forward a stool. As Caesar sat down, with a hint of a smile, Cassivellaunus gestured and a similar stool was planted ten feet from Caesar. There was a certain bravado as he, too, seated himself and crossed his legs.

One up for him, Caesar reflected. "Tell him," Caesar ordered Commius, "that we assume he is suing for peace."

Commius translated. The Briton uncrossed his legs and, gesticulating, poured forth a burst of rhetoric.

"What did he say?" Caesar asked.

"He says that you Romans invaded a peaceful people. He says that you have killed many and done much damage. All he wants, however, is an end to a war that does nothing but harm. Therefore, he will allow you to return to your ships and sail away without harassment."

Caesar's face was flushed. "Allow!" he exclaimed. "Who does he think he is?" He paused, then said coldly, "Tell him I've beaten his troops in battle, captured his headquarters, and ravaged his country to the mountains of the west and from the Tamesis to the next big river to the north. Remind him that the Trinovantes and five other tribes have joined me. Make it clear that unless he sues for peace, I'll march through all his country, burning and plundering, until not a single ally will be left him."

Commius spoke. The Briton got to his feet slowly. He spoke, quite quietly.

"Well?" Caesar asked.

"He says it is well known that you must return to Gaul before the equinoctial storms. Therefore, he repeats his offer."

Caesar stood up, his face controlled, his voice, too, quiet.

"Tell him that Romans do not treat with an enemy under arms. Make that clear, Commius. Make it clear that if he does not sue for peace, give hostages, and agree to pay tribute to Rome, I'll winter in Britain and to hell with Gaul. I mean it, Commius. This autumn and next spring I'll smash him and his people, and his own head will stare at his country from the top of a hundred-foot pole. I really mean it. No Briton defies me and lives."

He did mean it in the heat of the moment. As Commius

61

translated, Caesar saw Cassivellaunus glancing at him, estimating him anew. When he spoke again, it was with fewer gestures. Commius turned to Caesar.

"He says — " he began.

"Does he sue for peace?"

Commius decided not to translate all that Cassivellaunus had said. Most of it, in any case, had been directed to his chieftains to the effect that the Romans had a nuisance value and what did a few pledges matter. No wonder the Roman-appointed king was chewing at his moustache.

"In short, yes."

"Good," Caesar said, seating himself. "Now, we'll discuss terms."

It was an hour of haggling. Cassivellaunus agreed finally to give Caesar a hundred hostages and to pay an annual tribute to Rome of four thousand talents or their equivalent in gold, iron, and tin ingots.

"One other thing," Caesar added. "He must swear an oath not to attack any of the tribes which have joined me and, in particular, to leave the Trinovantes in peace."

Commius translated. Cassivellaunus hesitated an instant, then nodded.

"Make it clear to him that if he breaks any of his pledges, the hostages will die. Moreover, I myself with my legions will return to Britain to punish him."

When Commius had spoken, the Briton nodded again, this time with a suspicion of a smile under his moustache.

"Good," Caesar said, rising. "Have the altars set up here. At once. He will swear by his gods and I by the gods of Rome."

The oaths were sworn. As the Britons receded into the woods, Caesar walked slowly back to the camp. He had his semblance of a victory for his report to the Senate. Yet he knew, as Cassivellaunus knew, that he was not likely ever to return to this accursed island. No worthwhile loot. A cunning, skilful enemy. Mists, fogs, rains. Labienus had been right, after all. So what would Cassivellaunus do as soon as the Romans left?

Obvious. He'd give the hostages. He'd never send the tribute.

Before the winter was over the Trinovantes and the other tribes would be reconquered. He himself could put the hostages to death. But to what end, if he wasn't returning?

"Caesar's luck," as the troops called it, he thought bitterly. "Why should it have left me?"

## 3

"Like pickles in a barrel," Rullus grumbled. He hawked, spat, and wiped his nose. "If there's a storm, into the drink, that's us."

It was midnight and under the half-moon they were pulling away from shore on a sea that for the moment had no more than ripples on it. Their barge was overloaded. Fadius knew that. Every vessel was. Because of the loss of forty ships in the hurricane and because few of the boats Labienus had been building at Portus Itius had arrived, and because there were prisoners, hostages, and loot to carry, Caesar had sent half his load back in half the available transport. He had waited three days for that transport to return. When it hadn't, he'd piled everyone and everything into the remaining vessels.

"Look — back there," Rudex said. "The camp!"

Rullus and Fadius looked. On the receding shore the outlines of their first camp were darkly visible. Lights were dancing inside it.

"Britons!" Sporus observed. He, too, hawked, spat, and wiped his dripping nose with his fingers. "Didn't take the buggers long."

"If we were there with swords out!" Rudex exclaimed.

"We aren't," Rullus told him. "We won't be, ever again. That bloody island! Let 'em have it, bugger them."

Fadius said nothing. To the others, the veterans, that island was a complete loss. No loot, no women, nothing. But that island was where he'd found himself. He was a legionary. His fingers caressed the medal Caesar had given him.

On the stern of the flagship to the right of Fadius' barge, Caesar, too, was staring back at Britain. He was, as usual, facing facts. This invasion had accomplished nothing. As far as the Britons were concerned, it was a ripple which was receding. Yesterday, the Roman-sponsored king had arrived in camp with the news that Cassivellaunus' men were already into the territory of the Trinovantes. The British leader hadn't even done Caesar the courtesy of waiting until the Romans left.

Nothing he could do about it. Now or, it seemed, ever. He'd had to get away before the equinoctial storms.

Caesar turned from the stern and in that instant put the past behind him and concentrated on the present and the future. He glanced at the winking lights of his fleet. He knew that once again he was trusting to luck. If it held and if the sea remained calm, he'd be at Portus Itius by dawn. If a storm hit them, many of his overloaded boats and the men in them would sink. Why hadn't Labienus got the other ships back? He needed a chewing out, that man. A good, even a brilliant, second-in-command, but always grumbling. Always deliberate, taking his time. At times, there was no time to take time.

He shrugged his shoulders. If luck held, back in safety. Then, what to do about winter quarters for the legions? According to Labienus, the crops in Gaul were really bad. So, what to do?

As Caesar considered options, in the bow of a ship to his left Acco, Indutiomar, and Ambiorix were talking.

"So the demon can be beaten," Indutiomar was saying. "The Britons have proved it."

"What sort of plan do you have in mind?" Ambiorix asked.

"Gaul a province of Rome," Indutiomar went on. "A province! That demon promised that each tribe would still be free to pick its own king or chief magistrate. Free!" He snorted. "Free to pick Caesar's choices. Making that bastard, Cingetorix, king of the Treverans — instead of me!"

"What do we do, that's the question," Ambiorix pointed out.

Acco spoke. "The Council of all Gaul is to be held at Samarobriva as soon as we get back. Why don't we talk to those chieftains who are likely to agree with us? Form a league?"

"Agreed," Ambiorix said.

# 4

Before morning of that same night, in the palace of Verres in Massilia, Antony woke. He sat up, rubbed his eyes, and looked around. The room was a clutter of naked bodies, male and female.

Antony yawned. The lamps were guttering. He could make out Verres, his pot belly anchoring him to the cushions, his mouth open, a woman on either side. In the corner Lycisca, the madam from whose establishment the girls and boys had come, was propped against the wall, snoring, her dugs hanging to her navel. Quite an orgy, Antony thought. He and Aulus Cincius, another officer on his way to Caesar, had reached Massilia by boat from Ostia a day and a half ago. Cincius' father had been a friend of Verres, the former governor of Sicily, whom Cicero's orations sixteen years before this had sent into exile. Hence, their welcome.

Antony stretched. He had told his freedman, Hermogenes, to have horses ready for this morning. Over four hundred miles still to go, he reflected. The trader Lupinus had traced the route for him.

"Straight up the Rhone to Vienna," Lupinus had pointed out. "Then cut across to Lutetia, the chief town of the Parisians. It's on an island in the Sequana River. From Lutetia to Samarobriva, Caesar's headquarters, is about thirty miles to the northwest."

"Headquarters when he returns from Britain, you mean?"

"So I've been told." Lupinus had glanced at him. "After Vienna, keep your eyes open."

Antony had looked at him sharply. "Why?"

"There's rumours."

"What rumours?"

"I'd rather not say."

"Out with it, man."

"Well, keep it under your helmet but Sextus, Clodius' man, has been here in conference with your host. The rumour is that agents to stir trouble are moving up from Massilia into central Gaul."

Clodius again! Antony had thought. He'd tell Caesar when he joined him. The question was whether to leave Massilia this morning or not.

He looked around for Cincius. That young man was lying, dead to the world, with his head in the lap of a sleeping girl. Antony doubted if Cincius would be up to it. He'd drunk too much, so much that even during the exotic sexual exhibitions Lycisca had had her girls and boys put on, Cincius had had to struggle to live up to what was expected. Besides, what need was there to hurry? Another day wouldn't matter. Massilia was a harbour city that hummed. Ships from everywhere. Delicious sea-food. Every debauchery. No campaigning possible for the rest of this year, anyway.

Antony got to his feet. He glanced at the petite girl who had been his last partner. A miniature Venus, that one—and expert. He'd give her a bit extra, he decided, stepping over her and going to the entrance. In the peristyle was the light of early dawn.

"Hermogenes," he roared.


# 5


As the same dawn light picked out the cliffs of Portus Itius, Caesar's flagship was swimming up the estuary. His luck had held, Caesar was telling himself. Not a ship, not a soldier lost in the crossing.

He noted that Labienus was waiting with an escort on top of the cliff. He'd be full of excuses.

That didn't matter. His men were back safe. He thought of the dispatches and letters that would be waiting. One from Julia, he hoped, telling how she was, at least up to a month ago. Why hadn't somebody invented a faster means of communication than horses or boats, he wondered. Twenty-eight to thirty days for news from Rome. Twice that to hear from Athens. Still longer from Crassus. If you could send thoughts back and forth —

One had to make do with what one had. He raised a hand to signal his trumpeter to answer the trumpets blowing from the land. And there was the edge of the sun rising to the east. Sun!

# CHAPTER VII

IN THE SUN OF EARLY OCTOBER the legion of recruits, the Fifteenth, which had marched from Cisalpine Gaul during the summer, was at weapons drill outside the camp at Samarobriva. Caesar watched the men critically for a few moments, strolling from one squad to another. As he moved on, he glanced at the sky. The unnaturally dry and hot weather still held. That meant, as had been pointed out at the Council of all Gaul, starvation crops.

Part of his mind was considering this fact as it related to this morning's meeting with his legates. Another part was still worrying about Julia when he saw a party of Romans approaching. Of the two men riding at the head, one was as big as or bigger than any Gaul. That ought to be Marcus Antonius. In that case, the other, according to the letter that had been awaiting him on his return from Britain, would be young Cincius.

As they came closer, he saw that he was right. Antony and Cincius slipped from their horses and saluted him. Caesar greeted them warmly. Cincius was a slender young man, with candid eyes and dark hair. Caesar turned from him to Antony. When he'd known his cousin in Rome, he'd been a gay, reckless young man, usually half-seas over. He looked different now. Handsome as ever, but his face seemed to have taken on shape and character. Time, too. He'd be past twenty-nine. Caesar recalled the reports of his brilliance as leader of the cavalry during Gabinius' march into Egypt.

"You're most welcome," he repeated. "Unfortunately, I have a meeting in a few moments."

"One thing I think you really ought to know, Imperator," Antony said. He glanced at Cincius. "It's a private matter."

Caesar led him aside. Antony told him what he'd heard from Lupinus.

"Clodius, eh?" Caesar said. "Thanks, Antony. After dinner tonight, let's talk further."

"Oh, I almost forgot, Julius," Antony said. "I have a letter for you."

"Thank you." As Antony saluted and Caesar moved back toward the camp, he opened the letter. It was from Servilia, and in Greek. It told him that she was planning on an early visit to her villa at Comum in North Italy.

"Can scarcely wait to see you, darling," she wrote.

A smile curved Caesar's lips. Here was a compelling reason to get his legions into winter quarters and then post to Cisalpine Gaul.

And then he saw a scrawled postscript.

"I've just heard that Julia is going into labour," she had written.

Caesar stopped. So why hadn't he heard? Servilia—and Pompey, too — would know how anxious he was. His legates, however, were waiting in his headquarters tent. He moved on, putting out of his mind everything but the immediate problem. An hour later, he looked around at his legates.

"Well, gentlemen," he said. "Let's sum up our conclusions: We've decided that because of the crop failure, we must distribute the winter camps through northern Gaul where, we've determined from the recent Council, trouble spots, if any, may exist and where, too, the crop failure isn't as devastating. Agreed?"

"I mentioned the Senones and the Carnutes, south of us in the valley of the Liger," Labienus pointed out.

"I think we can discount them," Caesar observed. "Tasgetius, our nominee, is king of the Carnutes. He can hold both tribes in check. Now, gentlemen, you all have maps." He waited until they had pulled over the maps. "Let's review the placements."

As he bent over the map, the centurion Ceretus tiptoed in and leaned over to whisper to Trebonius, the nearest of the legates. Caesar looked up.

"He says that there's a courier from Pompey," Trebonius told him.

Caesar hesitated. But he couldn't wait.

"If you'll excuse me a moment," he said to the legates, then turned to the centurion. "Bring him in," he ordered.

The courier had obviously ridden hard. Caesar took Pompey's letter and waved dismissal to the courier and Ceretus. He made himself open the letter slowly. He read it. The words blurred. He looked up and the whole tent and the figures in it were tilting crazily. With an effort of will he brought the scene into focus. He reread the letter. Realization seeped into his mind. Julia — dead. Dead!

The legates were watching him. He laid the letter down carefully. The table seemed a long way off. He looked at the legates, not really seeing them.

"Well, gentlemen," he continued, "with respect to the winter camps — "

He could hear the words of the legates. He could hear his own replies. All the words — theirs and his — seemed to hang in space, a long way off. The faces of the legates kept wavering, dissolving, coming back again. He himself seemed to be outside himself, watching himself speaking calmly, making decisions. Whether they were good or bad didn't matter. She had lingered for a week, Pompey had written. A week!

"Well, gentlemen," he said finally, "that's decided. Labienus, you take a legion away to the east, to the borders of the Treverans. From that post you will watch Indutiomarus. The legion of recruits will go northwest of you under Sabinus to keep an eye on Ambiorix, and the Eburones and Atuatucans. We will add to Sabinus' force five cohorts of the Fourteenth under Cotta, but Sabinus will be the senior officer. The other five cohorts of the Fourteenth will be broken up among the other legions as replacements. You, Quintus Cicero, will place your legion among the Nervians. Those three camps will hold down northeastern Gaul and, if need be, assist each other."

"We ourselves pick the sites for our camps?" Quintus asked, unnecessarily, since the point had been covered.

"Yes. We'll send Roscius south of here with one legion to check on the Esuvians and the Venetans. For a central force we'll have one legion under Fabius at Portus Itius, another with Marcus Crassus Junior in command twenty-five miles south and east to overawe the Bellovacans, while Plancus with his legion will be at this point—again twenty-five miles away. Trebonius will sit here in Samarobriva with a legion. That way, while I'm gone, there will be four legions which can concentrate rapidly." Caesar sat back. "Any questions?"

"When do you go to Cisalpine Gaul?" Quintus Cicero asked.

No point now in hurrying. "After I'm informed by couriers that your troops are encamped. What is it, Labienus?"

"I'm at the far end, Caesar. I don't like a legion of recruits up there to the northwest of me. What good would they be if I needed help?"

"There are five cohorts of veterans to stiffen them."

"I don't like two men in command of the one camp, either. It's asking for trouble."

Caesar had had all that he could take. "Sabinus is senior to Cotta," he repeated and stood up to indicate that the meeting was over. "Dinner here in two hours," he said. Picking up Pompey's letter he turned abruptly and went into the inner tent. The legates stared after him, puzzled. In the inner tent, Caesar walked past Faberius without a word, into his sleeping cubicle, and flung himself face downward on the bed. Julia — dead. The child, a boy, dead too, a day or two later.

At the moment, the boy didn't matter. Julia—never to see her run to him again, arms outstretched, a smile on her lips. Julia—ashes by now. Julia!

## 2

In a curtained room of his palace, Pompey sat huddled on a sofa. Outside, a chill wind of mid-October was knocking down the leaves and scattering the petals of the flowers in the wide gardens.

71

It was a month since the funeral of Julia. His intention had been to inter her ashes in his family's tomb at Alba Longa, but the mob, stirred up by Clodius, had demanded burial in the Campus Martius, near Pompey's theatre. That fact had been flattering to him. So had all the principal nobles of Rome, walking in the funeral cortège.

No one, Pompey thought, could say he hadn't done her honour. But the house seemed empty. So did his bed. Nor could he shake off his lethargy. This morning Cato, blunt as ever, had demanded an audience.

"No consuls or praetors elected for next year," Cato had pointed out. "They should have been elected in July. Riots," Cato had stormed on, "the gangsters of your man, Milo, and Caesar's man, Clodius, fighting in the streets."

"Why come to me?" Pompey had asked. "I'm not consul."

Cato had stared. "You, Caesar, and Crassus have arranged to govern the Republic," he had said harshly. "A three-headed monster. If I could smash all three of you, I would. Since I can't, and since you're supposed to govern Italy, govern."

"I've no constitutional right to interfere in Rome."

"When did the constitution ever bother you, Gnaeus Pompeius Magnus, when you wanted something?"

That had been unfair, Pompey told himself now. He'd always acted according to the constitution. Even his extraordinary commands had always been passed by the Assembly.

"Bring in your troops," Cato had insisted. "Restore order. Hold elections."

According to the constitution, unless the Senate declared martial law, no one could bring troops into Rome. Pompey had shaken his head.

Cato was only one of the senators bothering him. Pompey stirred restlessly. Everyone always poking at him. He got up and wandered into the next salon. There were legions of slaves about. But the house seemed so empty.

Pompey rubbed the back of his head. Then he struck the gong on a nearby table. His freedman, Demetrius, hurried in.

"Flora," Pompey said heavily, not looking at Demetrius.

72

"Have her bring over one of her girls. A red-head."

He walked back into his bedroom. The master had always needed a woman about, Demetrius thought sympathetically as he sat down to write a note to Flora. He needed one badly now—to lock him to the living. And Flora, now Rome's foremost madam, had been his master's favourite.

Getting up, Demetrius summoned a slave and gave him the message. "And don't loiter," he added sternly.

# 3

A thousand miles to the north Ambiorix and Indutiomar had reached the point where their paths separated, Ambiorix to go further northward to the forested country around the Mosa River, Indutiomar east to the Treverans along the Rhenus. After the Council of the Gauls the two of them had visited chief after chief, and in particular Acco, leader of the Senones.

"So we're in accord," Indutiomar said now.

Ambiorix drew the hood of his cloak closer over his head. Yesterday evening, at long last, the drought had broken and it was raining. He reflected that he didn't trust Indutiomar, not altogether.

"I'm still walking cautiously," he answered.

"Why?" Indutiomar flung out an arm. "We know where the legionary camps are being placed—Labienus near my borders, Quintus Cicero among the Nervians, in your country Sabinus and Cotta. All three are leagues away from Samarobriva. We can pick them off one by one. You have the easiest job."

"A legion and a half to deal with!"

"That legion there is a legion of recruits. Recruits! Men who have never lifted a sword in battle."

Indutiomar moved his horse closer. "Only five veteran cohorts for you to handle. See?"

Ambiorix' eyes slid away from Indutiomar's gaze. He changed the subject.

"We should have heard from Acco by this time."

"He'll do what he promised. And as soon as I hear from you, Ambiorix, the Germans will be across the Rhenus. We can take the whole of northern Gaul. Let Caesar try to get it back." He moved his horse still closer. The two of them were in a glade with their men at the far end behind them, but Indutiomar lowered his voice. "Haven't you a sister that Sabinus ran after when he was freeing the Eburones from the Atuatucans? She wasn't unwilling, I've heard."

"The bitch!" Ambiorix said.

"Sabinus is a womanizer. Why not turn her loose on him?"

Ambiorix considered a moment. "It's an idea," he agreed. He glanced back. "Ah, here's the man you left with Acco to report."

Indutiomar nodded. He beckoned to the courier. The man rode to them.

"News?" Indutiomar asked.

"Tasget," the courier answered. "Dead. Killed in bed with his woman."

"You see?" Indutiomar exclaimed. "Acco said he'd bring it off. Tasget, king of the Carnutes by Caesar's command. That will stir the Roman."

"Plancus' legion is on the march to the Carnutes to find the killers," the courier added.

"One legion out of the way, Ambiorix. Now do you believe in Acco?"

He himself was cleverer than either Acco or Indutiomar, Ambiorix told himself. They thought he was their puppet, dancing. But if — when — they got rid of the Romans, they'd discover who was really in charge. King of northern Gaul, he thought. That was his aim and they never dreamed of it.

"I'll move," he promised. "But in my own time. Certainly not till that demon's out of Gaul and across the Alps."

"You heard what that trader reported in Cenabum. Turmoil in Rome. Caesar's daughter dead. Pompey, they say, moving toward those who hate Caesar. Maybe Caesar'll never return across the Alps. In any case, in two weeks he ought to be gone."

"I'll move against Sabinus," Ambiorix repeated. "Meanwhile, messengers back and forth each week, and as soon as you

74

hear I'm ready to attack, Germans across the Rhenus." He turned his horse and lifted his arm. "Salute."

# CHAPTER VIII

THERMUS' CENTURY WAS ON GUARD DUTY at the western gate of the winter camp of Sabinus and Cotta. The soldiers were at ease. Before them the ground sloped down to a forested ravine through which a stream ran westward to the Mosa River. The weather in this, the second week of November, was patchy, bits of sunlight alternating with drizzle driven by a wind from the northeast. Within the camp the thatched winter huts were arranged in orderly rows, and at the back the slaves and recruit legionaries had finished storing the last of the wheat brought in during the past few days by Ambiorix' Eburones. Outside, as Fadius, Rullus, and Sporus watched stolidly, squads of the recruit legion, the Fifteenth, were sweating at weapon drill. Other parties were out gathering firewood, water, and fodder for the horses of the Spanish and German cavalry.

"I wonder if the old Fourteenth will ever come together again," Rullus remarked idly.

"Five cohorts here, the rest split up as replacements," Sporus observed. "I doubt it."

"I heard," Fadius put in, "that recruits will be brought from Cisalpine Gaul. We'll be the core. The Fourteenth will march again."

"Who said that?" Sporus asked.

"The eagle-bearer. You know, Petrosidius." Fadius glanced at Thermus. "He was talking to my uncle."

"Oh-oh," Rullus said, just as Thermus barked, "Ten-shun."

Standing stiffly at attention, Fadius watched a mixed party of Spanish and Gallic horsemen emerge from the woods. At their head rode the legate, Sabinus, and the Gallic chieftain, Ambiorix. They were chatting and laughing. Fadius knew, as everyone in camp did, that for the past ten days, as the wheat was being brought in, Sabinus and Ambiorix had vied with each other in

76

hospitality. Sabinus had given dinners in his headquarters to Ambiorix. In turn Ambiorix had entertained Sabinus in his mansion near the river. There had been more to the entertainment than food. Everyone in camp knew that Sabinus was besotted with Ambiorix' sister, Fionna. A lovely-looking piece, the soldiers had agreed when she had ridden in to an afternoon dinner in Sabinus' tent — black-haired with creamy skin and rounded buttocks. Well, hair on the old bugger, the soldiers had said.

"Here's Cotta," Rullus said out of the side of his mouth, as Sabinus and Ambiorix paused in front of the gate.

Cotta walked out to meet them. He was a square-shouldered, chunky man in his early thirties. Keeping in shape was a fetish with him. He lifted weights. He sweated at weapon drill. Each day he ran in full armour around the perimeter of the camp. As he stood there now his face was impassive, but Fadius could sense a certain scorn in him.

Sabinus dismounted, his fat belly jiggling. Ambiorix slid from his horse. Cotta saluted. Sabinus, the senior officer, returned the salute negligently.

"I've just been thanking our friend,"—Sabinus draped an arm around Ambiorix' shoulders — "for bringing in his quota of wheat — all of it, too — so quickly."

"It's appreciated," Cotta said stiffly.

"More than appreciated," Sabinus said, withdrawing his arm to slap Ambiorix on the back. "Especially with the poor crops here. You must have had to put pressure on, friend."

"It wasn't too easy," Ambiorix replied modestly, lowering his eyes and not explaining that he had told his people, who were the Eburones, the People of the Boar, that if they followed him they'd get it all back — and more. "My people will be on short rations this winter. But I wasn't going to let you down, legates. That's why I came to my mansion on my southern frontier, to make sure it was done, to show you that the People of the Boar are loyal."

"Caesar shall know of it," Sabinus answered. "I promise you."

"Is Caesar still at Samarobriva?" Ambiorix asked casually.

77

"I doubt it. He was to leave for Cisalpine Gaul the end of last month. That's right, isn't it, Cotta?"

"That was the plan," Cotta answered stiffly.

Sabinus knew that Cotta was expressing disapproval. But Ambiorix had proved that he was a friend. Not only the wheat. The entertainment at his home, and each night Fionna slipping into his bed. Superb!

"Well, I must be off," Ambiorix said, turning toward his horse.

"Dinner with me tonight?" Sabinus asked.

Ambiorix paused, left foot on his groom's cupped hand. "I'll be your guest," he promised, and neither Sabinus nor Cotta noticed the smile on his lips as he mounted.

He rode away with his entourage, while Sabinus and Cotta walked into the camp. Thermus stood his men at ease. The sun came out. The squads broke off weapon drill and filed past them into the camp. Some of the foraging parties had returned but others were still out.

"Here comes the relief," Sporus said. Thermus called his men to attention, ready for the changing of the guard. As Lucanius, another centurion of the old Fourteenth, marched his squad up, there was a sudden wild yelling in the woods in front of the camp. Thermus looked and saw the glint of weapons.

"Man the towers," he roared. "Load the scorpions. Trumpeter, sound the alarm."

As Fadius and his comrades leaped up the steps of the towers, from the woods ran a half-dozen recruits, pursued by Gallic horsemen. The recruits were speared from behind. Out of the woods burst a mob of Gallic footmen, yelling. The horsemen galloped to the gate. A volley of javelins and scorpion-bolts repelled them. The footmen raced forward, piling into the ditch around the camp, setting up notched poles against the rampart to serve as ladders.

By this time the rampart was manned. The recruits, steadied by the veterans, hurled down spears, javelins, and stones. The Gallic infantry fell back. The horsemen rode around the camp, shouting and throwing spears.

78

Sabinus and Cotta had rushed up one of the towers at the main gate.

"I can't believe it," Sabinus cried.

"Over there," Corta said grimly. "See? Ambiorix."

Sabinus stared at Ambiorix. He was astride his horse, rallying his footmen and giving directions to his cavalry as they galloped around the camp, waving their spears.

"I still can't believe it!" Sabinus exclaimed.

Cotta turned to an aide. "Are the Spanish and German horse drawn up?" he asked.

"Ready, Legate."

"Spanish horse out the side gate, German out the front," Cotta ordered, without consulting Sabinus.

The disciplined cavalry thundered through the two gates and charged into the disorganized Gallic horsemen. Within twenty minutes it was over, the Gauls back in the forest, and the Spanish and German horse inside the camp again.

"I won't believe it," Sabinus mumbled. "Ambiorix — my friend."

He was in a state of shock, face grey, hands shaking. Sabinus had won a brilliant victory two years ago in southwestern Gaul against the Maritime tribes. Something had changed in him, Cotta thought.

"Not more than three hours since he left," Sabinus continued. "Dinner arranged. Something must have happened."

"He must have had his army waiting and ready," Cotta told Sabinus. "That was no spur-of-the-moment thing."

"Look, there he is now. Coming out of the wood. One of his men has an oak branch. He wants a parley, Cotta."

"No parley."

There was a flush of hope on Sabinus' face. "Ambiorix is my friend. I'll send out Arpineus here. And Junius. He knows Ambiorix. He used to carry messages to him from Caesar."

"But — "

"We'll have the parley."

Cotta turned his back in disgust. Sabinus anxiously watched the Roman envoys and Ambiorix. So did the legionaries. The parley went on and on, Ambiorix talking, gesticulating, pointing that way and this.

"What did he say?" Sabinus demanded when at last the Roman envoys returned.

"Headquarters," Cotta cut in. "Let's hear the report there."

Even so, the military tribunes and some of the senior centurions crowded into the headquarters hut. Arpineus' report, like the parley, went on and on. Cotta summed it up.

"Ambiorix claims he's our friend. He claims that when he left at mid-day, he found his tribesmen under the co-king of the Eburones already marching on our camp. He says he tried to dissuade them. He couldn't because today, all through Gaul, an attack is being made on every Roman camp." Cotta turned to Junius. "Do you believe Ambiorix?"

"It seems strange that a small tribe like the Eburones would attack by itself."

"I believe Ambiorix," Sabinus declared. "Remember, Cotta, he recalled all the favours we Romans have done for him and his tribe. I managed all that business. That's why I know him so well. He's my friend."

"Remember his offer, too," said Arpineus, a man who had joined the Roman army for loot, not for fighting. "All his people want is to have us Romans out of their country. So he promises safe conduct for you to lead your men to either Cicero's camp or that of Labienus."

"As if we'd trust Ambiorix," Cotta snorted.

"But he also said," Arpineus cried, his hands shaking, "that thousands of Germans have already crossed the Rhenus. They will be on us in two days. Two days!"

"We'll hold a Council of War," Sabinus decided.

"A Council of War!" Cotta exclaimed. "We can't—we won't—consider an offer like that, from a bastard like him—Ambiorix!"

"A Council of War," Sabinus insisted stubbornly.

It was a little after midnight. Thermus had called together his century. A good lot, he thought. What would happen to them tomorrow? He himself along with the other senior centurions had voted with Cotta to refuse any dealings with Ambiorix. The military tribunes and most of the junior centurions had gone along with Sabinus. The argument had lasted until a quarter of an hour ago. Finally, Cotta had had to concede to his senior officer and a messenger had been sent to Ambiorix, accepting his offer of safe conduct.

"You know we march out at dawn tomorrow," Thermus said. "I don't need to tell you not to overload yourselves with luggage like the recruits are doing. Get some sleep if you can, and get up in time to put some food under your belts."

He paused. There was a heavy sense of impending doom on him. He would like to have said that he thought Sabinus was crazy. He couldn't criticize his superior officer in public. Yet something needed to be said. He cleared his throat.

"I've been rough on you — for your own good," he went on brusquely. "Just want to say you're a good bunch — and — sharpen your swords tonight. Well — dismiss."

There was a muted cheer and the men broke ranks. Thermus fell in beside Fadius.

"Just want to say you're a good legionary, lad," he told him gruffly. "Whatever happens tomorrow, remember that. And good luck, lad. Good luck!"

He clapped his nephew on the shoulder. There was a lump in Fadius' throat as he watched his uncle clump away.

## 2

A watery sun rimmed the eastern sky as the head of the Roman column emerged from the western gate of the camp. Light-armed scouts led the way. Behind them in the van of the legionaries marched Thermus' century, the second century of the maniple following it. Their route ran northwestward for two miles, then dipped into a deep gorge almost a mile long. At the farther end of the gorge the road forked, one branch swinging southeast to Labienus' camp, the other west and south to Quintus Cicero's.

The thought of the wooded gorge was worrying the veterans. As the column curved toward it, Thermus fell into step beside Fadius.

"Look at our line of march," he said. Fadius glanced back. "Straggling," Thermus went on. "Those recruits—up all night, haggling about what to take and what not to take. Carts, wagons, and mules loaded. Women with us — and sutlers. By the armpit of Mars, we look like a bloody picnic."

"Maybe we'll get through."

"Here's the gorge. Eyes peeled, lad."

Thermus dropped back to check the century. Fadius shifted the pole that carried his baggage to sit more comfortably on his shoulder. The scouts dipped down the steep incline into the gorge. The column followed.

The gorge was lined on either side with wooded hills intersected by gullies thick with shrubs and bare-limbed trees. In the half-gloom, Thermus' century and the rest of the maniple tramped along stolidly, leading the legion through the mile-long defile. Cotta was striving to force the scouts to explore more deeply into the underbrush and trees on both sides, but without much success. Farther back in the column, recruits were bawling out a marching song, the one about Lalage, sweet Lalage, waiting under the chestnut tree for the boy who'd gone away. Was that, Fadius wondered, the glint of a spear-blade, there among the trees to the right?

Nothing happened. The whole column was now in the gorge, the carts, wagons, and mules just coming down the incline at its entrance. With a sense of relief Fadius saw the steep grade up from the defile, and light showing through the tall elms at the top of the rise. The scouts began to struggle up the grade.

Through, Fadius thought. Almost through — and war-horns brayed. Ahead of him a horde of Gauls leaped upon the light-armed troops. A split second later the woods along the whole length of the column seemed to explode into shouts, yells, and Gauls rushing upon the Romans, hurling spears, darts, and stones, and then slashing with their single-edged swords. Behind the veteran maniple, the attack cut through the recruits. The veterans had reacted automatically, tossing the baggage-poles outward, and falling into formation, four ranks facing outward on each side, casting javelins, then pulling their swords.

They beat back the Gauls. Behind them, with the other veteran maniples, it was the same story. For the recruits it was slaughter until their centurions got them steadied and into line with the help of Cotta and his horsemen. Behind, where Sabinus was, the Gauls killed mules and women until a cavalry charge drove them off.

The first onslaught was over. Cotta rode up to Thermus. He pointed to the rise from the gorge, now occupied by a mass of Gauls.

"Cut your way through," he shouted.

Thermus swung his century into the attack. As they slashed into the Gauls, at the top of the rise there was a crashing of timber. Thermus looked. Cotta looked. The big elms on the crest, obviously cut through beforehand to within a couple of inches, were being pulled down with ropes to form an impenetrable barrier, a tangle of trunks and branches twenty feet high. Cotta wiped his forehead with the back of his hand.

"All right, back," he ordered. "Fight back to camp."

An aide rode up, gesturing wildly. "They've blocked the way back," he cried. "The Gauls, I mean."

Cotta turned to his trumpeter. "Blow 'Form circle'," he ordered. "Blow, man."

The Gauls were attacking again. Cotta used his cavalry to seal off the gullies. Gradually he got the Romans to the one spot where a defensive circle could be formed. Here, about a quarter of a mile from the entrance to the gorge, two tiny converging streams had created a glade, a sort of natural amphitheatre surrounded by forested hills and ravines.

"Look, Cotta's ordered the wagons cut off," Sporus said, pointing.

"Makes sense," Thermus grunted, wiping blood from his sword with his cloak.

"The fools, the bloody fools," Rullus was shouting. "Look!"

The veterans looked. Recruits, breaking ranks, were running

to the wagons, carts, and mules to rescue their possessions. With howls of delight the Gauls charged them. The recruits were cut down by the dozens. Screaming and stumbling, the rest ran back. Finally, by mid-morning, Cotta got the circle formed, with the cavalry and light-armed troops inside it. The veterans looked out from it stolidly. The recruits shifted feet, glanced at each other, and sweated. The Gauls drew back. Sabinus came up to Cotta who, since his horse had been killed under him, had picked up a sword and shield from a dead legionary.

"It's a mistake," Sabinus cried shrilly. "A horrible mistake. It must be. Ambiorix promised safe-conduct, didn't he?"

"The bastard!" Cotta said. "The Jupiter-damned bastard!"

"Ambiorix — we must find Ambiorix."

"Pull yourself together, man," Cotta told him. "We can still win."

Sabinus turned a blank face to him. "Ambiorix — I must find him. Our only chance."

Cotta turned and shouted to the troops. "Kill Gauls. That way we win. Kill Gauls. Here they come, lads. Smash them. Then, charge out and back again."

It was a long morning for the Romans. There was rush after rush of yelling Gauls hurling spears, darts, and stones from ten to fifteen yards away and then dashing in with slashing swords. The Roman lines would hold. As the Gauls fell back, a cohort or a maniple would charge into the Gauls, following them into the brushwood, slicing and stabbing until the recall sounded. Then the legionaries would cut their way back to the circle. Here and there Romans fell. But they were killing ten times that number of Gauls. Satisfying, Fadius thought, as his cohort returned from a charge. They'd surrounded a mass of Gauls in a gully and put them down. The attacks began to lessen.

"They're getting a bellyful," Thermus grunted.

But then, abruptly, the Gallic tactics changed. The hand-to-hand onslaught stopped. Instead, the Gauls only came in close enough to hurl their missiles into the close-packed ranks of the Romans. When a maniple or cohort charged, instead of standing to fight, the Gauls ran back into the brushwood. When the recall sounded, they leaped back, raining missiles on the backs and unshielded right flanks of the Romans. Then the Gauls would be in again at the circle, throwing spears and darts, and slinging stones. The number of killed and wounded began to mount.

"If we had javelins — " Fadius said.

The javelins had been hurled long ago.

"Looks bad," Rullus grunted, bending to pick up a Gallic spear. He poised it, aimed, and cast. "Got that bugger," he said.

"Shields up," Thermus barked. "Shields up."

Cotta was thinking that this Ambiorix had more control over his men than most Gallic leaders. Something would have to be done — and soon. He watched another of the veteran maniples charge. As they turned to come back, the senior centurion tripped over a root. A Gallic spear went through both his thighs. A legionary ran out to help him. In an instant he, too, was surrounded. And there was the other centurion of the maniple, a man he recognized, rushing out.

He found his way to where Sabinus stood. "We'll have to cut our way back to camp," he said.

"But how? Wagons in the way. And trees — "

"Pull out three of the veteran cohorts. Give them the job. The other two can steady the recruits and cover the retreat."

"What about the wounded?"

"Leave them," Cotta said tersely. "We need another charge first." He turned to shout the order to Thermus and a stone caught him full in the face. Cotta staggered, dropped, then forced himself to his feet again, his nose and teeth smashed, his whole face a mask of blood. He waved to Thermus.

"Out, lads," Thermus roared. "On them."

The whole cohort charged, Thermus' century in the van. Again the Gauls melted away. They got one or two. They turned back. Immediately, the Gauls were all around them. As they turned back, Thermus' century was the rearguard. Fadius heard a cry and looked. It was Sporus, the second-in-command of the century, and he was down, a spear through his leg. Fadius stopped to get him up. Thermus was shouting, "Steady, lads, steady," when suddenly his shout was cut off. Fadius, in the act

85

of hauling Sporus to his feet, looked around. His uncle was on his knees, the feathered shaft of an arrow sticking from his throat. At the same instant two Gauls dashed in. Fadius slashed his sword into one — the other put a spear into Sporus' unprotected side. Fadius let go of his body, killed the other Gaul, and ran to his uncle. Rullus leaped out to help him. Between them they half-carried, half-dragged, Thermus into the ranks and back to the circle. Thermus was trying to speak.

"Quiet, uncle," Fadius said. "Keep quiet."

Thermus struggled to a sitting position. "Take over, lad," he said, his voice bubbling. "Take over." Then a gush of blood poured from his mouth and he fell back, eyes turning up so that only the whites showed.

"Uncle!" Fadius cried despairingly. "Uncle!"

It was over. Fadius gave a half-sob. Then, lips setting firmly, he pulled down his uncle's eyelids and stood up, a head taller than anyone in his century.

"Shields up!" he shouted powerfully. "Shields up!"

The ranks of the maniple steadied. Fadius looked and saw Sabinus arguing with Cotta, pointing, as he talked, to a knoll part-way up the ravine to the right. When Fadius stared at the knoll, there was Ambiorix in his gilded boar's-head helmet, directing the battle. Cotta, he noticed, was shaking his head. What was Sabinus urging? A charge against Ambiorix and his bodyguard?

He'd love that, Fadius thought, gripping the handle of his sword. Might as well charge as stand here and be killed by a flung spear. To his amazement, he saw Sabinus' friend, Arpineus, waving a white cloak and moving out to Ambiorix. Ambiorix shouted and flung out an arm. A Gallic war-horn brayed. Abruptly, the attacks ceased. The legionaries, who had now been fighting from dawn until well after mid-day, straightened their ranks, and the centurions grimly assessed the heavy losses. Almost half the troops were down. Fadius moved through his century. Some forty of its sixty men were still on their feet.

"What's up?" the men kept asking.

"Don't know," he would answer.

"Are we surrendering?" another would ask.

"Not me," Fadius would reply fiercely. "Not me."

They saw Arpineus return and then Sabinus and Cotta arguing again. Next, the legionaries saw Sabinus turn, leave Cotta, and wave to Arpineus and the military tribunes. The legionaries watched the party move up to the hillock, the veterans impassive, the recruits hoping, whispering to each other the rumours that had spread outward from the conference of their commanders. Fadius kept his gaze fixed on the meeting between Ambiorix and Sabinus. He saw Ambiorix command something. To Fadius' amazed disbelief, Sabinus laid his weapons on the ground and the other Romans followed. Now it was like being at a pantomime. Sabinus was obviously pleading earnestly, spreading out his hands; then Ambiorix would reply, gesticulating, pointing — and, all the while, groups of Gauls were stealthily moving through the brush, cutting off the party.

Fadius shouted a warning. A dozen centurions shouted. Cotta swung around and tried to shout. Even as he tried, the Gauls poured in on the unarmed group. There was an instant while Sabinus and his companions were hidden from sight, swords flashing above them. Then the Gauls drew back and Ambiorix stood triumphant, the Romans in a slaughtered tangle below him. There was an inarticulate groan of horror from the legionaries, and Ambiorix flung his reddened sword high above his head.

"Look out," Fadius roared, as the Gallic horns blared, and from all sides the attack came in, hand to hand this time. It was shout and slash and scream and stab. The veterans still held, but the recruits broke. The Gauls, howling like wolves, bored through the circle. In front of Fadius' century, the Gauls fell back to regroup. Fadius glanced around swiftly and had a quick glimpse over to his right of Cotta going down, sword still stabbing. A cold range burned in him. Were they to wait like sheep for their butcherers?

"Come on," he shouted to his men as the Gauls surged forward. "Charge. Kill the bastards. Kill!"

With a yell his men followed him to meet the Gauls head on.

They cut them down, slashed into those that ran, burst upon a fresh group, slew and slew, and abruptly there were no more Gauls in front of them.

Fadius pulled up, realizing that, with all the Gauls rushing to the attack, they had broken right through them. He stared back at the field of battle. In that short space of time the enemy had cut the Romans into little groups, each surrounded by a mob of yelling, slashing Gauls. Where was the eagle, he wondered, and saw it being carried by a party of fighting veterans through the Gauls, toward the entrance to the gorge.

"What now?" Rullus asked.

There was a fierce urge to rush back and kill, but Fadius suppressed the desire. He estimated his group. The other century of the maniple, its centurion already slain, had charged with his. He had about sixty men. Another glance down at the battle-ground told him that the fight was over. To charge back in an attempt to get to those with the eagle would bring the Gauls on his party, and would mean that every man would be killed to no purpose. They couldn't get through. That much was clear.

"Follow me," he said, and led his men up the hill and onto level ground.

The other group of veterans that Fadius had seen, led by the eagle-bearer, Petrosidius, had also cut their way through the attacking Gauls. They found the barrier at the entrance to the gorge unguarded and clambered over it. Once on level ground, Petrosidius could see the camp, two miles away. Walls there, he decided, and waved to his men to follow. They were only a couple of hundred yards away when a fresh force of Gauls, rushing to the battle, came upon them. In disciplined charges the Romans fought them off, continuing to retreat. They had almost won to the gate when a troop of Gallic cavalry came galloping to join their infantry.

"Inside," Petrosidius shouted to the Romans. "Hold the gate! Man the towers!"

With a powerful swing, he tossed the eagle over the rampart and, joined by a half-dozen others, turned to hold back the charge. He went down in the mêlée. So did his comrades. But when the Gauls turned to the gate, the legionaries were facing them at its inner entrance. From the curving walls and the towers, scorpion-bolts and spears came down.

There would be easier plunder at the scene of the battle. With yells of derision, the Gauls streamed away toward the gorge.

Meanwhile, after their first scrambling flight, Fadius and his men paused to decide whether to make for Cicero or Labienus. They had picked up more than a dozen stragglers in their retreat. Among them was a dismounted cavalryman who knew the route to Labienus' camp. That fact decided their course.

"March by night, hide by day," Fadius decided. He glanced at the sun, dipping now into a bank of clouds low down in the west. "Let's go."

As Fadius and his party slogged southeastward, back in the gorge the Gauls, wild with triumph, were killing the wounded, stripping the dead Romans of their armour, and looting the wagons and carts. Ambiorix, mounted now on his favourite steed, a black horse with white fetlocks and a white star on its forehead, looked on. Exultation was welling up in him. He'd done it, he wanted to shout, he'd done it! The invincible Romans, defeated! A legion and a half wiped out! His name would leap from mouth to mouth through Gaul. King! He'd be king of Gaul when the time came. In the meantime, let his men, the People of the Boar, have their fling.

That night, on the open ground to the west of the Roman camp, huge fires blazed. Around them, the Gauls drank the beer that somehow had been brought from somewhere and feasted on the charred flesh of mules and horses.

They yelled. They boasted. Men held up armour and severed heads as they ran up to taunt the Romans on the ramparts and then ran back again. Then someone had another idea. Lighting a bonfire close to the camp, they brought out Roman prisoners. With horrified eyes, the Romans watched as a screaming comrade, tied to an X-shaped cross, was gutted slowly, his intestines pulled out rope by rope, as the Gauls whooped in great bursts of laughter.

"Fenellus!" a veteran whispered, as another prisoner was

dragged forward, tied down, and flayed with loving deliberation, strip by strip. Another was emasculated and then speared a dozen times as he stumbled about, both hands clutching his groin. Next, stakes were brought out, sharpened, and the blunt end sunk in the ground. A screaming Roman was carried out, doubled up, and with his hands tied. The Gauls poised him over the first of the sharpened stakes.

"Impalement," the senior centurion said.

As the Romans watched, the Gauls put the end of the sharpened stake into the prisoner's rectum and shoved him down. His scream of agony shrilled into the dark sky. He struggled on the stake, each movement driving the stake in deeper. The Gauls roared with laughter. Another prisoner was brought out. The senior centurion looked around. He knew, as all of them did, that three hundred men couldn't hold a camp built for a legion and a half. In the morning they'd be overwhelmed—and if any one of them were unlucky enough to be captured, or merely wounded—

A second scream, joining the first man's cries, took his eyes back to the scene out there. The Gauls had rammed the second man's rectum down on the sharpened stake.

"Varus," a legionary near him said in a hushed voice. "My tent-mate—Varus."

It took hours to die that way, the stake piercing up inch by inch through one's bowels, and every split instant of every minute of each hour was sheer, unbelievable agony.

"That does it," the senior centurion said, as a third prisoner was carried to the stakes. He drew his sword, fitted the hilt carefully against the ground, point directed upward to enter just under the rib-cage. Then he fell forward on it. The nearest legionary looked at him, glanced once at the third screaming Roman out there, and began to draw his sword from the scabbard. So did the man beside him.

The next morning, when Ambiorix cautiously followed his men into a camp that, surprisingly, had offered no resistance, three hundred dead Romans were all that he found. He looked around at them.

"What do we do now?" his aged co-king, Catuvolcus, asked.

"Ride," Ambiorix said, rousing himself. "On to Quintus Cicero's camp. On to him before he knows we're coming."

"We're a small tribe," Catuvolcus quavered.

"The Nervians — the Atuatucans — they'll join us now." Ambiorix tossed up his spear and caught it by the shaft. "Us, the victors!"

"I don't like it. The Romans — "

"Stay here then, old man." Ambiorix turned to shout to the minor chieftains, "Get them moving. Everybody." He made his horse caracole. "We've got work to do," he cried. "Work, haven't we? Killing Romans."

A wild cheer answered him.

# CHAPTER IX

THE CAMP OF QUINTUS CICERO was sited on a gentle hill that sloped northward. Woods surrounded it, but the shrubbery between them and the ramparts had been cleared. A stream meandered along the eastern foot of the rise.

Within the ramparts, the thatched winter huts stood in neat rows, and commandeered wheat was being delivered, a little fitfully, but on the whole satisfactorily. Quintus Cicero, accompanied by his senior military tribune, Titus Flavius, who had finished inspecting the supplies, was walking back to headquarters. The November day was chill. Quintus drew his cloak closer, reflecting that he would be glad of the brazier in his hut.

Really, he thought, he was quite comfortably settled. At the moment his mind was occupied with a tragedy he was writing. But when he came to headquarters, the centurion in charge of the guard, Pullo, saluted and told him that the Nervian noble, Vertico, was waiting.

"Why did you let him in?" Quintus Cicero asked.

"He said he had news, Legate. Urgent news."

Quintus grunted. Vertico, after losing his case before the Nervian Council in a dispute with another noble about the possession of four farmsteads, had appealed to him for help. For this action the Council had expelled him so that he was now dependent on the Romans.

"Come in with me, Flavius," Quintus said. "You might as well listen, too."

They entered headquarters. Vertico, a tall, fine-looking man, came to meet them.

"If it's about that case of yours," Quintus began grumpily.

"Not that, Legate," Vertico, who spoke Latin, interrupted. "I've been informed that the Eburones are rushing to attack you, and that the Atuatucans and Nervians have joined them."

92

Quintus stared at him. The Nervians, years ago, had almost beaten Caesar in battle and had suffered enormous losses. As for the Atuatucans and Eburones, those tribes knew better than to provoke the Romans, and, besides, there was an old enmity between them.

"Where did you get that story?" Quintus demanded gruffly.

"You haven't heard the worst." Vertico took a step toward him. "Ambiorix and his Eburones have slaughtered Sabinus, Cotta, and their legion and a half."

"Impossible!" Quintus exclaimed.

"Ambiorix, I'm told, has the heads of Sabinus and Cotta—and the eagle, too."

"You're 'told'? You didn't see this in person?"

Vertico shrugged. "I'm outlawed," he said. "Fair game for my enemies. I decided to get here fast with my personal retainers."

Quintus Cicero pondered the information. Probably a rumour. A Roman camp could not be captured, surely. Gauls fed on rumours, the wilder the better. However —

"Double the guards at the gates, Flavius," he ordered. "Recall our foraging parties, too. Just in case. And," he added, "let this noble's entourage inside the camp. Again, just in case."

"Thank you, Legate," Vertico said.

Quintus waved a hand in dismissal, and turned to his comfortable quarters, his mind already on his writing. It was scarcely a half-hour later that he heard trumpets blaring, and, as realization came, he rushed out to the nearest rampart. One glance told him that Vertico had been right. From every side masses of yelling Gauls were pouring on the camp.

Quintus Cicero's men were veterans. They manned the ramparts. At the gates—led up to by curving walls and protected at the final entrance by towers on either side — the guards and the men on the walls and towers let the Gauls rush in, then methodically killed them with missiles and swords. At the ramparts, where the Gauls filled the ditch with fascines and set up scaling ladders, the defenders showered down javelins, scorpion-bolts, and stones.

The Gauls attacked again and again. They were slaughtered by

93

the hundreds. At dusk, they gave up. But their bivouacs and campfires ringed the camp.

"How many out there?" Quintus asked Vertico.

"I saw the insignia of the tribes subservient to the Atuatucans out there," Vertico answered. "So I'd guess sixty thousand."

Quintus had lost one foraging party and a number of wounded. He had, therefore, roughly thirty-two hundred legionaries, plus cavalry and auxiliaries.

"My thanks are due to you," he said to Vertico. He turned to Flavius, a stocky and competent fair-haired knight from Formiae. "Pick two couriers to send to Caesar," he ordered.

"Suppose the Imperator is already away to North Italy?"

"Trebonius will send help. Centurions, get your men to work. I want more towers along the ramparts, enough to give crossfire over every inch of space. Big siege spears, too. Heaps of stones for the ballistas. Bolts for the scorpions. Spare javelins. Everything ready."

The centurions saluted. Day by day the attacks came in. Day by day they were repelled. But day by day, too, the heads of Sabinus and Cotta were paraded before the Romans, and the couriers sent to Caesar were caught and tortured to death in front of the camp until no more couriers would go.

On the morning of the fifth day the attacks ceased. As the Romans stared down from their ramparts, two Nervian chieftains approached, asking for a parley. Quintus, who was ill from a cold and fatigue, ordered them admitted under a promise of safe-conduct. Standing in headquarters, tall, yellow-haired men, they spoke the words Ambiorix had put into their mouths. Their only quarrel with the Romans, they said in effect, was the winter camp in their territory. So, let the Romans march out wherever they wished, and not a Gaul would lift a spear or raise a sword against them.

Quintus Cicero, sitting heavily behind his table, ruddy face pale and thinner than it had been, spoke to the interpreter:

"Tell them a Roman never discusses terms with an enemy under arms. Tell them to lay down their arms and beg for mercy. Then I, Quintus Tullius Cicero, Legate, will recommend clem-

94

ency to Gaius Julius Caesar, Proconsul."

The two nobles listened, looked at each other, and burst into excited speech.

"They say," the interpreter translated, "that they have tens of thousands of armed men. They say, if you don't accept their terms, not a Roman in this camp will be left alive."

Quintus picked up a paper from the table. "Show them out," he said.

## 2

Toward evening of that same day, to the southeast of Quintus Cicero, Fadius led his party through a stream in front of Labienus' camp. He glanced up at the ramparts.

"Halt," he said to his men. He looked at them. They were mud-stained, bedraggled, weary.

"Form up," he ordered. He dressed the ranks and returned to the front. "We've made it," he said. "Now march in — like Romans."

The group marched up the slope to the main gate. The guard there stood to arms. The centurion in command stepped out.

"Who goes there?" he demanded.

"Halt," Fadius ordered. He saluted. "First Maniple of the First Cohort of the Fourteenth," he called. "From the camp of the legate Sabinus."

"From the camp of Sabinus!" the centurion exclaimed. Then, recovering, he spoke: "Enter, First Maniple of the First Cohort of the Fourteenth."

"By the right, quick march," Fadius barked. In perfect order, shields steady, right arms swinging, the legionaries marched through the gates to the two-hundred-foot space around the camp and halted. The centurion and his senior legionary had followed them in. He walked along the front. Every man stood at stiff attention.

"From the camp of Sabinus," the centurion repeated. He looked at Fadius, noting the medal for valour on his corselet.

95

"Your name and rank?"

"Titus Fadius Lupus, legionary."

"Stand your men easy." The centurion turned to his senior legionary. "Take charge of this maniple," he commanded; then, to Fadius, "Follow me."

Five minutes later, Fadius stood at attention in the headquarters of Labienus, while the centurion made his report. Labienus listened, his square, somewhat brutal face impassive. Then he said, quietly; "From the camp of Sabinus, eh? Report, soldier. Oh — and stand easy, both of you."

He listened again, not saying a word while Fadius tersely told of the first attack, the parley, the march out, the ambuscade, the slaughter. At this point, Labienus interrupted.

"The legates Sabinus and Cotta both dead?"

"I saw them killed, Legate."

"The whole legion and a half — slaughtered?"

"Except for us, Legate." Fadius hesitated an instant, then added, "I did see one group, with the eagle, trying to cut their way to the entrance of the gorge."

"Why didn't you join them?"

"No use, Legate. We'd cut our way through the Gauls by accident and luck, Legate. There were thousands of the enemy between us and those with the eagle. We would never have made it. My duty, as I saw it, was to get the news to you."

"Hmm," Labienus said. He was reflecting that he himself had objected to that legion of recruits being stationed up there, isolated. What this man had just reported, too, explained the rumours of a Roman defeat which his spies had been bringing in, but to which he hadn't given credence, since Gauls were always full of rumours. Besides, he himself had been walking a tightrope, like those fellows in the Circus Maximus in Rome. The Remans were loyal. Among the Treverans two factions were still in turmoil; Cingetorix, whom Caesar had made king, loyal; Indutiomarus, the malcontent, collecting troops and, it was reported, intriguing with the Germans across the Rhenus.

The news had probably reached Indutiomarus already, Labienus reflected. That fact would explain why he was march-

96

ing a force toward the camp. Well, Indutiomarus wouldn't catch him napping.

He remembered the two men in front of him. "Centurion, take this man and look after him." He looked at Fadius. "Legionary?" he asked.

"Yes, Legate."

"As of now, acting centurion." He stood up. "Dismiss."


# 3


On that same night, Ambiorix sat on a block of wood in a council of the Gallic nobles and knew that his position was precarious. Attack had failed. Trickery had failed. Hundreds had been killed or wounded. Some of the chiefs were for breaking off the siege. Others declared violently that it would be eternal disgrace if, with tens of thousands, they could not overwhelm one legion. Ambiorix, shrewd eyes darting from one noble to another, waited until they had talked themselves out. Then he stood up.

"There is only one thing to do," he said quietly. The nobles' faces turned to him. "Do as the Romans do. Dig a ditch and build an earthwork around the camp."

There was a stunned silence, and then an uproar. Ambiorix waited until Lugetorix, head chief of the Nervians, shouted above the din;

"I — and my men — are warriors, not diggers of ditches."

There were shouts of assent.

"Why do the Romans beat us, then?" Ambiorix shouted in his turn. "Are they braver? Are they better fighting-men?"

There was a roar of "No!".

"I'll tell you why," Ambiorix cried. "Because they aren't afraid to soil their hands. Because they fight and then they put up fortifications. Because if they can't carry a town by assault, they build a ditch and a wall around it and starve it into surrender. Well, I'm not ashamed to learn from the Romans. Not if it means victory."

They were silent. Ambiorix looked around him deliberately.

"If we don't win," he went on, spacing each word, "we're dead men, aren't we? Aren't we?"

"We have no spades," a voice shouted, uncertainly.

"No spades? We've swords, haven't we? And cloaks?" Ambiorix pulled out his sword and held it up. "With this sword tomorrow, I'll cut the first sod for a ditch, and with this cloak," he gathered it up with his other hand, "I'll carry the first lapful of dirt for an earthwork." He paused again, knowing he had them. "Then," he shouted, "when we have them pinned like cattle for the butchering, we'll throw up Roman siege-towers. We'll roll them up to their ramparts. We'll sweep into the camp. We'll kill them all — all — and the flame we've lit will leap from tribe to tribe across Gaul. We'll be sung of in story, chieftains. Wherever there's a harper or a bard, our deeds will be sung. Are you with me, nobles of Gaul?"

The cheers that answered him echoed back from the sky.

"What are those buggers yelling about?" a Roman sentry asked.

"Don't know," his mate answered. He drew his cloak closer against the night. "One thing's for sure — we've got bugger-all to cheer about."

Next morning, in amazement, the Romans watched thousands of Gauls digging a broad ditch and building an earthwork around the camp.

"A contravallation!" exclaimed Quintus Cicero, who had dragged himself from his sick-bed.

"And look," added Flavius. "Look over there. A siege-tower, by the ribs of Mars!"

"They learn fast, these Gauls," Pullo, the centurion, commented dryly.

"We'll have to get a courier through somehow," Quintus Cicero said heavily.

Pullo glanced up at the sky. "Mares'-tails," he observed. "Storm coming. Perhaps, if there's a storm, a man might get through."

"At this rate, they'll have that ditch and rampart built before night," said Flavius. "Then, how will anyone get through?"

The storm hit during the night. There was no rain. But by morning, gust after gust from the northwest was assaulting the camp at gale force, making the towers sway, swooping down into the camp itself to tear bits of thatch from the roofs of the huts, whirling along leaves, dust, cloaks, anything left loose. It shook the walls of Cicero's hut where he was lying in bed, alternating between flushes of heat and chills that set his whole body trembling. At least, he thought, between chills, today will be a quiet day.

But then the trumpets blew and Flavius rushed in.

"They're coming, Legate," he cried. "In thousands."

Cicero got out of bed, staggered, and clutched at Flavius. "Get me up to my command tower," he ordered.

They got him up to the command tower, wrapped in extra cloaks, the trumpeter beside him. The Gauls were attacking every side of the camp. It was evident, however, that the major assault was to come from the north and the west. It was well-organized, too; so well-organized that Cicero and every officer and every rank realized that this was to be the critical day.

Slingers and archers were in the Gallic vanguard, and next were masses of footmen carrying fascines to fill the Roman ditch. After them came men with firewood — what for, the Romans wondered. Still farther back, swaying along on logs used as rollers, were five siege-towers, and men steadying them against the wind with long poles. With the towers came mantlets in the Roman style, sheds to protect men tearing at the earthen rampart of the camp. Stolidly, the legionaries watched the advance. It halted. Out there, pits were being dug, and fires, shielded from above with cloaks, were being lit in them. Again the legionaries wondered — what for?

And then, like a black storm-cloud bursting, came the assault. The front masses rushed forward, shooting arrows and slinging stones, while between them other Gauls flung fascines into the ditch. The Roman towers and breastworks exploded into a hail of scorpion-bolts, javelins, and flights of spears from the

99

catapults, and, arcing into the masses behind the Gallic front ranks, stones, each as big as a cask of wine, hurtled from the ballistas.

The Gauls fell in heaps. But suddenly, from their firepits, men ran forward. Helped by the gale, spears and arrows, their points heated red-hot, soared over the breastworks into the camp, and, hurled even farther by slings, moulded balls of white-hot clay whistled overhead. Behind the legionaries there were panic shouts from the slaves and the mule-drivers of "Fire! Fire!" The thatched roofs of the nearest huts had caught, and the wind carried the spouting flames across the camp.

Seeing the smoke rise, with screams of exultation the Gauls burst forward; this was to be it, their final assault, on which victory or defeat would hang. Behind the legionaries, the Roman non-combatants had already been organized to beat out the flames. Water was in short supply. They used cloaks, hide tents dragged from the stores, anything and everything. It was futile. The fire gained. But scarce a legionary even glanced back to where their huts and possessions were going up in smoke. These men were veterans, and their lives were on the razor-edge. Below them, in spots all around the walk, the ditch was already filled with fascines and dead bodies. On them, scaling ladders were planted, and Gauls climbed up. Others with long hooks on the ends of poles tore at the breastworks. The Roman artillery rained death. Scaling ladders were pushed backward. Here and there Gauls got through the breastworks to meet the legionaries sword to sword. The siege-towers lurched closer. Over all was the roar of the wind, so that men seemed to die in a vacuum of sound. Wherever the Gauls seemed likely to break through, reserve squads rushed up the steps of the rampart to throw them back.

Still the Gauls came on. At last the five siege-towers reached the ditch. On the uneven footing of bodies and fascines, four wobbled in the wind and crashed down. Only one was planted opposite a Roman tower. The Gauls swarmed up it. Its gangplank smacked down on the top storey of the Roman tower. There, grim-faced veterans faced the Gauls, inviting them to charge across. The Gauls hesitated. The veterans swept across the gangplank, cutting down the attackers. Then came torches to turn the Gallic tower into a pillar of fire that finally collapsed on itself.

The attack had failed. Roman missiles still assailed the Gauls. As the wind began to die down, they withdrew behind their own ditch and rampart, leaving thousands of dead behind them.

"Well, what's your next plan?" a grim-faced Lugetorix asked of Ambiorix.

Ambiorix glanced sideways at him. "We've burnt their huts and their stores. Their stores, note that. We can starve them into surrender easily, if we have the guts."

"Hmm," Lugetorix said, thinking hard. "That is a point. Let's put it to the chieftains."

Within the camp, Quintus Cicero and his officers, including the senior centurions, were considering the same point.

"The huts don't matter too much," Quintus was saying, thinking at the same time that all his books and his manuscripts had been burnt. "We can all manage somehow. Wheat and water — how's the situation there, Calvus?"

Calvus, the quartermaster, answered, "The wheat, we concentrated on it, Legatus. Some of it scorched, but most of it saved. We have to get water somehow."

"I felt a drop of rain just then," Flavius said. He wetted a finger and held it up. "Wind's almost gone, by Jupiter."

"I've ordered every soldier to have a container ready in case," Calvus said.

"Good." Quintus looked around at the group. "Our losses are heavy. Not too many killed. But hundreds wounded. My orders are for every man who can draw a sword or cast a javelin or help work artillery to stay on duty, wound or no wound."

"How long can we hold out?" Flavius asked.

"As long as we have to," said Pullo. He looked at Quintus Cicero. "Any chance of getting a message through to the proconsul?"

"I have a slave," a voice said from the edge of the group, "who might try it."

101

The voice belonged to Vertico, the Nervian noble. Quintus waved him to come forward.

"Go on," Quintus said.

"He's a daring lad," Vertico went on. "He'd be a Gaul among Gauls, too. If the rewards promised were big enough — "

"I'll guarantee the rewards," Quintus Cicero broke in. "Anything he asks. Would you get him for us, Prince Vertico?"

# CHAPTER X

H E WALKS LIKE AN OLD MAN," Antony said to Trebonius.
"His daughter's death," Trebonius answered. "Ever since
then, it's been as if the heart had been squeezed out of him. He's
not our Caesar."

Along with a group of other officers, they were following
Caesar as he strolled, head down, hands clasped behind his back,
outside the eastern gate of the camp at Samarobriva. Trebonius
glanced over his shoulder at the sun. It was low in the sky.

"Perhaps," he said to Antony, "when he leaves in the morning
for Cisalpine Gaul, he'll come to himself."

Ahead of them Caesar paused to look at the woods to his right.
The woods were bare of leaves, desolate. Like himself, he
thought. Julia — dead.

He had loved Julia. That love had not prevented him from
marrying her off to Pompey to hold him in the triumvirate. And
that was what all those nobles and politicians coming up to
Cisalpine Gaul to curry favour would be recalling, even as they
nibbled at him with condolences.

If one could only go back in time, Caesar told himself. Yet he
must in some way shake off this lethargy, this feeling that
nothing mattered. Perhaps when he met Servilia in Comum nine
or ten days from now —

He turned back toward the camp and heard Antony call,

"Behind you, Imperator. A patrol, riding hard."

Caesar swung around. From the woods a group of cavalry was
galloping, Volusenus at its head. Beside him rode a Gaul. The
patrol pulled up a half-dozen paces away. Volusenus slipped
from his horse, came up to Caesar, the Gaul close behind him,
and saluted.

103

"A courier from Quintus Cicero," he said. "With a message, he says."

"Where's the message?"

Volusenus, a Roman who also knew Celtic, turned to the Gaul. The Gaul spilled words, pointing to his spear. Then, pulling a knife from his belt, he cut a lashing that strengthened the junction of the spear-point with its shaft. A sheet of papyrus appeared. The Gaul handed it to Volusenus, who passed it to Caesar. Caesar scanned it swiftly. His head came up.

"How long since that man left the camp of Quintus Cicero?" he asked.

Volusenus asked the Gaul, then turned to Caesar. "He says three nights and two days."

The Gaul spoke again, his words tumbling out. Volusenus listened.

"He says," he interpreted, "that he was promised his freedom, the woman he wants, and a gold torque."

"He'll get all three," Caesar answered, scanning the letter again more carefully. The Eburones, Nervians, and dependent tribes attacking, he read. Estimated at sixty thousand in all. The heads of Sabinus, Cotta, and the eagle of the recruit legion paraded, the rumour being that the whole legion and a half in Sabinus' camp had been slaughtered.

"I can't believe that," Caesar said aloud. Then, as Trebonius and Antony looked at him, he handed them the message. As they read it, Caesar was considering the situation—the message dated on the eighth day of the siege, so now the tenth or rather the eleventh day was coming up — huts burnt — supplies low — many casualties. By the time Trebonius and Antony finished reading, Caesar had made his plans.

"Get your legion ready to move," he ordered Trebonius. "A courier to Marcus Crassus the Younger, with instructions to march directly with his legion to our camp here at Samarobriva. As soon as his advance patrols come into sight we leave. His job will be to take our place at Samarobriva. Another courier to Fabius at Portus Itius. He and his legion are to cut across country to join us on the march. Still another courier, riding through friendly country — the Aeduans and the Lingones — to ask Labienus to come to us if he can." He turned to Antony. "We'll get as much cavalry for you as possible. Well, let's get cracking."

He set off for the camp in long strides.

"He's our Caesar again," Trebonius said to Antony.


## 2

It was on the evening of the fourth day of Caesar's march that a patrol brought into that evening's camp a Roman and a Gaul. Trebonius took them to Caesar.

"A message from Labienus," he reported.

Caesar, busy planning next day's march, took the message. It was a disappointment. Labienus wrote that Indutiomarus was threatening his camp so that he dare not leave. The disaster to Sabinus, about which the Roman courier could give details, had stirred up the Treverans.

Caesar drummed a brief tattoo on his table with the fingers of his right hand. He had marched Trebonius' legion twenty miles on the first day, and that evening had persuaded by rewards an Atrebatian Gaul to ride off to Quintus Cicero's camp with a letter in Greek characters to tell Quintus that he was on the way. On the second day the legion from Portus Itius had joined him. He had counted on Labienus' legion. Now he would have only two legions, roughly seven thousand legionaries, along with a thousand auxiliary troops and some four hundred cavalry, to face up to sixty thousand Gauls. But Quintus Cicero and his legion must be saved, no matter what the odds.

After he had made this decision he recalled that the Roman courier, Labienus had said, could tell him about Sabinus and Cotta. So was that report of a complete disaster really true? He glanced up at the Roman courier. His height and the medal for valour made Caesar cast his mind back.

"Titus Fadius Lupus, isn't it?" he asked.

"Yes, Imperator."

"Was there a massacre?"

"Yes, Imperator."

"Your uncle, Thermus?"

"Killed, Imperator."

Caesar looked at Trebonius. "Would you take the Gaul out?" he asked. "Give him food and a reward." He waited until the two had left. He waved his hand toward a stool. "Sit down, Fadius Lupus. Now tell me about it. All about it."

Fadius sat down. His face a mask, Caesar listened to his story —Ambiorix' promise of safe-conduct—Sabinus' acceptance of it — the ambuscade — the slaughter. To a general to whom each legionary was almost a son, the account bit deep. Within him was both anger at Sabinus' stupidity, and a blazing fury against Ambiorix. Somehow, at some time, that was one Gaul who would pay for his treachery, pay under the rods, he told himself. Meanwhile, there was this legionary to consider.

"You led those four-score men through enemy territory to Labienus," he commented.

"Yes, Imperator."

"What did Labienus, the Legate, say?"

"He made me acting centurion, Imperator."

"No longer 'acting'," Caesar told him. "Centurion." He stood up. Fadius immediately rose and stood at attention. Caesar liked the fact that he made no protestations of gratitude.

"Draw the proper crest for your helmet," he added. "For the moment, you'll be attached to my bodyguard."

"Could I ask one favour, Imperator?"

"What is it?"

"When there's fighting, can I get into it? It was my uncle those — those bastards killed."

"Granted," Caesar said. He held out his hand. "Good luck — Centurion."

## 3

It was the seventeenth day of the siege. There had been no further all-out assault, but each day attacks had been put in. There was still food, but water had run out, so Quintus Cicero and Flavius were discussing what to do. Send a force to the stream and risk its being cut off by the Gauls? Or what?

"The men are almost worn out," Flavius was saying as the centurion Pullo strode up and saluted.

"A message, Legatus," Pullo said. "Tied to this spear handle."

"Cut the lashing, man."

Pullo cut the lashing. Cicero looked at the words, puzzled at first, but then he realized that they were in Greek characters. A broad smile lightened his haggard face.

"Where and how did this message get here?" he asked, noting that the date was days ago.

"The legionary Florens saw a spear sticking in a tower, Legatus. He pulled it out, saw the message, and brought it to me. Neither of us could make head nor tail of it."

"Summon the troops to the tribunal," Quintus Cicero ordered.

The troops gathered at the central meeting point, exhausted, limping from wounds, staring up at Quintus Cicero. He raised a hand and shouted,

"Caesar's on the way. Caesar — "

The wild cheering from parched mouths drowned his voice. The legionaries were clapping one another on the back, embracing each other, shouting. As Quintus Cicero tried to continue, a centurion from the rampart rushed to the tribunal.

"Smoke," he shouted. "Burning villages. It's Caesar! Caesar!"

Within minutes the Gauls learned of Caesar's approach. The leaders met hurriedly. Here was Caesar, whom they had believed to be across the Alps, marching on them. Caesar!

"Let's scatter," Lugetorix, the Nervian, cried hoarsely. "Into our woods and swamps. Hide. Deep winter is almost on us. Even that demon can't attack in winter."

Ambiorix himself had felt a thrill of fear. What gods, what spirits could he have offended? Quintus Cicero's camp—in a few days it would have been his. But he'd gone too far to back down.

"What luck!" he shouted, throwing his sword up in the air.

107

"What unbelievable luck! Thank our gods, nobles of Gaul. Give thanks."

They stared at him as if he had gone mad. He jumped upon a stump so that he could be seen.

"Luck?" Catumaric of the Atuatucans bawled. "You call it luck! That devil —"

"Two legions!" Ambiorix interrupted. "Only two." He turned to Lugetorix. "When he fought you he had eight. Eight! And you almost beat him, didn't you?"

Lugetorix drew himself up proudly. "Almost? We had him beaten. If the tribes with us —"

"Exactly," Ambiorix broke in on him. "Now — two legions only. Can't you see? We can sweep down on him. Overwhelm him. Cut off the head of the snake that strangles Gaul." He flung up his sword again. "On to Caesar." His words carried them. From the gate-tower, Quintus Cicero watched them hurriedly assemble and pour westward.

"Caesar must be warned," he told Flavius. "Have Vertico get us another courier."

## 4

Quintus' courier reached Caesar just before midnight of the same day. He formulated his plan and immediately communicated it to his officers and centurions. On the following day, his two legions had marched for three hours when the patrols brought word that the Gauls were in sight. Caesar selected a valley with a wooded stream at its foot and had his men pitch camp at the top of the slope on the nearer side. Soon the Gauls occupied the opposite flank of the valley.

The Romans waited. So did the Gauls, all day. That evening Caesar called his officer and centurions together again.

"It's simple," he said. "We must entice the Gauls across the stream to attack us uphill. So we pretend we're afraid. Make that absolutely clear to your men, centurions."

"Do you think they'll really fall into that trap?" Antony asked.

108

"You don't know the Gauls yet, Antony," Caesar answered. "They believe what they want to believe. Besides, this lot has no supreme commander. Each tribe and each chieftain will want to show everyone else how brave they are. Get them started, that's all.

"That's to be your job tomorrow, Antony. Skirmish with your cavalry just across the stream down there. Some of their horsemen will be sure to attack. You let them chase you across the stream. They'll follow. Then, you gallop back to our camp. That ought to fetch them."

He turned to the others: "Is everything else understood?"

From the back, Fadius raised his hand.

"What is it, Centurion?" Caesar asked.

"A fighting post for me, Imperator."

"I'll assign one, Centurion. Now, dismiss."

On the next day from his command post Caesar watched his plan unfold.

The Gallic cavalry had followed Antony across the stream and, triumphant, had chased the Roman horse into the camp. They had ridden around the camp, hurling spears and insults. Then a chieftain had shouted to his footmen, waving them forward. Another had followed suit. At first in groups, then in a disorderly mass, they surged across the stream and up the slope. Within the camp, inside each of the four gates, the legionaries were drawn up, waiting.

"Now?" Trebonius asked.

Smiling a little, Caesar shook his head. Not a Roman was manning the ramparts. The Gallic horse and foot were pouring round the whole camp, shouting and throwing spears, and beginning to fill in the ditch and tear at the earthworks.

"Now!" Caesar said and raised a hand. The Roman trumpets blared. From each of the four gates the legionaries charged into the disorganized mob like ships' beaks ploughing water. Behind them rode Antony and his cavalry.

It was a massacre, not a battle. The Gallic horsemen, caught in scattered clumps, turned and bolted. trampling their own men in their panic. The mob of footmen tried to run from the slicing,

109

terrible, disciplined swords. A few got across the stream. The main mass, impeded by the willows and the muddy banks and their own hysteria, were slaughtered by the hundreds. When the rest did get over, the legionaries pursued them up the opposite slope, and Antony's cavalry speared them. At last, when the pursuit reached the opposite crest, Caesar ordered the trumpeters to blow the recall—for no one knew what swamps or forests might lie beyond.

Fadius, sword dripping red from hilt to point, turned reluctantly to rejoin his cohort and saw a Gaul get up from a heap of dead and start to run. He flung his sword and caught him in the back. Walking over, he recovered his sword and lopped off the Gaul's head.

"That's for your manes, Uncle," he said.

"Not a single Roman killed," Caesar said with satisfaction when the troops were formed up again. "Now on to Quintus Cicero."

At the second hour of the afternoon of that same day, Caesar marched at the head of his troops into Cicero's camp and halted them. Quintus had his men drawn up. Caesar clasped the legate's hand.

"Hail, Imperator," he said.

Quintus Cicero flushed with pleasure. The greeting given only to a victorious general, and to him!

"I've seen the enemy's fortifications and yours," Caesar added. "Now, stand your men easy."

With Quintus following him, he went along the lines, calling this veteran or that by name, asking about their wounds, and shaking hands with the senior centurions.

"A lot of wounded, I see," he said to Quintus. "How many?"

"Of those not killed, Imperator," Quintus answered, "only one in ten are without a wound. They fought on, wound or no wound."

"What men!" Caesar exclaimed. "What Romans! Have them break ranks, Quintus. I'll speak to them."

He mounted the tribunal. He looked down at the eager, upturned faces. In a few well-chosen phrases he praised Quintus

110

Cicero, his officers, and his soldiers — heroes all, he said. He paused. Then his words rang out:

"Beneath the eagle of this legion shall be added on a plaque a she-wolf at bay, the very symbol of Rome, and under it the word 'Unconquerable'. So shall the heroism of this legion live on in memory forever."

He waited for the cheering to die down, then lifted a hand. "To each soldier shall be given a medal in gold, with 'Unconquerable' on it, a memorial of your courage, for you and your children after you. Wear it with pride, my comrades."

Once again he stood while the cheering swelled and began to lessen. Then he raised his voice a notch.

"And to each shall be given a bonus" — he paused for a second — "a bonus of six months' pay."

This time the cheers seemed to hit the clouds above and reverberate.

Not a man here, Fadius thought, standing in Caesar's body-guard, but would march into Hades itself if he asked it.

# 5

Servilia threw Caesar's letter on the floor. She kicked at it, then went to the doorway of her Egyptian salon.

"Philhetaerus," she called to her steward. He came hurrying down the passageway. "Unpack!" she ordered.

The steward, a rotund Asiatic Greek, gaped at her.

"Don't stand there, you nit-wit," she lashed at him. "Don't ask questions, either. Not a one. A single one. Unpack!"

He scurried away. Servilia went back into the salon. She had been all packed, waiting for a note from her Julius. She had understood how crushed he had been by Julia's death, and how this had delayed his setting out. Her heart had been full of tender sympathy. She had been straining to meet him, to console him. Now, this!

She looked at the letter, picked it up, sat down, and scanned it again. The two battles did not interest her. Neither did his

111

protestations of sorrow nor his declarations of love. What she looked at were his reasons for cancelling his winter visit to Cisalpine Gaul — the effect on the Gauls of the slaughter of the legion and a half, the reports of envoys travelling from tribe to tribe, his fear of a widespread revolt . . .

Surely, she thought, he had generals who could look after that — for a month or so anyway.

"Zeus damn you!" she exclaimed aloud to herself. "Zeus damn all men!" She tossed the letter to the floor again and got up to wander restlessly about the room. What to do? All winter ahead of her. All winter!

An hour or so later, a few streets over from her, Caesar's most trusted personal agent in Rome was ushered into the African salon of Fulvia and Clodius. Clodius was leaning negligently against the base of a magnificent life-size bronze of an African panther. Fulvia was sitting on a sofa pretending to be busy embroidering.

Neither of them invited their visitor to be seated. Balbus, a Spaniard who had received Roman citizenship through Caesar, and whose black hair and beard were now flecked with grey, pulled a bench out from the wall and sat down. He looked at Clodius, a man he didn't like, but whose control of the voting guilds of Rome made him important to Caesar, and said, "I have a message for you." He glanced at Fulvia. "A personal message."

Clodius, the arrogance of the Claudians in his face and bearing, snapped, "She stays."

Balbus clapped both hands down on his knees. "Very well. Caesar knows what you've been up to. In Gaul, I mean. He advises you — no, orders you — to call off Sextus and Verres."

"No one," Clodius burst out, "no one orders me what to do — me, a Claudian!"

"No more payments to merchants to spread rumours," Balbus continued, as if Clodius had not spoken. "No more bribes to Gallic princes to stir revolt. Understood?"

Clodius, face white, took a step from the pedestal. "I do what I like. Tell your master that, Spaniard. Whatever I like. Understood?"

112

"Then, no more money. From Caesar anyway." Balbus got up, faced Clodius, feet planted firmly. "What you had better remember, Publius Clodius Pulcher, is that Caesar always wins. Always."

He turned and stalked through the door. Clodius spouted a torrent of obscenities, stamping around the room. Fulvia laid aside her embroidery, waiting until he'd finished. Then she said quietly, "There's more ways than one to hamstring a stallion, even a clever stallion."

Clodius rounded on her. "What do you mean?"

"Women," she said.

"Women?" Clodius flung out a hand. "Not with Caesar. He knows too much."

She got up and came over to him. "I don't mean Caesar, I mean the Gallic princes. Seem to yield, sweetheart. Recall Sextus. But Verres knows all the brothels. Gallic women lack perversions. Straight man-woman stuff—that's all they know. Let Verres pick whores from Gades, three-way girls from Syria. Send them up into Gaul, carrying lies, any lies you want. Promise them rewards. When a man is enthralled, he'll believe anything."

"Is that the way you work me?"

"Of course," she answered, fondling him.

"What then?"

"Obvious. Keep Caesar busy in Gaul. Meanwhile, stop elections. Create chaos — and still more chaos. Then, seize Rome when the moment comes."

"It's a thought," Clodius said. He squeezed her to him. "Oh yes, it is a thought."

# CHAPTER XI

SPRING, SCATTERING FLOWERS, was tripping lightly from east to west across the Mediterranean world. From Antioch, where his army had spent months in dissipation, Crassus was leading seven legions north eastward toward Upper Mesopotamia. During the winter he had seized the treasure of the temple of Yahweh in Jerusalem. But now, leaving two legions to guard Antioch and Syria, he was lusting for the riches of Parthia and India.

In Alexandria the Princess Cleopatra was leaning her forearms on a balustrade of the second storey of the palace. Below her the Great Harbour was crowded with shipping. When she lifted her eyes, on the eastern end of the island in front she could see one of the wonders of the world, the Pharos, the towering lighthouse, the beam of which could be seen in the night forty miles out at sea. Apollodorus had come to stand beside her.

"It's done," he whispered without turning his head.

Cleopatra did not turn her head either. "How?"

"A knife in the back. At Canopus. At its most crowded. Pleasure-seekers in throngs."

"No chance of anyone accusing you — or me?"

"None."

The princess stretched her arms above her head and yawned prettily. The Macedonian captain had become a bore. Dangerous too. Boastful. Arrogant. Demanding gold and promotion. So, good for Apollodorus. Canopus, the pleasure resort of Alexandria with its tunnels and love-bowers, where anything could — and did—happen, had certainly been the ideal place. He ought to be rewarded, she decided.

Lowering her arms and clasping them behind her neck, she whispered,

"Siesta — today."

"Oh, Princess!"

Across the Mediterranean that afternoon, Servilia's salon was humming. Through the atrium, the rooms off it and the peristyle, and in the sweet-smelling gardens, moved everyone who was anyone in Rome. There were other salons—those of Fulvia or Calpurnia, Caesar's wife, or of Fausta, daughter of the dead dictator Sulla, and now married to Clodius' antagonist, Milo. Servilia's salon was the most important, especially since she was known to be Caesar's confidante. So much could be learned or effected. One could hear all the latest scandals — who was in whose bed, for example, or who was bisexual or homosexual or what have you.

Such information was surface chit-chat. More important was news from abroad—the yield of crops in Egypt and North Africa for the granaries of Rome; the rumour that the Ptolemy was afflicted by a disease his physicians could neither diagnose nor cure; the fact that the Jews had called down the curse of Yahweh on the temple-robber Crassus, and whether that might have any influence on his success; a statement that last year's vintages in both Italy and Greece were below the best in quality, and how this would affect the prices — that sort of thing.

Inevitably, of course, politics in Rome came up for hints, discussions, and rumours. The elections for this current year had still not been held, thanks to Clodius, and Rome was without magistrates. What was Clodius aiming at? And why did Pompey sit and do nothing? Was it because he was waiting for the Senate to offer him a dictatorship? Or did Caesar's difficulties in Gaul have anything to do with his attitude?

Underneath all this were the opportunities for deals — political, economic, sexual — or the possibilities of them. Nor was it any drawback that Servilia always made certain that the food, drink, and service were excellent. The wine was the best and never ran out. Sweetmeats, tiny sausages kept hot on glowing gridirons, sturgeon's roe, sliced hard-boiled eggs, anchovies, cheeses, dainty slices of bread, fruits in season, artichoke hearts, bowls of beechnuts, hazelnuts, and the like, carefully shelled,

115

honey-cakes, pastries shaped into cunning forms by her master chef, and so on. Everywhere, too, were unobtrusive but efficient serving maids and men. A goblet was no sooner emptied than it was filled, and a demolished platter of sweets was immediately replaced.

It all took careful organization, Servilia thought, pausing for a moment on the tablinum to survey the atrium and the rooms off it, but it was worth the effort. In her salon she gathered information, made introductions, and suggested appointments, so that she kept increasing the debts of favours owed to her, and was able to feel the pulse of Rome for her reports to Caesar.

Caesar, she told herself somewhat bitterly, as she turned to move into the gardens, did not really deserve all that she did for him. No man should leave the woman he said he loved alone for so long. Latterly, too, his letters had been notes, hurried, casual, nothing between the lines on which a woman could feed her need for reassurance.

"And why is your face so sober-looking?" a voice said.

It was Memmius. Servilia glanced up at him. He had been courting her this winter and spring. Not that he limited himself. When women got together for women's chatter, there were giggles at Memmius' amorous exploits. He was said to be endowed well above the average and to have staying power. It was also known that he had a collection of nudes of his lady-loves, posed willingly, and had a rating for each with a description of her performance.

Memmius lowered his voice. "When will you say 'yes', Lady?"

"I'm afraid I'd be a beta minus," she said lightly.

"Never," Memmius said fervently. "You'll be an alpha plus. Maybe a double plus."

They had turned and were strolling back toward the chattering crowd. He did exude that aura of a man confident of his masculinity, Servilia felt. Handsome, too — and freshly bathed and scented.

"A compliment, coming from you," she answered. "Shall we leave it at that?"

"Never," he said, stopping.

One had to be careful how one handled anyone among the group of families, or clans rather — Memmii, Metelli, Julii, Domitii, Cornelii, and the rest — who dominated Roman society. Over the centuries those clans had, by intermarriage and adoption, woven an intricate network of relationships. One must always remember who was related to whom — herself to Cato, for instance, or her second husband a cousin to her first one.

"We're drawing attention," she said.

"I don't care. Look, Lady, you know and I know that your — friend doesn't limit himself. So, why not?"

Why not, indeed, Servilia thought suddenly. There'd be no real involvement with this man. And there was that Gallic princess her friends had been whispering about all winter. Could she be the reason her Julius had not come to Cisalpine Gaul this winter? Nor should he, she repeated to herself, have left her alone so long, too long.

"We can't talk here," she said, starting to move ahead. "But I will be looking over Hotep's jewellery in the Forum tomorrow morning."

"Lady!" he said, catching up to her.

"Don't count on anything," she said over her shoulder, and turned away from him to her daughter and her husband, Marcus Lepidus, one of the richest men in Rome, who had just come in.

"Darling," she said to her daughter, kissing her.


## 2


Spring found its way to central and northern Gaul, too, though later than in Italy. Caesar had not waited for it. At the beginning of March, Labienus, catching Indutiomarus off balance, had managed to rout his forces and kill him. Immediately thereafter, with snow still on the ground, Caesar had led four legions into Nervian territory. His men had been promised whatever booty was seized. As a result, the Nervians and Atuatucans had suffered

117

heavily for their part in the assault on the camp of Quintus Cicero. The slave-traders from Massilia had bought Nervians and Atuatucans at bargain prices.

Those two moves had not quelled the seething discontent. The Senones, under the leadership of Acco, had expelled the king whom Caesar had appointed, and the Carnutes had joined in league with them. So in early spring Caesar had leaped upon those two tribes as unexpectedly as he had rushed into Nervian territory. The tribes, caught off balance, had been compelled to submit.

Everyone expected him to sweep now upon Ambiorix and his Eburones. But Caesar had determined to isolate Ambiorix first. During the winter he had borrowed one of Pompey's north Italian legions and had recruited two new ones. With ten legions under arms, he was ready to begin his final moves. Since the kinsfolk of Indutiomarus were reassembling their slain leader's forces and were said to be trying to hire Germans to cross the Rhenus, he sent two veteran legions to raise Labienus' force to three. To the northeast of Ambiorix' realm was the one Gallic tribe that had never submitted to Rome, the Menapians, and their leaders were friendly to Ambiorix. With five legions Caesar marched into their country. By the end of April, by suntime, he was deep amid the fens and marshes, burning and plundering. Ambiorix, he kept reminding himself, *there* was the man he was after.

## 3

Verdant April clothed the Arduenna forest around Ambiorix' timbered lodge in a loop of the Mosa River. On this evening Ambiorix sat at the head of the long table in the great hall and surveyed his guests. Apart from the more important of his own minor chieftains and his own personal retainers, there were a couple of Menapian chieftains, a noble sent by Acco, and three Treveran envoys.

The timbered hall was alive with laughter and boasting. Slaves

118

hurried in with pigs cooked whole, piles of roasted duck, platters of venison, and jars of beer and mead. Dogs fought over and gnawed at bones tossed over the shoulders of the feasters. On a dais at the side, a half-dozen bards with harps took turns singing the heroic deeds of Gauls and Germans, since both Menapians and Eburones were originally from across the Rhenus. Every now and then the chieftains would stand up, waving their cups aloft as a song caught their attention.

Ambiorix' face was sombre as he watched. For a few days he had ridden the crest of success, and even after Caesar's victorious relief of Quintus Cicero's camp, Ambiorix' slaughter of the legion and a half had stirred all Gaul. A league stretching from the Atlantic to the Rhenus had been formed. But Indutiomar had been killed, and Caesar, the demon, had struck too soon and too rapidly for that league to get into action.

Yet Ambiorix and Acco had managed a new combination — the Carnutes and the Senones — with promises of help from the tribes along the Atlantic coast and the reconstituted Treverans. The Menapians, too, had promised to join. The expectation had been that Caesar would move directly against the Eburones. Instead, he had plunged into Menapian territory — and the Menapians were considering surrender, which Ambiorix could not let happen.

If one could only see into that demon's mind, Ambiorix thought. He beckoned to Celthir, his most trusted retainer, and slipped into a room behind the banquet hall. A few moments later the envoy of Acco, and the Treverans and the Menapians, along with the half-dozen principal Eburones' chieftains, were seated on stools in a semi-circle before him. Ambiorix clapped his hands. A score and a half of women slaves hurried in, bringing cups of Greek wine — not that his guests would enjoy it as much as beer, but it was a mark of honour and munificence.

Ambiorix himself sat in a chair of which the back and legs were carved in intricate and abstract representations of stags, wild boars, and the huge German ox, the aurochs.

"Yours," Ambiorix said with a negligent wave of his hand at the serving-women, "as soon as the conference is over." He

119

smiled and winked. "Don't quarrel over who gets which. There's plenty to choose from."

The women giggled. The men began to assess them, and Ambiorix took a sip of wine; then he set down his cup on the table beside him.

"You first," he said to Molnar, the leader of the Treveran envoys.

"We'll move next week," announced Molnar, a fair-haired, heavy-shouldered bear of a man.

"Explain to the others."

The slave-women were by now grouped against the wall, waiting. A burst of applause for one of the bards drifted in from the great hall. Molnar held out his cup for a refill. A slave-woman, deep-bosomed and broad-hipped, hurried over. Molnar took time to explore her buttocks before he went on,

"We Treverans have driven out that Roman-loving bastard Cingetorix. We, Indutiomar's kinsfolk, already have five times the forces Indutiomar had. All we're waiting for are the Germans."

"They're coming for sure?" Ambiorix asked.

Molnar nodded.

"Make it clear to our friends here."

Molnar finished his cup and held it out for another refill. The same woman came over. This time Molnar thrust a hand into her bosom to handle her breasts.

"She'll do," he observed, withdrawing his hand and giving her a slap on the buttocks. "Well, to business. The Ubians and the Sugambrians along the Rhenus turned us down. Afraid of the Romans. So we had to send deep into the country, to the Suebians. They're good fighters. It's costing us plenty. But thousands of them are on their way. As soon as they reach us — not more than a week from now — we sweep over the Rhenus camp of Labienus and his three legions."

Ambiorix glanced around, shrewd eyes assessing the effect of this information, particularly on the Menapian leaders.

"Now you, Coltan," he said to Acco's man.

120

Acco's man was long-winded. Ambiorix summed up his oration.

"Prince Acco assures us," he said, "that as soon as the Germans cross the Rhenus and the Treverans strike, the Senones and the Carnutes will revolt. Moreover, he has the oaths of the Atlantic tribes that they will swell the tide that will wash away the Romans." He turned to the Menapian chieftains. "You came to tell us you could not hold out any longer. One week is all we ask of you. One week and Caesar will have to retreat. Is that too much to ask for freedom? Freedom, nobles of the Menapians. Free men, not slaves — not slaves to the Romans!"

The leader of the Menapians said, "If we had fighting men from you, King Ambiorix?"

"You'll have them."

The Menapian stood up. "We'll fight on." He raised his hand high, clasping it into a fist. "There is my pledge—our pledge."

Ambiorix jumped to his feet. "Wine," he called. "Fill the cups, bitches. Quick." He waited. Then he raised his cup high. "Drink to victory," he cried. "To victory!"

With cries of "To victory", they drank. Ambiorix drained his cup. Then, with a wide smile, he pointed to the slave-women.

"They're yours," he called. "Ready. Waiting. Take your pick."

The women, with mock shrieks, pretended to try to escape. The men, laughing and cursing, seized them and bore them to the floor. Soon, as Ambiorix looked on, naked limbs were tangled together in grunting, giggling couples. He had won again, he was thinking. If luck was with him, if all the gods of darkness aided him, he could still overset the demon. A hecatomb of slaves to be burned alive to Lugh, to all the gods of Gaul, he vowed aloud, stretching both arms to the ceiling. Yes, a hecatomb for victory. Victory!

Later, midway between midnight and dawn, Ambiorix stepped out the postern door of his lodge. Behind him there was a lull in the orgy. In front, a brook murmured and chuckled as it ran over stones and pebbles on its way to the nearby river.

121

Ambiorix stepped over the stream. On three sides the thick trees of the Arduenna forest stood tall and dark. Above, the sky was bright with stars. Somewhere out in the Mosa a fish splashed.

Quiet, Ambiorix was thinking. Peaceful. Secure, too; for posted all around in the trees were his men.

Ambiorix was a man of considerable complexity. Ambition surged in him. There was also a strong instinct, which he had had to conceal far too often, never to be forced to bow to any man, and, somewhat surprisingly, that feeling extended to every Gaul, to every tribe. If one could only inspire the tribes to act as one, he thought now, not to fight as a Treveran or an Eburonian or a Senonian, but to put all Gaul first.

Impossible, he realized. One would have to work with what one had, to hope that a common front against the Romans could be maintained long enough to drive them out — and then — then he himself might be the one who could over-master northern and central Gaul, at least.

Well, he told himself, he had bought time tonight by persuading the Menapians to continue the fight, knowing that the Treverans would soon join in; and in the meantime, his own special woman was awaiting him, a Greek girl, traded all the way from Cyprus to this remote forest. She was good at pleasing him, he remembered, feeling heat in his loins.

He turned to go back into the lodge, but from the edge of the forest he heard a challenge and an answer. He stopped, hearing the guard say, "He'll have your ass at this hour. Mine, too."

"This hour or not, he'll have my balls if I don't tell him."

That was the voice of Melhir, his spy among the Treverans. "Let him through," Ambiorix called.

Melhir came running to him and fell on his knees. "Swear you won't flog me," he begged.

Bad news, then. "Up, man," Ambiorix told him. "Now, come with me."

He led him along the brook to the pier at the river's edge. "Out with it," he ordered.

"The Treverans — "

"Speak softly, by the Horned One."

"Beaten. Thousands killed. No army left."

A rush of blood to his head made Ambiorix dizzy for an instant.

"The Germans?" he got out.

"Labienus pretended to be scared to death. The Treverans believed it. They attacked uphill. Uphill!"

Ambiorix seized him by the shoulders and shook him. "The Germans, I said."

"The Treverans fought before the Germans got there, master. When the Germans heard, they turned back. No Treveran host —no Germans."

Ambiorix released Melhir. Disaster! He couldn't think. He must think. Buy time—that was the thought that came to him. A courier to Acco begging him to rise, Treverans or no Treverans. Above all, keep the Menapians fighting. If he could get their envoys away early this coming morning, before they could hear of the Treveran disaster, they'd tell their men to fight on. Yes, buy time. But no one must know about the Treverans, not until the Menapians were away. No one.

"A gold piece for you," he said to Melhir. "Here."

Melhir held out his hand. Ambiorix seized it, pulled him to him, and with his left hand slipped in the knife he'd had ready. Out in the river another fish splashed, a big one.


# 4


"You don't have to go yet, surely," Memmius protested.

Servilia slipped off the couch. "I must," she said, and, walking over to the mirror of polished bronze, took up comb and brush and began to restore her hair-do. Memmius came up behind her and fitted his body to hers, looking over her shoulder and reaching around with both hands to caress her nipples.

"Don't," Servilia said. "You're distracting me."

"That's what I'm after," Memmius answered. "See, they're ready again. Feel him? He's ready, too."

Servilia hesitated an instant. This was her second visit to

123

Memmius' villa on the right bank of the Tiber. The physical release had been excellent. As a sexual athlete, Memmius matched his reputation.

"I haven't time," she answered, but weakening a little.

"There are positions we haven't tried yet," Memmius said, squeezing her breasts and hugging her more closely. "That one over there. Look. I like that one. You would, too."

Servilia looked. Memmius had the walls of his loving-room, as he called it, painted with postures of love-making, brilliantly coloured, and done, obviously, from living models, and the room itself was kept well lit. That sort of thing seemed to stir men. After the first examination, they had the opposite effect on her.

"Come," Memmius said, drawing her away from the mirror. "We'll use that chair there — the big one."

"No!" she said decisively, disengaging herself. "I told you I haven't time."

"What's so important? — More important?"

"It's my birthday today. My daughters — "

"Why didn't you tell me?" Memmius cried. "I'd have had flowers for you — jewels — "

"It doesn't matter," Servilia answered, returning to her hair.

"Next time," Memmius said, almost boyishly, "I will surprise you, I promise."

"Please don't," Servilia told him, giving the last little pats to her coiffure. "Now, help me with my breast-band, please."

He came behind her to fasten it, and then put his hand on each side of her waist. "Time for a quick one, surely," he said. "I won't mess your hair-do. Promise."

Servilia disengaged herself again. "No," she repeated. "No time. My daughters are putting on the celebration. No, please, Memmius. Wait till next time." She gathered her tunic and stola and began to put them on.

"When?" he asked eagerly.

"I'll have to let you know," she answered, arranging the folds of her stola.

He came close. "And next time," he said, dropping his voice, "you'll let me have my artist in? Such lovely nudes he does. Any pose, sweet. Whichever one you'd like."

That does it, she thought. That really does it.

"I'll think about it," she said, smiling sweetly. "No, don't mess my make-up. I'll see you."

"Soon, I hope," he said, catching up a robe so as to escort her from the room to the postern gate, where her litter was waiting. At the exit he held her arm an instant.

"Good, wasn't it," he said, making it a statement, not a question.

"Tremendous," she answered, giving him a peck on the cheek and then walking to her litter, knowing that he was lounging in the exit, a confident, satisfied smile on his face. Men, she thought, settling herself among the cushions, so certain that to make a woman subservient all they had to do was give her overpowering sexual satisfaction. As the eight Gallic slaves, all presents from Caesar, lifted the litter carefully, she glanced out at the gardens around her. It was May by suntime, even though by the creaky Roman calendar it was early in April, so the apple and cherry trees were in exuberant bloom. She sniffed the fragrance before she drew the curtains of the litter. Her escort was waiting outside the back entrance to the grounds, and she had no desire to advertise her visit here too blatantly.

So now she knew, she reflected. She had tried Memmius twice to make sure. It might suit other women, these casual pairings. For her there had to be more than the physical. As she analysed it now, what she needed was a melding of the mental and the spiritual with the physical, otherwise there was no real union — or, putting it another way, the physical became the ultimate, the natural, the absolutely perfect expression of something far deeper than the physical — an almost ethereal delight in giving oneself without reserve. As with Julius. But why only with him?

The litter-bearers were on their way toward the bridge over the Tiber. Zeus damn Gaius Julius Caesar, she told herself resentfully. He could — and did — take other women. Why couldn't she take other men, just as casually? Yes, Zeus damn him.

The bearers were passing over the stone bridge to her side of the Tiber. Her thoughts veered. Now, how to get rid of this Memmius, tactfully. It shouldn't be too difficult. He wasn't noted for constancy. But she must be careful, very careful, not to offend his masculine pride.

She turned the problem over in her mind and recalled that Memmius, an Epicurean, was the patron of that Lucretius, who had just published his poem on "The Nature of Things". It was a brilliant poem, but it was a defence and an exposition of Epicureanism, with its twin theories of the universe come by chance and of pleasure as the chief end of life. Her son, Marcus Brutus, a Stoic, abhorred Epicureanism — and he had drunk in his abhorrence from his uncle and her half-brother, Cato. Cato had a rough tongue. He called it speaking the truth. So, if at her salon next week she could inveigle Cato to attend and get him into conflict with Memmius, a man he despised and had once formally charged with electoral corruption — well, that could be a start.

She sighed and leaned back. What was Caesar doing at this moment, she wondered.

# CHAPTER XII

AMBIORIX HAD WITHDRAWN STILL DEEPER into the Arduenna forest, his schemes scattered around him like broken eggshells. His courier to Acco had returned with bad news. Acco had tried to raise the tribes, but the Treveran defeat had overawed them. Worse still, the Menapian resistance had collapsed. They had surrendered, and Comm, the traitor, had been left with his Atrebatian cavalry to keep them under control.

In a frenzy of activity, Ambiorix had called his chieftains together to prepare guerrilla warfare of the sort that he had seen in Britain, against the attack that he thought would be launched immediately. Instead, a spy came to tell him that Caesar was preparing to march into Germany.

"What for?" Ambiorix demanded of Celthir. "Why doesn't he attack us? This waiting — ah, if I could only see into his mind." He rumpled his hair, jumped up, sat down again, and beckoned Celthir to come close. "Could we find a man — no, three men — to kill the demon?" he whispered. "When he returns from Germany, I mean? Desperate men? Men with nothing to lose? I'd give a reward. A big one."

Celthir had been staring at his king, his mind clicking fast. "Menapians!" he exclaimed.

"Keep your voice down."

Celthir leaned down. "Refugees," he whispered hoarsely. "I know one, a peasant. The Romans raped his wife to death and killed his son. You wouldn't need a reward — not for him."

Ambiorix jumped up. "Two others like him. Find them. They could stalk the demon and when the moment came — "

They stared at each other an instant. Then, half laughing, Ambiorix hugged his henchman. "If we can settle his porridge, Celthir! If our gods smile on us for once."

127

# 2

On this mid-day in late May, Caesar was standing with Antony in a glade on a bluff overlooking the Rhenus. In the trees behind them an oriole was singing. Under their feet was a carpet of yellow dandelions. From below floated up shouts, orders, and the clang of hammers as the bridge crept toward the German shore.

"You aren't against it, then, like Labienus?" Caesar said.

"Whatever you do suits me, Julius. Besides, it ought to be fun."

"German wenches are cows, Antony."

Antony shrugged his shoulders. "Well, as the saying goes, 'Any port'."

"I've two reasons, Antony. Or, rather, three. First of all, to teach those beggars never to cross the Rhenus. Secondly, to make clear that no one is to give refuge to Ambiorix, when and if he runs. Next, I'd like to have the crops ripe for reaping when I hit the Eburones." Caesar hesitated, bent down, picked up a pebble, and fondled it with his fingers. "There's another reason. Not a military one. I saw a little of Germany two years ago. I'd like to learn more."

Antony grunted. Caesar glanced back at his bodyguard and lowered his voice: "Anyway, you won't be going."

"What! For Jupiter's sake, why?"

Caesar tossed the pebble up in the air and caught it. "You're off to Rome tomorrow — to run for a quaestorship."

"Whatever for?"

"Every aristocrat must go through the offices — quaestor, aedile or tribune, praetor, then, if possible, consul. You know that. Besides, each year I need people in office who are my supporters." Caesar flung up and caught the pebble again. "In your case, once you're elected you'll return as my quaestor in Gaul."

"I still don't like it," Antony grumbled. "I'm a fighting-man, not a politician."

128

Caesar tossed the pebble down the bluff. "Keep an eye on Clodius, will you?"

Antony thought of the red-haired Fulvia. "I'll do that."

"And Pompey," Caesar added. "Not that he can make much of a move. Not with my legions here and the army of Crassus in the Near East."

# 3

If Caesar could have seen many miles eastward, he would have been horrified. There in the desert between the Euphrates and Tigris rivers, under a brassy sun, four of Crassus' legions stood in a square, with the other three behind them as a reserve. Across their front, from a huge semicircle, Parthian horse-archers were pouring in arrows from their powerful, composite bows.

Those arrows were piercing armour and men. Crassus, sitting on his horse in the centre of the square, was gnawing at his nether lip. Legionaries ought to defeat cavalry easily. But these horse-archers shot from beyond the range of the Roman archers and slingers; and if a cohort charged, they retreated, firing back from over their horses' rumps.

So what to do? It didn't help his temper that his quaestor, Cassius, had an "I told you so" look on his lean, bitter face.

Crassus thought back over his moves. When he had marched from Antioch in early April, the Parthian commander-in-chief, titled the Surena, had been attacking with all his cavalry the garrisons in the cities across the Euphrates that Crassus had captured last year. Then news came that the Parthian king was using his infantry to assault Armenia—an ally of Rome—where Crassus intended to establish his base for the final assault upon Parthia. In the Council of War Cassius had advocated a round-about route to the hills of Armenia so as to avoid the desert and the Parthian cavalry.

Crassus had refused to abandon his garrisons. He had led his army across the Euphrates at Zeugma. The Parthians had retreated. Cassius had wanted to halt or else to follow the left bank of the Euphrates downsteam. But the Abgar of Edessa, who had led his cavalry to join Crassus, maintained that the Surena and his horsemen were retreating in order to join the Parthian infantry and convoy all the Parthian treasures from their rich cities in Lower Mesopotamia into the uplands behind the riverine plain. Pursue the Surena, he had urged. Crassus had agreed. Then, this morning, after the Romans had marched from the city of Carrhae, scouts had ridden back to report the advance of the Parthian host.

The Romans were on their side of a tributary river. Again Cassius had advised a halt. But Crassus wanted to smash the Surena. He had formed square and led his army across the stream. Suddenly, when they were well out in the boiling desert, the Parthian mailed cavalry had burst upon the Romans, and the Abgar of Edessa and his horsemen had deserted.

The legionaries had repulsed the mailed cavalry. Then had come the horse-archers and the killing hail of arrows. So what to do?

Crassus wiped sweat from his forehead. Too many of his men, he thought regretfully, were recruits. His senior legate, Octavius, rode up to him.

"Surely, Imperator, we can't just stand here and be killed," he said. He pointed to the ridge behind the horse-archers where a long line of camels stood. "They aren't going to run out of arrows, sir."

"Retreat to Carrhae," Cassius said abruptly.

Crassus wiped sweat from his forehead again. "What about the wounded?" he asked.

Before Cassius could answer, young Publius Crassus joined them. "Let me take my Gauls," he said eagerly. "They'd break those bastards."

Cassius glanced at Publius thoughtfully. "It might work," he observed. "Take the Syrian horse, too. And cohorts to hold the ground."

"How many?" Publius asked, as if his father were not there.

130

"Eight, I'd say — from the reserve legions."

"Well, sir?" Octavius asked.

"Oh, do what you want," Crassus answered irritably. "But don't go too far, lad. That heavy cavalry of theirs — it's somewhere."

Publius rode off, face alight. The legionaries watched. The Gauls, fine-looking yellow-haired men, and the dark Syrians charged in unison. They broke the Parthian horse-archers' line, and turned right and left to drive them off. The cohorts trotted up to hold the ground. The horse-archers re-formed. Publius led his men in another charge, and still another, and yet another, until his force and the horse-archers were lost in dust beyond the ridge. The arrow-sleet was gone. The legionaries relaxed, munching dates, drinking water. Crassus took off his helmet. It had turned out all right after all, he thought. Publius was a good lad — a good lad.

"Hadn't we better get the troops up on the ridge, sir?" Octavius asked.

Crassus nodded. The troops plodded to the new position and halted again. By this time of mid-afternoon the heat was even more intense. Wherever one looked, that brassy sun was reflected from nothing but sand, rock, and scrub. But at least there was no hail of arrows.

"Publius ought to be back," Cassius remarked after a while, peering toward the horizon and then, exhaling in relief, "See, there's a messenger coming."

But when the messenger got to them, his face was a mask of fear and despair.

"Help," he croaked. "Surrounded — out there." He pointed. "Their mailed cavalry—boiling out of the wadis. Help, sir. Your son must have help."

Crassus grabbed at his helmet. "Get the men moving," he cried.

The legions slogged forward. They had made barely half a mile when out of a cloud of dust the mailed cavalry charged. The Romans repulsed them. But a squad rode forward. At their head the leader held up a lance with a red and black object on its point.

"What's that?" Crassus asked, peering. "What's that?"

Octavius looked at him. "Your son," he said, hesitatingly. "Your son's head, sir."

Both he and Cassius expected the old man to collapse. Crassus sat very still for an instant. Along the ranks of the square, one could hear exclamations of horror. The general's chin came up.

"Do we retreat now, sir?" Octavius asked.

"If we do, the men will break," Crassus said. He raised his voice and it was strong and clear. "Tell the men I've lost a son. My loss, not theirs. Tell them to stand firm."

"Here come the horse-archers again," Cassius announced. To Crassus he said with respect in his voice, "It's well past mid-afternoon, sir. If we can hold out till the sun goes down, we have a chance."

"Tell the centurions that," Crassus ordered, thinking that he meant that they might be able to retire when darkness came.

The Romans stood under the arrow-storm for two more hours. Then, as the sun dipped to the horizon, the Parthian army began to ride off.

"Why?" Crassus asked.

"Parthian tactics, sir," Cassius answered. "They have no commissariat. They're off to the oases till morning."

"Very well. Now we retreat to Carrhae."

"The wounded, sir."

Crassus' face was stern. "Leave them."

At that moment a group rode back from the receding Parthians, the Abgar of Edessa at their head. He shouted something, waved his hand, and rode away.

"What did he say?" Crassus asked.

Octavius hesitated, then spoke. "He said they are giving you till morning to grieve for your son."

If he could ever get that traitor in his hands, Crassus thought. "Give the order to move," he said.

By morning the Romans were safe behind the walls of Carrhae, except for four cohorts which had lost their way during the night. Along with the abandoned wounded, they were massacred by the Parthians. Cassius now advised retreating to Antioch. But Crassus had turned obstinate again. He pointed out that if they marched by night, they could avoid attacks from the Parthians and reach Armenia. From there, with Armenian reinforcements, they could plunge once again into Lower Mesopotamia and exact revenge; secretly, he was obsessed with killing the Abgar of Edessa. Octavius opted for staying where they were.

The Council of War went on and on into the next day, until the senior centurions came in a body to tell the Council that emissaries from the Surena had promised the Romans safety if they surrendered Crassus and Cassius — and that the troops were considering the offer seriously.

"But's that's ridiculous!" Octavius exclaimed. The leading centurion shook his head.

"Recruits, sir," he said. "Too many of them. They're scared." He paused and added reluctantly, "So are some of the veterans. It's close to mutiny."

Crassus stood up. "That settles it. Tonight we start for Armenia!"

Five days later came the finale. In spite of losses, the Romans had reached the fortress of Sinnaca, one day's march from Armenia's foothills. En route, after a violent dispute over plans, Cassius, at the invitation of Crassus, had galloped away with five hundred cavalry toward Carrhae and Antioch.

The Roman army was by this time thoroughly demoralized. The Parthians, after following them all the way, had now surrounded Sinnaca. Their Surena, through a Roman prisoner, asked for a parley outside the walls, offering for a high ransom safe-conduct into Armenia and a treaty of peace. When Crassus refused, his troops swarmed round him, shouting insults and waving their swords. Crassus looked at the tumult, his face drawn but his chin up.

"'Tell them I'll go to the parley," he said to Octavius.

"Why, sir?"

"Sooner be killed by Parthian spears than Roman swords," said Crassus shortly.

133

A couple of hours later, Crassus, accompanied by Octavius and his military tribunes, rode from the main gate of Sinnaca to a plateau where the Surena and his cortège waited. Romans and Parthians dismounted and surveyed each other. The Surena saw a white-haired old man who looked unexpectedly calm and dignified. Crassus found himself confronted by a lean, hawk-faced man with piercing black eyes and an air of accustomed authority.

The two groups moved slowly toward each other and halted, the Romans in armour, daggers at their sides, the Parthians in long, brilliantly coloured robes, with no visible weapons. An interpreter stood between. Speaking through him, the Surena thanked Crassus for the honour done him and to his monarch, Orodes, King of Kings, Lord of the East, Mighty Conqueror, Wonder of the World, by the consent to the parley. Then he waved a hand. A noble stallion, richly caparisoned, was led forward. This, the Surena explained was a gift from his royal master, the king, to Marcus Crassus, Proconsul of Syria. He added a suggestion with a wave of his hand.

"He begs you," the interpreter translated, "to mount the steed his royal master has sent for you."

"The terms for the safe-conduct and the treaty," Crassus said, not moving.

"Mount, noble Roman," a familiar voice urged, and a hand took his arm.

Crassus turned and found himself looking into the sneering face of the treacherous Abgar of Edessa. With an inarticulate cry he wrenched his arm free and smashed the Abgar in the face. As the Abgar staggered back, a Parthian drew a sword from under his long robe and swung it up. Octavius sprang forward, dagger in hand, and plunged it into the Parthian. Then swords and daggers were out. Crassus stuck his dagger into the nearest enemy and drove toward the Abgar, careless of the swords that swung toward him. The Abgar shrank back. Crassus, wounded in half a dozen places, fell to his knees. With his last ounce of strength, he thrust upward deep into the Abgar's groin and fell forward, dead.

All the Romans were dead. As his men cleaned their swords, the Surena glanced up at Sinnaca. The troops up there, leaderless, would be easy spoil. He looked down at the body of Crassus and thought of his royal master, the king.

"Strike off his head," he ordered.

# CHAPTER XIII

CRASSUS KILLED! Seven legions destroyed! At the wedding feast of the Armenian king's daughter to the Parthian king's son — and what else could Armenia do but submit — a troupe of Greek actors, presenting the *Bacchae* of Euripides, at the appropriate moment in the play tossed the head of Crassus to roll forward and come to rest before the throne of the Parthian king.

In Jerusalem, the high priest of Yahweh proclaimed to a throng of cheering Jews that Yahweh had struck down the violator of His temple. In Alexandria, the eunuch Pothinus, now the virtual master of Egypt, said to the shrunken and desperately ill Ptolemy, "Now, not a sesterce to Rome. Not a single sesterce."

On her upper balcony, reclining on a couch as her maids swung fans against the heat, Cleopatra said to Apollodorus, "How far will the Parthians drive? To our borders?"

Apollodorus shook his head.

"Why not? They've beaten the legions."

"In the desert, Princess. With horse-archers and cavalry. Cavalry isn't any good in hill country, and Parthian infantry can't match the legions. Besides, the Parthians have no skill in siege operations." Apollodorus paused. "It's reported, too, that this Cassius is a good general — though he won't be popular in Rome."

"Why?"

Apollodorus shrugged his shoulders. "The Romans have what I call 'the always-brave ethic'. A Roman noble is supposed to die with his commander, no matter what a mess that commander has made of it, not leave him, as Cassius did."

"That's stupid. But Apollodorus, this Parthian Surena must

be clever. Terribly clever. Suppose he finds a way to capture Antioch, Cassius or no Cassius?"

Apollodorus smiled at her. "Suppose, Princess, you had a commander-in-chief like this Surena, who had won a greater victory than you had ever won, who was cheered louder in the streets than you. Well, what would you do?"

"Mmm," Cleopatra murmured. She picked a couple of grapes from the bowl beside her, ate them, and spat out the seeds. "I see." With a lithe movement she swung her body upright, waved her maids back, and beckoned to Apollodorus to come close.

"My father," she whispered, "how bad is he?"

"You've seen him," Apollodorus whispered back. "All the flab gone. A wizened monkey of a man."

"How long will he last?"

"The physicians don't know. Maybe months, maybe a couple of years. Yesterday I heard," Apollodorus lowered his voice still more, "that the Ptolemy plans for you and your brother to marry and inherit."

"That pimply ten-year-old—ugh!" Cleopatra reached an arm upward, drawing Apollodorus' ear down almost to her lips: "Pothinus hates me — because he senses he won't be able to manage me. He knows he can dominate my brother. So we must start to make plans. My room, tonight — subtle plans."

She released Apollodorus' head, then clapped her hands. "Music," she announced. "I want music."


## 2


Crassus dead! His army destroyed! The news did not reach Rome until early July, just as the long-delayed elections were being held. In public the Conservatives expressed horror, in private they whispered to each other that now that one of the triumvirs and his army had been destroyed, chances for the Senate to recover its power had improved enormously. Was not Caesar in trouble in Gaul? As for Pompey, one could wait and see what happened.

In his villa outside Praeneste, Pompey worked his lips out and in, considering his situation. He had sent troops into Rome to ensure that the elections could be held. With Crassus and his army lost, the Conservatives were not likely now to give him the constitutional dictatorship he craved. The thing to do, he decided, was to strengthen Milo's gangsters so as to offset Clodius' bully-boys. If enough anarchy resulted, the Conservatives would be forced to come to him.

On the afternoon of that same day, Clodius came into his palace just as Fulvia was giving orders to her steward about housecleaning the atrium. Careless of the troops of slaves with mops, brooms, and jars of water, she did a gay pirouette and swirled into her husband's arms.

"What's that for?" he wanted to know.

She planted a kiss on his lips, swirled away, and came back.

"Crassus dead!" she exclaimed. "Dead!"

"Well?"

"Crassus dead — his army gone," she repeated. "Gaul? Can you imagine the Gauls when they hear the news? They'll keep Caesar busy. Pompey? He'll sit like a frog on a lily-pad, puffing its throat in and out."

"Fishing for mullets in roiled water, eh?"

"Big, fat mullets, lover."

"And we keep stirring the water?"

"Of course."

Clodius was planning rapidly. "Elections for this year just being held. Elections for next year due ten days from now."

"You running for praetor and Milo for consul."

"So we prevent them being held."

"Riots. Beatings. Burnings. Murders." Fulvia did another pirouette and faced her husband again. "And sometime, somehow, a dagger into Milo. Fun!"

Clodius swept her into his arms. "Power, darling. First Rome — then Italy. Power!"

A few blocks away in the summer-house in Servilia's gardens,

Balbus and she were concluding a conference. They had agreed on the damage done to Caesar's political position by the destruction of Crassus' army, and on the danger of Pompey's now being won over by the Conservatives.

"Pompey, fortunately, will want a dictatorship offered," Balbus said, "and the Conservatives are tortoises."

"The real danger that I see," Servilia observed, "is that, with Crassus gone, there's no buffer between Caesar and Pompey."

She paused. "First Julia — then Crassus," she remarked. "Somehow we must re-establish a link between the two men."

"What do you have in mind, Lady?"

"I'll have to think," Servilia answered. She rose as a sign that their conference was over. They walked together to the doorway. Servilia paused, looking out at the brilliant beds of flowers. "The Memmius episode is over," she added casually.

Balbus made a noncommittal sound.

"Young Antony," Servilia went on, "what do you think of him?"

"Not subtle," Balbus replied. "Completely loyal to Caesar, though."

"My impression, too. His quaestorship?"

"No trouble, I'd say. Provided the elections for next year take place."

"Clodius?"

Balbus nodded again.

"Your courier to Caesar?"

"Off within the hour. Relays of horses ready."

"Have him pick up a letter from me, will you?" She turned to face him. "We must keep in close touch, friend."

They clasped hands.


# 3


In a retreat deep in the Arduenna forest, guarded by his most trusted retainers, Ambiorix surveyed the three men Celthir had selected. For three weeks they had been well-fed and well-

139

trained. All three were sturdy fellows, their leader a blond, bigger than the other two, with pale-blue eyes in a seamed, leathery face. Ambiorix walked around them, studying their equipment — boots, trousers, and jerkins green to match the foliage; helmets, spears, daggers, single-edged Gallic swords, and long, narrow Gallic shields; food in the leather bags at their sides.

He faced them again. "Let's go over it once more. We know that Caesar is recrossing the Rhenus. My spies tell me he intends to march to the camp of Sabinus and Cotta, the camp where we slaughtered a legion and a half. A good omen, that. Your job is to stalk him. Wait until the chances are good — then strike — and strike home."

"You can be sure we will, King Ambiorix," the leader said.

"You've told no one of your mission?"

"No, King of the Eburones. Nor will we."

"When you come back, Caesar dead, there'll be gifts."

"I need no gifts. The Roman dead — that's my reward and my revenge. The reward of all three of us." His face was grim. "My wife — dead. My son — dead. My friends here — Roman rape and Roman murder. Oh yes, to kill the man who ordered it — that's all we want."

"There'll still be gifts — lands, gold, women. Now, go. And may the One Who Walks by Night and all the gods of Gaul go with you."

The three merged with the forest.

Ambiorix looked after them. His spies had also brought word that Caesar was ready at last to leap upon him and his Eburones. Those three men were his final throw of the knuckle-bones. If they could kill the demon — if only they could kill him —

He turned back to his lodge.


# 4


The summer sun was hot. Caesar, bodyguard following, was riding with Quintus Cicero behind the advance cohort of the

Tenth, with cavalry patrols in front and on the flanks. He was leading the Tenth and one of the recruit legions, numbered as the Fourteenth in place of Sabinus' slaughtered legion, toward what had been the camp of Sabinus and Cotta. Scouts had reported its fortifications to be almost intact. The other eight legions had been left with Labienus.

Caesar and Quintus were moving up a long rise. Caesar glanced back. There, along the winding road, gleamed the standards of the cohorts. Between them, at intervals, were scores of wagons, carts, and mules, carrying Caesar's own treasure chests, the heavy baggage of his ten legions, including the loot of all his troops, and the Romans who had been wounded in the Menapian and German campaigns. There were sutlers, too, and dozens of camp-women.

"Your job, Quintus, is to keep all that safe," Caesar said, with a wave of his hand at the long cortège, "until I've finished with the Eburones. I'll stay a day or two, until the camp's shipshape," he added. "Then, the Tenth will return with me."

Quintus Cicero cleared his throat. "I'd be happier if you left me the Tenth, not this legion of recruits."

"No need to worry, Quintus. We smashed the Atuatucans this spring. The Nervians, too. Besides, remember that I've sent riders out inviting the tribes in to plunder the Eburones. What's left of the Atuatucans and Nervians will be off on a looting spree."

"Fellow Gauls? Allies last November?"

"You don't really know the Gauls yet, Quintus. Free loot — they'll be in there. All the tribes will be there, as fast as they can make it." Caesar smiled. "That will spare Roman lives, too. So, to repeat, you'll be as safe as if you were in Rome."

Quintus Cicero grunted. He looked over the countryside, the copses, woods, and fields of yellow grain smiling in the sun.

"Well, it's better than Germany anyway," he said.

Caesar thought briefly of his incursion into Germany. No battle. Day after day spent marching through endless woodlands, broken only by the odd clearing, and with only herds of swine and cattle as plunder. When he found that the Suebians had

141

retreated to the dense forest on their eastern frontier, he had turned back. Possibly, though, it would make the Suebians think twice about crossing the Rhenus into Gaul.

They had reached the top of the rise—and there was a cavalry patrol trotting past the advance-guard. Caesar shaded his eyes against the sun.

"They're escorting a courier," he said, and rode forward to meet the patrol.

The courier passed him a bag of dispatches. Returning to his position, Caesar leafed through them as he rode. Coming to Servilia's letter and Balbus' dispatch, Caesar passed the bag back to the courier and opened Balbus' communication first, then, quickly, Servilia's letter. Holding the two in his hand, he looked ahead of him unseeingly, his mind working rapidly.

Crassus—dead! His army destroyed! One of the vital bastions of his whole position shattered! How could it have happened?

He put the question aside at once. Face facts. Power came from the swords of the legions and the money to pay them. So, what did he have now against the menace of the die-hard Conservatives and the possiblity that they could persuade Pompey to throw his legions over to them? Ten legions and Gaul. That, in essence, was all.

He realized that Quintus Cicero was looking at him and said, "News. I'll tell you tonight."

At the same instant he was realizing that crushing the Eburones was more than retaliation for the slaughter of the legion and a half. Now, the fate of the Eburones must be made an example and a deterrent for all Gaul. Gaul must be pacified so that his legions would be free to move.

Conciliation, he told himself grimly, he'd tried that. What had it brought him? Except for a few loyal tribes, such as the Boians, the Aeduans — and they still had an anti-Roman faction — the Lingones, the Atrebatians under Commius, and the Arvernians led by Vercingetorix, everywhere it had been revolt. So, reward the loyal, smite the disaffected. Take Acco of the Senones, for example. A trouble-maker. So, devastate the Eburones in such a way that no tribe would dare even to think of revolt in future.

For behind his legions he must have a pacified Gaul.

"About an hour more," Quintus remarked. "To the camp, I mean."

Caesar agreed without hearing himself agree. His mind turned briefly to Crassus. In the days when he was struggling up the slippery road to political power, Crassus had financed his campaign to become the leader of the Populares, and he in turn had been Crassus' henchman. Later on, he had been the intermediary between Pompey and Crassus to set up the dictatorship of the three of them. Still later he had used Crassus as a check against any alliance between Pompey and the Conservatives. Now Crassus was of no further use. Caesar felt a momentary pang, too, for the death of Publius — a promising young man whose decisive action five years ago had saved Caesar's entire army in the battle against the German, Ariovistus.

Still, Publius, too, was dead, So, turn to making plans, not only for the Eburones and Gaul, but also about what to do in Rome. Problems on problems, he told himself. But he, he thought with a strong surge of confidence, he, Caesar, could surmount any problem.

As he concentrated on his current problems, behind him in the bodyguard Fadius was enjoying the ride. Crops were good this year, he thought idly, looking at the patches of golden wheat. So different, too, this pleasant, sun-warmed countryside, from the gloomy forests of Germany.

They were moving now down a long, gentle slope and up the opposite side. As Caesar had done, Fadius glanced back at the long procession. Rullus was back there — Rullus, now a centurion in the new Fourteenth.

"Don't want the bloody, buggering job," Rullus had said. "Can't you get me out of it, Titus?"

But the recruit Fourteenth needed veterans to train them, and Rullus was already proving his worth.

Fadius took another glance back. Somewhere among the camp-women, there'd be Chione, the half-Greek, half-Spanish girl from Massilia. This last winter and spring, Fadius, weary of casual cohabitation, had developed affection for her. She was a light-hearted girl and not, Fadius reflected now, as all-fired greedy as most of them. He was smiling a little as he thought of her when, beside him, Paulus said, "That's the camp, isn't it?"

They had reached the top of the rise. Across the valley, Fadius caught a glimpse of the deserted ramparts, those ramparts that he'd seen that bleak morning of last November. One glance at them and his mood of lazy well-being vanished. His lips were dry, remembering. No, if he had his way, he'd never enter that camp again. Never!

## 5

The feeling of unease was still stronger in him as he rode with Caesar the next morning, followed by a half-dozen of his body-guard, along the two-mile stretch to the gorge.

"Centurion," Caesar had said, "you know the way to the ambush. Lead me to it."

Last November there had been lowering clouds and flecks of sleet. Today was blue sky, hot sun, and a carpet of green grass, ox-eyed daisies, and yellow buttercups. Yet Fadius could feel, as if it were yesterday, the flecks of sleet, almost hear the marching feet of the column, the creaking of the cart-wheels, the muttered talk of the soldiers, the barked commands of the centurions. Uncle Thermus—where was his spirit now? Did it hover around him? Was it trying to warn him?

"Dismount here," Fadius heard Caesar say, and he jerked out of the hazy world that had seemed to be enveloping him. They had reached, he realized, the dip down into the gorge. A couple of guards were left with the horses.

"Lead on, Centurion," Caesar said.

He saw Caesar glance at the remnants of carts and wagons, and the scattered bones among them, as they made their way through the trees the Gauls had felled and then moved down into the gorge. Last November the trees had been bare and a dust of snow had mantled the ground. Today, through green leaves, sunlight dappled the road. When they reached the glade where the Romans had made their stand, Caesar halted. The bodyguard halted. Here the bones lay in heaps. The Gauls had stripped off the armour last November. Since then the bodies of the dead Romans had been ravaged by wolves and carrion crows, but bits of dried flesh still clung to their bones.

Caesar stared down at them. So did the bodyguard. Fadius looked at Caesar and the bodyguard. They all stood in hushed silence. But they did not, could not, know how it had been. It was so peaceful now — sunlight filtering through the leaves, green grass speckled with yellow buttercups and blue violets, a squirrel chattering, a song-sparrow carolling, and, farther off, crows cawing. But then it had been shouts and groans and cries and swords, spears and arms clashing, and from the bare-limbed trees and shrubs wild-eyed Gauls hurtling with swinging swords.

The smell of death was in Fadius' nostrils. Those heaps of bones — and from them he felt ghostly fingers reaching out to him, and voices crying soundlessly. Danger! those voices seemed to be crying. Danger!

Beside him, Caesar, too, was conscious of the hushed silence of his bodyguard, of some sort of emanation from those heaps of bones. He had never believed in the gods, in any gods. To him this one life through which one walked was all there was, so one should make the most of it. Yet was it possible, he found himself wondering, that where men had died in anguish, some sort of emotion lingered?

"Uncle Thermus!" he heard Fadius whisper. With an unconscious jerk of his arm, Caesar repelled his thoughts. He broke the hushed silence.

"We'll give them burial," he said, his voice rough. "A Roman burial." He paused, thinking of Roman superstition. "So their manes shall no longer roam the world, homeless." He turned to Fadius. "Now show me where Sabinus was killed."

Fadius glanced to the right, to the little knoll he remembered. It was green now, and the copses about it were in full leaf. Unwillingly, his footsteps slow, he led Caesar to it, the bodyguard following a few paces behind. There was a heap of bones

145

on the nearer flank of the knoll, all that was left of Sabinus and his officers. Again Caesar halted and stared down. You will pay for this, Ambiorix, he was thinking. Not by a quick death—no, by a slow one under the rods.

He turned to walk back. The bodyguard wheeled around to follow him. Fadius took one last look and, as he turned, the corner of his eye caught a glint of metal in the nearest copse. With a shout he whirled to jump between Caesar and the copse. Two spears thudded against his shield as he pulled his sword, and at the same instant three Gauls leaped from the copse to race toward Caesar. Fadius flung himself in front of them. He got the foremost one with a thrust into his guts, checked the second with his shield, and then, seeing the third, with his spear-arm pulled back to cast at Caesar, threw himself at him in a desperate tackle. The Gaul staggered back, his cast spoiled. Fadius tried to jump up and his right ankle gave way. Sprained, he realized as he fell sideways and felt something slice hotly across his left buttock. Around him there were shouts, the bodyguard back and in action. Fadius got to his right knee and heard Caesar shouting, "Don't kill that one. Take him alive."

Fadius glanced around. Two of the Gauls were dead, and the third, blood flowing from his scalp and from a stab wound in his thigh, was having his hands tied behind him. Fadius tried to stand but had to sink back on his knee.

"You're bleeding," the voice of Caesar said.

Fadius looked up. "A scratch, Imperator," he said. "That's all. But this damned ankle—if I could have a stick or something to lean on — "

"Stanch his wound, Paulus," Caesar ordered. He took off his cloak. "That and a couple of spears for a stretcher." He looked at the Gaul. "Stanch his wounds, too. I want him for the questioners."

Later that evening he summoned Basilus, the leader of his cavalry contingent, to his tent, told him to sit down, and poured him a cup of wine.

"This is most secret," he said, leaning across the table. "No

146

one except the two of us, not even Quintus Cicero, is to know why I'm sending you out with the cavalry."

"I understand, Imperator."

Caesar leaned back. "The questioners have found out from that Gaul exactly where Ambiorix is."

"Oh."

"Come around here. See this point on the map, deep in the forest?" Basilus nodded. "You will take the cavalry and drive straight for it. No fires. No one to get ahead of you. At the last, a quick foray with not more than three-score horse — or less. Surprise this Ambiorix. Capture him." Caesar looked at Basilus. "I want him alive. Understand?"

"I understand, Imperator."

"A bonus for your men if you get him alive." Caesar held out his hand. "May luck ride with you, Basilus."

Still later Fadius was lying on his face in the sick bay when he heard a stirring around him. The convalescents had been having fun with him. "In the ass, eh," one would say. "Running away," another would suggest. "His woman's man must have caught him bare-assed, eh? That'll larn you," still another would quip.

Now everyone was quiet. "How goes it, Titus?" Caesar's voice said.

Fadius twisted his head. "Like I said, just a scratch, Imperator."

"A cut only," the voice of the physician said. "I've stitched it. It and the sprained ankle will keep him here a few days."

Caesar put a hand on his shoulder. "Want to thank you, Titus." He turned so that he could be heard through the sick bay. "This man put himself between me and three assassins. He's getting a medal — his second."

There was a cheer from those who could cheer. Caesar smiled, turned to leave, then noticed the man lying on the pallet next to Fadius, and stepped toward him.

"Baculus!" he exclaimed. "What ails you, man?"

Baculus was the eagle-bearer who had distinguished himself during the first expedition to Britain, and before that in the

147

critical battle four years ago that had shattered the power of the Nervians. He struggled to a sitting position.

"That dart from that Menapian weeks ago, Imperator," he answered. "Bloody hole won't seem to mend."

"He can't seem to keep much on his stomach either," the physician added.

"Lie back, man," Caesar said. He touched the grizzled head affectionately. "Can't afford to lose you, friend."

"You won't Imperator." Baculus managed a laugh. "You know me. I'm an ornery bastard."

Caesar laughed, too, patted his head again and left the bay. Baculus looked across at Fadius.

"So you stopped the buggers."

"Just doing my job, that's all."

"Cup of wine with me, eh? When I get out."

"Glad to."


# 6

Ambiorix was sleeping on his back, snoring. In the glade outside, the only sounds were the purling of the brook and the stamping of horses in the horse-lines. Celthir glanced up at the moon, a slice of silver above the tall trees, then around the glade at the dimly discerned shapes that were the sleeping retainers of Ambiorix. Time to turn in, he thought, and wondered how the three Menapians were faring. At that moment somewhere off to the right in the forest he heard a stick snap.

Something out there, he thought, listening. Could it be the Menapians returning?

Over in the horse-lines there was a whinny. Was that an answering whinny, cut off? From the horse-lines came another whinny and the stamp of a hoof. Horses, Celthir knew, sensed other horses. And then, he heard a second stick crack.

"Everybody up," Celthir shouted. "To arms! To arms!"

As the Gauls rushed to their horses, there were shouts in the forest and the rush of horses with muffled hooves through the undergrowth. The Gauls were in disorder as Basilus and his picked horsemen charged into the glade. But the Gauls were knights, tied by custom and oath to die, if need be, for Ambiorix. They flung themselves between Basilus' horsemen and the lodge, fighting furiously. Celthir took one look, called three knights to him, and ran to the lodge and burst in.

"Up, master," he shouted, shaking Ambiorix roughly. "The Romans. Up!"

Ambiorix was sitting up, still struggling out of sleep. Celthir caught one arm, a knight the other. The second knight caught up a cloak, and the third seized Ambiorix' sword from the wall.

"My helmet," Ambiorix sputtered. "In the other room."

"No time," Celthir told him. "We've horses waiting." He and his comrade half carried, half dragged, Ambiorix out the postern door and helped him onto a horse. The knight with the cloak flung it around the king. Just as Basilus with a half-dozen of his picked men broke through the fierce resistance, he saw four horsemen leaping the stream and disappearing into the dense forest beyond.

"Almost, but not quite," Caesar said when Basilus reported. He picked up Ambiorix' gilded helmet and examined it.

"Yes, Imperator."

Caesar put down the helmet. "Tell your men they'll get half the bonus, all the same," he said.

# CHAPTER XIV

OUTSIDE QUINTUS CICERO'S CAMP, Caesar was about to mount his horse.

"You're quite clear about the operation, are you, Quintus?" he asked. "Three armies of three legions each, Labienus in command on the right, Trebonius on the left, myself driving through the Arduenna forest in the centre?"

Quintus nodded. "I still don't like only a legion of recruits on guard," he grumbled. "Think of it, Julius — all that treasure."

"What possible danger can there be? Our armies will prevent anything from the Eburones. As for the other tribes, they're ready to rush in to loot. Besides your legion, you have two hundred cavalry. I and my army will be back on the seventh day. Your only precaution, Quintus, must be not to let a single man outside the camp or, at least, beyond its immediate environs."

"Well, if you're back in seven days — "

"I will be." Caesar mounted. "Hail and farewell, Quintus, or rather, farewell and hail on the seventh day."

With a wave of his hand he rode off. The Tenth had already marched. Quintus looked after his commander-in-chief. With nothing but camp routine, he could get on with the rewrite of the play that had been destroyed during the siege of his camp last November.

## 2

Caesar was strolling along the rampart of his camp. It was the sixth day of his sweep, and he would be, he knew, late for his rendezvous with Quintus Cicero. But the pursuit of Ambiorix had led him farther than he had intended. Once a detachment had

150

almost captured the king. He had got away with three companions only, long hair streaming behind him as he galloped along a forest path.

However, Caesar told himself, this was only his first incursion. The Eburones were fighting a guerrilla war, one that limited the damage from the Romans but could not protect them from the looting by their fellow Gauls. Catuvolcus, the aged co-king, had already drunk poison made from the yew tree. When he had finished with the Eburones, only a few miserable, starving remnants would be left, an example of Roman vengeance to all the tribes.

Caesar stopped to look over the palisade. The countryside was still thickly wooded, and the sun was setting behind the trees. He'd capture Ambiorix, he swore to himself, take him alive. As for Quintus, he'd send Volusenus ahead with the cavalry northwestward, to let him know where he was. Besides, Quintus was in no danger. He turned to descend from the rampart and go to his headquarters.

If Caesar could have seen eastward, he would have lost his complacency. There, some four thousand Germans were settling in for the night. They were Sugambrians. When the news of the licence to loot had reached them, their war-king, Saewulf, a jovial but unpredictable man, had assembled two thousand horsemen and the same number of footmen, trained in the German fashion either to ride double, or to charge with the mounted men holding on to the horses' manes. He had got them across the Rhenus on boats and rafts, and had ridden into the Eburonian country.

But Labienus' army had passed that way and the amount of loot left was not at all satisfactory. Now the Germans sat around their campfires, drinking beer, grumbling, and gorging themselves on slaughtered swine and cattle. There was a group of Eburonian captives, too. As Saewulf finished gnawing a bone and tossed it aside, one of the captives, sitting with ankles bound, a noble by his dress, spoke to him.

"Why are you looting our poor remnants," he asked, "when so much treasure lies near you, ready for the taking?"

151

Saewulf paused in the act of drinking. "What do you mean, slave?"

"The loot of all Gaul — gold and silver cups, jewels, bars of bronze, silver, and gold. Women, too. Everything you can think of. Three to four hours' ride away."

Saewulf put down his beechwood cup. "Where?"

The Eburonian pointed northward. "In the Roman camp we captured last year."

"Inside a Roman camp? Fool!" Saewulf reached forward to give the Eburonian a buffet that sent him reeling. "Inside a Roman camp!" he repeated, picking up his cup. "You brass-balled idiot." He drained the cup and leaned to spear a succulent gobbet of pork.

"Wait," the Eburonian said, recovering. "Hear me out, noble king. One legion of recruits. That's all. Recruits! Men who've never tested battle. Are you Germans afraid of boys?"

Saewulf swallowed a bit of the pork, belched, and thought. "What's your name?" he asked.

"Celthir, noble king. Think of the loot. All Caesar's treasure. Yours to take, if you have the guts."

Saewulf stood up. "War-leaders," he bellowed. "Here."

"What about me?" Celthir asked. "What do I get?"

"You guide us," Saewulf flung at him. "Do it right — and you're a free man again. Wrong — and I skin you alive."

# 3

The early morning sun was bright. Quintus Cicero stood at the eastern gate of his camp, watching benevolently as five cohorts, half of his recruit legion, formed up. A deputation of senior centurions had approached him at dawn. They had pointed out that, thanks to the mob of women, sutlers, and slave-traders in the camp, all of them anticipating the loot which the returning armies would bring, the food had run out. Yet, less than two miles away were fields of wheat, ripe for the cutting. So, why not send out a force to bring in wheat?

Quintus had discussed the request briefly with his military

tribunes. They and he could see no harm in acceding to it. It was the seventh day, but there had not been a single word from Caesar. The Atuatucans and the neighbouring tribes were off looting the Eburonian country. Besides, Quintus thought to himself, a general was entitled to use his own judgement.

"Very well," he had decided. "Half the force today, the other half tomorrow. You, Plancus, in command. Select your five cohorts by lot."

Plancus was the senior tribune. Another military tribune, Trebonius, spoke up: "Why not give the convalescents an outing, too?"

"No harm in that," Quintus answered. "Will you see to it?" He paused. "I'll send the cavalry with you. They can patrol."

So now he watched the head of the procession dip down into the first ravine to the east of the camp. Between the cohorts straggled carts, wagons, and mules to bring back the wheat, along with sutlers' carts carrying wine and sweetmeats. A number of the camp-women, too, had decided to enjoy the outing. The cavalry had ridden on ahead. The convalescents, some three hundred veterans, were the rearguard.

Quintus Cicero waited until the rearguard had vanished. Then he walked back through the gate, thinking comfortably that he could have a morning at writing.

Fadius, although he still had a slight limp, was among the convalescents. He was delighted to be out. The sun was pleasantly warm, the leaves were green, the birds were singing, squirrels were chattering, and the air he breathed was fresh and invigorating. Ahead, legs dangling from the back of a sutler's cart, Chione waved to him.

Fadius waved back. A really nice wench, he thought with warmth. Tender. Considerate. Pretty, too, with that glossy black hair and lovely white skin. Later, sickle in hand, mingling his sweat with the scent of wheat, thistles, clover, and scarlet poppies, he felt even better. When it was his turn to stand guard, he thought idly that he'd love to carry Chione to that copse over there and make love to her tenderly while the crows cawed in the trees and a meadowlark spiralled upward, carolling. So peaceful, Fadius told himself, drawing in a deep breath.

153

It was peaceful, too, back at camp. The recruits, given a rare holiday from drill, lazed about inside the camp or outside the rear gate, dickering with the sutlers and the wenches. Between the camp-followers' booths and the woods, two hundred yards away, the grass was dotted with marguerites and yellow buttercups. The guards at the gate were at ease, and Rullus, who was in command, let them lounge. He listened with a smile as the recruits called out obscenities to two girls passing by carrying wicker baskets heaped with the red of wild raspberries. The recruits were suggesting what they would do to those girls as soon as the tour of duty was over.

"I'll throw you so high you'll never come down," one of the two, a bold-faced wench, called back.

"Screw all of you," the other called, buttocks twitching insolently as she walked away.

It was at this moment that from the woods burst a horde of yelling Germans, brandishing swords and spears, footmen racing even with the horsemen. The two girls took one startled look, dropped the raspberries, and ran, screaming, for the gate. At the same instant Rullus roared at his gaping-mouthed recruits, trying to beat them into line. But the rest of the camp-women and all the sutlers had also stampeded for the gate, making it almost impossible for the soldiers to form a defensive wall.

Into the tangled mass drove the Germans, slashing and stabbing. In one of the towers above the mêlée, a trumpeter, coming to his senses, blew the alarm. Quintus, who had fallen into a pleasant doze, ran out of headquarters just as he was, rubbing his eyes and staring around him. Everywhere the recruits were milling about, some of them rushing for their armour, others standing dazed, still others dashing first this way, then that, not sure of what they ought to do. Fortunately, it took the Germans a few moments to find and assault the other gates. In that time the centurions in command, all veterans, got their guards into formation and the scorpions and catapults in the gate-towers manned.

But at the rear gate the Germans, big men wild with bloodlust, hacked down women and sutlers and clove through to Rullus and his recruits. They were holding, but only just, when Baculus, leaping from his sick-bed, snatched sword and shield from a dazed recruit, shouted to three centurions he saw, and with them plunged into the fight. Rullus joined them. In a savage sortie the four centurions put down a half-dozen Germans. That rallied the recruits, but Baculus took a sword slash on his shoulder and went down. Rullus jumped forward, killed the German, and dragged Baculus into safety. Then, shouting curses and not knowing what he was shouting, he beat his men forward. A moment later—at last—scorpion bolts from the towers began to tear into the Germans.

The first savage onslaught had been checked. But the ramparts were still not manned. Saewulf, who was directing the assault near the main gates, realized that there was panic and confusion inside the camp. He roared at his war-leaders to regroup their men, to fill the ditch with fascines cut from the woods, and then to clamber over the walls. Meanwhile, half his horsemen rode around the camp, yelling and hurling spears over the palisades.

In the meantime the foragers, carts and wagons filled and mules laden, were making a lazy journey back. The cavalry rode in front, bridles slack, horses at a walk. The convalescent veterans marched next, out of habit keeping a more or less disciplined formation. Behind them the recruit cohorts were strung out over three-quarters of a mile of ground and separated from each other by the lines of mules, carts, and wagons. The recruits were bantering with each other and with the drivers, sutlers, and girls. Fadius himself was pleasantly weary as the convalescents turned into the last ravine that led to the camp.

"Just watch me eat tonight," he said to Turbatus, the grizzled veteran next to him.

"Me, too," Turbatus agreed. He looked back. "That girl of yours is waving to you again." Turbatus laughed. "You'll have to work tonight, too, lad. Get your pecker ready."

Fadius grinned, turned to wave back, and checked.

"What's that?" he said.

"What's what?"

"I hear yelling."

Turbatus listened. "By Mars, you're right. Look, Trebonius

has heard it, too. He's riding to the cavalry."

A moment later, they saw the cavalry go forward. Trebonius rode back. He barked commands. The veterans put their helmets on, loosened their swords in their scabbards, and hefted their shields and javelins.

"Can't be anything," Fadius said. "How could it be?"

Turbatus spat. "When you've had as many years in the army as me, you'll have learned that whatever can't possibly happen always happens."

At the camp, the Germans were already hauling themselves up the ramparts at half a dozen places when suddenly Saewulf saw the first squadron of Roman cavalry emerging from the ravine. Then he heard the creaking of carts and wagons. He turned to Celthir in quick suspicion that the man had led him into a trap.

"What's that?" he bellowed, lifting his sword. "What's that?"

"Foragers," Celthir cried to him. "Foragers."

"War-horns," Saewulf roared.

The war-horns brayed. The Germans were well trained. Deserting the attack on the camp, they regrouped rapidly; then, led by Saewulf, they flung themselves on the Roman cavalry, drove it back into the ravine, and burst upon the veterans, the non-combatants, and the first two cohorts of recruits. The women screamed and, with the sutlers and drivers, bolted for the ridge on the left. A group of Germans drove them back. They fled to the cohorts, throwing them into still more confusion. The veterans prevented an immediate and indiscriminate massacre. Automatically they were in fighting formation. Flights of javelins and slashing swords checked the Germans. In the interval of time won, Trebonius and Plancus conferred briefly.

"To the ridge," Plancus shouted. "Form up there."

"Cut our way through," Trebonius shouted back.

"No, the ridge," Plancus ordered, turning back to where the centurions were beating the recruits into formation.

Trebonius would have none of the ridge.

"Form wedge," he shouted to the veterans. "Form wedge."

As the veterans slid smoothly into the wedge formation, Trebonius rode to Cornficius, the leader of the cavalry.

"Get the women and sutlers inside the wedge," he ordered. "As many as you can. Then, follow."

At that moment more Germans erupted into the ravine. Fadius looked for Chione. A German footman had her by the hair, his sword lifted. Fadius still had his javelin. His cast went right through the German. Dashing out, he seized Chione, carried her into the wedge, and jumped back into his place. The trumpet blared the advance. Smoothly, relentlessly, the veterans shore through the German hordes. As they came out of the ravine, behind them they could see the Germans attacking the first two cohorts as they reached the ridge and tried to make a stand. But they themselves were on the cleared ground around the camp and making for the nearest gate, the cavalry with them, and the women and sutlers they'd saved inside the wedge.

Quintus Cicero was awaiting them, his ruddy face grey with shock.

"The cohorts," he cried to Trebonius as the wedge halted. "What's happening? Where are they?"

Trebonius gestured toward the ravine. They could hear the yelling, the screaming, the shouting.

"We'll have to send in a cohort or two to save them, sir," he said.

Quintus shook his head. "The camp comes first. It must. We're getting the walls manned — at last. Recruits," he added bitterly. "Your veterans will steady them."

Trebonius looked stubborn. The women and sutlers had already fled through the gate.

"We can't let them be killed, sir," he said, "and not do anything. Five cohorts!"

"Thousands of Germans," Quintus said. "Where in the name of Mars and Jupiter, too, did they come from? Caesar must have been beaten."

"Not Caesar, sir."

Quintus didn't hear him. "No, save the camp," he repeated. "Our only chance. Save the camp."

Trebonius had turned to look toward the ravine. The sound of fighting was coming nearer. He spun round.

"They're off the ridge," he cried. "They're fighting their way in. One charge, sir — the veterans and the cavalry."

He scarcely waited for Quintus' nod to give the order.

"Here we go again, dammit," Turbatus grumbled as the veterans got into formation. Fadius didn't answer. The veterans reached the entrance to the ravine. Trebonius halted them there. In front was a tangled mêlée, German horse and footmen attacking jumbled formations of Romans, their centurions fighting desperately in the rear to hold back the enemy.

"Charge," the order came.

The veterans and the cavalry took the Germans in the rear and scattered them. While the Roman recruits got through and ran for the camp, their centurions joined the veterans in another charge. The Germans broke off the action. With derisive yells they turned to join in the assault on the other recruit cohorts, which, still a half-mile or so away, were being broken into disorganized groups. Trebonius looked toward them regretfully and shook his head. In that ravine his small force could be overwhelmed. He gave the order to retreat to camp. Not too long afterwards, the Germans came out of the ravine, waving Roman heads and Roman armour.

But the ramparts were manned by now, and catapults and ballistas began to shoot at the attackers. At the same time a cluster of Germans who had been at the far end of the ravine rode up to Saewulf.

"Roman cavalry," the leader exclaimed. "Coming from the northwest."

"Where's that Eburonian?" Saewulf shouted.

Celthir was nowhere to be found. Saewulf reached a quick decision. The horns blew a signal. Almost as rapidly as they had appeared, the Germans vanished. A half-hour later Volusenus rode in with Caesar's cavalry and the news that Caesar himself was on his way. Quintus Cicero sat down heavily in his headquarters. It was already clear that over half the men who had set out so blithely that morning had perished. But who could have previsaged the Germans? That's what he would have to explain to Caesar.

In his tent Fadius removed his armour, realizing that he was bone-weary and not as fit as he'd thought. He sat down, thinking that he didn't even feel like eating. Then he recalled Chione. Before she'd left with the other women, she'd flung her arms around his neck and whispered, "Come to my booth tonight. You won't be sorry."

Fadius stood up, and there was a spring in his step as he walked to the rear gate.

# CHAPTER XV

SUMMER WAS OVER. The wealthy of Rome had returned to the city. Antony in his candidate's toga, chalked white, had collected a cortège of clients and armed slaves. Riots day after day prevented elections, while Pompey sat in Praeneste and did nothing. But his supporters had let it be known that if the Senate were to offer him an official position to restore order, he would accept it. As a result, Servilia and Balbus were holding a conference in her palace on the Palatine.

"I may have a solution," Servilia was saying, her candid grey-blue eyes thoughtful.

Balbus waited. They were sitting in her Greek salon.

"Pompey always needs a woman," Servilia went on. "Remember Julia and her influence on him? Also, he likes them young. Well, Caesar's grand-niece, Octavia, is nubile — and pretty. So why not a marriage between her and Pompey?"

Balbus glanced at one of the statuettes in the room, a pert Venus looking over her shoulder. Hellenistic period, he decided.

"It's a thought," he said cautiously.

"More than a thought," Servilia answered with a certain asperity. "We both know that a Pompey-Conservative alliance must be prevented. Otherwise, it could be — civil war."

"I don't like using women in politics."

"That's stupid," Servilia said bluntly. "In today's Rome women, in one way or another, either as pawns or as actors — like Fulvia, like Clodia in her time, or like myself, for that matter — are a force to be reckoned with. I have a second marriage in mind — Julius and Pompey's daughter."

Balbus stared at her. "How will Calpurnia react?" he asked.

Servilia shrugged her lovely shoulders. "Hers was a political marriage. Like my two." She laughed. "You know the rules. Marriages and divorces arranged by the families concerned to benefit the families. Affairs after marriage? Fine, as long as the woman is discreet—though even that rule in today's Rome has been flung into the Tiber."

Balbus thought of Memmius. Servilia thought of him, too. One reason, she knew, for the keenness of her desire to aid Caesar was a sense of guilt—though that was absurd, considering the licence he allowed himself. That thought put sharpness into her voice as she said,

"The point is that Calpurnia would understand. My question, Balbus, is this. If Julius approves my suggestions, will you convey them to Pompey? You have always been their go-between."

"As long as you, not I, write Julius. Then, if he agrees, yes."

"I'll write."

## 2

When Caesar received Servilia's letter, he had just returned to the camp at Atuatuca from his fourth foray into the Eburonian territory. It was raining, as it had been for days on end, and he had the sniffles, a bad case, just as it had been in Britain. He was too busy to give any attention to his runny nose. The rain was destroying what crops were left to the remnants of the Eburones, and their fellow-Gauls had done a thorough job of plundering the country. Yet Ambiorix had still escaped him. Therefore, he'd make one last incursion—objective: to capture Ambiorix.

There was another pressing item of business. Caesar wiped his nose. He had proof now that Acco of the Senones had conspired continuously against him. The murderers of Tasgetius, the Caesar-appointed king of the Carnutes, when put to the torture had confessed that Acco had paid them. Now, under his hand were written messages from Acco to the chief men of the Atlantic tribes, urging them to revolt while Caesar's legions were occupied with the Eburones. The fool, Caesar thought, to put it in writing.

Now, what to do about him? Acco was a tall, handsome man, and popular. He wiped his nose again. Acco could not be allowed

161

to continue with this sort of thing — not if Gaul was to be pacified.

As he was considering the question, his secretary, Faberius, brought in Servilia's letter. At first, he was reading with only part of his mind. Then, his attention sharpened.

"You need desperately," she wrote, "to re-establish a close relationship with Pompey. Otherwise, I assure you, he is very likely to go over to the Conservatives, and your man, Clodius, whether he realizes it or not, is helping to push him there. So, what I suggest is this."

She went on to give in detail her proposals to Balbus, and his reaction.

Caesar laid the letter down on the table. He respected Servilia's intelligence and also her intuition. Time after time where a man would have considered a problem carefully, step by step, he had seen Servilia, in a flash, reach a conclusion which one knew at once was correct. So, if she felt an imminent danger of a Pompey-Conservative alliance, one must pay attention. Her suggestions, though — one would have to consider them carefully and, if one accepted them, plan even more carefully how to present them to Pompey.

But not now. Now he had two jobs to do. He'd wait until he got to Cisalpine Gaul. As he thought this he remembered one bit in the letter and picked it up to reread it. It was in the proposal that he ask for the hand in marriage of Pompey's daughter by Mucia.

"That might intrigue you," Servilia had written. "First the mother and then the daughter, you lecherous bastard."

Caesar grinned, put down the letter, blew his nose vigorously, and turned back to Acco's letters. Gaul must be completely subdued, he told himself, before he could leave for Cisalpine Gaul. So take a legion. Sweep upon the Senones and arrest Acco. Then, back for his final attempt to capture Ambiorix. Next, before he left, a Council of the Gauls so that he could review his legions in front of them, show them his power.

He started to rise, then checked himself. Better take Gauls with him against Acco, he decided. He struck the gong on the table. When Faberius entered, he ordered, "Send an aide to invite Vercingetorix to headquarters."

162

# 3

All was ready for the spectacle that bright October day on the parade site outside of Durocortum, the capital of the Remans. Caesar, in glittering armour, followed by his lictors carrying their fasces with the polished axe-heads protruding, mounted the steps behind the long platform, walked to the dais set in the centre, climbed its steps, and paused for a moment before his curule chair to survey the scene. In front, backed by woods, was a great rectangle, carefully smoothed and prepared for the review. To the left in the neighbouring fields, the marshals had the troops aligned and ready. On either side of the dais were his lictors, protected in the rear and on the flanks by his bodyguard. Next, again on either side on the long platform, were the Gallic chiefs. Well, today, Caesar thought, they would realize the might of Rome — and Caesar.

He sat down. Out there in the centre of the parade ground a post with a cross-beam had been planted, a log beside it. He could sense the Gallic princes and nobles staring at it, wondering, whispering. Would Caesar dare or wouldn't he? That would be what they'd be whispering.

His face was impassive as he waited, letting the suspense build. The fate of the Eburones was fresh in everyone's mind; of the tribe nothing remained except a few starving fugitives, hiding deep in the forests. Ambiorix, though, had escaped — across the Rhenus into Germany, rumour had it. If he had captured him, Caesar thought, this spectacle would be complete. Still, the Gauls had learned. For the first time, at the great Council held during the last few days at Durocortum, all the principal kings, princes, and chieftains had attended, willing to agree to whatever he suggested. He had been right, he told himself, reflecting on the execution of the murderers of King Tasgetius of the Carnutes. The Gauls understood force. Still, there were a few who had responded to conciliation and friendship.

The thought led him to signal the chief lictor.

"Bring me King Commius and Prince Vercingetorix," he ordered.

When the two arrived he stood up to greet them, then placed

Commius on his right and Vercingetorix on his left. Let the Gauls see, he thought as he seated himself again, that loyalty was rewarded. Now it was time. He lifted his hand. On the ground in front of the dais a score of trumpeters raised their trumpets and blew a single high note. On cue from the left came a band of flautists shrilling a martial tune. Behind them, in troops, marched the lithe Balearic slingers, next the Cretan archers, then the light-armed troops with spears and light, round shields. As each troop passed, its commander shouted, "Eyes right." Caesar raised his arm to acknowledge the salute, and "Eyes front" resounded.

Those troops wheeled left to take up position at the far end of the parade ground. Next, buglers rode in leading the cavalry, again troop by troop. After the ride past, half of them positioned themselves to the right of the platform, half to the left.

That much had already been impressive. Caesar signalled again. Again the trumpets blew that single, clear, high note. In answer, to the left a massed band burst into the greatest of marching songs — "Fight, Romans, Fight, Glory Awaits You" — and in marched the first cohort of the Tenth, its manipular standards gleaming, its legate in the lead, stiff and straight on his horse, the eagle-bearer behind him holding the silver eagle high, and behind him the legionaries, sixteen abreast, crested helmets, gilded armour, and bronze shields glittering, javelins and rust-red cloaks swinging in perfect unison, footsteps coming down as one in the quick-march of parade.

His men! Caesar's heart, his whole being, seemed to him to swell as the first cohort came abreast and the sharp commands were shouted, and the javelins were raised as if by a single arm, and the heads snapped right. He stood up and snapped his return salute.

The first cohort passed. The second cohort swung by, then the third. Yes, let them look, those Gauls. Let them realize the might of Rome and of him, Gaius Julius Caesar. His men!

Fadius, standing in the front rank of the bodyguard, was sharing a somewhat similar exaltation. Gone were the memories of camp routine, of ceaseless drill, of long, slogging marches. As the Tenth went by and legion after legion followed, he wished that he were out there, all sense of individualism swallowed up, a unit in that mighty, irresistible force moving as one. "Fight, Romans, Fight." As the last legion marched by and took up position, unconsciously he exhaled. What magnificence of power, he thought.

The legions were now arranged on three sides of the great rectangle, of which the long platform was the fourth. As Caesar sat down, Fadius looked around him and noticed that the lictors had disappeared.

What now? he wondered—and a bugle blew. From each side a troop of cavalry trotted in, one of matched blacks, the other of matched roans. The two troops met, swung round to face Caesar, lifted their spears, shouted, "Hail, Caesar," then separated to wheel and face outward, one troop on each side of the front of the dais, the men motionless. From underneath the dais, the twelve lictors emerged. In the midst of them, two dragged along Acco, Prince of the Senones. From the Gauls all along the platform came a single exhalation of breath, almost a moan. In his chair Caesar sat, his face impassive, as if carved from marble. Let those Gauls watch this, he was thinking.

Fadius stared, almost as unbelieving as the Gauls, as the lictors marched Prince Acco to the post with the crossbar in the centre of the parade-ground. Two of them tied his wrists, one to each end of the crossbar. Two others ripped his shirt from his back. The next two stepped forward, each wielding a heavy rod as thick as a man's wrist. They waited. Caesar raised his hand. A bugle blew. The lictor on the right struck, the thud startlingly loud in the shocked silence. Acco's body jerked under the impact. The lictor on the left struck. Acco cried out. There was a gasp from the Gallic nobles. One of them stepped forward, looked at the massed legions, and stepped back. Caesar sat impassive. Out in the centre the blows were thudding one after another. Fadius had heard how in ancient days this sort of death had been the Roman penalty for traitors.

But, as blow after blow came down, and as two other lictors with rods took the place of the first two, his whole being cried out in protest. Acco was guilty of attempting revolt. The troops knew that much. But this kind of death. A quick killing in battle — a man trying to kill you — yes. But this —

His exaltation was gone. He wanted to retch but dared not. He lifted his eyes to the woods behind the parade-ground, bronzed and still in the sun, trying to shut out the sound of the blows, of Acco's screams, and the sight of his body jerking under the blows. It was going on so long — so long.

In his chair Caesar, motionless, watched. If one ordered it, one must look at it. That man out there, after Ambiorix, had been the prime mover in the attempt to form a league of tribes against him. So let this drive the lesson home to the Gauls. Without turning, he could sense Commius and Vercingetorix staring at the ground, and farther along on each side he could hear the Gallic nobles shuffling their feet and muttering to each other. Well, let them all learn, even Commius and Vercingetorix. Let them know who was master.

There was not even a moan now from Acco. Caesar raised his arm once more. The bugle blew. On the parade-ground the lictors with rods stepped back. Two others untied Acco's wrists. They lifted the bloody hunk of meat that had been Prince Acco and laid the neck across the log that was ready. The senior lictor lifted his axe. It flashed down. The head of Acco fell to the grass, rolled once, and stopped. Caesar stood up.

"Justice has been done," he said in a high, clear voice, "according to the custom of our ancestors." He paused, the silence building. "Dismiss," he said. The trumpets blew.


# 4


That evening, under a vast marquee outside Durocortum, Caesar, accompanied by his officers, gave a lavish banquet for the nobles of the Gauls. On the long trestle tables were snails, mussels, olives, tiny sausages over glowing gridirons, slices of melon, reed-birds stuffed with anchovies and hard-boiled eggs. There were platters of venison, of roasted ducks and geese and baked pheasants. Suckling pigs and wild boars roasted whole were brought in, along with spiced herrings, plates of pike, salmon, and bearded mullet; lentils, lettuces, turnips, leeks, and onions; and sweetmeats fashioned into cunning forms — everything that caterers and chefs imported from Massilia could supply and devise. Among the feasters slaves moved, filling the cups, beakers, and goblets with wine or beer, according to the banqueter's choice. Everywhere, too, tall candelabra gave light to the scene.

Caesar, a few picked men from his bodyguard keeping watch near him, as usual ate and drank abstemiously and was at his charming best — joking, smiling, raising his goblet in a toast to this or that one of the Gallic nobles. Yet, even after the wine and beer took hold, he could sense a sullen resentment.

The fact did not worry him. These Gauls, he had decided, were as mercurial as the sea, today seething with rage, tomorrow gay and friendly. Besides, a part of his mind was concerned with all that must be done before he left for Cisalpine Gaul the day after tomorrow, there to deal with the administrative backlog of a year and a half's absence and, more importantly, with his political problem in Rome.

As if on cue, his secretary, Faberius, appeared bringing dispatches just arrived. Caesar excused himself, opened one from Balbus, and skimmed its contents. No elections for next year yet, he learned. Riots. Anarchy. Cicero almost killed on the Sacred Way. Antony, sword out, chasing Clodius through the Forum until Clodius, evading him, hid under the steps of the Temple of Safety — the red-head, Fulvia, reported as the cause of the fracas.

Caesar grinned at the picture the words evoked. He riffled through the rest of the correspondence. It could all wait until he was on his way, two secretaries with him in his coach, and he dictating first to one on one subject, then to the other on another, as was his habit. But look, a letter from Servilia.

He opened it. It was a burst of joy at the news that soon he would be in Cisalpine Gaul.

"I'll be waiting, darling, at Mediolanum. So hurry, dearest. If

you're walking, run. If you're running, gallop. Think of it, lover
—together at last, together—limbs entwined, my breast against
yours."

The words brought back the first time, in hot-blooded youth,
they had come together. Even then, when they were joined, they
had drawn back a little, looking into each other's eyes as they
sensed that this was going to be more than the physical, much
more, and then had seized each other in molten passion. The
memory put fire in his loins. But, meantime, this banquet—and
later, the green-eyed Fiammar.

Reluctantly, he tucked Servilia's letter in his sleeve and looked
around. Two tables away, Mamurra, more than half-seas-over,
had pulled a serving-wench into his lap. Across from Caesar
were Commius and Vercingetorix. He raised his goblet to them,
smiling, and took a sip of wine. They responded, but their smiles
were strained and their eyes slid away from his. Well, let them,
too, realize who ruled, Caesar thought, putting down his goblet.

# 5

Over in the camp and in Durocortum, Caesar's legionaries were
spending the bonus he had given them, drinking, bawling songs,
and wenching with the Massilian tarts and the thousands of
Gallic women who had flocked in to give themselves to the
conquerors.

In the room in Durocortum that he'd managed to get, Fadius
was lying with Chione. The two of them had looked forward
eagerly to the comfort of a room, secure, no time on them. But at
first Fadius was withdrawn.

"What is it, lover?" she asked anxiously. "Tell me—please."
He did not answer.

"Don't I please you, darling? Look." She showed herself,
turning this way and that. "See, my breasts." She cupped them
with her hands. "The nipples are ready for your lips. See."

Still he didn't respond. She flung herself on her knees beside
him. "Please, Titus, please."

168

"That flogging today," he said. He turned to her. "I can still hear the thuds. I can still see his body jerking. To kill a man — yes. But not that way. Not that way."

He was staring at her, eyes glazed. In a swift movement, she was up and gathering his face and head to her breasts. "There, dearest, there," she murmured, holding his face close. "Come to me," she said. "Let Chione take care of you, dearest."

The first love-making was violent, almost vicious in Fadius' roughness. But the second was slow and close and tender. Afterward they lay side by side, both of them thoughtful.

"So you leave with Caesar, day after tomorrow," Chione said slowly.

"On furlough," Fadius answered, hands behind his head. "First to Massilia. Then, home."

"So tonight is good-bye?"

Fadius turned toward her, resting on one elbow. "There's still tomorrow."

"Tomorrow won't be much good. Not with us both knowing you're leaving." She turned toward him. "I'd sooner face it, Titus. Maybe next spring we'll see each other again. Maybe not. A girl like me has to eat."

Fadius lay back and by the light of the single candle looked at the flickering shadows on the ceiling.

"I've been thinking," he said, speaking as if each word was being pulled out of him.

"What, darling?"

What Fadius was thinking confusedly was that you enter into a casual relationship that you expect to put an end to without anyone being hurt, and suddenly you can't bear for it to end.

"Why," he said even more reluctantly, "shouldn't you come with me as far as Massilia?"

"Massilia?" She shrugged her shoulders. "How would I manage? Don't be silly, dearest."

Fadius turned to her and now the words came in a rush: "I've saved a lot of loot. I've never spent much. I could manage a room in Massilia for you until I came back — that is, if you'd like?"

Chione was very still for an instant. Then, with a little sob, she flung herself upon him, crying, "My own — my very own."

"No one else, remember."

"No one," she said, kissing him. "No one," she repeated, starting to kiss him all over. "And now," she added breathlessly between kisses, "I'm going to do everything for you. Everything!"

6

At that same moment, in a room of the stone house he had commandeered in Durocortum, Caesar was lying relaxed beside Fiammar, the green-eyed princess of the Senones. They had made sensuous, participatory love. Now part of him was appreciating the full, pink-nippled breasts, the breathless insink to the waist and flare out to the rounded hips, and the long, tapering legs, and thinking that the enjoyment of a woman like this was the ultimate reward for all one's efforts. Another part of his mind was considering his journey and, at the end of it, Servilia.

The thought of her was beginning to make him tumescent again when suddenly Fiammar said, "You made a mistake today, lover."

"What do you mean?"

"Acco."

Caesar sat up. "Not a mistake. Gauls only understand one thing — force, or power, if you like."

Fiammar rolled over to rest her face on her hand supported by a bent elbow. "Still a mistake. To flog him to death in front of the nobles, I mean."

"Why? Gauls do worse things to other Gauls. Like killing Dumnorix. Like burning Vercingetorix's father alive."

"That was Gauls doing things to Gauls. But Acco—you didn't even bring his case before the Council of the Gauls. Instead, he was killed by your decision. No veil over it. That was where you made your mistake."

Caesar looked at her. "I still say it was not a mistake. Now the Gauls know who rules."

Fiammar sat up. "You don't understand. Gauls live by illusion. As long as the nobles — forget the peasants, they don't matter — as long as the nobles could pretend that it was really they who made the decisions — like the killing of Dumnorix, though that killing did spark a revolt—but as long as they could still pretend, it was all right. Now you've stripped illusion from them. That's dangerous, lover."

"I'm right," Caesar said stubbornly. "The Gauls bow to force. They'll be angry tonight, perhaps. By tomorrow, they'll have forgotten. Gaul is at peace. That destruction of the Eburones, that beating to death of Acco — "

"Because you couldn't catch Ambiorix, wasn't it?"

Part of the truth, Caesar admitted to himself. Not all the truth, though.

"Look, I'll repeat," he said. "I tried conciliation and friendship. That failed. So now I've shown them what happens to rebels. That will work. Gaul will be at peace. I've made it so."

Fiammar glanced at him. No use arguing with a man who had made up his mind. She looked down.

"Almost ready again," she said, fondling him. She bent over, long hair brushing his belly. "You're a woman's delight, lover."

# 7

As Caesar looked down at Fiammar, fantasizing, had she known it, that those were Servilia's lips, in a cottage deep in a forest some four miles away Comm and Vercingetorix faced each other. Their retainers were outside. Inside, logs blazed in a fireplace.

"Well, what's on your mind?" Comm asked.

"I saw how you felt today. I feel the same."

Comm considered the tall, yellow-haired Arvernian prince. Vercingetorix' chin was up and his eyes steel-blue and steady. Comm took a block of wood, up-ended it, and sat down.

"I'll speak right out, if you will."

Vercingetorix up-ended another block and sat down opposite Comm.

"Agreed," he answered.

"I told myself," Comm said, "that Caesar was putting an end to our senseless intertribal wars, that he would bring order, that, as he told us, under the aegis of Rome we would still rule our tribes but would develop from a semi-barbarous to a civilized people. I believed him, I suppose, because I wanted to."

"Besides, he made you king of the Atrebatians."

"That was part of it, I admit."

"Well," Vercingetorix said, "I believed in Caesar, too — his value to us Gauls, I mean. Not to mention that he flattered me, called me his friend, charmed me. The killing of Dumnorix did bother me." He scratched at his cheek. "But we Gauls killed him — in battle. Besides, he was an Aeduan."

"And an enemy of you Arvernians."

"Right." Vercingetorix clapped a hand down on his knee. "What's wrong with us Gauls? You holding down the Menapians. All the neighbouring tribes looting the Eburones. Me helping to arrest Acco."

"You tell me."

Vercingetorix jumped to his feet. "What's wrong is that, in the pinch, we don't think of ourselves as Gauls but as Arvernians, Atrebatians, Cadurcans, Senones, or what have you. That's our trouble, by the Horned One."

"So, what?"

Vercingetorix paced around the room, came to a halt in front of Comm.

"Am I right in saying that this afternoon Caesar overstepped the mark?"

"You're right. This afternoon Caesar showed too nakedly that Rome — and he — are the conquerors, and we Gauls the conquered."

"And that, at his whim, any noble can be flogged to death. And here, Comm, is our chance. Gauls will forget much. The nobles can't — won't — forget that fact."

Comm, too, got to his feet. "What do you propose, then?"

"We can still throw out the Romans, if we fight as Gauls—not as Arvernians or Atrebatians or Senones or Carnutes, but as

172

Gauls. We'll go to the nobles. We'll unite them. Then, we'll fight as Gauls, free Gauls. Are you with me, Comm?"

Comm held out his hand. "I'm with you."

# CHAPTER XVI

I T HAD BEEN A LONG DAY at Mediolanum. Caesar's war had brimmed the cup of Cisalpine Gaul's prosperity — the purchase of grain and the like; the manufacture of clothes and other essentials for the army; the supply depots for weapons brought up from Puteoli, the centre of Italian iron and steel workings; the transport trains into Gaul — all the necessities for keeping Caesar's troops in the field. So there had been cheering mobs as Caesar's coach rode into the city; then speeches of welcome, deputations, and finally a banquet in the town hall.

Now, at last, Caesar and Servilia were alone in a villa outside the city, one loaned by Hirtius, Caesar's quartermaster. Oak and beech logs crackled in the fireplace, its flickering light the only illumination. The two of them sat in front of it on cushions piled on bearskin rugs. Their first, fierce physical need had been assuaged.

"No one like you, ever," Caesar said, tightening his arm around Servilia's waist.

"And no one like you, darling." She thought of Memmius and snuggled into Caesar. "No one," she repeated with an almost savage intensity. "But don't ever leave me so long again."

"No need. Gaul is at peace."

"All winter? In Cisalpine Gaul, I mean?"

Caesar nodded. "Courts. Disputes. Checking of accounts. All that sort of thing, all the way to Ravenna. But," he drew her closer to him, "with Decius, your son, here on furlough to satisfy the conventions, there will still be plenty of time for us."

"Wonderful!" She kissed his neck. Caesar leaned over to touch her lips with his, then said, "Those marriage proposals of yours, they seem a possible idea. Tell me, what's my grand-niece, Octavia, like? Remember, I haven't seen her since she was a youngster."

174

Servilia freed herself and sat up. "Young," she said. "Shy. Gentle. The way Pompey likes them."

"He's seen her?"

"At my salon. He noticed her, all right." She glanced at Caesar. "About your marriage to Pompey's daughter — will you miss Calpurnia?"

Caesar rubbed his hand across his chin. "Yes. She's been dignified. Hasn't minded my long absences. She'll understand, though."

"One problem, Julius."

"What?"

Servilia spoke slowly. "Pompey is attracted, I hear, to Cornelia, the daughter of Metellus Scipio."

Caesar thought a moment. "I think he'll see the political advantages of your proposals, dear."

"You'll write him?"

"Provided you'll draft the letter."

"Glad to, sweetheart."

"And now, dearest," Caesar said, turning to her.

"No, Julius, please. I'd like to talk first."

"Of course. What's on your mind?"

Servilia sat up, her face serious in the flickering light. "Rome today," she said. "Chaos. No elections for next year. That's only one symptom of a deeper malaise — greed. Everyone trying to grab all he can get for himself and to Hades with the rest of society. Our upper class? Unbelievable luxury. In debt, too. Get now, pay later, as if possessions were all that mattered. Meanwhile, out in the country, the peasants are bankrupt, and in Rome tens of thousands on the dole — "

"That's because slave labour has ousted free labour and because the huge thousand-acre plantations have driven the peasants off their little farms."

"I know." Servilia drew up her knees and clasped her arms around them. "A society of beggars and millionaires, that's us. Morality?" She glanced at Caesar. "I shouldn't talk, naked here with you. But our orators, like Cicero, declaim about the stern virtues of old that made Rome great. Meantime, bribery rampant and, as Jugurtha once said, anything in Rome — votes,

175

foreign policies, governorships, contracts, what have you—can be bought. Sex? Every possible variation. Our ancestors would have called them 'perversions'. Not that I mind. But that permissiveness is a symptom, too, of a general breakdown." She glanced at Caesar again. "It gives me a feeling that our society is hurtling toward a precipice. So, is there an answer, Julius?"

"Reform. Drastic reforms."

"How? By consent? Or imposed?"

"Imposed."

"What about freedom?" She let go of her knees and turned to face him. "The freedom to say what one thinks, to do, within reason, what one wants?"

She looked charming, the firelight playing in light and shadow over her naked body. But Caesar respected her intelligence.

" 'Drastic' was the word I used, dearest," he answered. "The rot in Rome is too deep for anything but surgery."

"And meanwhile," Servilia said, shifting her position to look at him even more directly, "Crassus and his army gone. You with Gaul and your ten legions, and Pompey with his five legions in Spain and the right to raise more in Italy. No other army. No, listen, Julius. You and I grew up amid civil war. That's the abyss I fear."

"No civil war," Caesar said. "I promise you that. No Sullan-type dictatorship either. You'll see. Somehow, I'll work it out with Pompey. This marriage proposal is the first step. In any case, no civil war, darling."

"Oh, Julius." She opened her arms. "Come to me."

"You," he said between kisses, "and Gaul at peace."

"Your other women?" she whispered.

"No one to equal you, ever."

"As long as I'm first—always," she said fiercely, holding him back an instant. "As long as I'm first, I don't mind. Make sure I'm first."

"You are. Always."

"Come into me then. Quick."

## 2

At Brixia, Fadius, leaving the group on furlough, had turned from the main highroad to a side road leading to his home. Evening was beginning to close in on afternoon. He missed Rullus who had gone off at Mediolanum to visit his family on the farm in the Sabine hills. So Fadius was riding alone, a bitter wind from the Alps at his back — his helmet off, a bag of knick-knacks he had bought in Massilia strapped behind him on the horse's back, his head turning from side to side to take in the bronzed leaves of the oaks and beeches, the grunting swine nosing for acorns, the farmers guiding their horned oxen with their long goads as they turned them back and forth to finish the ploughing.

It was all so familiar that the months in Gaul and Britain seemed to be falling away from him. He drew in deep breaths, thinking that the rhythm of country life was so different from the army. Here, year after year it was the same: long, slow days, season passing into season, and each season with its own appointed, recurring jobs — the sowing, the harvesting, the ploughing, the housing and feeding of the stock—a secure life, of the earth and for the earth.

In this atmosphere, even the memory of Chione had receded. In any case, he knew that she was safe and comfortable in Massilia. Next spring, he could consider again what he could do for her. As he was thinking this, a bend in the road brought him over a knoll, and there, nestled among the tall poplars, was his home. He reined in his horse, surprised at the surge of emotion within him. Home!

Carefully he took off the extra cloak he'd been wearing and folded it in front of him. Then, reaching for his helmet, he put it on, slung his shield with its leathern cover on his left arm, and freed his javelin and took it in his right hand. At last, ready, he gathered the reins, chirruped to his horse, and cantered to the single entrance of the farmhouse and through it into the courtyard. Behind him and to right and left were the storerooms and the stables. In the centre were the remains of the manure-pile — most of it, he remembered, already spread over the fields to be ploughed under for next year's crops. Beyond, closing the courtyard, was the long, low, whitewashed house. In front children, his own nephews and nieces, were playing, shouting, and shrieking in the midst of a game of Romans against wild tribesmen from the Alps.

Fadius rode on toward them. A blunt wooden arrow banged on his armour and fell off. The boy who had shot it saw him.

"A soldier," he yelled. "Look, a soldier!"

They all froze where they were, staring at him. Fadius started to dismount. The eldest of the children, a girl, ran into the house, shouting, "Mother! A soldier! Mother!" A woman—that would be Marcia, his second-eldest brother's wife—came to the doorway to peer at him. Fadius, grinning, led his horse up to her.

"Don't you remember me?"

A look of recognition flashed into her face.

"Titus!" she exclaimed. "It's Titus!" Then, she shouted back into the house. "It's Titus! Home! Titus!"

He heard scurrying feet and next his mother was in the doorway, grey hair straggling across her lined, weather-beaten face, hands and arms covered to the elbow with bits of the dough she'd been kneading. Fadius stuck the butt-end of his javelin into the ground, let the reins fall, and stepped forward, opening his arms, shield and all. She ran into them. He hugged her, forgetting his armour. She didn't notice it either.

"My boy!" she was saying between sobs. "My boy! Is it really you? Titus!"

There were tears in Fadius' own eyes.

Later, armour and weapons stacked in a corner, the whole family summoned, the presents he had brought distributed — lead soldiers for the boys, carved wooden dolls for the girls, necklaces and bracelets for his brothers' wives and his younger sister, who had married a neighbour while he was away, a cameo brooch for his mother, a Gallic sickle with embossed handle for his father — he sat with the others at the rough table. It was loaded with the food the scurrying women had got ready—lamb stew, fish, home-baked bread, pickles, buns, preserved jams and jellies, his favorite oatmeal cakes, nuts, olives, cheese, and cup after cup of home-made wine. Fadius ate and ate. They all ate. When they finally got up from the table, it was the children's turn to sit down. Fadius watched them benevolently, trying to sort out the eight of them. But then, with the room smoky from the brazier and light flickering from the beeswax candles, he realized that they all, even the children, were beginning to look at him expectantly. He stirred uneasily. He had learned during the meal that, thanks to the prosperity in Cisalpine Gaul caused by Caesar's war, the family had bought more land, and that his eldest brother, Tiberius, had established his own barns and house.

"Sell everything, anything we can grow," Tiberius had boasted. "Wheat. Oats. Olives. Horses. Mules. Cattle. Pigs. Melons. Nuts even. You ought to have stayed on the farm, Wart."

Wart had been his nickname. Now Tiberius was asking, "How do you like it, the army, I mean?"

"It's a job."

"Lots of loot, eh?"

A warning bell tinkled in Fadius' mind as he remembered that Tiberius had mentioned an orchard he'd like to buy.

"Not too bad," Fadius admitted. "It's all in the army bank, though. Up in Gaul."

Tiberius grunted.

"What's the land like?" his father wanted to know. "For crops, I mean?"

Fadius glanced at the lean, work-hardened face, one knotted hand wrapped around a beechwood cup.

"Good," he said earnestly. "Never seen better. Especially around Lutetia."

"Where's Lutetia?" a childish voice piped.

How could you explain that? Fadius shrugged his shoulders.

"What's the fighting like?" his sister's husband asked.

How could he tell them? They were civilians. He did his best. The British chariots interested them, especially the women. Women—and children—seemed to like to hear about violence. But Fadius, even as he exaggerated a bit, knew that he couldn't

179

really get across to any of them what the army was like — the long hours of drill, the sweat as you built a camp, the slog, slog, slog of one foot after another, hour on hour; or the feeling just before the charge, the heart thumping, the inner core of fear, the surge of determination to fight better than anyone, and then the savage exultation as you charged and slashed and stabbed and felt the enemy giving way and knew you'd won—and you were still alive — alive!

"How many men did you kill, Uncle Titus?" the second-eldest boy, a sturdy, tow-haired youngster, wanted to know.

He looked at the youngster. Before he could answer, another voice piped, "Can I play with your sword, Uncle Titus?"

"The idea," the child's mother, Marcia, scolded. "Cut yourself. I should say not."

His father spoke slowly, heavily. "How was your Uncle Thermus killed, Titus?"

How could he ever make that day clear, the sleet in their faces, the yelling Gauls, the confusion?

"We were ambushed," he answered gruffly.

"A legion and a half killed," Tiberius put in. "A legion and a half! How could that happen if our troops are as good as they say?"

There was a sneer in his voice. His mother cut in.

"Did you bury my brother?"

"How could I? I just barely got away."

"You should have. Think of his ghost." His mother stifled a sob. "Wandering. Homeless. Moaning."

Women were always bound up in religion. "I did, later," Fadius said hastily. "When we went back to that camp."

"You're sure it was my brother?"

Fadius thought of the tumbled heaps of bones. He lied.

"I picked up his bones myself," he said. "I gave them proper burial."

There were a few more questions, perfunctory ones. The women began to hustle the children off to bed. The men began to talk of the olive crop, of the fields that still had to be ploughed, of the cow that was sick, of how many piglets the old sow might

180

have—that sort of thing. Fadius sat back, melancholy engulfing him. Time had flowed by, for him and for them, cutting an abyss between them. Perhaps, though, with all the winter before him, he could get back to them — and the land — back close.

## 3

Snow lay deep on Gaul. But the flogging to death of Prince Acco had not, as Caesar had expected, been forgotten. On this day of late November, in a glade deep in the forest south of Cenabum, the capital of the Carnutes, were gathered over a score of the principal chieftains of the Atlantic and central tribes, who had responded to visits by Comm and Vercingetorix. Before them rose an ancient and sacred oak. In front of it was an altar. By that altar, motionless, a golden sickle in his hand, stood the eldest and the holiest of the Druids of Gaul, robed in black. Behind him were ranged three other black-robed Druids. Two of them held a slave by the arms, the third cherished a golden bowl.

All was in readiness for the most sacred, the most binding ceremony among the Gauls. During the previous night, the chieftains had held a council in Cenabum. In that council they had chosen Vercingetorix as leader, decided not to approach the tribes loyal to Rome or those crushed by Caesar last summer, approved Vercingetorix' plan of striking while Caesar was away, decided the contingents that each of the tribes was to supply for the army of Gaul, granted to Cotuat, leader of the Carnutes, his request to ignite the fire of freedom's fight in Cenabum when the appointed day came, and sworn mutual oaths.

Now the chieftains waited, their eyes on the black-robed Druids. They were tall, yellow-haired men, these nobles. Golden torques encircled their throats. Bands of gold, set with gems, enriched their arms. Tartan cloaks and trousers, bright with colour, clothed them. Their swords hung at their sides, and each held in his right hand the standard of his tribe. Above them the winter clouds leaned down, heavy. Their faces were turned toward the oak, the altar, and the Druid. Comm nudged Vercingetorix.

"It's time," he whispered.

Vercingetorix, tall, handsome, face like a hawk, took one step forward, the snow crunching beneath his foot, and pointed his standard toward the altar and the Druid. At the signal the eldest of the Druids turned toward the sacred oak. Raising the golden sickle, slowly and reverentially he cut from it a sprig of sacred mistletoe and laid the sprig on the altar.

He placed the sickle on top of the mistletoe. Then, with uplifted arms facing north, east, south, and west in turn, from each quarter he invoked the gods of the Gauls to approach and bless this holy ceremony. Finally, hands pointing downward to the earth beneath the snow, he called upon the greatest of the gods, Him Who Rules the Darkness, by whose nights the seasons and the days of each man's life are numbered, to grant his blessing.

He turned to take up the golden sickle again. He faced the chieftains and beckoned with his left hand behind him. Two other Druids led the slave, unresisting, around to face him. They forced the slave to his knees in the snow. The eldest of the Druids seized him by the hair, lifted up his head, and sliced the golden sickle across his throat. One of his black-robed assistants sank to his knees and held up the golden bowl to receive the spurting blood. When it was finished the eldest of the Druids laid the sickle on the altar once more, took the bowl in one hand and the sprig of mistletoe in the other, and walked toward the chieftains. As he moved away, the other Druids raised the body of the slave and bore it to the forest.

The eldest of the Druids reached the chieftains. He dipped the sprig of mistletoe into the bowl and sprinkled Vercingetorix, and next Comm, and then each of the chieftains in turn with drops of the blood. As he sprinkled them, redipping the mistletoe, he repeated three phrases in a language so old that no one knew the meaning.

When he had finished, he stepped to one side.

"Place the standards," he ordered.

As one man, the chieftains moved to the altar and the oak and laid the massed standards against them.

"Each man keep his right hand upon his standard and face toward me," the eldest of the Druids commanded.

The chieftains obeyed.

"Now, repeat after me," the Druid said. Then, phrase by phrase, he intoned the most sacred of oaths. In concert, phrase by phrase, the chieftains repeated the oath, ending by calling down on themselves, in this life and in all succeeding lives, such terrible penalties for breaking faith that each man shuddered as he spoke them aloud.

"May it so be, ye gods of the Gauls," the Druid called.

"May it so be," the chieftains answered.

The Druid dropped his uplifted arms. The chieftains stepped back from the massed standards, their faces awed. At that instant, a shaft of sunlight broke through the heavy clouds to fall full upon the massed standards.

"An omen!" the Druid cried. He raised his hand high. "I accept the omen, gods of the Gauls. I accept it."

"And I accept it," Vercingetorix exclaimed. In a swift, impulsive movement he pulled his sword from its scabbard and raised it high.

"Up the Gauls!" he shouted. "Up the free Gauls!"

As one man the chieftains, too, flung up their swords.

"Up the Gauls!" they roared.

As the Gallic chieftains began to travel back to their tribes, snow lay deep on the valley of the Po. For Fadius in these days it was as if he were sloughing off one skin and putting on another. Occasionally the memory of Chione crossed his mind. But she was safe and comfortable, and spring and the army seemed far away. Meanwhile on the farm it was like old times. Once again he was feeding the cattle and swine, enjoying the odours and the steamy warmth as he cleaned out the pig-pens and the cattle-byres to add to the growing manure pile in the courtyard. He went out, too, with his brothers to cut firewood and drag it home. In the evenings he sat with the others in front of the blazing fire, the children playing, the women cooking or weaving or sewing, he and his brothers and their friends eating apples or home-made honey-cakes, or cracking hickory nuts and picking out the meat.

There were no more questions about army life. Instead, it was the slow talk of farmers about crops and cattle and prices, and what fields to sow to what crop when spring came. Now and then he would tramp through the snow to visit this uncle or that. At home, at night the slave-girl who had initiated him in sex would come to his bed, smelling of wool and cheese, and giggling as he taught the refinements of lovemaking taught him by Chione. But Chione and spring were still so far away that the future was like a misty dream.

## 5

In Ravenna the snow was slush, although a chill wind from the Adriatic blew across the waterfront and through the streets of the town. On this day, which by the Roman calendar was the first week in January, Caesar stood in the Salon of Spring in the mansion that was his headquarters.

There was a frown on his face. His journey from Mediolanum to Ravenna had been a triumphal tour—cheering mobs in Brixia, Verona, Parma, Bononia, and all the towns and villages in between. It had also been a slow trip — courts to be held, accounts to be examined, disputes to be settled, all the backlog of administration to be cleared. Each night, though, it had been Servilia and he and such a perfect meshing of bodies, minds, and spirits that each morning he rose clear-minded and invigorated. Here in Ravenna it had been the same. His headquarters faced on the main square. She had a mansion a street away and a villa outside the walls, both loaned by her daughter, the one married to Cassius, who was still in Syria.

But this afternoon Balbus had arrived from Rome. At the moment, he was warming his hands over a brazier while Servilia sat in a chair under a fresco in soft yellows and greens of spring scattering flowers. She was watching the frown on her lover's

184

face and the sheets of papyrus crumpled in his hand.

"So Pompey refuses the marriage proposals," Caesar said. "Why?"

Balbus turned from the brazier. "It's in my report," he answered. "Because he says both girls are already betrothed."

"The real reason?"

Balbus shrugged. "Because," he said bluntly, "he's fascinated by Cornelia, the daughter of Metellus Scipio."

·"A Conservative noble," Caesar said, still frowning.

"What's she like? I mean, I've seen her. I don't know her well."

That was Servilia. Balbus turned to her.

"Good-looking in a cool sort of way. An intellectual. I think that's what intrigues Pompey. She knows the works of the Greek philosophers, tragedians, lyric poets, what have you—and can, and does, talk about them knowledgeably. A new kind of woman for Pompey."

"You say here," Caesar said, smoothing out a sheet of the papyrus, "that he's supporting this Metellus Scipio for consul. What about his man, Milo?"

Balbus chuckled. He seated himself on a stool.

"Pompey has abandoned Milo," he answered. "That intrigues all Rome. So the Conservatives, to thumb their nose at Pompey, are backing Milo. Clodius is furious—at them and at Pompey."

"Still no elections?" Servilia inquired.

"No interrex either," Balbus told her. "It's all in that report. For the second year in succession, Rome begins January with no consuls or praetors, but this time Clodius had a tribune, Munatius Plancus, refuse to permit the Senate to appoint an interrex." He spread his hands. "No one at all in charge. Sheer chaos."

"So, what will you do now, Julius?" Servilia asked.

Caesar had been thinking it over. "This refusal of the marriages is a shock," he said slowly. "On the other hand, if the Conservatives and Pompey are at odds, the danger of a Pompey-Conservative alliance is, for the moment anyway, out of the picture." He paced to the brazier and back again. "Return to Rome, my friend," he went on, putting a hand on Balbus' shoulder. "Propose to Pompey that, since by law I can't leave my province, we meet at Lucca as we did four years ago this spring."

Servilia rose from her chair. "What have you to offer this time, Julius?"

Caesar glanced at her. "Gaul is at peace. So I can afford to offer Pompey five more years as governor, in absentia, of Spain. Furthermore, I have soldiers on furlough in Rome. Pompey wants elections. By means of those soldiers I can put pressure on Clodius to permit elections. Nothing in writing, of course. But Pompey is to understand that a meeting at Lucca is a prerequisite. Once we meet face to face, we can arrange everything—particularly with a pacified Gaul behind me."

"It may well work," Balbus agreed, getting up. "I'll get ready to go."

"Tomorrow, not tonight," Caesar said. "Meanwhile, as Servilia knows, I must make a tour of Illyricum. There's a mountain tribe there making trouble. By the time I return, my friend, you'll be back, I hope, with Pompey's agreement to a meeting."

"Shall I go to Rome with Balbus?" Servilia asked. "While you're away, I mean?"

Caesar put an arm about her and smiled down at her.

"No, darling. The roads across the Apennines in winter can be treacherous. Wait here. I'll hurry — and then we'll meet with Pompey."

So he spoke, not knowing that as he spoke the fates were busy spinning new threads for Rome, for Gaul, and for him.

# CHAPTER XVII

A FEW DAYS AFTER BALBUS REACHED ROME, but before he
could get in touch with Pompey, Titus Annius Milo, muffled in a travelling cloak, was riding in a coach along the Appian
Way, escorted by a score and a half of gladiators and armed
slaves. It was late of a wintry afternoon. A chill wind was
blowing and clouds hung low. At Milo's side his wife, Fausta,
was nattering about buying a palace on the Palatine Hill.

Except for a grunt or two, Milo, a broad-faced, broad-beamed
man, made no reply. That day's meeting of the Senate had
dragged on and on — that ass, Cicero, as Milo regarded him, off
on one of his interminable harangues about how he, single-
handed, had destroyed the revolutionary Catiline. When, finally, Milo had reached home, he had found that his wife still
wasn't ready to leave for Lanuvium.

Lanuvium was Milo's birthplace. Last year, in recognition of
his meteoric rise in Rome, its citizens had elected him "Dictator", an obsolete title that went back to the days when
Lanuvium was important and Rome merely a few miserable
villages by the Tiber. The title meant that tomorrow, in an
elaborate ceremony, he was to appoint a flamen, that ancient
priest, for Lanuvium's tutelary deity, Juno Sospita.

He'd come a long way, Milo was thinking comfortably, since
he'd been a boy in Lanuvium, the son of its richest man, lounging
on the main street and clicking his tongue at the girls as they
walked by. His father, a banker, hadn't wanted him to leave for
Rome. But he had felt within himself a talent for stirring the
mob. And look where he was now! Running for consul! Consul!

Milo yawned. He was conscious and not conscious of the
coach rattling over the paving-stones, of the coachman up front
and the creaking of harness, of the clattering of the hooves of his

187

escort's horses, and of the nattering of his wife. It wasn't fair of Pompey not to support him for consul, he told himself resentfully, not after all he'd done for the bastard. On the other hand, it was flattering to have Cato, Bibulus, Domitius, and other Conservative nobles speaking in his favour, when he himself was middle-class, not an aristocrat.

"It's sleeting!" Fausta exclaimed. "Stop the coach, Titus. The curtains — have them put on."

His wife was a florid woman, known for obvious reasons as the "gladiators' remount". But he was lucky to have got to marry her, a daughter of the aristocratic dictator, Sulla. Resignedly, Milo had the coach stopped and the leather curtains attached. As they started on again, his wife peered out.

"Look," she said. "There's the tomb of my mother." She sat back. "The tomb of Caecilia Metella, the biggest tomb on the Appian Way. The very biggest. D'you realize that?"

Milo grunted. But the words "Appian Way" had stuck in his mind. This road beneath the wheels of his coach, the first of the great Roman roads, had been built over two and a half centuries ago by Appius Claudius — and Appius Claudius was a direct ancestor of the sneering son-of-a-bitch, Clodius. Dull anger surged in Milo. Clodius hadn't attended the Senate today. Whenever he was there, in that arrogant upper-class accent of his he enjoyed himself by baiting middle-class Milo. "Hog-butcher" he'd called him last week, just because Milo's father had once seized a herd of swine from a bankrupt debtor. The senators had snickered. "Frog-face," he'd sneered, making fun of Milo's broad face and bulging eyes, and a couple of senators had laughed. And three days ago, he had drawled in the Senate that if the honourable pig-sticker from Lanuvium — no, drawer-out-of-guts was more accurate — had any brains, he'd comprehend that it was an insult to the Republic for a man still smelling of manure to run for consul.

He'd pig-stick him if he got the chance, Milo told himself, and began to fantasize scenes in which that sneering patrician was on his knees in front of him, begging for mercy. He did not know it, but at this moment Clodius, head down against the sleet, a score

188

of mounted retainers accompanying him, was riding towards him. For two days he had been at Aricia, where he owned property, conducting meetings of the town council. The mayor had invited him to stay the night. But in Rome there was Fulvia, and with that lecher, Antony, in the city, Clodius had decided to hurry home.

Midway between the two leaders was Bovillae, a small town with a long and narrow main street, lined on each side with houses and half a dozen taverns. Just at dusk, as Clodius and his men clip-clopped into one end of that street, Milo's coach and escort clattered into the other. The two parties met. The men in front of each group began to jostle, shouting for the other to pull to one side.

"What's this — what's this!" Clodius exclaimed, pushing his horse forward.

"Give way," a gladiator was shouting. "Give way for Titus Annius Milo."

"Give way yourself," Clodius shouted in his turn, "you dung-hill feeder," and struck the gladiator in the face with his riding-crop. The gladiator lugged out his sword. Clodius pulled his own. In an instant swords were out everywhere, blades clashing. At this moment, Milo, wakened from his semi-doze, stuck his broad face out between the leather curtains of the coach, and saw Clodius not more than a dozen feet away.

"You!" he bellowed. "You!"

"Get your pigs out of the way, Frog-face," Clodius shouted back at him. "Get your pigs off my road."

Inside the coach, Fausta was screaming. Milo shrugged off his cloak and tumbled out, sword in hand. By this time the darkening street, with the inhabitants of the town cowering inside their houses, windows hastily shuttered and barred, was a mêlée of cursing, slashing men and tangled, snorting, rearing horses. The sleet drove down, making the whole scene still more confused. In the fighting Clodius was carried past Milo's coach. Turning his horse he tried to cut his way back to it, his intention being to stick his sword into Milo's flat, broad face. A gladiator barred his way. Clodius sliced at him. His sword slid off the

189

man's armour, throwing his arm wide, leaving his unarmoured body open. The gladiator thrust. To avoid the blow, Clodius jerked his horse away, but the horse's hooves slipped on the sleet-iced paving-stones and it stumbled. The thrust bit into Clodius' side. As he started to fall from his horse, one of his men caught him and, dismounting, eased his master to the ground. Two more of Clodius' escort jumped from their horses to help. The three carried their master to the nearest tavern, broke down the door, lugged him inside, laid him on a bench, and shouted for cloths to stanch the wound. Outside, Thrax, the leader of Milo's gladiators, called to his master, who was standing by the coach, travelling cloak wrapped round his left arm, defending himself against a couple of Clodius' horsemen.

"He's down!" Thrax shouted. "The bastard's down. Clodius —he's down!"

Clodius' two men drew back. The rest of his escort began to mill about, leaderless. The gladiators drove in on them. Within a couple of minutes, Clodius' men turned tail and galloped back down the street. Milo, sweating and angry, sheathed his sword. Inside the coach, Fausta was still screaming at the top of her lungs. Milo thrust in his face.

"Shut up, bitch!" he yelled. She was so astonished that she stopped in mid-scream, mouth open. Milo pulled back his head and said to Thrax.

"Where is he, the son of a bitch?"

"In that tavern," Thrax said, pointing. "Bad hurt, I'd say." He leaned down from his horse toward Milo. "Good chance to finish him off, master," he suggested, lowering his voice. "Not more than three men with him. I could drag him out to the street. They'd think he was killed in the fighting."

Milo's lips worked in and out. To murder a patrician, the darling of the Roman mob, would be dangerous. Yet there were already several bodies lying in the street. If one could pretend that the killing was done without one's knowledge or consent—

"Get the coach turned round," he said to the coachman. He waited. When it was facing toward Rome again, he said to Thrax,

"I'm going back. I'll take half the men. You stay here with the

190

rest, Thrax. Clean up the mess." He lowered his voice and winked at his henchman. "Clean it up properly. Understand? You won't be sorry." He stepped into the coach. "Back to Rome," he said to the coachman.

## 2

Late that night a senator named Lucius Regillus, returning from a visit to his farms near Fregellae, came across the body of Clodius in the main street of Bovillae. Recognizing the corpse, he had it put into his coach, brought it to Clodius' palace on the Palatine, and had it carried in and laid on a couch in a salon off the atrium. The Lady Fulvia, just wakened, her torrent of copper-red hair spilling down over her robe, stood looking down at her dead husband's face. The senator had expected shrieks, screams, tossing arms. Instead her voice was ice-cold.

"Who?" she said, fists clenched, still staring down. "Who?"

"Milo's men," the senator answered. "Or so," he led forward a man with a bandage around his head, "this man says."

Fulvia whirled on the man. "And you, still alive!" she shouted, knocking him back with a full swing of her arm. "You, alive — and your master dead!"

She advanced on the man. The senator checked her.

"We found this man in the street beside his master," he told her. "Unconscious. Obviously they thought he was dead, too."

Fulvia stared at the man for an instant. She swung back to her husband's body. Now it will come, the senator thought, the screams, the shrieks. Instead, she said as if to herself,

"He'll pay for it. Milo. All of them — Cato, Domitus — all of them." She turned to her steward. "Have the lamps lit," she told him in a flat, controlled voice, "every lamp in the house. No, wait. Send messengers first. To Plancus. To Quintus Rufus. To Sallustius Crispus. To each gang leader in Rome. Have them here. Within the hour."

The steward stared at her.

"Move," Fulvia exploded. "D'you want the cross?"

191

For three days, the body of Clodius had lain in state. For three days the tribunes and the gang leaders had filed past it to gather in groups throughout the palace, eating, drinking, talking. Balbus, who had already sent off a courier to Caesar, had come to pay his respects. So had those senators who belonged to the Caesar clique. Even Antony, accompanied by Curio, had put in a somewhat embarrassed appearance.

Now, on the fourth day, the body, its wounds exposed, lay on a bier placed on the Rostra. Above, high clouds drifted. Below, the Forum was packed with an excited, jostling crowd, staring up at the bier and at the vivid pictures displayed behind it: on the right, Clodius proclaiming free grain for the thousands on the dole; on the left, Clodius protecting the proletariat from the menacing advance of a group of Conservative nobles; in the centre, largest of all, Clodius dragged, wounded, from the tavern in Bovillae, while a huge gladiator thrust a sword into him — and in the background was the broad face of Milo, backed by smirking nobles.

One by one the tribunes of the Popularist party stepped forward on the Rostra. One by one, in shrill, excited voices, they reminded the mob of all Clodius had done for them — the free banquets, the rescue of man after man from the courts, the free spectacles in the Circus Maximus, and, most of all, the free grain for everyone. His reward for all that? Each of them flung his hand toward the central picture. Ambushed, wounded — then, dragged out like a dog and murdered.

There were groans, shouts from the mob, fists thrust upward, while on the brow of the Palatine Hill, a group of nobles, including Cato, Domitius, and Bibulus, watched. Cicero watched too. So did Antony and Curio. As they watched, suddenly, against all precedent, there was Fulvia on the Rostra, clothes rent, hair dishevelled. Plancus the tribune caught at her to pull her back. With a thrust of her elbow she sent him stumbling. She raised her hands high.

"Look at me, citizens of Rome," she cried. "Look! His widow

— bereaved!" She swung around to point at the bier and the picture behind it. "My husband! But your champion!" She turned back, reaching out to the crowd. "Vengeance! Shall we not call for vengeance?"

A wild roar of assent answered her.

"Milo—the murderer," she shrilled. "Oh, I could tear his guts out with my hands. These hands!" She held them out curved like grasping talons. "He isn't here — Milo," she said, dropping her hands and lowering her voice to a dramatic but hoarse and carrying tone. "The other murderers — those behind Milo," she, gestured to the central picture, "they aren't here. But over there," she swung to her left to point to the Senate-House close by, "that's where they plotted against him. My Clodius! Your Clodius! Egging on Milo. Over there. Right there." She took a step forward, throwing her arms and hands toward the en-thralled mob. "Shall we light a fire for him? Over there? For your hero — your Clodius?"

She paused for a split instant, then shrieked, "Will you follow me? A funeral-pyre for your hero — and mine. The Senate-House?"

"The Senate-House!" the mob roared. Led by Fulvia and Plancus, it surged across to the Senate-House and began to beat on the tall bronze doors. On the brow of the Palatine Curio turned to Antony.

"A Medea!" he exclaimed. "A veritable Medea!"

"They wouldn't dare!" Cicero was saying, as he watched beams being hammered against the bronze doors. "Surely not!"

"Look," Cato said grimly.

As they looked the mob beat down the doors. They rushed into the Senate-House. Under Plancus' direction they seized benches, tables, and chairs, splintered them, and heaped them in a huge pile in the centre of the great hall. From the shops round about, from the records building, from anywhere and every-where, piles of papyrus, along with shop counters split into kindling-wood, curtains, tapestries, anything flammable, were pushed onto the huge funeral-pyre. A score of hands brought torches and thrust them in. The papyrus caught. A few moments passed as the fire began to feed on the splintered wood, the curtains, the broken furniture; then, abruptly, there was a blazing pyramid of flames. Those flames reached out to lay hold of the beams and woodwork of the ceiling and the walls. The mob, driven back by the flames and the heat, danced and cheered. A wall collapsed. With a tremendous crash, the roof fell inward and showers of sparks along with smoke laced with flames soared up toward the clouds. The ancient and adjacent Basilica Aemilia caught fire. No one cared. As the first fury of the fire began to decline, the mob turned to looting the shops around the Forum, grabbing cottons from India, gold and silver cups, priceless vases, jewels and silks from the far-off Silk People. Then it began to spill out into the streets, bursting into taverns and restaurants, guzzling jars of wine, stuffing stomachs with sausages, hams, fish, olives, whatever was handiest.

And, meanwhile, Plancus and Fulvia, followed by a band of rioters, had rushed to Milo's palace on the Quirinal. But Milo had fled the city, and his palace was protected by gladiators, with armed men on the roof hurling down flights of spears. They fell back.

"I'm not done yet," Fulvia raved that night. "You'll see. Yes, you'll see."

That night, too, groups of nobles, accompanied by armed escorts, stood on the edge of the Palatine Hill and looked down at the Forum. It was empty. But from farther off came shouts and cries.

"If I only had my herdsmen here," roared Domitius, who had broad ranchlands in Picenum and Apulia, "I'd show them."

"A legion—no, a cohort," said Bibulus, who was married to Porcia, Cato's daughter. "I'd tame that rabble."

"Shouldn't we go to Pompey?" Cicero, who was on the fringe of the group, asked. "Ask him to become dictator?"

"No interrex," Cato said flatly. "Unconstitutional."

"We'll have to protect Milo," observed Marcellus.

Cicero thought of what Clodius had done to him—exile, for instance, and the burning of his house. "We ought," he said, with a nervous giggle, "to vote a Thanksgiving to Milo."

"Unconstitutional," Cato said again, looking sombrely at the pillar of smoke rising from the Senate-House toward the winter stars, now winking down between the clouds.

"What a woman!" Curio, standing next to Antony on the terrace of the House of the Vestal Virgins, said in wonder.

Above them, on the lip of the Palatine Hill, Balbus was thinking, "Now Pompey may get his chance."

# 4

Clodius killed! The Senate-House burned! The news galloped outward. Caesar, deep in Illyricum, sped back to Ravenna. In Gaul, the nobles hurried along the assembling of troops for the national revolt. In Rome, events trod on each other's heels. Plancus, frightened by the violence of the rioting, agreed to permit the Senate to appoint an interrex to govern the city, provided that the interrex was Marcus Lepidus, Servilia's son-in-law.

The city became quieter. The shops opened. Milo returned to his palace. But at the funeral banquet to Clodius, Fulvia inflamed the mob to another riot. Surging crowds looted and raped. Rioters attacked the mansions of Milo and Lepidus, the interrex, until they were driven back by flights of spears and arrows. Chaos ruled again. So Plancus led a delegation to Pompey, begging him to become dictator.

Pompey refused, saying that only the Senate, constitutionally, could confer the dictatorship. That refusal was a signal to the Conservatives. When Lepidus, infuriated by the attack on his palace, summoned the Senate to meet in the great hall in the Campus Martius that Pompey had had built, it decreed martial law and a levy of troops throughout Italy. Furthermore, it called on Lepidus as interrex and Pompey as proconsul to enforce those decrees.

Pompey sent in enough troops to stop the rioting but did nothing decisive. In Ravenna, to which each day couriers from Balbus came, Servilia said to her lover, "Will Pompey join the Conservatives now, Julius?"

"The Conservatives are too stupid to forgive and forget. And

Pompey wants the dictatorship served up to him on a platter —
like a roasted pheasant. He won't ask for it. He'll wait." Caesar
paused. "Besides," he added, "Pompey is a man who takes a step
forward, then one sideways, then one back. I'll offer him what he
wants — five more years as an absentee governor of Spain and its
legions. He'll meet with me at Lucca finally — or so Balbus
thinks."

"Meanwhile?"

Caesar, who had begun a levy of his own in Cisalpine Gaul,
drew her to him. "Meanwhile, we wait, dearest. That isn't too
boring, is it?"

"Oh no, Julius!"

"Don't worry, sweet. Everything will turn out all right."

He spoke confidently — and did not know that Fortune was
already considering how next to spin her wheel.

# CHAPTER XVIII

IT WAS MIDWINTER. In his palace on the Palatine, Marcus Bibulus surveyed the inner group of the Conservatives. Bibulus, a bulky, middle-aged man, could see that they were all ignoring Cicero, who did not really belong. But Bibulus had invited the orator with a purpose in mind. Bibulus was as rigid as his confrères. He, too, disliked and despised Pompey. On the other hand, his hatred of Caesar was more vindictive than that of any man here, except perhaps Cato, Bibulus' father-in-law. Bibulus had never forgotten his co-consulship with Caesar seven years ago. He had opposed Caesar, who was by-passing the Senate and presenting his self-serving laws directly to the Assembly. Early in the year, as he was returning from the Forum after interposing his veto, a basket of the vilest dung had been dumped on his head from the upper window of a shop — on Caesar's order, he was certain. So, Bibulus had shut himself up in his palace and announced by messenger that he had "seen lightning" every time Caesar had a law brought forward, even if the day were one of brilliant sunlight. By Roman law the seeing of lightning by a consul required the immediate dissolution of the Assembly. Instead, Caesar had ignored the announcement and passed his laws. The wags of Rome had in fact designated the year as "the consulship of Julius and Caesar".

It was this long-nurtured hatred which had finally caused Bibulus to listen to the arguments of Metellus Scipio, revolve them in his mind, and, at last, since disorder still afflicted Rome, come to a decision. In that decision, he was regarding Pompey as merely a necessary piece on the board of draughts.

This was what was occupying his mind as he surveyed his colleagues. He raised a hand.

"Shall we come to the purpose of this meeting, gentlemen?"

he said. He leaned forward. "It may surprise you," he went on heavily, "but our friend Metellus Scipio has convinced me. To end disorder, the Senate must decree that Gnaeus Pompeius Magnus be appointed" — he paused — "dictator."

"Never!" Cato exclaimed. "Not ever!"

"Wait," Bibulus said. "Listen a moment. Who is most dangerous to the Republic — Gnaeus Pompeius Magnus or Gaius Julius Caesar, the renegade?"

"Caesar!"

The chorus was unanimous.

"Well then," Bibulus went on, "let us look at it this way. We rule the Senate, but we have no army. Levies could never face Caesar's trained legions. Pompey has five legions in Spain. And Pompey, gentlemen, is the best general in today's world. Forget Caesar." Bibulus waved a hand contemptuously. "He announced that he had conquered Gaul. What's happened since? Revolt after revolt. When Pompey put down the Popularist leader, Sertorius, in Spain, Spain stayed peaceful. When Pompey swept the pirates from the seas, he did a thorough job. When he defeated Mithridates the Great and conquered the East, the East remained conquered."

"Which does not excuse the fact," Cato said, high-bridged nose arrogant, "that this Gnaeus Pompeius Magnus joined Marcus Crassus and Julius Caesar to overturn the Senate and negate the Republic." He glared around him. "We're all agreed on that point, surely."

"We use this Pompey to destroy Caesar," Bibulus argued. "After he's served his purpose, we can — ah — persuade him to retire."

Cicero was fidgeting on his chair. He could sense that most of the Conservatives were almost convinced. Here, almost won, was his own basic policy, the "Harmony of the Orders", as he had so often called it: senators, knights, and plebs united, but each class staying in its proper niche, presided over by Pompey — a true Roman Republic, stable and permanent. Did he dare speak? At that instant Cato got to his feet.

"It's a matter of principle," he said. He stared around him and none of the Conservatives could meet his eyes. "My great-grandfather, that exemplar of the virtues of our forefathers, would never have agreed. 'A man who betrayed the Republic—Dictator!' he would have said. 'Never.' That's what I say. Pompey — Dictator? Never. Not while I live."

It came to Cicero as if flashed to him by the gods.

"May I speak?" he asked.

Bibulus nodded assent. Cicero rose. He expressed his gratitude and his pleasure at being included in this conference. He could not forbear reminding these nobles how long and how faithfully, even at a bitter cost to himself, he had served the Republic. Next he admitted that, as they knew, he had always admired and respected Gnaeus Pompeius Magnus, and had felt that he had been misguided in joining with Marcus Crassus and Gaius Julius Caesar.

"I am certain, in fact completely confident in my own mind, that he has regretted that action," he said. "Essentially," he looked around him, "Gnaeus Pompeius Magnus is completely devoted to the Republic. However, in spite of my own friendship with him and my admiration of him, I agree with Marcus Porcius Cato. He should not be offered the dictatorship." He waited for the movements and mutterings of surprise to die down. "What I propose, gentlemen, is that the Senate decree that Gnaeus Pompeius Magnus, to save the Republic, be appointed Sole Consul."

The Conservatives looked at each other. Bibulus stared at Cicero, his slow mind gradually absorbing the proposal and then turning it over and over, examining it.

"With the proviso," Cicero added quickly, "that, once the crisis is over and order restored, Gnaeus Pompeius Magnus co-opt a second consul. Thus, the constitution will be observed and the Senate—the Senate, gentlemen, not the Assembly—will once more take its proper place as the leader of the Republic."

He saw Bibulus' face clear and sat down, knowing that he had won. Bibulus clapped a hand on his knee.

"I will so move in the Senate this afternoon." He turned to Cato. "Will you second that motion, Marcus Porcius Cato?"

Cato, who was younger than his son-in-law, sat there, his lips in a stubborn line. The others were calling on him to agree.

"For the welfare of the Republic," Bibulus urged, leaning toward him.

"I don't approve of it," Cato said slowly. "But yes, for the good of the Republic, I will second the motion."

Cicero sat back, a glow of accomplishment warming him. It had been genius, sheer genius. Once more he, Marcus Tullius Cicero, had saved the Republic.

Late that afternoon a delegation of Bibulus, Cato, and Metellus Scipio went to Pompey. He listened to the decree of the Senate, his lips moving in and out. He had expected the offer of the dictatorship. "Sole Consul". Was that appropriate to his dignity?

"If you'll pardon me a moment," he said, rising to his feet and then, with their consent, limping from the room. Two doors down was Cornelia, who had come over to visit him, chaperoned by her aunt. He told her the proposal. Cornelia, a tall woman who carried herself as erect as a pillar but whose face was relieved by lovely, intelligent eyes, had a genuine admiration for Pompey's achievements. She considered the situation.

"It ought to be the dictatorship," she said, "in view of all you've done for Rome. Besides," — she turned to him, her blue eyes warm — "you are the only man, Gnaeus, who can save Rome. However — 'Sole Consul' — doesn't that mean that, in effect, you will be in complete control?"

Pompey nodded.

"If you made it a condition that they extend your governorship of Spain," she said, a frown on her high forehead.

"I have never asked anybody for anything," Pompey answered stiffly. "And never will."

"I know, Gnaeus," Cornelia said, coming over to him swiftly. "I can speak to my father, can't I?"

"You think I ought to accept, then?"

"For the good of Rome, yes—darling," she said and gave him a light kiss on his cheek.

That same evening, in Balbus' modest mansion on the Quirinal, he and Oppius considered Pompey's acceptance of the post of Sole Consul.

"Alliance between the Conservatives and Pompey, that's evident — and dangerous," Oppius, a stoop-shouldered Roman whose family came from Alba Longa, observed.

The black-bearded Spaniard nodded. "We must discover what's going on behind the scenes," he said. "Now, who — who?" He paced back and forth, frowning, hands clasped behind his back. "Metellus Scipio!" he exclaimed, stopping. "All puffed up with his new importance. He'll talk. He'll tell me what the Conservatives are planning. Then we can protect Caesar."

And they did not know that Fortune had already given another flick to her wheel.


## 2

Snow lay deep on the valley of the Liger. In Cenabum, capital of the Carnutes, it was market-day. Already, although the sun was not quite up, in the market-place and in the narrow, twisting streets leading to it the snow was trampled and muddy. Before first light the peasants from the prosperous homesteads on the plain had brought in their produce and set up their stalls. The townsfolk, stamping their feet and flailing their arms to keep warm, were chatting to each other and to the stall-keepers as they examined the cured hams, the heaps of winter apples, the bowls of hazel, beech, and hickory nuts, the huge cheeses, the jars of home-made beer, the sacks of wheat, oats, barley, and rye, the beans, peas, dried apples, and other produce.

In another section, cattle were bawling, sheep bleating, pigs grunting, and horses stamping as prospective purchasers gathered around. In still another area, Italian and Greek traders, up from Massilia and Narbonese Gaul were arranging their wares — cheap brooches, armlets, necklaces, cameos, toys, and the like — to tempt the wives of the peasants and the townsfolk. For the nobles and the wealthy they offered woollens in bright colours, rich rugs and tapestries, finely turned vases, jars of

Greek wine, and other luxury wares. In the streets off the market-place, coopers, blacksmiths, and metal-workers were busy.

It was a typical market-day. In a stone house some distance up the street along the river, Cita, one of Caesar's quartermasters, yawned as he breakfasted off pieces of bread dipped in wine and examined his lists of requirements for Caesar's legions. More wheat and oats were obvious necessities.

"We'll see what's available in the market first," he told his secretary, "then ride out to the homesteads." He yawned again and began to put on his corselet. "The troop ready?"

"Yes, master," the secretary, a half-Greek, half-Syrian slave from Smyrna, answered.

Cita, a slight, dark-haired young man in his middle twenties, asked for his helmet. As he was fitting it on, his troop-leader, a Spaniard from Baetica, rushed in.

"Gauls," he blurted, "rushing across the bridge. Hordes. Hostiles."

Cita snatched his dagger, belting it on as he hurried outside. A yelling surge of Gauls was riding up the river road. Behind the horsemen ran a swarm of footmen. Cita leaped onto his horse.

"Make for the bridge," he shouted to his men.

He and his troop did not make it. They were pulled from their horses and killed, and then had their heads lopped off. Through the market-place and the whole town Prince Cotuat and his Carnutes raged, slaughtering the Italian and Greek traders and stuffing their genitalia into their mouths, raping their women and then slitting their bellies open. At the end of the massacre, Prince Cotuat leaped from his horse to embrace his second-in-command, Conconnetodumn.

"We've done it," he shouted. "We've lit the flame."


# 3


The Carntes had slaughtered the Romans in Cenabum! The news was shouted from homestead to village to homestead across central Gaul. By the middle of the first watch of that night the report had reached Gergovia, the capital of the Arvernians, a hundred and forty miles away.

The news was the signal a tense and expectant Vercingetorix had been awaiting. His retainers were already assembled in a forest three miles away from Gergovia's walls. Now, resplendent in armour, with an escort of supporters, he rode up the flat-topped hill on which Gergovia sat and through its northern gate, demanding a meeting of the Arvernian Council. By midnight that Council had been hurriedly assembled, all of its members cognizant of the massacre at Cenabum. Vercingetorix, gilded helmet on his head, sword with jewelled hilt at his side, gold torque around his neck, strode into the Council-Hall. From his seat on the dais at the end of the hall, his father's brother, Gubannitio, regarded his nephew dourly.

Vercingetorix did not notice. Standing there, tall, confident, he called upon the Arvernian nobles for immediate action.

"Arm every Arvernian," he cried to the Council. "Kill every Roman. Free Gaul."

There was a shout of assent from half a dozen chieftains. The older men sat silent, their faces closed. So was the face of his uncle, Gubannitio.

"You are out of your mind," he said in a cold, disdainful tone, and a dozen voices murmured agreement.

Vercingetorix could not believe it. He stared around him.

"Can't you comprehend?" he exclaimed. "All Gaul is ready. I've seen to that. So has Comm, Lucter, a dozen others. We're ready to strike, not just Arvernians and Carnutes, but Atrebatians, Senones, Venetans, Parisians, Cadurcans — all of us united." He flung his arms wide. "The Gauls a nation — at last. Now is the moment. Caesar away. Riots in Rome to keep him across the Alps. The legions leaderless. Strike now — and we win. Win!"

His uncle stood up. "Sit down," he told Vercingetorix. As Vercingetorix slowly, unbelievingly, found a bench, his uncle, too, looked around the hall.

"We've heard this story before," he said. "Revolt!" He

203

snorted. "It's been tried. Indutiomar? Where is he now? Or Dumnorix? Or Ambiorix and his Eburones? Do we want their fate to befall us and our people when Caesar comes, we whose southern border abuts Narbonese Gaul?"

Vercingetorix jumped to his feet. "The Cebennes Mountains protect us," he cried. "It's winter. The passes are deep with snow. Even if Caesar does come — "

"Sit down, I told you," his uncle ordered. Shouts from others backed him. Vercingetorix seated himself again, slowly, glaring around him.

"The Aeduans, too, would leap upon us," his uncle went on. "As things are, the Romans protect us. Under the cloak they've flung over us, we prosper. So why disrupt the Roman peace?" He paused, then raised his voice. "I rule that the Arvernians do not revolt. Stand up, those who agree with me."

In amazement Vercingetorix saw three-quarters of the Council rise, among them half a dozen whom he had regarded as certain supporters. He leaped to his feet.

"Cowards," he stormed. "Roman boot-lickers."

"I propose," his uncle said coldly, "that this—this fire-dragon be exiled."

Vercingetorix did not wait for the vote. Striding from the hall, he jumped onto his horse and with his escort clattered out of Gergovia. At dawn, leading three thousand men from the forest, he stormed into the city again. It was the turn of his uncle and his followers to be expelled. At mid-morning, in the great square, the townsfolk watched as Vercingetorix, lifted high on the shields of his followers, was proclaimed King of the Arvernians. King of Gaul next, he thought. And then he thought of his wife, the Princess Guenome, watching. She would see him now in full glory—King! Getting to his feet carefully and balancing himself on the shields, he pulled his sword from its enamelled scabbard and raised it high.

"Freedom for Gaul," he shouted. "Freedom."

# 4

In Ravenna, Caesar had no knowledge of the events in Cenabum or in Gergovia. Neither had Balbus. Ten days after Vercingetorix had seized the kingship and had immediately begun to set his forces in motion, the Spaniard descended from the coach that had brought him from Rome and walked stiffly through a light drizzle flecked with snow to the entrance of Servilia's villa outside Ravenna. In the hallway, Faberius, the secretary whom Balbus considered to be too clever by half, bowed low in greeting.

"Where's your master?" Balbus demanded.

"In the solarium."

"Announce me," Balbus ordered and followed close on his heels.

"Lucius!" Caesar exclaimed in surprise, coming to greet him. "What brings you here?"

"You're half-frozen," Servilia said, rising. "Come to the brazier." She turned to Faberius. "Take his cloak. And bring wine — mulled and spiced."

"My news is serious," Balbus said, walking to the brazier and holding his hands over it. "I wrote you about the Senate appointing Pompey Sole Consul," he said over his shoulder. "And about his decisive action in sending troops into Rome and restoring order."

"I received those letters," Caesar said. A slave entered with a goblet of mulled wine and pastries on a tray. Balbus turned from the brazier, picked up the goblet, and took a deep drink.

"I needed that," he said, setting down the goblet and wiping his lips. "Those Apennine passes in winter — b-r-r." He looked at Caesar and Servilia. "My first item — Pompey has announced that Milo is to be tried for the murder of Clodius."

"No more use for Milo," Servilia commented, glancing at Caesar. "So he's dumping him."

Caesar nodded.

"My second item, secured from Metellus Scipio — he is so puffed up he can't forbear boasting — is that Pompey is shortly to marry Scipio's daughter, Cornelia. My third is that it is already arranged that Pompey's proconsulship in absentia of Spain is to be extended for five years. That removes one of your bargaining points, Julius. It also proves definitely that the Conservatives have embraced Pompey — are hugging him close, in fact." Balbus took another gulp of the wine. "You know Cato, Domitius, Bibulus, the rest of that clique. They won't rest, Julius, until they have destroyed you."

Caesar was frowning thoughtfully. "I'm well protected," he said slowly. "Consider. My proconsulship of the three Gauls and Illyricum ends officially on the Kalends of March, three years from now. A law was passed after the conference at Lucca that my successor cannot be discussed until the Kalends of March two years hence. By Roman procedure that means that I cannot be replaced except by the consuls of the next year — that is, of my last year. They cannot become proconsuls until their consulships are over, that is, not until the Kalends of January of the following year, almost four years from now. So, in effect, I will have ten extra months as proconsul."

"But," Balbus began.

"No, wait," Caesar said. "Furthermore, as you know, early this winter I had the ten tribunes pass a law that, during those ten extra months, I can stand for the consulship in absentia. It cost me a sizeable amount. To sum it up, I have provided carefully that I pass directly from proconsulship to consulship. No Roman can be prosecuted while he is a magistrate in office. I'm protected, Lucius. Let Cato rave. And Bibulus. They can't touch me."

"The Conservatives — and Pompey — plan to destroy your protection," Balbus said quietly. "That fact is what brought me here."

"How?" Caesar asked sharply.

Balbus came closer and lowered his voice. "A law is already drafted that the consuls, instead of becoming proconsuls at the end of their consulships, must wait five years for a proconsulship."

Caesar's head came up. "That leaves a five-year interval. How is that to be filled?"

"That same law provides that, during that five-year interval, all ex-consuls who have never been proconsul in a province — like Cicero, for instance — must take over a province as proconsul. You won't have those ten extra months, Julius. There will be an ex-consul ready to step into your sandals — or shoes — immediately your term ends on the Kalends of March three years from now."

"Naked to your enemies!" Servilia exclaimed.

Caesar was watching Balbus. "And next?" he asked.

"Another law is ready," Balbus said quietly, "that no one, absolutely no one, can stand for the consulship in absentia."

"But the law I had passed — " Caesar began.

"The Conservatives are manipulating Pompey," Balbus interrupted. "He'll see to it that both laws are passed."

"Oh, Julius," Servilia exclaimed, coming to Caesar. "Prosecution. Exile. What will you do?"

"I see, as you do, darling, the minds of Cato, Domitius, and Bibulus behind those laws." Caesar turned to Balbus. "Now, Pompey must be *compelled* to meet with me at Lucca."

"How?" Balbus spread his hands. "He has evaded every attempt, every appeal I've made to him."

"You will return to Rome," Caesar said calmly. "This time you will be blunt. Tell him I will not wait like a patient ox to be knocked on the head by the Conservatives. Tell him that unless he meets me, my legions will march south."

"Not civil war!" Servilia cried.

Caesar turned to her. "I know Pompey. He'll sulk, but he'll come. All I need is to meet him face to face. I can win him back. And Gaul is at peace."

At that moment, as if on cue, Faberius kicked at the doorway. "Dispatches from Gaul, master," he called. "Two couriers. Urgent."

Caesar turned. "Send them in."

The two couriers entered, weary, travel-stained.

"From the legate Labienus, Imperator," the first one said and held out a dispatch.

Caesar took it, broke the seal, and read, the colour draining from his cheeks. Labienus reported the massacre at Cenabum, and told of revolt in Gaul and of a rumour that Vercingetorix had seized the kingship of the Arvernians.

"I heard from reliable sources," Labienus went on, "that the Atrebatian Commius was conspiring against us. Therefore, I sent a centurion with a body of troops to lure him to a conference and assassinate him. However, the centurion bungled the job — only wounded him — and Commius escaped."

"The idiot!" Caesar exclaimed.

"What is it, Julius?" Servilia asked.

Caesar waved a hand at her. He had been referring to Labienus. He read on.

"However, there is no need to worry," Labienus wrote. "I have put the camps on alert. Moreover, the Boians, Remans, Lingones, Sequanans, and of course the Aeduans are loyal. Naturally, one cannot campaign in winter. When spring comes, I'll lead out the legions."

Caesar finished the dispatch and, without speaking, handed it to Servilia. She and Balbus crowded together to read it. The second courier held out his dispatch.

"From Decimus Brutus, Imperator," he announced. "Governor by your appointment of Narbonese Gaul."

Caesar made himself open the dispatch calmly. Decimus Brutus, since he was nearer to Ravenna, had later news.

"All the maritime and central tribes are in revolt," he reported. "Even among the Aeduans the relatives and friends of Dumnorix are putting together an anti-Roman faction. Your friend Vercingetorix is commander-in-chief of the revolt. It is said that he has instituted strict discipline. Hands are cut off, eyes gouged out if there is any infraction of his orders. More importantly, he is moving fast. Half his forces under Prince Lucterius of the Cadurcans are already advancing against Narbo. He himself is reported to be marching against the Bituriges to force them to join his league.

"My problem is that, besides the attack on Narbo, the whole frontier of Narbonese Gaul seems on fire. All I have are a few garrison troops and local levies. You are needed here at once, Imperator. Otherwise the whole province, including Massilia,

208

could be lost. So, hasten, Imperator, I implore you."

Caesar passed this dispatch in turn to Servilia and Balbus.

"Take the couriers out," he said to Faberius. "Give orders to have them fed and looked after. Then come back here."

Leaving Servilia and Balbus to finish reading the dispatch from Decimus Brutus, he turned to look at the flecks of snow and sleet outside. Vercingetorix, whom he had treated as a friend, an intimate, he thought with a flare of anger.

He suppressed the anger. His face set in its eagle lines as he estimated, considered, decided.

"What will you do, Julius?" Servilia behind him cried in alarm.

Faberius had re-entered the room. Caesar turned to him.

"Get couriers ready," he ordered. "Send a secretary here. I'll dictate orders to concentrate the new levies and to bring back the men on furlough. Meanwhile, Faberius, get everything ready for me to leave tomorrow morning, early."

"Oh, Julius!"

That was Servilia, and there was anguish in her voice. Caesar could understand. Their togetherness at Ravenna had been perfect. He went over to take her in his arms, tenderly.

"I'm sorry, dearest one," he said. "So sorry."

"And we had till spring," she said, with a half-sob. "Till spring!"

Her voice was muffled by his shoulder.

"You can't leave," Balbus exclaimed. "Not now! Rome — Cato — Pompey!"

"I must save my legions," Caesar said over Servilia's head. "They're my men, Balbus. My—my comrades. Labienus—fine in a battle. In a crisis like this, no. My legions, they depend on me. On me!"

"If you go now," Balbus argued, "you'll lose Rome. The Conservatives will smother Pompey in their togas."

"And without my legions, Balbus, what am I? Nothing. You can see that."

Our togetherness gone, Servilia was thinking. Our — our honeymoon—like blossoms when the frost hits. But she was in control of herself again. She stepped back.

"Do what you have to do, Caesar," she said. "But tell Balbus — and me — what to do while you're gone."

Caesar thought a moment.

"Go to Pompey," he told Balbus. "Make sure he sticks to that law that my successor is not to be discussed until the Kalends of March in the year just before my term ends. That's the first point. The second is to remind him that he promised at Lucca three years ago that I could stand for the consulship in absentia, and now there's a law confirming that promise."

Balbus thought rapidly. "One curious item I forgot to mention," he said. "Curio is fascinated by Fulvia."

"Curio!" Servilia exclaimed. "That homosexual!"

"And Fulvia," Balbus went on, "controls what's left of the Clodian gangs."

"Get Curio for me," Caesar said abruptly.

"He will be expensive."

"Doesn't matter. And Balbus, suggest to him that he run for tribune—at my expense—and thereafter that he should still seem to oppose me, as he's always done, while really working for me." Caesar smiled grimly. "Curio has a devious mind. He'll like that sort of method. Also, Balbus, encourage this thing for Fulvia. Fulvia and he united could be useful."

"I can see that."

"And now," Caesar said briskly, "I must move."

Servilia took a step forward. "How long?" she asked.

Caesar turned to her. "I can't tell, dear. This time," he raised an open hand and closed it slowly until it was a tight-clenched fist, "this time I will squeeze rebellion out of them — like that."

# CHAPTER XIX

FADIUS WAS CLEANING THE PIGPENS when word came, carried by Silius, a centurion whom he knew.

"Titus Fadius," Silius said formally, "you are to report immediately to Brixia."

Fadius looked at the sow lying comfortably on her side and grunting in a sort of purring way as ten newly born piglets tugged at her teats.

"Nice, aren't they?" he said. And then, "What's up?"

"Trouble in Gaul. That's the talk."

"Have I time to finish this pen?"

Silius shook his head. "Our Caesar is already on his way. There's a group of the new levy at Brixia. You'll have one century. I'll have the other. Orders are to get them to Massilia, double-quick."

Fadius leaned his spade in a corner of the pen, climbed over the fence somewhat heavily, took one last look at the sow and the piglets, then went out and down to the horse-stable. He put a bridle on his mare, flung the rug over her back, and fastened a strap around it. He led her out into the courtyard and gave the reins to Silius. The mare and Silius' gelding sniffed at each other.

"Be out in a minute," he said, and tramped to the house and in, calling for his mother.

She bustled in from a back room.

"Got to go," Fadius said.

His mother stopped, shock showing on her face.

"I'll get my armour on," Fadius said, walking to the corner where it was stored. As he began to put it on, his mother recovered.

"I'll get you something to eat."

"Can't wait. My comrade is outside, holding Doll."

211

"Bring him in, Titus. I'll have something ready right away."

Fadius shook his head. "Give me bread and cheese, please. We'll eat as we ride."

"Wait for your father, Titus, at least. He's in the back field, I think. I'll send a youngster."

Titus was in his armour. He slipped his sword-belt on, sheathed his sword, and swung his helmet around his neck. After picking up his cloak, he took his javelin and came to the centre of the room.

"No time," he said. "You'll have to say good-bye for me to him — to everybody."

His mother had been hurrying around. She put a saddlebag in his hand.

Bread there," she said. "Cheese. A few olives. A small jar of wine. Best I can do unless you'll wait."

"Can't, Mother," Titus repeated.

She stepped back, looked up at him, moistened her lips, and said, "How long this time, Titus?"

"Don't know."

They stood there an instant, gazing at each other. Then, suddenly, she came in to embrace him, hugging him tightly.

"My son," she said. "My son."

Titus hugged her back. "Mother!"

His mother broke the embrace, stepped back, wiped the tears from her work-lined face, and said,

"If you have to go, you have to."

"Bye, Mother. Bye."

Fadius turned to go.

"Take care, son," he heard his mother say. "Oh, take care."

Somewhat blindly Fadius walked out to join Silius. They mounted in silence and in silence rode from the courtyard and up the road. At the little knoll overlooking the farmhouse, Fadius stopped his mare and turned her for one last look. It seemed ages now since that day he had stopped here on his return for his first look. He felt an almost overpowering desire to ride back. In these long weeks at home he had become knitted to it and to the slow life of the farm, peaceful, no worries, no — no killing, except of

212

animals and fowl for food. He had been of the earth and for the earth. If one could only stay.

He felt tears and an almost overwhelming longing for that home down there. When would he see it again—if ever? His eyes were brimming.

Silius coughed. Fadius wiped the tears away and turned his mare.

"Well, let's go," he said.

## 2

The news of the revolt in Gaul had reached Rome. The Conservatives, joyful, hugged the news.

"See," Bibulus said to Cato. "What did I tell you? Caesar a general. He could be a centurion, perhaps. General — pouf!"

"I hope he gets himself killed," Marcellus spat out.

"Then we could proclaim a twenty-day Thanksgiving for the Gauls," Metellus Scipio suggested slyly.

"The important thing is that that renegade can no longer interfere with our plans," Cato pointed out. "Now we must get Pompey to commit himself so completely to anti-Caesar measures that he can't back out."

The four of them were in Bibulus' palace on the Palatine. Meanwhile, Balbus sat with Curio in a tavern near the Tiber, a place chosen by the Spaniard because the bargees and wagoners who frequented it made such a racket that one was not likely to be overheard.

"I'll have to think about it," Curio said of the proposal to go over to Caesar.

"You're so deep in the debt-dungeon that you can never climb out—not without help," Balbus pointed out. "Caesar offers that help. Besides, the deviousness of the method ought to intrigue you."

"It does. Oh yes, it does," Curio answered. He lifted a limp wrist to arrange a lock of his curled hair and glanced at the table where his latest fancy, an acrobat from the shows in the Circus

Maximus, was sitting. "However, I have an appointment right now."

"Fulvia?" Balbus asked, knowing that he was overstepping the bounds of good taste, but wanting to test Curio.

Curio looked at him sharply. Before Balbus' eyes he seemed to shed his languidity, his affectation. The transformation made Balbus recall that in the sports in the Campus Martius, this Curio had proved himself to be a powerful swimmer, a competent wrestler, and an excellent fencer. Well, Caesar at one time had swung both ways, too.

"As a matter of fact, yes," Curio answered, rising.

"You'll think about the proposal?"

"Most certainly, Balbus. Yes, certainly."

He crooked a finger at his acrobat, who got up and somewhat sulkily joined Curio to walk with him to the waiting escort of a dozen slaves. Balbus watched him go. I believe he'll swallow the bait, he was thinking. He's more than a dandy, though, that young man. Much more.

# 3

Baculus, the hero of the German assault the previous summer on the camp at Atuatuca, had been discharged from the army, his last wound having left him with a stiff leg. His loot and a generous bonus from Caesar had made it possible for him to buy a tavern in Massilia well up from the harbour-front, so that, as he had confided to Fadius, his clientele was from a better class.

At this moment of mid-afternoon, Fadius and Chione, cups of wine before them, were sitting at a table in the tavern, Fadius' arm around Chione's waist and she snuggled in against him. Fadius, in fact, had been surprised at the torrent of emotion that had engulfed him when, arriving in Massilia, he had hurried to her room and with a cry of joy she had run to him, arms outstretched. The rapidity with which the home farm had receded, when he thought about it, had amazed him, too. It was as if he had never been away from army life.

Baculus came stumping over to them, bringing a cup of wine with him. He sat down, his right leg, the game leg, stretched out to one side.

"So you're off tomorrow," he said.

"To Nicaea," Fadius answered. "After that, don't know where. We're still a long way from the legions."

"Our Caesar will figure out something." Baculus took a drink from his cup. "What a job he's done," he said admiringly. "At Narbo. All along the frontier. Like summer lightning flashing. With make-do troops, too. The Gauls checked. What a man!" He turned to Chione, whom he had come to know well in the last few days. "Your last night together, eh?"

Chione nodded.

"Make good use of it," Baculus said.

"We will," Chione answered. "Oh yes, we will."

Fadius tightened his clasp round her waist. He looked through the open doorway. There was a nip to the air, and down below one could see whitecaps tossing on the blue water; but the grass was green, and the palms were tall and crested with long leaves. The worst part of the army, he was thinking. Always going somewhere. No chance to put down roots.

Baculus took another drink and set down his cup.

"I've a proposition," he said, speaking to Fadius. "It's up to you, of course. The fact is that my business has grown. I need a serving-wench. If Chione would like the job, she can have it."

Chione sat up straight. "You mean that?"

Baculus nodded. "There's an extra room upstairs, too. She could have that — for free."

Fadius was sitting up straight, too. "She has a room," he said. "There's money to pay for it, too."

Chione turned to him. "Why not, darling? You'll be away — we don't know how long."

"Doesn't matter."

"I'd be happier."

Fadius turned to her, startled.

"Look, darling," she said, catching at his arm. "When you're away the days—and nights—are long. Nothing to do. Can't you

215

see I'd be happier doing something — and — and earning a little toward my keep?"

Fadius sat looking at the table, stubborn, a frown on his forehead. Chione reached up to kiss him.

"Please, honey. There still won't be anyone else. I swear it."

"I'll see to that," Baculus said gruffly. As Fadius looked up, Baculus reached a hand across the table. "You can trust me, comrade."

Fadius met his eyes then clasped the proffered hand. The two held the clasp a long moment. As they released their grip, Chione flung her arms around Fadius' neck, kissing him again and again. Baculus looked at them, then, getting up, stumped to his bar and went behind it. He came back with a sealed jar and plunked it down on the table.

"That's settled then," Baculus said. "Now, off with you."

"It's Rhodian wine!" Chione exclaimed, examining the seal. "Expensive. Much too expensive."

"Not for me to give to you two. Come on, get. As I said before, make good use of this last night."

"Oh, we will," Chione repeated, smiling. "Oh yes, you can bet your tavern we will." She picked up the jar, tucked it under one arm, and caught Fadius' arm with the other. "Come, dearest dear. Our bed is ready. And I'm ready too."

Fadius was blushing as he got up. "Thanks," he said over his shoulder as they went toward the door.

Baculus, smiling to himself, watched them leave. There was, though, a touch of envy in the smile.


# 4

Just as Baculus had said, Fadius thought wryly, Caesar had figured out a way. His own feet were wet and cold, and he had to watch his face for frost-bite from the wind that poured up the pass. Meanwhile, he sweated as he swung his shovel into the six-foot-deep snow-drift and shouted to the levies on either side to put their backs into it. It was almost unbelievable that a few days ago he had been where the grass was green and flowers blossomed.

"Give me that shovel," Caesar's voice said behind him.

"Imperator!" Fadius exclaimed, turning and saluting. "We'll do the job for you, Imperator. You—" But Caesar had already tossed his cloak to an aide. He took the shovel, then bent his back and dug into the packed snow. Fadius saw the levies on either side glance sideways at their commander and then turn to the drift with redoubled energy.

What a commander! Fadius thought, wiping his nose with the back of his mitten. He himself and the other veterans knew the general plan: to break through the passes of the Cebennes Mountains and be upon the Arvernians before they could believe it. So they had marched westward from the Rhodanus River and up the first pass. The snow was piled high. The cavalry had tried to ride through. Their horses had bogged down, floundering in the drifts. The shovels had made a slow way and that first night had been misery, huddled together around fires that kept going out, fighting frost-bite, gnawing cold rations. Next, higher up, there had been moorland, swept bare of snow by a whistling wind that froze your cheeks and nose before you knew it, and a second night almost worse than the first. When they turned from the moorland into another pass, this one leading downward, again there was the piled snow. Thanks be to Mars, this was the last of the passes.

As Fadius thought this, he caught a glimpse of Caesar's face as he swung sideways to throw back a shovelful of snow.

"Imperator!" Fadius cried, jumping forward.

Caesar turned and straightened up.

"Stand still," Fadius ordered, rapidly scooping up with both hands a heaping handful of snow. As Caesar stared at him in amazement, Fadius rubbed it on his commander's cheeks and nose.

"Frost-bite, Imperator," Fadius said, stepping back. "Pardon, Imperator. No time to lose."

Caesar, feeling the sharp tingle of returning circulation, rubbed his face and smiled at Fadius.

217

"Thanks, Fadius," he said.

"Now, if you'll give me that shovel, Imperator."

Caesar relinquished it and stood for a moment watching the men dig. Then, he took his cloak from the aide, put it on, and glanced downward. He could already glimpse the open country beyond this pass. He patted his nose and cheeks. Tender, but nothing serious. Wiping his nose with a linen cloth, he turned to the digging troops.

"Almost through, lads," he shouted. They stopped to listen. "Almost there," he went on. "A few more drifts and we've made it. Tonight you'll sleep warm. Food. Dry wood for fires. Women, too." He laughed. "That is, if you're up to it."

A cheer answered him, and the levies swung to work, furiously. What a man! Fadius thought again.

Behind him, accompanied by his aides, Caesar tramped back along the infantry column, tossing a joke here, an exhortation there. He himself felt marvellous. Somehow, the greater the challenge, the swifter his mind and body seemed to respond. Rome? Servilia? They had been put on a shelf to be taken down when this fierce effort was over. Meanwhile, the whole of his being was concentrated on the crisis.

He had reached the cavalry. The men had dismounted and were stamping their feet and beating their hands together to keep warm.

"How long?" Decimus Brutus, the cavalry commander, asked.

"Mid-afternoon, I'd say," Caesar answered. "Time to build a camp and get the men comfortable before dark. But you'll start your cavalry raiding as soon as we arrive, Decimus." He smiled grimly. "The Arvernians will think we've dropped from the moon. Their messengers will gallop to Vercingetorix, bring him scurrying back from attacking the Boians. The Arvernians are his own people, his power-base."

"And then what, Imperator? You're still a long way from the legions, and we can't fight a pitched battle with just the levies."

Caesar looked at his subordinate. Decimus Brutus was a compact, quick-moving man in his early thirties, and one of the best

218

of his legates. Four years ago he had led the fleet which had destroyed the Venetan navy in their home waters in the Atlantic, and his tactics and decisions had been excellent. But not even to Decimus would he disclose his plan. No one, absolutely no one, knew the destination of the two hundred horsemen he had sent off a week ago, their commander carrying sealed orders to be opened at their first stop.

"We'll improvise," he said. He waved an arm toward the coast. "Can you imagine it? Over there, not too many miles away, blue sea, green grass, flowers, palm trees." He laughed. "And us freezing here."

# 5

The camp was built. From it the Romans raided outward, burning and pillaging. Reports came in that Vercingetorix and his army were hurrying back. Two days later, Fadius found himself one of a score of horsemen, all veterans, escorting Caesar back through the passes.

They had left camp before first light, the story being that Caesar was off to the coast to bring in reinforcements. Fortunately, there had been a thaw so that, this time, there were no new drifts. But when they reached the level ground of the Rhodanus valley, Caesar ordered his escort to gather around him.

"We're riding north, not south," he told them. "A hundred miles up the river at Vienna are two hundred cavalry I sent there before we entered the passes. They're awaiting us."

He paused to look around him. "It will be a tough ride," he went on. "Day and night. Brief halts for fresh horses and food. Dangerous, too. If Vercingetorix should hear of it, he'll send a force to cut us off. Even after Vienna, there's risk. Most of the Aeduans are loyal, but there are hostiles among them. No rest either, not until we reach the legions—and that's at least another two hundred and fifty miles."

He paused again, then said, raising his voice,

"If any one of you doesn't feel he's up to it, say so now."
No one spoke.

"Good," Caesar said and turned his horse northward, urging it to a trot. The escort followed him.

At mid-morning of the eighth day they came in sight of the main camp at Agedincum, some fifty miles southeast of Lutetia. A half a mile away, Caesar stopped his force. A few of the men had had to drop out, but he still had over two hundred horsemen.

"Form squadrons," he ordered, "and dress ranks."

He rode along the ranks, then put himself at the head, had his banner raised, and ordered the advance. Carefully, as if on parade, the travel-stained horses and men moved towards the ramparts.

"Signal," Caesar said to his trumpeter as they came within a couple of hundred yards.

The trumpet blew a high, clear note three times, Caesar's own signal. Almost instantaneously, or so it seemed, out the main gate poured the guard, to draw up in two formations, one on either side of a passageway for Caesar and his cavalry. As Caesar began to lead his force through, on either side the ramparts were suddenly filled with shouting, cheering legionaries. It was the same reception as when he had stopped briefly at the smaller camp among the Lingones.

"Caesar! Caesar!" the shouts billowed up to the blue winter sky.

Later, Caesar sat in the headquarters hut, Labienus across from him. His second-in-command, Caesar knew, was somewhat disgruntled.

"There was no need to take that risk, Julius," Labienus said stiffly. He puffed out his cheeks. "Two hundred horsemen," he exploded. "Didn't you stop to consider what would happen if Vercingetorix got news of your—your mad gallop and cut you off? Or if the Aeduans turned on you? Two hundred horse!" He snorted. "Asking for disaster."

He'd reached his legions, Caesar told himself. So he could afford to mollify Labienus.

"I know, Titus," he said. "I know. I was luckier than I deserved."

"We were perfectly all right here, too," Labienus went on. "The camp's on alert. The troops ready. Completely safe, Julius."

"I know, Titus," Caesar repeated. "As always, your dispositions are excellent. Superb, in fact."

Labienus' heavy face softened. He leaned back and picked at his nose before he said,

"Well, you were lucky this time, Julius. You do take too many risks, though." He paused. "That was a good move you made through the Cebennes," he said, as if conferring an accolade. "My reports are that Vercingetorix left the Boians and rushed south as if all his Gallic demons were after him."

"He'll be back," Caesar said quietly. "So we must decide how to stop him."

Labienus sat up. "You can't be thinking of campaigning before spring!"

"We must."

"Snow still on the ground! The legions won't like it."

"Oh yes they will." Caesar's smile was tight-lipped. "With the rewards I'll offer, they will."

# CHAPTER XX

CAESAR LOOKED DOWN AT CENABUM. To his left his legionaries were building a camp, grumbling at the snow, at their cold feet and hands, at the speed of their march. Soldiers always grumbled. What interested Caesar were the reports deserters had just given him of panic and disorder inside Cenabum. He reviewed the situation. Discovering that he had been deceived by the Roman camp set up in Arvernian territory, and learning that Caesar had managed to rejoin his legions, Vercingetorix had moved back north to besiege the Boian capital. Caesar had already concentrated his forces at Agedincum. Now he told Labienus that he would leave him two legions and would march against the Gauls with eight.

Labienus, as usual, had disapproved.

"Campaign in winter?" he had said. "Where can you get supplies? You can't live off the country, not in winter."

"It will be your job to keep supply trains from the Lingones and Aeduans moving after me," Caesar had answered.

"Suppose the Gauls cut them off?"

"See to it that they don't, Titus."

"With my small force? I still don't like it, Julius."

"The Boians are our loyal allies. If we fail to protect them, think of the effect on the Gauls, particularly the Lingones and Aeduans. No, winter or not, I must march. Besides, Titus," Caesar had smiled, "I have a plan that will puzzle Vercingetorix."

The plan had been successful. Vercingetorix had expected Caesar to move directly to raise the siege of the Boian capital. Instead the legions had tramped northwest. On the fifth day out from Agedincum they had captured Vallaunodunum, an important town of the Senones. Then Caesar had turned toward

Cenabum, eager to avenge its recent massacre of Romans and Italians. Two days later, in mid-afternoon, he had suddenly appeared before the city—and Vercingetorix was leagues away.

Now Caesar digested the news of panic and complete disorganization within Cenabum. Prince Cotuat, he gathered, had expected Vallaunodunum to delay the Romans for weeks, and had not prepared a defence. Typical of the Gauls, Caesar thought contemptuously. He turned to the legate Trebonius, who was standing beside him.

"We'll have a Council of War," he said.

At the Council, he outlined the situation rapidly to his officers and senior centurions.

"One report has it that this Prince Cotuat is planning to evacuate the city by the single bridge across the Liger," he concluded. "Therefore, I'm putting the Tenth and the Eighth on alert." He turned to the senior centurions of those two legions. "Detail parties at once to make battering-rams and assault ladders. If word comes of an attempted evacuation, your legates will order an immediate attack." He paused and spoke to the whole Council. "Remember that those streets in there have run red with Roman blood. So tell your men, all of them, that whatever lies behind the walls of Cenabum is theirs to seize and keep."

As they walked from the Council, Fadius, who had been put into the Eighth to replace a wounded centurion, said to Rullus, who was now a centurion in the same legion, "The men will be ravening sons of the she-wolf when we take that city."

"We'll rape it, then burn it," Rullus answered and spat a blob of phelgm into the snow. "As our Caesar said, those sons-of-bitches in there killed men, women, and children of ours. By the phallus of Mars, we won't spare a one."

It was midnight when a deserter slipped out to inform Caesar that the Gauls were starting to flee across the bridge in a tangled mass of soldiers, men, women, and children. The assault went in. Resistance was minimal. The Tenth rushed down the river road to the bridge, cutting down the confused mass on it, and seizing it to prevent further egress. The Eighth poured into the

223

streets. The other legions followed. From midnight until after dawn the Romans raped and looted and killed and killed, as if slaughtering pigs. Finally fires were lit throughout Cenabum. In the early afternoon of the following day, Caesar sat on his favorite steed, Five-Toes, and looked back at pillars of smoke. Then he glanced at his legionaries gathering in march formation. In the intervals between them were long lines of prisoners, destined to be sold as slaves, and wagons, carts, mules, and donkeys piled high with loot.

The legionaries, he knew, were now ready, winter notwithstanding, to march anywhere, attempt anything. A few blows like this, Caesar thought and, as always, the Gallic league would dissolve. So now into the country of the Bituriges. He raised his hand as a signal for the trumpets to sound the march.

Three days later he sat in a captured Biturigan town. There had been a cavalry battle first, since Vercingetorix had at last led his forces from Boian territory to meet him. The Romans had won, thanks to Caesar's four hundred German horsemen.

Everything is flowing my way, Caesar was thinking that night. Stores of food from the town and from Cenabum were keeping the men happy. So were the Gallic women.

On to Avaricum, Caesar was deciding. "Queen of Cities", as the Bituriges called it. Vercingetorix' forces must be almost ready to desert him. Take Avaricum and that traitor would be finished.


2


At that moment, in wooded country a few miles away, Vercingetorix was facing a mutinous council of chieftains. The young Arvernian king knew that it was a crucial hour. Cenabum lost — their cavalry beaten — Caesar back with his legions — Vercingetorix a useless leader — that was what they were thinking.

Vercingetorix began his speech quietly. He told the chieftains that Caesar had outfoxed him by crossing the Cebennes Mountains in winter, by drawing him south by his camp and the feinting raids, while Caesar himself was riding north to rejoin his legions.

"These were moves that I never anticipated," he continued. "None of you, either, dreamed them possible. His last move — against Cenabum — was one I ought to have foreseen as a possibility, particularly since he marched in winter. I did not — and so I reacted too late."

"That you did," Prince Cotuat agreed sourly; with a few followers he had got away from Cenabum before the Romans seized the bridge. A murmur of assent rippled through the chieftains. Vercingetorix could have turned on Cotuat for not having prepared for defence long ago. Instead, he said calmly,

"I admit my error. Our defeat today — that was the failure of all of us." He looked around the gathering. "I know what Caesar expects. He is thinking at this instant that, as usual after our defeats, each of you will run home with his tribesmen—whipped dogs with tails between their legs." He considered the chieftains for a moment, then went on. "I myself have heard him say, 'Gauls! Brave as panthers one moment — run like rabbits the next.' Is that what you are ready to do, chieftains and nobles of Gaul? Run like rabbits?"

He watched the chieftains look at each other uneasily, shuffling their feet. He raised his hand and his voice rang out:

"If you are ready to surrender, take my head to Caesar," he said. "We can still win. But he will accept my head. Comm, Lucter, Cotuat, whomsoever else he chooses, will die under the rods—like Acco. The rest of you will live—slaves to Rome." He dropped his hand. "I have spoken. Now, decide."

The chieftains whispered and muttered to each other. Comm spoke:

"You said, 'We can still win.' How?"

Vercingetorix took a step forward. "Starve the Romans," he said. He watched the nobles glance at each other, then look back at him. "It's still winter," he continued. "No crops for the Romans to cut. No fodder growing for their horses. So, destroy every mowful of hay, every bin of wheat, barley, oats. Burn

225

every homestead, hamlet, town."

"Burn!" Ruorix, principal chieftain of the Biturges, said in a shocked voice.

"Make the land around the legions a waste, as bare of food as a licked platter."

"They will still get convoys of food — from the Boians, the Aeduans, the Lingones," Ruorix objected.

"With our cavalry, we can cut those off," Vercingetorix told him. "Make sure not a single scrap of food or bale of fodder gets through." He raised his voice. "Don't you see? So far we've played Caesar's game—and lost. Now, we make him play ours. Ten legions, auxiliary troops, cavalry, slaves, mules, drivers — how long will Caesar's supplies hold out?" Vercingetorix slammed his right fist into the palm of his left hand. "If we're men we can win."

"I'm for it," Comm shouted.

"I am, too," Lucter put in.

"What about us?" Ruorix cried, pushing his way forward to face Vercingetorix. "The Romans are in our country, the land of the Bituriges. It's our hamlets, our towns, our grain, our fodder that will go up in smoke. You can't ask that of us."

"I promise on my honour," Vercingetorix told him, spacing each word, "and on the honour of the Arvernians, that your losses will be replaced." He looked around. "Who else will pledge this much?" he cried. "For a free Gaul? For victory!"

Comm was the first to shout, "I and my Atrebates."

His enthusiasm brought cheers from the others.

"Well, Ruorix?" Vercingetorix asked.

Ruorix nodded, reluctantly. "Organize our parties then," Vercingetorix commanded. "Send them out. Destroy. Burn. Don't leave a single bundle of hay, a single kernel of grain, a single homestead, hamlet, or town. Let the Romans look on desolation and shudder."

"But not Avaricum!" Ruorix cried.

Vercingetorix turned on him. "It must go, too."

"No!" Ruorix exclaimed. "Not Avaricum. Not our Queen of Cities." He turned to his subordinate chieftains. "Are you with me?"

226

In an instant they were crowding around him agreeing, shouting, "Not Avaricum." The other chieftains shouted back, demanding the burning. Hands began to go to swords.

"Quiet," Vercingetorix roared. Then, as the clamour sank down, he said to Ruorix, "Why not? Why not Avaricum?"

Ruorix faced him, blue eyes flashing. He was as tall as Vercingetorix and his shoulders were just as broad and his chest as powerful.

"Everything else," he answered in a fierce voice, "for a free Gaul—yes. But not Avaricum." He flung an arm wide. "Tens of thousands dwell in it. It's stocked with great bins of grain, with heaps of iron from our mines, with silver, with gold. It can withstand any attack. Consider, Vercingetorix. High walls, surrounded by three rivers with marshland in between. Let Caesar assault Avaricum and beat out his brains against it. Well?"

To his left Vercingetorix saw Comm give a slight sign.

"I still think it should go," Vercingetorix said slowly. "But, put that way, Ruorix, I'll grant you Avaricum. Everything else, though?"

"Everything else," Ruorix agreed vehemently. "We of the Bituriges will start the burning." He turned to his sub-chiefs. "At once."

That evening, standing on the wall of his captured town, Caesar watched smoke and flames blossoming in every direction. A sub-chief of the Bituriges, resenting the decision, had deserted and had informed him about the new strategy. Caesar had begun to admit a certain admiration for Vercingetorix. That admiration did not lessen his burning resentment against the man, a man whom he had regarded as a loyal friend—and now look at him! But he had expected that the capture of Cenabum piled on top of the other defeats would have caused the tribes to defect from him. Yet he seemed to have a stronger hold on them than before.

The sub-chief, he remembered, had also told him that Avaricum was to be spared. So on to it. Capture it and not even Vercingetorix could hold the tribes together.

It was the twenty-fifth day of the siege. Soon, Caesar thought as he stood on a knoll to the southeast of Avaricum, hood over his head against a gust of rain, and looked at the ramp his legionaries had built almost to the wall of the city. Because of the rivers and the marshland, Avaricum could not be starved into surrender by a contravallation around it. The Roman engineers had found only one point from which its forty-foot-high walls could be assaulted. From the knoll on which Caesar stood, the Roman camp behind him, a narrow neck of dry land ran up close to the city. Even at that point Avaricum was protected by a deep, though narrow, ravine so that in actuality its walls towered eighty feet above ground level.

But the legionaries, working furiously, had built, in terrace upon terrace, a ramp three hundred and thirty feet wide, rising to a height of eighty feet to match the city wall. That ramp had been flung together from logs, beams, stones, and earth. On either side of it, on sloping runways, storey upon storey, towered two massive assault towers, covered with hides wetted against fire. At the moment, pushed forward and crammed with catapults and scorpions, those towers poured missiles upon the defenders on the walls to cover the men working under mantlets on the ramp.

What men! Caesar thought in a surge of feeling. Thanks to Vercingetorix' cavalry, who had encamped northeast of Avaricum, and had cut off convoys and foragers, the Romans were on short rations. But, though he himself had offered to raise the siege, the legionaries had refused to quit. They had endured shortage of food, missiles from the walls, sorties from the city, underground tunnels dug from within Avaricum designed to come up beneath the ramp and let the defenders set fire to it, and showers of rain and sleet, and they had never faltered. But now, soon, the ramp would be completed and the attack could go in.

The gust of rain had stopped. Caesar slipped the hood off his head. He took a last glance at the ramp and then at the wall beyond it. Clever, those Gauls, he told himself. Look at the towers they had built on that wall to match his own. And Vercingetorix' tactics had been admirable, too. Starving the Romans. Tempting him, Caesar, to a battle by leaving his infantry without cavalry and sending a reputed deserter to inform Caesar. Yet when Caesar had hurriedly led six legions to attack, he had found the Gauls in an unassailable position and had had to march back to his camp. Then Vercingetorix had used that retreat to send in ten thousand men across the causeways through the marshes to the north to reinforce Avaricum. No, he thought, don't underestimate your enemy.

He turned to walk back to his headquarters, head down, reflecting that tonight it would be the Eighth and the Tenth on alert in front of the camp with strong drafts from them on guard at the ramp. Soon, tomorrow perhaps, he could order the assault. And then — then his men, enraged by their privations, would be like lions.

He would promise them all the loot in that city behind him, he decided abruptly. Then, as at Cenabum, they would be wolves and lions — and nothing could stop them!

# 4

The night was as black as the Styx. Fadius and Rullus, each in command of a century of the two maniples of the Eighth which were on guard on the right of the ramp, while two maniples from the Tenth protected the left flank, had met for a moment. Their cloaks were wrapped around them against the biting wind.

"A man don't get much sleep," Rullus grumbled. He glanced back toward the camp in front of which the rest of the Eighth and the Tenth had bivouacked. "Damn little to eat, too. The two sides of my stomach are rubbing each other."

"Plenty in there," Fadius answered, gesturing toward Avaricum. "Once we get in."

Rullus, too, glanced toward the walls. Then his eyes caught sight of something.

"Look, Titus," he cried. "Look! Fire!"

Fadius looked. From the forward edge of the ramp flames were flickering.

"The buggers!" Fadius gasped. "They've tunnelled."

They turned to their centuries. Before either could utter a command, from the gates to right and left of the ramp surged hordes of yelling Gauls carrying flaming torches.

"Form line," both Fadius and Rullus shouted to their men, and then, as the Gauls charged, "Javelins — cast. Out swords."

From behind them Roman trumpets blared. Before reinforcements could reach them, torrents of Gauls had forced back the maniples of both the Eighth and the Tenth, seizing the forward end of the ramp, tossing in torches to feed the blaze, and setting fire to the assault towers. Fresh Roman troops drove back the Gauls for the moment. One assault tower was dragged back, scorched but still intact. The other was a pillar of fire.

The Gauls came on again. It was a wild struggle in the darkness, the only light the tongues of fire from the ramp and the blazing tower. The Gauls strove to keep the flames burning, shooting fire-arrows, breaking through to toss in torches and balls of grease and pitch. The Romans fought to drive them back while a chain of legionaries passed along jars of water to douse the conflagration. As Fadius rallied his century, he saw a gigantic Gaul on the forward edge of the ramp, taking balls of grease and pitch passed to him by a line of men and throwing them into the fire. A scorpion-bolt felled him. Another jumped into his place and then still another.

"Guts," Fadius thought, even as he fought.

The fight went on. Not until dawn, when a sudden downpour of rain helped put out the fires, did the Gauls withdraw. A little later Caesar, grim-faced, assessed the damage. Great pits in the ramp still smoked, and one assault tower had collapsed.

"A week's work, just to get those pits filled," grumbled Mamurra, who had accompanied him.

"You have twenty-four hours," Caesar said.

"Impossible."

"Make it possible," Caesar answered, turning away.

That night, as the Romans laboured furiously in spite of a

raging wind and spits of rain, they heard screams and cries inside Avaricum. The legionaries on guard prepared for another sortie. But deserters, clambering over the wall, brought the news that the garrison had decided to evacuate the city but had been prevented by the women.

Typical of the Gauls, Caesar thought, even as he sent cavalry patrols to watch all the gates. He himself had neither slept nor thought of sleeping during the day or the night. By morning the ramp was repaired. At dawn, although the clouds now allowed only a dim light, he walked back toward the camp. At the main gate he stopped. A slash of rain had caught him on the cheek. He turned. There from the northeast a dark mass of clouds was rushing forward, and behind it, a band that stretched greyish-white from horizon to horizon.

Caesar drew in his breath. He knew storms. If that dark mass and the greyish-white behind it presaged what he thought it did —

Five minutes later a wind to end all winds struck. An instant later rain poured down, driven in fierce, solid sheets.

"Better get under cover, Imperator," Mamurra said.

Caesar shook his head. Bending forward and steadying himself against the buffeting of the wind, he peered at the walls of Avaricum. He could scarcely see them. Without a word, Mamurra and the legate Trebonius following, Caesar, crouched almost double, managed to reach the cover of the forward mantlets. Here the ramp was even with the wall except for the Gallic towers, raised at intervals along its top. The Gallic sentries, Caesar saw with exultation, had deserted their posts because of the storm. Even on their towers no watch was being kept.

Cupping his hands around his mouth so as to be heard over the roar of the wind and the beating of the rain, he shouted to his companions:

"Back to camp. I'm calling a Council of War. At once."

At that council, Caesar gave swift orders to push up the one usable tower and fill it with assault troops. Other assault legionaries were to be concealed behind the mantlets, the protected sheds on the forward edge of the ramp; the rest were to be arrayed, crouched down, in the shelter of the terraces.

"When the trumpets sound, have your men leap forward like wolves," he told the centurions. "Once you have a lodgement, don't jump down. Run along the walls each way first until you've made a ring of iron around the enemy. Not one must get away. Not one."

He paused, looking at the centurions. They looked back at him.

"Tell your men again," Caesar said, speaking slowly and deliberately, "that, to repay them for their labours, their endurance, as at Cenabum, everything within Avaricum is theirs." He paused again. "Furthermore, to the first man on those walls, a bonus — a year's extra pay. To the first dozen after him, a half a year's extra pay."

He saw the eyes of the centurions light up as they shifted their feet.

"I'll earn that bonus, Imperator," a veteran centurion growled.

Caesar raised a hand. "Remember," he said, "this time we teach those bastards never to challenge Romans. So, kill and slay. Make your swords red, comrades."

A cheer answered him.

The Romans moved fast. The rain was still slashing down and the gale roaring when the bridge of the tower slammed down on the opposing tower and the first assault troops rushed across, while from the mantlets legionaries poured onto the wall. The few sentries still at their posts were killed. So were the Gauls sheltering in the adjoining towers. Inside the city, too late, war-horns brayed. Gallic warriors rushed from the houses in which they had sheltered. A disorganized attempt to charge up the stairways inside the walls and throw off the Romans failed. The wind and rain still swooped down into the streets. Finally the Gauls massed in the squares, spears and swords ready, awaiting the assault.

No attack came. Instead, word leapt among them that the Romans were spreading along the top of the great wall. From the southeastern gate came news that Roman cavalry was posted outside.

Surrounded! No chance! "Let's get out," someone shouted. "The gates! To the gates," someone else cried, throwing away his sword and shield and starting to run to the northern gates. Beyond those gates was marshland, and beyond that the camp of Vercingetorix. Those nearest the fleeing man flung down their weapons and followed. In an instant, the whole Gallic host was rushing, a stampeding mass, down the narrow, twisting streets toward the northern gates.

At that moment, from the whole circuit of the walls, the legionaries pounced. For men trained to kill, forced by the obstinate Gallic resistance to face death, to suffer and endure, this was the hour of frenzied release. Amid the roar of the wind and the downbeat of the rain, they slew and slew, slaughtering men, women, and children as if gripped by madness.

Fadius, too, was seized by the hysteria. Shouting like the men he led, like them he killed and killed. It was when a woman, caught in a doorway, seized her child and, sinking to the ground, bowed her neck to his stroke that a sort of fog seemed to begin to clear from his brain. Lowering his upraised sword he looked at the blade. It was dripping red. As he stared, almost not comprehending, a legionary tried to thrust his sword-blade past him into the woman. With a blow of his shield, Fadius sent him reeling. He glanced down the street. To his right another legionary seized an infant by its legs and swung its head against the stone wall of a house.

"This is madness," Fadius said aloud, not knowing that he had spoken. He looked down at the woman. She was still crouched over her child, waiting.

"You're safe," he shouted above the wind in the clumsy Celtic he'd picked up. "You and the child. Do you hear? Safe."

Later, when the violence of the storm had blown itself out, Caesar, with his aides and Trebonius, entered the city. Above him a watery sun was struggling amid scudding clouds. He looked with distaste at the tangled heaps of butchered bodies. However, if one could order it, one ought to look at it.

"How many got away?" he asked Trebonius.

"Not more than a thousand, according to our estimate," Trebonius answered.

"Captives?"

"Not too many, Imperator."

"Ah, here's Hirtius," Caesar said, seeing his quartermaster-general approaching. "What about stores, Legate?"

Hirtius' face was beaming. "Huge bins of grain, Imperator. Enough to feed the legions for weeks."

Caesar glanced again at the heaps of dead, among them the best troops of the Gauls.

"This day will finish Vercingetorix," he pronounced. "Avaricum on top of Cenabum — not even he can hold the tribes together now."

# 5

Caesar had underestimated Vercingetorix. While Caesar was feeding and resting his men, Vercingetorix managed to delay a confrontation with the chieftains until he was prepared. Then, he summoned them to a council. Arms folded, he listened to their denunciations of his leadership.

"And what have you to say?" Camulogen, aged leader of the Parisians, demanded finally.

Vercingetorix still said nothing.

"Avaricum, our Queen of Cities," Ruorix cried hysterically for the dozenth time. "Captured! Destroyed!"

Vercingetorix turned on him. "And who begged, implored, went on his knees to me not to burn it?" he demanded. "You." He looked round the semicircle. "And who supported him? You! All of you! Fighting Caesar's war for him."

"I'm off to the forests," Ruorix cried. "What's left of my men with me." He shook his fist at Vercingetorix. "If we'd had one battle, at least. But no, you wouldn't let us fight a battle."

"So you haven't learned," Vercingetorix said in a cold, contemptuous voice. His eyes measured the chieftains. "After all these years of Roman victories none of you, it seems, have learned. Our infantry? Brave enough. But in battle, a mob." He flung out an arm. "The legions? Trained, disciplined killers. If

234

you want to see your men slaughtered like milling sheep with the wolves upon them, all right, I'll order a battle."

They were silent a moment. Camulogen, who had been sitting on a stool, got up. "All the same, I'm leading my Parisians back to Lutetia — today."

"Wait," Vercingetorix said. He stepped forward. He surveyed the chieftains, his blue eyes vivid, compelling.

"Avaricum is lost," he said, "and thousands on thousands of fighting-men with it. Granted. But how many tens of thousands of warriors are left in Gaul? You know as well as I. Brave men. Men ready to fight for freedom. Kings, princes, nobles, you know as well as I that, if we set a contingent for each tribe, within a month we'll be stronger than ever. Is freedom worth that much? Or more?"

He could feel the chieftains waver.

"I have news for you," he said. He beckoned. "Come forward, Cotrix, envoy of Teutomar, king of the Nitiobriges."

The chieftains looked at each other. The Nitiobriges were a tribe close to the Pyrenees.

"Tell them, Cotrix," Vercingetorix ordered.

Cotrix, a man whose blue eyes contrasted sharply with his black hair and eyebrows, somewhat puffed up with his importance, spoke with flamboyant gestures and oratorical flourishes. Summed up, his words spelled out that King Teutomar was leading all his cavalry, along with hired Aquitanian archers, to join Vercingetorix.

The chieftains were impressed. As Cotrix stepped back, Vercingetorix gestured to a man who had just entered. He came forward, a tall, yellow-haired noble in his early forties. As he stood there, exclamations and murmurs ran like little tongues of flame from one to another of the chieftains.

"Prince Eporedorix of the Aeduans," Vercingetorix announced.

Eporedorix was the general who, years ago, had led the Aeduans in their successful war against the Arvernians. What did this mean, the chieftains were wondering. Could it mean —

"Speak, Prince Eporedorix," Vercingetorix said.

Eporedorix looked around him. The Gauls loved and appreciated oratory. Eporedorix did not disappoint them. With gestures and tricks of tone, he described the might, wealth, and long history of the Aeduans. He dropped his voice to tell of Aeduan suffering under Ariovistus, the German invader. He pleaded with them to understand why those sufferings and the incursion of the Helvetians had, to the ultimate misfortune of all Gaul, led Diviciac to call on Caesar for help. Though from the beginning, one hero—he wiped away tears, his voice breaking—Dumnorix, had resisted Caesar and they, all of them, knew his fate.

He paused.

"But you, kings, princes, nobles of the Gauls," he cried, pointing a finger at them, "you shared in the murder of that noble soul, that hero who died for freedom's sake. Do you wonder that those of us who in our hearts were against the Romans shrank from putting trust in any of you?"

He glanced at them. Then, abruptly he changed the timbre of his voice.

"But now," he declared, "now that we see that all Gaul is ready to vomit forth the Romans, we, in our turn, are ready to assume our rightful place — in the forefront of the Freedom Fighters." He paused again. "It will take time. There are, as among your Arvernians," he gestured toward Vercingetorix, "among us, too," he spat out the words, "Roman-lovers. We must be wary. But when the moment comes," he raised his voice, "when the moment comes, the Aeduans will throw off the Roman yoke, as if it were a sack of feathers, and drench their swords in Roman blood. I have spoken."

He stood, head held high. Vercingetorix did not mention the bags of gold he had sent to Eporedorix and to noble after noble of the Aeduans. Instead, as if impulsively, he reached out to grasp Eporedorix' hand.

"Cheer," he cried to the chieftains, "cheer for Eporedorix, the Aeduan."

The shouting and the clanging of swords against shields filled the glade. Vercingetorix stood tall and proud. Once more he was in command.

# CHAPTER XXI

I T WAS A SUN-BRIGHT MORNING late in May. From the watchtower of his main camp Caesar stared up at Gergovia, capital of the Arvernians. It sat over two thousand yards away on its mile-long flat-topped hill and seemed to mock him.

Caesar clenched his hands on the rail of the tower. After Avaricum he had waited for the Gallic army to dissolve. Instead, it had grown stronger, and agents had reported serious unrest among the Aeduans.

Control of the Aeduans was essential. He had marched to one of their border towns to decide a quarrel about who was to succeed to the chief magistracy, and he had sensed duplicity. Meanwhile, the news from Rome was unfavourable. Milo, found guilty of Clodius' murder, had been exiled to Massilia. The two laws that shattered his own protection had been passed, although after the law that no one could stand for the consulship in absentia had been sanctioned, Pompey, at Balbus' insistence, had put in an addendum that Caesar was to be excepted from that law. The legality of that addendum could, naturally, be questioned. Then Servilia had written about the marriage of Cornelia to Pompey and the extension for five years of his governorship of Spain.

"So, as I've told you before, dearest," Servilia had added, "Pompey no longer needs you. Beware of Milo's fate."

He must, Caesar had decided, crush this revolt at once. Leaving the new recruits to hold the camp at Agedincum, he had sent Labienus with four legions to overwhelm the Parisians and the Senones, while he himself with six had marched southwest into the Arvernian country. Vercingetorix had followed him. But instead of meeting Caesar in the battle that the Romans craved, he had flung his army into Gergovia, a city that could not be surrounded by six legions. The best Caesar could do was to pitch

237

his main camp on level ground to the southeast of Gergovia, and then draw lines from the camp along the southern flank of the city to a smaller camp in the west.

Stalemate, Caesar thought, still staring up at the city. Part way down its rugged southern slope, Vercingetorix had had built a six-foot-high breastwork. Between it and Gergovia's walls were the encampments of the Gallic tribes.

Caesar examined the scene for the hundredth time. Below the breastwork, the hillside was sprinkled with scrub trees, tufts of grass, and thousands of ox-eyed daisies and yellow buttercups. Up in the blue sky larks flew, carolling. If one could be a lark — or, better still, an eagle, Caesar told himself. As it was, he could not attack uphill over that rough terrain. Nor could he stay here, day after day, doing nothing while the revolt spread and strengthened.

He drew in a lungful of the fresh, clean air, then turned to look at his smaller camp built on a hill three thousand yards to the west. Trenches led to it. Well, better inspect it, he decided.

It was while he and Lucius Sextius, commander of the smaller camp, were on its watchtower that Caesar spotted something. Gergovia's one weakness was that from a hill on its western side a saddle of rock ran to the city's wall. Yesterday Vercingetorix had had troops on that hill. Today, it seemed to be deserted. Instead, the next hill, farther west, appeared to swarm with activity.

"What's that about?" Caesar asked sharply.

Sextius shrugged. "The patrols say that the Gauls are fortifying that second hill. I suppose they're afraid of an attack along the saddle."

"And look," Caesar said, "the encampments between the breastwork and the city walls are empty."

He stood very still a moment, considering, then deciding: Yes, there was a chance.


2


Early the next morning Caesar summoned Eporedorix and his cousin, Viridomarus. These two nobles were now the leaders of the ten thousand Aeduan footmen Caesar had requisitioned. Their original general, Litaviccus, with his personal retainers, had defected to Vercingetorix.

"Are you clear about your route?" he asked the nobles.

Eporedorix put his finger on the map. "Roundabout," he said, "this way to the eastern gates. Keeping ourselves out of sight until the assault comes in."

"Good — and your men with bared right shoulders to show they are friends, not hostiles." Caesar stood up. "Good luck — and start now."

He watched the Aeduans move out. Then, a smoke signal from the main camp initiated the second piece of his plan. As the sun peeked over the eastern horizon, a long line of muleteers, wearing helmets and riding baggage animals, moved out from the smaller camp toward the western hill that Vercingetorix' men were fortifying. In that line were a few cavalrymen and behind followed the Eighth legion, standards glittering in the rising sun.

The objective of this exercise was to persuade Vercingetorix that an attack was to be put in on the western hill, so as to hold him and his men right where they were; then, as the attack progressed, the Aeduans would take the eastern gate. From his watchtower in the main camp Caesar looked west again. Just this side of the smaller camp, Roman assault troops crouched in folds of the terrain which hid them from watchers on Gergovia's walls. They had been put there during the night, their faces, hands, and armour blackened. Even their standards had been taken away.

Caesar drew in a long breath of the spring-scented air. It was against all Roman military tactics to attack uphill — and Gergovia's slopes were steep. But, perhaps, if his luck held —

He let out the breath and raised a hand. Another smoke signal spiralled up in the lazy air. The assault troops rose and raced uphill. Caesar ran down the watchtower's steps, two at a time. The Tenth was already drawn up. Caesar, scarlet mantle on, leaped on Five-Toes and led the Tenth up the hill to form a reserve.

From that point, he watched. After the first spurt, his assault

239

troops had slowed down, panting, grabbing at rocks and shrubs to help them up the steep slope. In Gergovia, faintly heard at this distance, war-horns were braying. But now, at last, his men had reached the undefended breastwork and were spilling over it. Caesar urged Five-Toes farther upward for a closer view. Then he cursed. His assault troops were disorganized! Some—bloody fools—were looting the encampments. Others were running in groups to the city walls, by now lined with screaming women.

Yet the plan, explained carefully to the centurions, was to capture the breastwork and then re-form, either to fight a battle between it and the walls or, if the Gallic army didn't appear, to carry the walls. Those walls were not like those at Avaricum. They were low and assailable. But the troops must re-form first.

"Blow the halt," Caesar snapped to his bugler. "Blow, man."

The bugler blew. Some of the units up there halted and began to re-form ranks. But others continued to loot or to rush toward the walls.

And then Caesar saw Gallic cavalry riding into view around the western edge of Gergovia. Tight-lipped, he signalled the Tenth to move up closer to the breastwork. By the time it was in position, the enemy cavalry had slaughtered the groups attempting to scale Gergovia's walls. Next, the Gallic infantry poured into sight, rushing in to attack, tribe by tribe.

Caesar had already sent aides to Sextius ordering him to lead out half the cohorts in the smaller camp and to recall the Eighth from its feint against the western hill. Now he saw the ten thousand Aeduans appear before the city's eastern gates. Now was their chance; why didn't they rush in?

But they only stood and watched. Meanwhile, the Roman assault troops were in confusion.

Defeat! Perhaps disaster!

"Blow the retreat," Caesar ordered.

The bugler blew. From the Tenth Caesar sent forward three maniples to the breastwork. With their help his assault troops got back over. A few Gauls, yelling, followed. The three maniples of the Tenth cut them down. Meanwhile, Caesar, riding Five-Toes furiously, got his assault troops into line and back down the hill.

Beyond the breastwork, the Gauls were also reorganizing just as hastily. With his legions in line on level ground, Caesar turned to look upward. If they will only attack now, he was praying. By all the gods, surely they will attack, he thought — and saw Vercingetorix urging his jet-black horse along the breastwork, his sword out. Obviously he was striving to restrain his men. Surely, Caesar thought again, not even Vercingetorix can hold the Gauls back, not after this success!

The chieftains were milling around Vercingetorix, waving their swords. "Attack," they were howling in wild excitement. "Give the order. Charge."

Vercingetorix shook his head.

"Then I and my Atrebatians will charge," Comm shouted.

"I, too," Lucter cried, forcing his horse forward.

"And have your men cut to pieces," Vercingetorix shouted back. He pointed with his sword. "Look! Those lines. Ready!"

"We can break them!" Teutomar yelled.

"Haven't you learned?" Vercingetorix shouted. "Have none of you learned? We've won here. That's enough."

Ruorix of the Bituriges pushed his horse up to him.

"Vengeance for Avaricum!" he bawled at Vercingetorix. "Vengeance!" He turned to wave his sword at his men. "Come on. Charge!"

Vercingetorix' sword-point was suddenly at Ruorix' throat. "Who commands here?" he said in a voice as cold as the steel of his sword.

Ruorix felt the prick of the point. His sword dropped.

"Order your men back," Vercingetorix commanded.

Sullenly, Ruorix called the order.


# 3


That night Caesar again stood on his watchtower. A full moon bathed Gergovia and the breastwork and the rugged hill below. The moon watched, peaceful, remote. Down below between the breastwork and Gergovia, fires were burning, lights were tossing, and, borne on the still air, bursts of song came floating faintly.

As they had two mornings ago, Caesar's hands clenched tightly on the rail. Between that breastwork up there and the city beyond it, seven hundred legionaries and forty-six centurions lay dead. Five times that number had been wounded.

His first personal defeat, Caesar thought sombrely. By this time the news, shouted from hamlet to village to farmstead, and exaggerated a hundredfold, would be spreading across the countryside to Bibracte, the Aeduan capital. So, what to do?

He stared up at Gergovia, hands still clenched on the rail. Today, after the failure of his attack, he had waited, legions in line, hoping, praying that Vercingetorix would find it impossible to restrain his tribesmen from attacking. But he had restrained them.

No other Gallic commander could have done it. Caesar had long ago discovered that the vast majority of men were followers. Only a few were leaders; and among those leaders still fewer exuded that peculiar aura, or whatever one called it, that inspired a blind loyalty or devotion among his followers. He knew that he himself possessed that special quality. It now appeared that Vercingetorix, too, possessed it — which made him much more dangerous, the first truly national leader the Gauls had produced.

His own mistake, Caesar admitted grimly to himself. What was it the green-eyed Fiammar had said to him after he had had Acco flogged to death?

"You've gone too far," she had said.

Well, she had been right. That act, obviously, had turned Vercingetorix from loyal friend to traitor. Equally obviously it had united the Gallic nobles behind him.

The past was past. Unclenching his hands, Caesar turned to survey the sleeping camp beneath him. The ten thousand Aeduans, he recalled, had not joined in the battle on either side. Instead, after watching, they had melted away and returned to camp. But, once again, what to do? No use staying here. The great, the most immediate, danger was a revolt of the Aeduans, since peace with them was the very keystone, to use a cliché, of

242

his presence in Gaul. So, send those ten thousand Aeduans back to Bibracte, with a warning to Eporedorix, a man who probably could be trusted to remain neutral at least, to prevent an Aeduan revolt. Meanwhile, draw up his legions for battle tomorrow—a question of morale for them after today's defeat — and then, post-haste, march back to Agedincum to reunite his legions.

He heaved a deep sigh. Defeat was bitter — and think of the effect in Rome when it became known. Hands clasped behind his back, he began to walk to the steps down from the tower, and heard a voice booming out at the gates below him. Caesar's chin came up. That voice—Antony! He went down the steps. By the time he reached ground-level Antony and his escort had ridden in. With a broad grin on his face, Antony slid from his horse and strode forward.

"Your quaestor, Imperator," he said, saluting. "Reporting for duty."

Ignoring the salute, Caesar stepped up to him for a quick embrace.

"You're late," he said, stepping back.

Antony shrugged. "You know our Senate, when it comes to confirming an appointment." He looked at Caesar. "What goes on here, Julius?"

"What do you mean?"

"We were attacked twice this afternoon — in Aeduan territory." Antony gestured behind him to his escort. "We took a couple of prisoners."

"What did they tell you?"

"That you'd had the living daylights kicked out of you," Antony said bluntly.

"Come to my tent," Caesar said. "We'll talk there."

Sitting across the table from Caesar, Antony had little that was new to report from Rome, except that Pompey had co-opted his father-in-law as the second consul, and that Marcus Cicero, to his disgust, had been appointed governor of Cilicia for the next ensuing year.

Antony leaned forward. "Just what is the situation here, Julius?" he asked. "One of my prisoners boasted that an Aeduan noble — I couldn't make out his name — is on his way from Vercingetorix to Bibracte to persuade the Aeduan Council to revolt."

"Was that name Litaviccus?" Caesar asked sharply.

"Sounds like it."

Caesar rose. "We'll talk later," he said. "Right now I must get off a courier to Noviodunum."

"Noviodunum?"

"That town to the north in Aeduan territory. All my hostages from all over Gaul are there, Antony. So are the remounts for the cavalry, stocks of grain, armour, my war-chest. I stripped the garrison pretty lean when I marched here. So a warning courier must ride at once."

He strode from the tent. Antony sat back. He'd seldom seen Caesar so worried, he was thinking.

# 4

Eporedorix and Viridomar, on their way to Bibracte with the ten thousand Aeduans, were well ahead of Caesar's army, encumbered as it was by wounded men, baggage, and artillery.

"You don't think we should act right now?" Viridomar was saying.

The morning was fresh and beautiful, tall clumps of trees in full foliage, grass green, flowers in profusion, and on either side rich fields of grain, rippling in a gentle breeze that seemed to caress one's skin. Eporedorix glanced ahead. They were approaching a junction. From it one road swung eastward to Bibracte; the other drove north to Noviodunum.

"There's the saying," Eporedorix observed, " 'Don't dive off the cliff until you're sure there are no rocks below the surface of the lake.' Let's wait until we reach Bibracte. See how the Council feels."

They were just reaching the junction.

"Look!" Viridomar exclaimed, pointing.

Down the long slope on the road from Bibracte an imposing

244

cortège was riding. With a wave of his hand Eporedorix gathered their personal retainers around them, lances ready. Behind their horses the Aeduan infantry halted. The cortège approached.

"The banner of Litavic," Viridomar said.

They both knew that Litavic had ridden from Gergovia to Bibracte. Eporedorix pulled at his long moustache, recognizing a dozen of the principal Aeduan nobles among Litavic's followers. The cortège halted. Even after the peace sign had been given and returned, Eporedorix regarded Litavic warily. When Litavic had defected, Eporedorix had opposed the move.

But Litavic, a bold, sanguine man whose black, heavy eyebrows contrasted sharply with his yellow hair, was too excited to remember the dispute. He rode forward. In a gush of words he told Eporedorix that the Aeduan Council had voted to join the revolt, that every Roman and Italian trader in Bibracte had been massacred, and that he himself was leading a delegation to Vercingetorix.

"To Vercingetorix!" Eporedorix exclaimed. "An Arvernian!"

"What does that matter now?" Litavic waved an arm. "Let Caesar find a grave in Gaul. Then we Aeduans once again will dominate."

Eporedorix, always a cautious man, pulled at his moustache again, considering the situation.

"Are you with us?" Litavic demanded.

Viridomar looked at his cousin. Eporedorix nodded. As one man the two leaders drew their swords and raised them high.

"For Gaul!" they shouted.

"Good!" Litavic cried. He turned to his cortège. With a sweep of his arm, he led it down the road toward Gergovia. Eporedorix watched the group ride past the waiting Aeduan infantry.

"Now what?" Viridomar asked.

Eporedorix turned to look north. "Noviodunum!" he said. "Noviodunum!"

"All Caesar's stores," Eporedorix explained. "His hostages. His war-chest. We have ten thousand men — and friends inside that town. Capture it and all that's in it and who, Viridomar, will be greater heroes in Bibracte than we?"

"By the gods of darkness and the night, you've hit it," Viridomar cried. "Let's go!"

"Softly, softly, cousin. This must be planned — carefully."

# 5

Noviodunum sat on its hill. Below it, along the Liger River, swollen with melting snow from the Cebennes Mountains, were Caesar's warehouses. To the northeast, beyond the walls, was the corral for the remounts and the compound for the hostages — men, women, and children — from the Gallic tribes.

The Roman commander, Quintus Pediculus, a solid military veteran, had commandeered a stone house in the principal square. He had listened to Caesar's courier but was not unduly disturbed. He had alerted his men, but, after all, Noviodunum was an Aeduan town and for years the Aeduans had been loyal allies. Besides, this afternoon another courier had informed him that Caesar and his legions were within three days' march. So he had told a frightened deputation from the Italian traders, who swarmed in the town, not to piss their legs. In the evening he inspected the guards at the warehouses and the gates, and took the trouble to walk out to the corral and the compounds.

"We're spread a little thin, aren't we, sir?" the senior centurion ventured to say as he was leaving.

"We've always been," Pediculus answered a little testily.

"Three hundred and fifty fit for duty, all ranks, sir," the centurion went on. "The hostages are on tenterhooks. They've heard the Aeduans are joining Vercingetorix. Is that a fact, sir?"

"Nonsense." Pediculus reflected a moment. "Tell your men to relax. The legions will be here in three days."

"Thank you, sir."

The centurion saluted. As Pediculus walked back to the town he considered whether he ought to cancel the dinner at the home of Noviodunum's chief magistrate. At this juncture, though, it was important to act as if everything were normal.

Dinner had reached the second tables — and really, Pediculus

246

was thinking, this Meroviccus had gone to a great deal of trouble to make sure that everything was done in Roman style. At that moment one of his escort burst into the dining-room.

"Fighting, sir!" he cried. "Hordes of Gauls, attacking."

At that instant a score of armed Gauls poured in from behind the curtains at the back. Pediculus barely had time to realize that his host had prepared for this action before he was killed. Meanwhile in the outer room his half-dozen soldiers, who, armour off, had been drinking and relaxing with the women slaves of the household, had hastily seized their swords and formed a circle. Not only from the back but from the front, Gauls burst upon them. They went down one by one.

What happened in the chief magistrate's home was a prelude to the slaughter throughout Noviodunum. Eporedorix' emissaries had found the townsfolk ready to join him. They opened the gates. Eporedorix' men poured in. Led by shouting allies, they rushed upon the homes of the Italian traders and merchants. Scarcely any escaped, except that the girls and women were reserved for further sport. Meanwhile — for Eporedorix had planned his operation carefully — cavalry and infantry seized the hostages. Down by the warehouses there was stiff fighting. The guards beat back the first attack, and the second. Eporedorix himself organized the next assault. Under sheer weight of numbers, the Romans were cut down. By dawn, Noviodunum, the hostages, and all Caesar's supplies were in Gallic hands.

Eporedorix finished the operation swiftly and efficiently. The hostages were sent to Bibracte under escort. Caesar's war-chest was divided between himself and Viridomar. Caesar's remounts, along with every additional mule, horse, wagon, and cart that could be found, all loaded with Caesar's supplies of grain and armour, were also forwarded to Bibracte. Other stocks of grain were carried to barges and boats to be sent downriver. Next, the town was set on fire to deny it to the Romans. Whatever stores were left were tossed into the flames.

"Now," he said to Viridomar, "we picket the Liger. If we can prevent Caesar from crossing it, he's done."

"A courier to Vercingetorix," Viridomar suggested.

"Already sent off. His cavalry is pressing on Caesar's rear."

"We're heroes!" Viridomar exclaimed. "Heroes!" He embraced Eporedorix. "Who else but you, cousin, ought to lead the army of Gaul? Think of it. Commander-in-Chief of Gaul."

"Exactly," Eporedorix said.


# 6

Caesar was within a day's march of Noviodunum when the first of the few surviving Italian fugitives from the town reached him. He listened to them, questioned them, then halted his legions and summoned his legates. In brief, concise terms he described the situation. The legates looked at each other.

"Our options are limited," Caesar concluded. "We can retreat to Narbonese Gaul, fighting our way through the passes of the Cebennes. That course of action would leave Labienus and his four legions isolated. Secondly, we can march against Bibracte. With the Aeduans in revolt, and Vercingetorix pressing upon us and refusing battle in the open field, we could piss away our strength. Our third option, the one I've chosen, is to cross the Liger, recall Labienus, and reunite our legions at Agedincum. Any questions, gentlemen?"

"The Liger is swollen with meltwater," Trebonius said. "Suppose we can't cross?"

"We will," Caesar answered. To all the legates he said, "Hurry up the march! We must cross before the enemy garrisons the fords." He turned to Antony. "Take a hundred of the German horse. Find a passable ford — and find it quick."

Antony found a ford. It was guarded by a small Aeduan picket. Antony swam his cavalry across and routed them. When the legions arrived, Caesar put one line of horsemen upstream to break the force of the icy current and another downstream to rescue anyone who was swept off his feet. The legionaries found themselves in water up to their armpits. But Caesar got his army across without the loss of a single man. Vercingetorix made no attempt to cross. Instead, he reorganized his army and made for

Bibracte. At Bibracte, he sensed intuitively, with the arrogant Aeduans at last in revolt, there would soon be a decision about who was to be Commander-in-Chief of the combined forces; and he was determined not to be overlooked.

## 7

At Agedincum, Labienus and Caesar were consulting about what to do. Labienus was secretly exultant and at the same time somewhat patronizing toward his superior. Labienus' own operation had been an unqualified success. With his four legions he had destroyed the combined army of the Parisians and the Senones and had killed its aged and respected leader, Camulogenus.

"To attack uphill, Julius," he was repeating. "That was against all sound military practice."

They were in Caesar's tent.

"You took chances yourself, against Camulogenus," Caesar answered.

"Only with sound tactics, Julius."

Caesar controlled a spurt of irritation. "I saw a chance to end the revolt," he said equably. "It was worth the risk, I decided." He shrugged. "It didn't come off, that's all."

Labienus plucked a hair from his ear, bit it, then put it on the table.

"As a result the Aeduans are in revolt. The effects of that —"

"I know them," Caesar cut in. "The question is what to do now."

"My advice is to retreat to Narbonese Gaul," Labienus answered. "Regroup and return."

Caesar shook his head. He got up and paced around.

"All we need is one battle on even terms," he said. "Just one battle."

"I still advise —"

"We stay in Gaul," Caesar said, turning to face him. "And that's final, Titus."

Labienus flushed and got up. "Very well," he said stiffly. "Don't blame me if we lose."

"I won't," Caesar answered.

But later that evening he summoned Antony.

"I've a job for you," he said without any preliminaries.

"Whatever you say, Julius."

"Sit down," Caesar told him. When they were facing each other, he leaned across the table. "I want this to be confidential— and secret, Antony," he said.

"Very well, cousin."

"We're short, terribly short, of cavalry, Antony. The Aeduan horse have gone. So have the horsemen of almost all the Gallic tribes. They're with Vercingetorix. So he is superior in numbers and, except for the Germans, in quality." Caesar leaned closer. "I'd like four thousand more German cavalry — and if possible without Vercingetorix knowing about them—at first, anyway." He leaned back. "Will you take on that job, Antony?"

"Of course."

"It could be dangerous."

"That just adds spice, cousin."

"How many men do you want as an escort, Antony?"

Antony pondered a moment. "Not too many," he answered. "How about fifty of the Germans?"

"Fine." Caesar leaned across and grabbed Antony's hand tightly. "I can always depend on you, cousin."

Antony flushed. "Think nothing of it, Julius."

# CHAPTER XXII

HE JUNE SUN BEAT DOWN. Outside the Great Harbour of
Alexandria, Cleopatra and Apollodorus sat, presumably
fishing, under an awning on a boat manned by deaf-mutes,
discussing what to do when the Ptolemy died.

"Six to eight months at the most, the physicians say," Apollodorus told the Princess.

"And at that point I have to marry that pimply half-brother of
mine and share the throne. No change in my father's will,
Apollodorus?"

He shook his head. "Meanwhile, Pothinus controls Egypt,
and will try to keep the reins in his hands."

Cleopatra felt a tug at her line but did not set the hook.

"Power!" she said fiercely. "Egypt must be mine, Apollodorus. If Pothinus tries to tell me what to do, out with him."

As she said this, Marcus Cicero sat in the cool rock-garden of
his villa at Arpinum.

"Cilicia," he was thinking petulantly. "I don't want to leave
Italy."

He got up. My books, my writing, all this, he was thinking as
he strolled past the plashing fountain and among the trees, the
flowers. He sighed. "I suppose I have to go," he told himself. "I
helped Pompey put through the law about the five-year interval
between the consulship and proconsulship and how that gap was
to be filled. So I have to go."

To the south of him, Pompey reclined on a sofa in the pergola
of his Cumaean villa. A fraction of his drowsy mind was listening to his wife, Cornelia, expound the differences in the tenets
and moral objectives of Epicureanism and Stoicism. The rest was
reflecting that everything was turning out for the best. In Rome
and Italy he was recognized, as he ought to have been long ago,

as the director of Rome and the Empire. No need to do anything, either. Gergovia had completely discredited his one possible rival, Caesar — and he himself had his veteran legions in Spain. No, it was the best of all possible worlds.

"I've decided for Stoicism," his wife was saying vehemently. "It isn't permissive in morals, like Epicureanism."

Pompey glanced at her. She was sitting up straight, a becoming flush on her cheeks and her fine eyes flashing. He felt a flicker of desire but not keen enough to stir him to action. Tonight would be time enough, he decided comfortably. His thoughts turned to Caesar again. Attacking uphill, he remembered. No, Caesar was no longer a rival. What would he do now after Gergovia? Perhaps he would be wiped out. What was the name of that Gallic leader — Vercin-something or other? Oh well, it didn't matter. He settled himself more comfortably and closed his eyes.

At that moment in his encampment outside Bibracte, the Aeduan capital, Vercingetorix stood beside his black stallion and, a smile on his lips, looked down at his wife, Guenome. Guenome was a noble's daughter, married originally to Vercingetorix to unite two Arvernian clans, but now the political marriage had become a love match. Beautiful, he thought once again — that hair, black and smooth as sable, that skin, soft and white as ivory, those dark-blue, velvety eyes gazing up at him adoringly. To him, she and their two young sons were almost as dear as his ambition.

"Don't worry, my love," he said to her.

"The Aeduans are against you."

Vercingetorix glanced over his shoulder at Bibracte on its hill. Within those walls in the great hall, the Council of all Gaul was meeting. Clustered to right and left of his own tents were the encampments of the principal nobles and chieftains of the tribes. To the west on a hill was the camp of his army, and to its right on another hill the camp of the Aeduan soldiers. Eporedorix, Vercingetorix knew, was his rival for the position of Commander-in-Chief of the combined forces.

"Today is the day they vote, isn't it?" Guenome asked.

Vercingetorix nodded. "Don't worry," he repeated and bent to kiss her. Her arms went around his neck and she hugged him to her fiercely, almost savagely.

"Take care," she whispered. "Oh, my love, take care."

He disengaged himself gently. "Until tonight, sweet," he said and, turning, vaulted onto his stallion. Gathering the reins he began the ride up to Bibracte, his gaily dressed retinue falling in behind him.

Guenome gazed after him. He was so handsome, this lover-husband of hers. Today he had chosen a helmet adorned with flared-back wings of gold, and his tartan trousers and cloak were brilliant with reds and bright blues. So wonderful, she thought. If only he could have been content to have remained what he was, an Arvernian prince, rich, respected, and safe. Now he was a king — a king who had beaten Caesar! But that meant fighting and still more fighting — and intrigues, and, perhaps, even treachery.

So sure of himself, she thought, watching his helmet sparkle in the sun as he and his escort receded from her. Nothing could go wrong, could it? No, surely not. With a sigh, she turned back to the tent and her sons.


## 2


The twisting streets of Bibracte were lined with people. As Vercingetorix rode through them to the Council Hall, there were cheers for the hero of Gergovia. Yet here and there were silent, sullen faces — Aeduans mostly. Dismounting before the Council Hall, Vercingetorix strode in. It was thronged with nobles. At the far end on a dais were two chairs, one for Vercingetorix as acting Commander-in-Chief, the other for the official host and chairman, the chief magistrate of the Aeduans. The two of them took their places. The meeting began.

Gauls loved oratory. Chieftain after chieftain came forward to extol the courage and tremendous achievements of his particular tribe, while the critical audience assessed the gestures, the phrasing, the tricks of voice, and applauded accordingly. Finally, when the audience began to move restlessly, the chief magistrate rose. In a flowery speech he reminded the chieftains that they were to vote on who was to be the Commander-in-Chief of united Gaul, a man, he pointed out, who must have the confidence of all and be an experienced general.

He went on and on. When he sat down, as if on cue Viridomar, the captor of Noviodunum, sprang to his feet. His oration, too, was lengthy; he began with the history, achievements, and importance of the Aeduans, to prove that the leader of united Gaul ought to be an Aeduan. When, at last, he neared his nomination, he paid a brief tribute to the noble king of the Arvernians who, thanks to the courage of the chieftains with him, had defeated the Romans at Gergovia.

There were cheers from the throng. Viridomar waited. Then, raising his voice, he told them that, great though the victory of King Vercingetorix was, there was a man who had achieved more. Because of him, Caesar's stores had been captured or destroyed — and he went into detail. Because of him, he continued, at this instant the hostages from all Gaul were in Bibracte, and through them this Council held a sword over the tribes from east to west and north to south.

"And who is the prince, the hero who has achieved all this?" he cried. "The general from whom the demon Caesar barely escaped with his skin? — in fact pieces of that skin were left behind on Aeduan spear-points when he forded the Liger. I'll tell you," he shouted, flinging his arms wide, "Eporedorix the famous, Eporedorix the general, Eporedorix with years of experience in warfare, Eporedorix whom all men know and trust. Stand up, Prince Eporedorix," he roared, turning to him. "Let all men see you."

Eporedorix stood up, hand on his sword, golden helmet glittering.

"I give you Eporedorix," Viridomar cried. "The hero who will lead us all to victory!"

The Aeduans in the hall shouted and cheered and stamped their feet. So did the leaders of their client tribes. Vercingetorix sat impassive. As the cheering died, Comm, King of the Atrebatians, mounted the dais. He faced the chieftains.

"I need no oratory," he said flatly. "His deeds speak for him. I nominate the greatest of us all, the one man who has defeated Caesar himself, King Vercingetorix."

The roar of cheers seemed almost to lift the roof and burst the walls. The chief magistrate got to his feet, waving his arms to quell the tumult. It was in his mind to get other chieftains onto the dais to destroy the impression Comm had made. Before he could speak, Lucter of the Cadurcans was on his feet.

"Vote!" he was shouting. "Call the vote."

A hundred other voices took up the cry. The chief magistrate tried to speak. The clamour defeated him. With a helpless gesture, he held up his staff, the signal for the vote. The room grew quiet.

"Those for Prince Eporedorix," he called. The Aeduans shouted, but only a half-dozen others joined them.

"For King Vercingetorix."

A roar answered him as the chieftains, rising, flooded forward and onto the dais, lifting Vercingetorix, raising him high. The chief magistrate turned away. Down in the hall, Eporedorix stared up at the dais, lips pressed tightly together, face contorted. Viridomar joined him.

"Let's leave," he said.

The two turned and went out from the Council Hall. Inside, Vercingetorix, lifted on high, face flushed, felt as if his being would burst. Leader of all Gaul, he was thinking. At the apex of success. How proud of him Guenome would be!

# 3

The news reached Caesar.

"What now?" asked Labienus, who had brought in the messenger.

"A battle," Caesar said confidently.

"What makes you think that, Julius?"

255

Caesar got to his feet. "The more tribes and the bigger his army, the more problems for Vercingetorix. The hot-heads will demand a battle. And the Aeduans, I predict, will be furious that Eporedorix was not chosen. So, we'll march, Titus, into Aeduan territory. The Aeduans will force Vercingetorix to fight."

"We haven't enough cavalry, Julius."

"The legions will win," Caesar replied; but at the same time he was wondering if and when Antony would return with German horsemen.

## 4

On that same afternoon, beakers of mead in their hands, Antony and his second-in-command, Trifanius, were sitting on chunks of up-ended logs in a clearing outside the village of Saewulf, the war-chief of the Sugambrians. In his trip down the right bank of the Rhenus River, Antony had found that he liked the Germans. They were uncomplicated men — no Druids, no slavery to religion, their chief interests hunting, fighting, eating, and tossing down beaker on beaker of beer and mead.

They seemed to take to him, too. He was as big as their best warriors. He could match them beaker for beaker, and occasionally, without any fuss about dignity, he would throw off his cloak and tumble their best wrestlers. Yet, so far he had been able to enlist only a thousand horsemen, which was what had brought him to Saewulf's village.

He glanced at Saewulf who, beaker in hand, was sitting to his right on another chunk of up-ended log. Antony had already sensed a scornful attitude in this burly and, as he'd been told by his interpreter, unpredictable chieftain. Perhaps, he thought, that attitude derived from his raid on Quintus Cicero's camp a year ago, a raid that had come within an eyewink of being successful. At any rate, his slaughter of almost three Roman cohorts had given Saewulf a formidable reputation among the Germans.

Saewulf finished his mead and held his beaker behind him for a slave to refill. Then he rumbled a few words.

Antony's interpreter, a man whose unpronounceable name Antony had reduced to Hermann, leaned forward from his position behind Antony and Saewulf.

"He says, 'So you Romans are begging for help,' " he translated.

Antony, in turn, tossed down his mead and held out his beaker for a refill. In the time this took he made a quick assessment of his situation. To his right, grouped in the clearing, were his fifty Germans and the dozen mounted Roman legionaries that Caesar had added as he was leaving the camp at Agedincum. To the left were clustered Saewulf's armed warriors, and behind them was a ring of tow-headed youngsters and women. Farther back was the palisaded village and the few plots of ground the women cultivated. What he noted particularly was that Saewulf's warriors outnumbered his own men by at least four to one.

The beaker was passed back to him. Antony took a gulp from it.

"Tell him," he said to Hermann, "that a Roman never begs for help, that all I'm here for is to offer his young men a chance for pay and loot. Tell him I thought Germans loved to fight. However, if the chance I offer doesn't appeal, it doesn't matter. I'll leave."

He waited until Hermann had finished. Saewulf opened his mouth to speak, but Antony raised a hand to check him.

"Tell him again that we Romans don't need help. Tell him that a single Roman can lick a dozen, no, a score of Gauls — and for that matter a brace of Germans."

He watched. When Hermann spoke of one Roman defeating two Germans, Saewulf's head jerked up and his broad face flushed beet-red. He roared something, then, with a wave of his hand, washed it out and spoke in a quieter voice.

"He asks how many horsemen you want."

"Three thousand from him — and the foot-soldiers to go with them."

Saewulf listened. Then he drained his beaker, wiped his lips, and spoke.

"He says," Hermann told Antony, "since you say one Roman can lick two Germans, he'd like to see if you can. Two of his best fighters. If you beat them, you'll have your three thousand horsemen and three thousand foot-soldiers. If not—" Hermann shrugged.

Antony saw Saewulf grinning at him. He got to his feet.

"Get me a legionary's sword and shield," he said to Trifanius.

Trifanius jumped up. "You can't. It's crazy—"

"Get them!" Antony ordered. He turned to Hermann. "Tell that bastard 'No body armour. No helmets either. Close combat. No spears.' " He took the sword and shield Trifanius had brought and hefted them. "Tell him to pick his men."

Saewulf got up. He roared orders. The log seats were thrown out. Saewulf went around pushing people back until a complete circle of spectators—warriors, soldiers, women, and children— was made. In the centre was the cleared ring. Two Germans stepped into it. One had an axe and shield, the other a long sword and shield.

Antony faced them, a short two-edged Roman sword in his right hand, a heavy oblong Roman shield on his left arm. A glance at the Germans told him that, big as he himself was, they were just as big. Then, swiftly, he scanned the ground for holes and obstacles. Next, he noted that the sunlight was slanting down above the tall trees from his right to his left. In the circle of spectators Saewulf's warriors and his own men were shouting bets across the ring. Saewulf, he saw, had his sword raised high. Antony lifted his shield to cover himself from mid-thigh to just below his eyes.

"Now," Saewulf cried, slashing down his sword.

Antony turned and ran swiftly to his right. Jeers followed him. So did the two Germans. In the shadow of the trees, Antony swung around and faced them. The Germans stopped, the sun in their eyes. They were slow-witted, Antony realized. The man with the sword was a little in front, and neither of them had thought of spreading out so as to come in on two sides.

Before they could think of it, Antony leaped upon the man with the sword, starting a savage swing from right to left at his

258

face. The German's shield went up to guard against the blow. Quick as a panther, Antony checked his swing, dropped to one knee, and thrust upward. His sword-point went up under the German's shield and in under his rib-cage to his heart. In the same split second as he pulled out his sword, Antony was on his feet and pivoting to his left to take a blow from the axe on his shield.

The force of the blow sent him reeling back. The axeman swung another mighty blow that would have lopped Antony's head from his shoulders except for the quick lift of his shield. This time the axe cut through leather and canvas deep into the two layers of wood that formed the shield's core. The German, grunting, had to wrench it free. The circle of spectators was shouting, cheering. But the moment's pause as the German pulled had given Antony time to recover his balance. With a thrust of his powerful legs and thighs he was on the German, cutting, stabbing, giving him no time to get set for another blow of the axe. But the German jumped forward, thrusting his shield against Antony's. They stood for a moment chest to chest, too close for any effective blow. Straining and grunting, each tried to shove the other back, and could not. So, in a concerted movement, the two jumped backward.

They faced each other again. Antony had been impressed with the ease and speed with which his opponent swung the heavy axe, as if it were a cane. He feinted at the German's face. Instead of raising his shield, the German countered with a lightning-like slash at Antony's outstretched arm, and Antony barely got it out of the way in time.

By now there was a continuous roar from the spectators. Antony didn't hear it. He began to circle the German, moving to his own right and feinting with his sword.

The German was not to be drawn. He turned in a tight circle, axe poised. This could go on and on, Antony realized. Suddenly raising his shield — for it, too, was a weapon — he swung the metal-edged rim at the German, face high. The German's shield went up to check it and his axe struck. At the same instant, as Antony lunged forward and downward under the blow, his sword sliced deep into the German's left thigh. As the German toppled, still trying to strike upward with his axe, Antony stepped back. He looked down at his opponent. The shouting had stopped. Should he finish him or not?

Turning, he walked over to Saewulf.

"Well?" he said.

Saewulf looked at the dead swordsman and the wounded axeman. He was scowling. In the circle of spectators some of the German warriors were shouting and brandishing spears and swords, calling, obviously, on their war-chief to give the order to take vengeance on the Roman. Saewulf turned and yelled. Then, grinning broadly, he swung to Antony and held out his hand. Antony passed his sword to Trifanius and clasped the hand for a moment. Saewulf spoke. Hermann, whose face had returned to its normal colour, translated.

"You'll have your horsemen, he says."

"Good," Antony said.

"He also says that for tonight you'll have his choicest slave-woman."

"Tell him to send three," Antony answered.

Hermann translated. Saewulf burst into laughter and clapped Antony on the back.

"We understand each other," was what, obviously, he said.


# 5

It had taken time to collect the Germans. It was late in July when, dark thunder-tops on the horizon, Antony and Saewulf led them on the last stage of the march toward Caesar's camp. About mid-afternoon Caesar himself, escorted by a powerful contingent of cavalry and legionaries, met them. He was all charm and smiles as he was introduced to Saewulf and his sub-chiefs. He looked critically at the ponies most of the Germans rode.

"Have the interpreter tell Saewulf that I have provided for big horses for them," he instructed Antony.

Saewulf and his sub-chiefs were pleased. But underneath

260

Caesar's manner, Antony had detected a certain preoccupation. He was not surprised when, as soon as was convenient, Caesar drew him aside, ostensibly to say how delighted he'd been when Antony's advance courier had reached him.

"What's up, Julius?" Antony asked.

Caesar drew his horse close beside Antony's.

"We march south, the day after tomorrow," he said grimly.

"South! — Where?"

"Back to Narbonese Gaul."

"Narbonese Gaul! Why, Julius, why?"

"Vercingetorix won't fight a battle. When I march into Aeduan or Arvernian territory, he simply falls back. He's even got his men to build camps in our style, Roman style. And he hasn't been idle. Oh no!"

"Tell me."

Caesar turned a bitter face to Antony.

"He has flung three armies against Narbonese Gaul. In the centre, the Arvernians have already defeated the Helvians and confined them to their fortresses. On our right and his left, the Allobroges are holding against ten thousand Aeduans, but only just. In the far west, Lucter is leading the Rutenians and his Cadurcans against Tolosa and Narbo and making headway. Narbonese Gaul is screaming for help."

"Can't they hold?"

"Ten thousand troops, mostly levies. No, I have to save Narbonese Gaul, and also my legions. If Narbonese Gaul is overrun, where would they—and I—be? No base. No supplies. No communications with Cisalpine Gaul and Italy."

"And then?"

Caesar was staring straight ahead. "Then, I'll reconquer Gaul, starting in the west — that is, unless the Senate stabs me in the back. Yet, so long as I have my legions — "

"I see."

Not altogether, Caesar thought. No one but he himself could understand the bitterness of this retreat. A year ago, at the pinnacle of success. Today, Gaul lost — and all because of one man, Vercingetorix. If only that man could have been tempted to a battle in the open field — but, for once, he had met a Gallic leader who could estimate the strengths and weaknesses of his people, devise a strategy to utilize them, and, furthermore, control the tribes.

One man — only.

Defeat, he thought, the bitterness wrenching at him, almost destroying him. In a surge of defiance, he put up his chin. He glanced at the thunderheads. Let Fate sling all her arrows at him. He'd still win — somehow.

# CHAPTER XXIII

T HE LEGIONS WERE RETREATING to Narbonese Gaul! That was the news that was shouted from village to homestead to hamlet across the countryside. From a wood on a hill overlooking the Roman line of march, Vercingetorix, accompanied by Comm and their escort, stared down at Caesar's columns, some three-quarters of a mile away. Those columns were marching, legion by legion, the baggage of each legion just behind it. Their line extended for miles.

I've won, Vercingetorix was thinking in exultation. Gaul is free. Beside him, Comm was fingering his moustache.

"Trouble coming," he said.

Vercingetorix turned to him. "Trouble?"

"When we got the news," Comm went on slowly, "you left our fortress at Alesia and brought your army here to Caesar's western flank."

"Correct," Vercingetorix answered. "Our cavalry has cut off convoys to Caesar and has slaughtered any of his patrols that ventured too far from the legions. We're hustling him out of Gaul, Comm — a wounded wolf that can only turn to snap and snarl before it runs again."

"And now your chieftains are wild to attack. I've heard them. 'Let him get away scot-free?' they're saying. 'No. Smash him!' "

Vercingetorix' eyes flashed. "I'm in command."

"You may have to throw them a sop."

Vercingetorix shook his head. "No battle. I won't risk that. Let him go." He waved his hand at Caesar's columns. "He's heading for Sequanian territory. Then he'll have to push through the Allobroges. We'll hurry him along. That's all. Well, back to camp."

They turned their horses around.

263

## 2

Down in the valley Fadius, once more in Caesar's bodyguard, was riding several files away from his commander. He, like everyone in the army, knew that they were marching to Narbonese Gaul.

It did not worry him. Caesar knew best. Rullus had expressed the previous evening what he, Fadius, and the legionaries felt.

"Wonder if we'll get leave?" Rullus had said. "Nicaea! Massilia! Girls! By the phallus of Mars, I can use them."

Fadius himself was thinking pleasurably of Chione in Massilia. How surprised she would be! He drew in deep breaths. It was a golden day today, sun bright but not too hot, green in the valley, green on the hills and clothing the forests on either side; and it was pleasant to be on a horse again, instead of trudging along with the Eighth.

Over to the left, Caesar was staring at Five-Toes' ears. It was a bitter reflection that this was the same countryside he had traversed six years back on his way toward his first great victory over the Helvetians. It was still more bitter to recall that a year ago he had held Gaul in his cupped hands, conquered at last, he had thought. Yet here he was, all because of one man, a friend turned traitor. Traitor!

He suppressed the fury and glanced about him. It was a vagrant thought that he ought to send orders to his cavalry patrols to scout deeper into the hills and woods on either side. It did not seem necessary. He had hoped that by sending alleged deserters with stories of dejection among the legions he might stir the Gauls into an attack. None had come. Vercingetorix obviously had them under control.

He heaved a deep sigh. Retreat! Would he ever return?

## 3

On the evening of that same day, at the insistence of Eporedorix and the other Aeduan leaders, Vercingetorix had summoned the chieftains to a Council. His army had been put in three camps on the southwestern side of a steep-banked stream, past which Caesar would be marching next day. Now, the Council was meeting on a hilltop above the principal camp. It had already been a stormy session. Comm had been right. Discontent was bubbling like water soon ready to boil over the side of the pot.

"No battle," Vercingetorix repeated, towering a head above them.

"Will you let them get away from us?" Eporedorix shouted. "Beaten men? Ready to break? No, by Midhir of the lightnings!"

Cheers applauded Eporedorix. Vercingetorix sat with a frown on his forehead. His own judgment was to let the Romans go. Harry them, yes. But not risk anything. Not when one had already achieved this retreat from Gaul.

"Who commands here?" he said, eyes flashing.

The question did not quell Eporedorix. He was on his feet, gesturing wildly.

"Here we are, the best fighting-men in Gaul, which means the best in the world." He waited for the roar of assent to die. "Eighty thousand foot-soldiers," he went on hotly. "Fifteen thousand cavalry. And you say, 'No battle!'"

The Aeduan and younger chieftains were up, shouting in support of Eporedorix. Vercingetorix jumped to his feet.

"Silence!" he shouted. "Silence!"

Comm echoed his cry. "Silence!"

Vercingetorix glared around at the chieftains, then fixed his gaze on Eporedorix.

"If anyone wishes to challenge my leadership," he said coldly, "let him come forward." He drew himself up to his great height and put his hand on the hilt of his sword. "Let him fight me — here and now."

Eporedorix did not accept the challenge. Vercingetorix took his hand away from his sword-hilt. He was reflecting that Caesar's line of march was long. A cavalry onslaught on its flanks could break through. Caesar had only his Roman and Spanish horse, a few squadrons of Gallic cavalry, and his four hundred Germans. There was, indeed, a rumour that more

265

German cavalry had been brought across the Rhenus, but that rumour might have been planted by Caesar to disguise his weakness in horsemen. In any case, Vercingetorix decided there could not be too many Germans, and his own cavalry was definitely superior in numbers and morale. So, why not, as Comm had suggested, throw these turbulent chieftains a sop?

"You chafe at the bit," he said. "I will not, I repeat, risk a set battle — our tribesmen against the legions. But are you not, as you claim, the best cavalry in the world? Caesar's long line of march is vulnerable. Will you ride through that line of march, if I let you loose?"

The roar of assent was deafening. The chieftains were yelling, shouting, tossing their swords into the air and catching them.

"An oath," the high-pitched voice of Viridomar was shrilling above the din. "An oath!"

"Yes, an oath," the deeper voice of Eporedorix shouted. As the chieftains, quietening, turned toward him, he stood forth, tall and confident, sword raised high. "An oath that each of us will ride twice through the Roman lines, or henceforth," he paused as the hill-top grew still, "be homeless, never again to be welcomed by parents, children, and wife. Twice through the Roman lines. Will you swear that oath, nobles of Gaul?"

There was a split-second's pause. Then, the chieftains crowded around Eporedorix.

"The oath!" they were shouting. "Bring the Druids. Swear the oath. Twice through the Roman lines."

Vercingetorix looked at them somewhat wryly. Eporedorix, he realized, had taken the moment away from him.

# 4

It was another golden morning, the sun just up, a line of green hills to their right, and on their left clumps of forest, the trees still and peaceful. Fadius was riding in Caesar's escort. His commander had been inspecting part of the line of march, and they were about a half a mile from the head of the Tenth, which led the van.

In front and on either flank was the Roman cavalry. Antony and Saewulf and the German horsemen were guarding the rear.

Such a gorgeous day, Fadius thought, and drew in a deep lungful of the fresh and scented air. At that instant down from the hills to the right a half a mile away, and from the clumps of forest on the left, rode masses of yelling, cheering Gallic horsemen; and from up front there were shouts and Roman bugles blowing.

As Fadius, in shock, reined in his horse, he heard Caesar shouting to his trumpeter.

"Form square!" Caesar was shouting. "Blow the signal. Form square."

The trumpeter blew. It was touch and go. The Roman cavalry, caught by surprise, still had time to arrange their squadrons and meet the attacks from the front and the flanks. Their resistance, in turn, bought time for the legions, one by one, to form squares, baggage in each case in the centre. The legates and the centurions, in fact, had not needed the trumpet-signal to act. Now, the legionaries stood, weapons ready, blank, incurious faces looking at the cavalry battles.

"Support the cavalry," the trumpets ordered.

Again the legions' officers did not need the signal. Wherever the Gallic horsemen broke through on them, the charge of a cohort threw them back. Wherever the commanders saw a Roman squadron encircled or being cut down, a similar charge freed them. Within half an hour, the battle had settled down into three separate cavalry engagements, one Gallic force attacking the van of the Romans, the other two Gallic cavalry contingents assaulting the right and left flanks of the foremost legions.

Why hadn't Antony brought up his Germans from the rear, Caesar wondered. And where was Vercingetorix' infantry? Would they attack?

He had to know. Leading a cohort in reconnaissance around a bend in the road a hundred yards away, he found the Gallic footmen. They were massed in phalanx behind a steep riverbank, shouting and waving spears but not attempting to advance. But where was Antony?

Away to the rear, he heard faint bugles. Careless of danger, his bodyguard around him, he galloped Five-Toes back half a mile, then reined him, exultation within him. At last the German horse and foot soldiers were pouring along the ridge on the right, driving Gallic cavalry before them. Caesar watched. Soon he was able to see Antony and Saewulf side by side in the lead. Then, swinging to their left, they swooped upon the Gauls in the plain.

For Vercingetorix' men it was disaster. They fled; and, between the gaps in the squares of the legions, Saewulf led squadrons that put the Gallic horse on the other flank to flight. In front other squadrons, commanded by Antony, scattered the Gauls who had been attacking the van.

"Into battle-line," Caesar shouted to the legion next to him, then rode furiously to the Eighth and then the Tenth with the same order.

On the height from which he had been watching the fight, Vercingetorix, his face ravaged, turned to Comm.

"Come, let's get our men away," he said.

"Why not fight?" Comm cried in despair.

Vercingetorix swept an arm to the scene below. "Our cavalry —see! Galloping away, the Germans after them."

"They swore!" Comm exclaimed in anguish. "Twice through the Roman lines, they swore!"

"Now they're fleeing through our own infantry. And look, the legions are forming into battle-line. If we give them time, they'll carve through our footmen like a butcher slicing meat. Back to Alesia. Come. Let's get them back."

As he rode down the hill, Vercingetorix was reproaching himself bitterly. He should never have allowed the cavalry to charge. Never.

## 5

The Gallic army was streaming away. Caesar watched it run, cursing the fact that it took time to transform a ten-legion-long line of march into a battle-front. He had sent Antony and his Germans in pursuit. For the moment that was all he could do. Labienus rode up to him. His expression was smug.

"No more trouble now, Julius," he commented.

Caesar turned a blank face to him.

"In getting back to Narbonese Gaul, I mean," Labienus explained.

"Narbonese Gaul!" Caesar exploded. He waved an arm toward the fleeing Gauls. "I'm going to finish them now."

"Finish them?"

"Two legions to guard the baggage. The others—after them."

"Alesia is impregnable, Julius. If you — "

"Impregnable or not, I'll take it. Titus, will you see to the baggage? The Sixth and the Fourth as guards."

Caesar rode off. Labienus looked after him for an instant; then, shaking his head, he turned to his job.

That evening, Caesar built his camp on the road to Alesia. Antony came in with his report.

"I estimate three thousand of them killed in their retreat, Imperator," he said.

"Good."

Antony grinned. "I have some interesting prisoners, too, Julius."

Caesar stood up. "Who?"

Antony called an order. In came Saewulf and half a dozen of his Germans, herding three Aeduan nobles. The first of them was Eporedorix. Caesar glanced at the two others. One was Cotus, leader of the Aeduan cavalry. The other was Cavarillus, commander of the Aeduan infantry.

Caesar's gaze came back to Eporedorix, the man who had captured Noviodunum and ordered the massacre of the Romans and Italians in it.

"Shall I take them out and lop off their heads, Imperator?" Antony asked.

Caesar's face was stern. Eporedorix took one look, fell to his knees, and scrabbled forward on them.

"Mercy, Imperator," he begged. "Have pity."

269

Caesar looked down at the Aeduan. It was passing through his mind that Eporedorix had a grudge against Vercingetorix over the Gallic leadership. Could one make use of him?

"Take them away," he ordered. "Keep them under guard. Close guard."

## 6

Before evening fell, the story of disaster had reached Bibracte, south of Alesia. In the stone house in which her husband had placed her, their two sons, and their slaves, Guenome sat down, got up, went into a room, then left it for another; she was wild with anxiety. Was her husband still alive? If he was, what would happen to him? Why, oh why, had he ever started this revolt or, worse still, taken the command? What would Caesar do to him?

When, late that evening, a messenger from Vercingetorix reached her house, she swept the guards at the door away and grabbed at him.

"Is he alive?" she demanded. "Quick. Does he live?"

"Yes, lady, yes," the messenger told her.

She stepped back, releasing him, and drew in a long breath. "Praise be to the Shining One!" she said. And then, sharply, "What news, men? What does he say?"

The messenger rearranged his cloak.

"He's in Alesia — safe. He and his army. He says not to worry."

"Not worry! Don't be foolish."

"He also bids you to take his sons and go to Gergovia. He wants them — and you — safe."

"But I want to be near him. As near as I can be."

The messenger looked around him and lowered his voice.

"He doesn't trust the Aeduans, Lady. In Gergovia, in your own home among the Arvernians, you'll be secure."

"All the same, if he's in danger — "

"Don't trouble yourself, Lady," the messenger interrupted. "Alesia is even stronger than Gergovia. Let the Romans beat

270

their heads out against it, if they want to. Alesia can't be captured."

"Well — "

"And—and," the messenger went on, somewhat embarrassed and looking at his toes, "he ordered me to say something else—"

"What?"

"That he sends his deepest love to his dearest wife — and his sons, yours and his."

To think that he had taken time for this in the midst of the rout! Her two sons were beside her, staring up wide-eyed at the messenger. Guenome put her arms around them and lifted her chin.

"Go back," she said. "Tell him that his sons and I go to Gergovia. Tell him we wait there for him to join us—victorious. And tell him that I, his wife, send him a love that is all-encompassing, a love that is even deeper than his—I, and his sons — our sons."

The messenger bowed in acknowledgment. Guenome stood even straighter.

"Tell him I believe in him. Victorious, I said. Victor always— even over Caesar."

# CHAPTER XXIV

A S GUENOME AND HER SONS journeyed from Bibracte toward Gergovia, her husband stood with Comm on Alesia's walls. Behind them was the town, a mile in length and roughly half that distance in width, its streets and squares swarming with infantry and cavalrymen. Below the walls were rocky, precipitous outcrops. The main entrance was at the eastern end. Circling the town was a ring of wooded hills, of approximately the same height as Alesia, except that on its western flank a level plain, traversed by two streams, extended to Alesia's southwestern corner.

Vercingetorix and Comm stared down at that plain. On it ant-sized figures could be seen, the Romans digging trenches. It was clear that Caesar intended to draw lines around Alesia to starve it into surrender.

"Who could have believed it?" Comm exclaimed vehemently. "Six miles around the base of this hill. It will mean ten miles of trenching."

"I wish — " Vercingetorix began and stopped.

Comm turned to him. "I know," he said roughly. "You're wishing you'd never permitted that cavalry battle. You can blame it on me."

Vercingetorix shook his head. "I am the commander. I made the decision."

"They swore," Comm said violently. " 'Twice through the Roman lines.' Bah."

He spat.

"If I'd known about the Germans," Vercingetorix muttered. "I mean, how many there were of them."

"The Germans again yesterday," Comm said.

He was referring to the cavalry battle down there in the plain.

272

The Gauls had been winning, until the Germans had charged and driven Vercingetorix' horsemen almost to the gates of Alesia.

"Well, what now?" Comm asked. "Food is in short supply."

"I have a plan, Comm. I'm calling a Council." He glanced southwestward. By this time Guenome and his sons should be safely out of Bibracte. He turned to descend the wall.

The Council, at first, was tumultuous, the chieftains blaming one another for yesterday's defeat.

"The Aeduans," Vercingetorix' cousin, Vercaswallon, was shouting, "they were the first to turn tail."

"Liar," Viridomar shouted back. "Braggart. If you Arvernians —"

Others broke in. Vercingetorix sat and let the chieftains squabble. It was when swords were drawn that Comm roared, "Put up your swords, you fools. D'you want to do Caesar's work for him?"

"Caesar—he has us trapped," Viridomar cried. He pointed his sword at Vercingetorix. "You let us be trapped. If you hadn't ordered that battle, a battle you knew we'd lose — now you've trapped us. All of us!"

Vercingetorix got slowly to his feet, thinking that, at least, he did not have Eporedorix — taken prisoner, it was said — to oppose him.

"So you think you're trapped, do you?" he asked.

Those nearest to him turned on him, shouting, waving swords.

"Silence," Comm roared again. Vercingetorix waited. Then, with slow deliberation, he said,

"It's Caesar who's trapped, not we."

The chieftains gaped.

"Those busy little men down there," Vercingetorix flung a gesture toward where the plain was, "are sweating, digging a ditch to hem us in. But, suppose the Romans are attacked from without as well as from within? Who's the victim then?"

The chieftains still gaped at him.

Vercingetorix took a stride forward, once more tall, confident. In brief sentences he pointed out that the Romans had only

273

begun to dig their lines around Alesia. There were gaps, many of them. So that night all the cavalry was to ride through those gaps.

He saw the chieftains look at each other, hope and relief in their eyes. They were realizing, Vercingetorix thought sardonically, that they themselves would be safe. He raised his voice a notch.

"Then, get together an army. From all Gaul. March here. Sweep over Caesar's men like a wave curling to break, and from these walls, Alesia's walls, another wave will swell forward to meet you. In those two floods the legions will be drowned."

"And you?" Vercaswallon asked. "Do you ride out with us?"

Vercingetorix shook his head. "I'm needed here." He paused. "And ride fast. I've checked our stores. I and my seventy-five thousand men have food for thirty days. Go and return. May all our gods go with you. But, return."

Later that night, when the contingents of cavalry were already on their way, he spoke briefly with Comm.

"I'd prefer to stay here with you," Comm said for the tenth time.

"I have Critognat here," Vercingetorix answered. "You're needed outside. You and my cousin, Vercaswallon, will make sure that an army is brought back in time. I repeat, in time."

"I promise."

"And Comm," Vercingetorix said, somewhat hesitantly.

"What is it?"

"If anything happens—you know—death in battle—will you take care of my wife and sons?"

Comm held out his hand for Vercingetorix to clasp.

"My oath," he said. "By all our gods, I swear it."

"Till we meet," Vercingetorix said.

"Till we meet," Comm repeated.


## 2


Vercingetorix stood for the hundredth time on Alesia's walls and stared over the tip of the plain at the hill to the southwest. Would the relieving army never come? He had told the chieftains thirty days' food. Here it was, seven weeks — forty-nine nights and days — and still no sign.

At first, messengers had got through. He had learned that the Council had sent out orders to each tribe to raise contingents and concentrate at Bibracte. He had also been informed that, somehow, Eporedorix had escaped from Roman custody—news that had caused a flicker of unease within him. He had dismissed the unease. With Comm and Vercaswallon out there things would move.

But now for weeks, ever since Caesar had completed his first encircling line, there had been no news. What could have happened? Why wasn't the army here? Forty-nine days. Not a rat, not a mouse was left in Alesia—nor a kernel of grain, nor a single animal, except his own black stallion.

He looked down at the plain. There under the sun of a golden autumn morning, the Romans were still busy. One could not have believed it possible. Two lines of defence works, one hemming in Alesia, the other facing outward, with space to manoeuvre between them. Eight camps, four for the Roman cavalry, four for the infantry. Twenty-three redoubts. On the rampart and the palisade, towers crammed with artillery only eighty yards apart. Special defences in the plain. He had tested those defences time after time. Unbreakable. The only hope was the army from outside.

Vercingetorix glanced again beyond the Roman lines at the southwestern hill. The Romans had cut down its trees, the stately elms, the billowing horse chestnuts, leaves already bronzed by autumn. Would he ever see Gallic spear-points there?

Like everyone else's inside the starving city, his face was gaunt and seamed. He turned to descend from the wall. Critognat, the principal Arvernian sub-chief, who had been standing on the wall with him, grasped his arm.

"You'll be forced to my plan, Vercingetorix," he warned.

Vercingetorix paused. Critognat had urged cannibalism, as adopted half a century before when the Cimbrians and the Teutones, pouring in from the north, had locked the Arvernians inside their towns and cities. The lines on Vercingetorix' face deepened. On the thirty-third day of the siege he had expelled every non-combatant from Alesia — men, women, children — and left them to die between the town and the Roman lines. But to eat human flesh —

"We'll wait one more day," he said.


# 3

At that moment, Caesar was on his tall command-tower on the western slope of the south hill. He glanced up at Alesia, its walls outlined against the sky. Somewhere up there was his former friend, turned enemy. It had come, finally, to a duel between the two of them — the prize, Gaul. He turned to consider his entrenchments. Labienus had grumbled that it couldn't be done; and, after the news of the assembling of a great relief army, he had advised abandonment of the siege.

"Caught in the proverbial nutcracker, we'll be," he had pronounced. "Seventy-five thousand desperate men up there," he had waved at Alesia, "and hundreds of thousands from outside, Julius. Thirty-five thousand legionaries. Outnumbered like that, how can we win against attacks from front and rear?"

Caesar had known with men such as his he could, as the saying went, pile Mount Ossa on Mount Pelion. Every man — legionary, auxiliary, cavalry-man, mule-driver, slave — had been tossed into the work. The inner line, over ten miles in all, had been flung around Alesia. In the plain, where the defences were most vulnerable, a broad trench, twenty feet deep, had been dug. Some four hundred yards behind it, two other trenches, each fifteen feet deep and nine feet wide—the one nearest Alesia being the one that ran around the town—had been added. Behind the second one a rampart and a palisade twelve feet high had been erected. The same sort of trenches and rampart-cum-palisade protected every other weak point in his contravallation. Everywhere they might be needed, too, were the towers replete with artillery and siege-pikes.

Then he had turned his men to building a circumvallation over twelve miles in all, the line to face the relieving army. It had only a single trench in front of its rampart, palisade, and towers. Within the two lines, foraging and working parties had stored ammunition for the artillery, stocks of arrows, bolts, and spare javelins, and fuel and food for men and beasts for thirty days.

What men! Caesar thought now, with an upswelling in his heart. He turned to look toward the same hill to the southwest at which Vercingetorix had been staring. His agents and spies had kept him informed about the Gallic host — the contingents ordered from the tribes, the assembling of the army at Bibracte, the disputes over the leadership, the boasting and the banqueting. The release of Eporedorix had been a calculated move that had paid off. Thanks to the deal that Caesar had made with him, Eporedorix had managed to delay the Gallic force's departure time after time. But now, at last, it was on its way under four commanders — Comm, Vercingetorix' cousin, Vercaswallon, and two Aeduans, Eporedorix and Viridomarus.

It was these two men on whom he was counting—except that one could never be sure of Gauls. For instance, practically every second day a deserter from Alesia would come in, so he, Caesar, knew the desperate straits of the town's garrison.

He turned to glance up at Alesia briefly. It had been a hard thing when his opponent had turned out men, women, and children to die between the town and his lines; but he had forbidden his men to feed them. Who knew how long the Romans would have to hold out between their two lines of defences?

Caesar moved his gaze from Alesia. Was there anything else to do before the Gallic host arrived? Only one really weak spot in his lines, he decided, his glance lifting to a lofty hill northwest of Alesia. That hill was far enough back that he had had to construct a camp on its nearer flank. It could be attacked from uphill. Still, the camp ought to hold against an onslaught there. He looked down at the plain. His men were still working. His mind ran rapidly over the extra defences he had devised — the limbs of trees thrust in between the earthen rampart and the palisade with

277

the branches outward. The men called them "deerhorns". Next, beyond the two trenches were the "tombstones" — slit trenches, each five feet deep in five rows, with pointed logs planted in them. Beyond them were conical pits, arranged in five rows so that in each row a pit three feet deep with sharpened stakes protruding covered a gap in the row in front; and finally came rows of wooden pegs a foot and a half deep, carrying iron barbs. The men had found names for these two devices, too — "lilies" and "spurs".

If Vercingetorix tried to attack across the plain, Caesar thought grimly, those devices would cost him. Yes, all was as ready as one could make it — and the seven weeks had made it possible.


# 4


That afternoon Vercingetorix, Critognat with him, once more climbed Alesia's wall to look southwest, shading their eyes against the sun with cupped hands. There was still nothing, no matter how hard Vercingetorix stared. Forty-nine days. What could have happened?

"The men are eating roots, grass, boiled hides, crickets, grasshoppers," Critognat said. "You'll have to come to it. Surrender, or charge out to die. Or eat human flesh."

Human flesh! Well, better that than surrender. Vercingetorix started to turn away and remembered that far away to the southwest was Gergovia, Guenome, and his sons. He stopped to send his thoughts across the distance to Guenome and saw something.

He looked, brushed his hands across his eyes, and looked again.

"It's real," he whispered. "Real."

"What did you say?" Critognat, who had turned to go, asked.

"Look! On that hill to the southwest. See? Dust! And now, look, spear-points! Spear-points in the sun!"

"By the god of night and darkness, you're right!" Critognat exclaimed.

"They've come!" Vercingetorix cried, his gaunt face alive with exultation. "They're here!" He turned to shake his fist at the Roman lines. "And now, Gaius Julius Caesar, look to yourself. Your course is run, Gaius Julius Caesar. Wait. Just wait — and tremble."

# 5

On his watchtower Caesar, too, his face impassive, was watching the Gallic host flood over the hill and begin to set up their encampments. Now the final hour was approaching. Now came the battle for Gaul.

Along the walls on either side his legionaries were also watching. They knew that they were badly outnumbered. They realized that they would be attacked from front and rear. But after the long days of labour and waiting, it was a relief to know that at last the decisive moment was almost upon them.

"Now you know why our Caesar made us work our asses off," Crastinus, a grizzled centurion of the Tenth, said.

"We'll kick them in the balls," Rullus said. "Wait till they try our spurs, our lilies, our tombstones. Eh, Fadius?"

Fadius was on active duty again, this time as a centurion with the Tenth. His face was sombre. It was not because he was afraid. Like Rullus and Crastinus he had complete confidence that the lines and the legionaries would hold. He turned to look behind him at the parapet of the rampart facing Alesia and beyond it. Out there a few wraiths of the men, women, and children still lived.

Why was it that in war the innocent suffered, he was thinking. After Avaricum he had sworn to himself never again to kill a child, or a woman, or anyone except a fighting-man. Yet Caesar, his commander, his idol, had given the order that meant that all those poor wretches out there must starve to death. He had watched them beg, plead, lift up their hands for pity.

It had squeezed his heart. In spite of the order, in spite of the danger to himself if he were caught, he had helped a dozen women and children through the Roman lines. It was a mere

279

handful. Yet, like the starving kitten he had once picked up at home on the farm, if the helpless crossed your path, surely you had to do something, even if you knew that for hundreds and thousands there was nothing but slow death waiting. Now a quick fate would seize the few misery-ridden wretches who were still alive out there.

Rullus nudged him in the ribs.

"Eh, Fadius?" he repeated.

Fadius turned back and forced a grin. "We'll spill their guts," he agreed.

Up on the hill Viridomar and Eporedorix, as if by accident, came together.

"You sent the messenger?" Eporedorix asked.

Viridomar nodded. "He'll be with Caesar by now." He paused. "You're sure of our reward?"

Eporedorix nodded. "Remember," he said, his voice low, "we step cautiously, as if watching for vipers in underbrush. We hold back our men. But if it looks as if the Gauls are winning, then we rush in. But not too soon, cousin. Not too soon."

## 6

Far away to the southwest, in Gergovia, in the pillared mansion her husband had had built by Greek architects from Massilia, Guenome sat down in a chair, got up again, went into the kitchens to scold the slaves there, came out again, moved a Greek vase from one marble table to another, looked at it, moved it back again, then stood still.

If only she could know, she thought. For days and days she had waited for word that the relieving host had set out from Bibracte, asking herself in anguish why it did not hasten. She had even gone to her husband's uncle, Gubannitio, who had returned to Gergovia. He had shrugged.

"I was the one who strove to prevent the Arvernians from joining the revolt," he had said coldly. "Vercingetorix chose not to listen."

"But he was winning," she had cried.

He had shrugged his shoulders again.

"Why doesn't our army leave?" she had asked. "At once. Why? Why?"

"Your husband was told time and time again never to trust an Aeduan," he had answered. "Again he made his choice."

She had dropped to her knees. "Will you go to Bibracte?" she had begged. "Thirty days, we were told. Now it's over forty-five and the army is still there. Will you go to Bibracte, uncle? Will you find out what's wrong?"

He had shaken his head. But today she had heard that the army had marched. That was why she stood as if frozen, one thought skittering after another through her brain. What was happening to him? Now. Right now.

The Druids, she thought suddenly. I'll go to them. Ask them to pray for him. Give them my jewels. Beg them to sacrifice. Which of my slaves? Which? My two favourites, of course. Yes, those two. Their lives to save his, my husband's —

She turned. "Bring me my cloak," she cried.


# 7


On the next afternoon, in the Egyptian salon of her palace on the Palatine, Servilia and Balbus had been conferring. Ever since the victory in the first cavalry battle, communications between Caesar and Rome had been restored.

"He's written me that this battle at a place called Alesia will be the final battle," Servilia was saying.

"The same to me," Balbus answered. He rose from the sofa and wandered around the salon, picking up a gilded statuette of Isis and putting it down, glancing at the black-painted wall, relieved high up by lozenges of a hard, bright red.

"What Julius does not realize," he said over his shoulder, "is that this revolt has destroyed his reputation. Even his ardent supporters are wavering."

"If he wins this battle?" Servilia suggested.

281

Balbus turned toward her, his face heavy. "He may not win. I have an agent in Pompey's palace. He reports a letter from Labienus to Pompey."

"Oh?"

"Labienus says that a great Gallic army is assembling. He says that the legions and the whole army — auxiliaries and cavalry, somewhere like sixty thousand men in all—will be outnumbered and attacked from front and rear. He tells Pompey that he has begged Julius to give up the siege and retreat to the safety of Narbonese Gaul, but Julius will not listen. He finished by pointing out that if the army is destroyed, it will not be his fault."

"What was Pompey's reaction?"

"He flung down the letter and said Caesar was a fool to take such a risk."

"Julius has always taken risks."

"There's an old saying," Balbus answered; "if you take the jar to the well once too often — "

Servilia got up. "I don't believe it. I won't. Labienus is protecting his own reputation. Gaius Julius Caesar is going to win. He must win."

But after she had escorted Balbus to the doorway — clouds above and a biting unseasonable east wind — she shivered and pulled her cloak around her as she re-entered the salon. What was Julius doing at this instant, she wondered. Was he in danger?

She, too, wandered about the salon, touching this and that abstractedly. Like her lover, she had long ago lost her belief in the gods of Rome. Yet, perhaps, at this moment of crisis —

She thought about it. There were her own household gods — Vesta, goddess of the hearth; Diana, the virgin huntress; and Venus, the mother—and Venus was the goddess from whom the Julian clan claimed descent. There would be no harm in sacrifices and prayers to them. No harm, certainly. And perhaps, perhaps —

"Yes, my love," she said aloud. "I'll pray for you. For you, I'll go to my knees and pray. May you win, my own. Win!"

# CHAPTER XXV

AT ALESIA, it was the sixth day since the relieving army had come. There had been two battles, both in the plain. In the first, the Gallic cavalry had poured down to meet the Roman horse outside the circumvallation, while Vercingetorix' gaunt warriors had assailed the inner lines. In the second, fought at midnight, Gallic infantry had attacked the outer defences, while Vercingetorix had once more striven to breach the interior lines.

It had been a wild and desperate struggle in the darkness — Gauls shrieking as the spurs, lilies, and tombstones impaled them, but pressing on to bridge the ditches with fascines and plant scaling ladders and mount them; the Roman artillery shooting bolts and stones into the dark masses of the enemy; the legionaries using huge siege-pikes to topple the ladders; and everywhere shouts, screams, yells, death-rattles; and everywhere, too, spears, javelins, and arrows in a missile-storm, death darting out of the blackness.

The Roman losses had been heavy. Ten times as many Gauls had fallen. But they had kept on coming until, at the first streaks of dawn, the Gauls outside, fearing sorties on their flanks from the cavalry camps, had begun to retire, and, as in the first battle, the Aeduans had been the first to retreat. From the inner lines, Vercingetorix' men, dejected, had withdrawn to Alesia.

So the Roman lines had held. Yet for two days now there had been no onslaught. No messenger, either from Viridomar or from Eporedorix.

Those facts worried Caesar. Before both battles he had been forewarned by the two Aeduan leaders. Through their messages he also knew that the relieving host had food for only eight days; so the Gauls must attack soon. But when? And at what point?

For the fifth time that morning he climbed his watchtower. He had had it placed on the edge of the southern hill, just above the junction with the western plain. When he reached the platform on top, he surveyed the scene. It was a bright morning, so warm that it seemed like a renewal of summer rather than an autumn day. Nor was there a breath of wind. Over to his left the Gallic encampment seemed to slumber on its hill. His own lines were somnolent. He examined them thoughtfully, his gaze lingering a moment on the weakest point in his defences, the hill to the northwest of Alesia, the one he had not been able to include in his lines but had had to defend by a camp on its nearer slope. That camp had two legions in it and an outpost on the summit of the hill, so it ought to hold. Well, better inspect his defences.

As he went down the steps, in Alesia, a mile away to the north, Vercingetorix, too, was staring at the Gallic encampment. It was as obvious to him as to Caesar that the relieving army must attack soon. But when—and where? His own starving men were prepared, and he himself had devised a new plan. Everything was ready for that plan. Yet nothing seemed to be stirring.

As he considered this fact, in the Gallic encampment Viridomar and Eporedorix were speaking to each other in whispers.

"Do we dare?" Viridomar was asking.

Eporedorix shook his head. "No messenger to Caesar. Comm has men watching us. He's a hawk, ready to pounce. He knows that twice our men have been the first to retreat. Besides," he glanced at the northwestern hill, "this time we Gauls might win."


## 2


At this moment, behind a shoulder of that northwestern hill, sixty thousand picked Gallic warriors began to stir, yawn, and sit up. During the night Vercaswallon, Vercingetorix' cousin, had led them by a roundabout route to this valley, then ordered them to eat and rest. As the men stirred, Vercaswallon glanced at the sun. It would soon be at the zenith, the time arranged with Comm for the attack. He signalled with his hand to his chieftains.

"Time to get ready," he said.

There were no horns blown. Instead, the chieftains moved quietly among the men, forming them into phalanxes and making certain that each group understood its task: some were to charge, others to convey fascines or cloakfuls of earth to fill the trench of the Roman camp and build a ramp up to its breastworks, still others to carry scaling-ladders and poles with long hooks at their ends to tear down those breastworks. Then, the whole force began to tramp upwards, crushing bluebells, daisies, and yellow buttercups, but still directed by hand signal only.

Vercaswallon, riding a bay mare up the hill, surveyed his force, rippling waves of tall, moustachioed, tartan-trousered men. This time, he thought, we have to break through—or free Gaul is finished.

# 3

For the eighth time that morning, Caesar had climbed his watchtower. Still nothing, but intuitively he felt that somewhere, somehow, a pot was bubbling, ready to boil over. Under the watchful eyes of his aides and his trumpeter he paced back and forth, surveying the Gallic encampment, his own lines, and Alesia. Everything was quiet. He glanced up at the sun. It was at its zenith. He decided to descend for a cup of wine, a couple of cold, hardboiled eggs, and a chunk of bread. As he started toward the steps something made him check and look at the northwestern hill. Two eagles were circling above its summit.

He watched them for an instant, then glanced at the summit. What was that glinting in the sun? Spear-points, by Jupiter! And there, from the Gallic encampment, war-horns were braying, and cavalry and infantry were streaming.

"Sound the alarm!" Caesar shouted to his trumpeter. "Sound it!"

An instant before, Vercingetorix, too, had seen the spear-points. He turned to rush down from his tower.

"At last!" he cried over his shoulder to Critognat. "At last!"

285

# 4

The stillness was shattered. War-horns blared. Roman trumpets shrilled. In the plain, Gallic fighting-men shouted, flung missiles, and here and there assaulted the outer lines. On the Roman towers the catapults and ballistae thudded against their stop-bars as they shot flights of spears or hurled stones as big as wine kegs. Caesar stood on his tower, watching. From Alesia a torrent of gaunt warriors crossed the twenty-foot ditch and began to stumble among the spurs, lilies, and tombstones toward the double trenches guarding the ramparts across the plain.

But Caesar saw that Vercingetorix' main force was assembled but not committed. A glance toward the northwestern hill told him that his outpost had been overrun, and that the Gauls, miniature figures at this distance, were assaulting the camp. Well, the two legions there should hold them. He looked toward his right and suppressed an exclamation. Vercingetorix' main force from the city was not rushing toward the lines in the plain. Instead, they were charging eastward toward the contravallation to his right, along the flank of the south hill, carrying fascines, ladders, and long poles with hooks in the end.

It would be uphill for them, but sound tactics, Caesar realized. The lines in the plain had held, yet Gauls outside and inside were pinning down Roman troops all across that wide expanse. And at the point where Vercingetorix had chosen to attack there was only a single ditch and no spurs, lilies, or tombstones.

Caesar watched, lips in a straight line. In spite of the artillery and the defenders on the rampart, Vercingetorix' lean, wolf-hungry men bridged the ditch with fascines, put up scaling-ladders under the protection of overlapping shields — the so-called tortoise formation learned from the Romans — and tore at the breastworks with their grappling-hooks. Now, groups of the attackers were actually on top of the rampart. This was serious.

Caesar turned to glance toward the northwestern hill and saw a mounted courier riding hard between the lines toward his command tower. He hurried down the steps. It was the knight Gnaeus Racilius.

286

"The situation?" Caesar barked as Racilius slid from his mount.

"Bad, Imperator. The Gauls have filled the trench, built a ramp, and broken into the camp. They're flinging in fresh men."

Labienus was in command of an infantry camp to the north.

"Gallop to Labienus," Caesar ordered. "Tell him to take six cohorts from his camp. If that isn't enough, have him pull in troops from the nearest redoubts. Now, repeat."

Racilius repeated the orders, leaped on his horse, and galloped away to the left. At that instant a courier rushed up from the right.

"Vercingetorix is inside the line, Imperator," he gasped.

Caesar turned and leaped up the steps of the watchtower two at a time. From the top he surveyed the battle. His lines in the plain were holding. The men from Alesia were fighting furiously, but the Gauls from the encampment were doing little except hurling missiles, brandishing spears, and shouting. They had obviously had enough of the spurs, lilies and tombstones. Suppose, though, they were to attack the outer defences opposite where Vercingetorix was fighting?

As he thought this, an aide from Labienus struggled up the steps. The six cohorts, Caesar was informed, had not been enough. Labienus was pulling in eleven more cohorts from the redoubts to stop the Gauls, who were now pushing forward inside the camp on the northwestern hill.

Two legions and now almost another two to be committed at that point, Caesar told himself grimly. Soon he would run out of troops. He turned to look at the battle to his right. Vercingetorix' men were down from the rampart and forcing the Romans back. Two legions there — and not holding! A courier from Decimus Brutus clambered up the steps.

"Request for help, Imperator," he gasped. "Immediate. Most immediate!"

There was an infantry camp on the summit of the hill behind where Vercingetorix had broken through the contravallation, a camp commanded by Marcus Cicero and Gaius Fabius. It held reserves. Caesar glanced at his lines in the plain. If at this moment a serious attack were put in down there, then his reserves would

287

be needed. On the other hand —

He decided to gamble. He turned to two of his aides.

"To the legate Decimus Brutus," he ordered. "Tell him and Gaius Fabius to take a dozen cohorts and stop Vercingetorix. Repeat."

Caesar stood still an instant, making a rapid assessment. Another glance at the battle to his right and he saw that Vercingetorix' men, uphill or not, were still advancing. Desperate gamble or not, Vercingetorix must be stopped.

"To Antony in the plain," he ordered an aide. "Tell him to put cavalrymen on the ramparts."

Then, leaping down the steps, he jumped on Five-Toes, waved to his bodyguard to follow, and rode toward the battle to his right, collecting cohorts from the redoubts as he went. He reached the battle-scene at a gallop. A glance made the situation clear. The Gauls had won half the camp; careless of death, Vercingetorix' men were tearing away the legionaries' shields with their hands so that, as they themselves fell, their comrades behind could leap in and kill; and they outnumbered the Romans ten to one.

They could smell victory. But their right flank, overlapping the Roman left, was exposed. Caesar jumped from Five-Toes, seized a sword from a legionary, and ordered his trumpeter to sound the charge. The bodyguard and the cohorts sliced into Vercingetorix' right rear. Decimus Brutus' legionaries raised a cheer and held. The Gauls fought furiously, Vercingetorix in the forefront. Step by step they were forced back from the centre of the camp. At the rampart the fight hung static. A fresh cohort, rushing in, decided the issue. The rampart was cleared. As Vercingetorix strove to rally his men, Caesar, standing on the re-won rampart, stared down. Those gaunt men were spent. In spite of Vercingetorix' attempts, they were turning to trudge back up the hill to Alesia.

At that moment, a galloper from Labienus caught at his scarlet mantle.

"Imperator," he panted, "we're losing. Losing! The Gauls have almost carried the northwest camp."

288

"Cohorts from the redoubts?"

"The legate Labienus is bringing more in. But the Gauls are almost through. Through, Imperator!"

It was another moment of decision, not that there was much choice. If the Gauls broke through to join Vercingetorix' men, then the assault would come all along the enfeebled lines, and the Romans would be done for. Caesar turned to Decimus Brutus.

"You will hold here," he said, "with the troops you have. I'm off."

Waving to his bodyguard to follow and mounting Five-Toes, he rode down to the lines in the plain. Antony met him. Caesar reined in Five-Toes.

"Take a half-dozen men," he told him. "Gallop between the lines to the cavalry camp in the north. Lead horsemen outside our lines and around to come in on the Gallic rear," Caesar pointed to the northwestern camp, "up there."

"The lines here? In the plain, I mean?"

"We gamble, Antony. Our last throw. Off with you."

As Antony galloped off, Caesar rode on between the lines, collecting four cohorts and a detachment of cavalry from the redoubts along the route. They were his last reserves, his very last. Pray Mars and Venus, too, that the Gauls outside did not attack the lines in the plain.

He reached the northwestern camp and rode in its southern gates. It was a scene to appal him. The Gauls had won three-quarters of the camp. The tents behind them were down, the ground covered with dead and wounded men, and they scented victory. Their leader—Caesar knew him as Vercassivellaunus—was feeding in fresh troops. Behind the Roman lines Labienus, mounted on a powerful roan, had just received two new cohorts from the redoubts along the northern line and, waving his arms emphatically, was sending them in. Caesar led his bodyguard and the cavalry he had gathered in an attack on the Gallic right flank. It cost him a hundred men as the Gauls rushed reserves to meet him. But that charge and Labienus' two fresh cohorts did check the Gallic advance. As the cavalry extricated itself, Caesar's four cohorts arrived. Caesar put one to face the Gallic reserves and led the other three behind the Roman lines, shouting to the centurions, putting in a maniple here, and another there, to stiffen the line. The Gauls recognized his scarlet mantle. So did Vercaswallon.

For a moment the whole battle paused, as if both sides realized that here was to be the final, the deciding, hour. Vercaswallon moved fresh men into his line. On their side, Caesar and Labienus reconstituted their front.

"More cohorts?" Caesar shouted to Labienus.

"Three more to come," Labienus shouted back. "All we've got."

The two battle-lines were ready. With a roar both sides charged. Above, the eagles soared higher. From below the sounds of battle rose, steel on steel, shouts, yells, moans, shrieks, cries.

Caesar watched. The Romans were fighting uphill. They were holding against the downhill charge, but just barely.

He must not lose! Caesar leaped from Five-Toes, waved to his bodyguard to dismount, and, sword still in his hand, led them into the battle. Along the Roman lines the word spread. Caesar himself fighting! Foot by hard-won foot the legionaries began to push back the Gauls. Vercaswallon poured in fresh men again and again. Labienus, taking charge behind the Romans, fed in rested maniples. Foot by foot the Romans advanced until the Gauls were back on the steps of the ramparts they had breached and won.

There the battle hung. Caesar rushed back to Labienus. The three fresh cohorts had just come in. Caesar waved to them.

"Follow me!" he shouted, waving a red-dripping sword.

"Julius!" Labienus shouted. "Julius — come back!"

Caesar was already on his way. The cohorts he led forced back the centre of Vercaswallon's line and won that part of the rampart; and at that instant, riding hard, Antony's cavalry came over the summit. With a yell they charged downhill on to the Gallic rear. With an answering yell all along the line, the legionaries charged the faltering tribesmen.

The Gauls broke. The cavalry was amongst them, stabbing,

slicing. The legionaries joined in, slaying any group that still resisted and slaughtering those that fled. Caesar paused on the rampart. The battle for Gaul had been won. Won!

In the sky the eagles circled lower and still lower.


# 5


The next afternoon Fadius stood at the head of his century, crest on his helmet, rust-red cloak hanging from his shoulders. To his left, on a tribunal erected just inside the contravallation where Vercingetorix' men had broken through, Caesar sat bareheaded, face impassive, in his richly brocaded proconsul's robe. Beside him stood his lictors. Behind him were ranged his legates, and in a semicircle around the tribunal his bodyguard was on the alert. On either side of the plot of levelled ground, as far as the gap made in the fortifications, centuries picked from the legions were drawn up, parade armour glittering in the sun.

Fadius was sweating. Today was as cloudless and as warm as yesterday. The gaunt thousands of Alesia's garrison had already stumbled down the hill and through the gap to fling their weapons down and be herded into compounds. The legionaries had watched them speculatively. Last night Caesar had promised each Roman soldier one of those prisoners as a slave to use or sell as he wished—and that was a bonus to add to the three months' extra pay already guaranteed.

Fadius wondered casually what he would do with his prisoner-slave, thinking at the same time that those men had been brave fighters. His gaze returned to the tribunal. The Gallic nobles, disarmed, were kneeling one by one in front of Caesar, bowing their heads to the ground in token of submission; then, at a casual wave of Caesar's hand, two guards would lead each one away to the camp behind the tribunal. But where, Fadius asked himself, was Vercingetorix? He turned to glance up at Alesia, its battlements etched against the blue sky.

# 6

Caesar looked down at the chieftain kneeling before him. He knew the man. It was Critognat. So he kept him on his knees. Let him look at the captured Gallic standards—carved poles portraying defiant boars, slavering wolves, snarling panthers, and the like, flung carelessly in a tumbled heap in front of the tribunal— eighty-four taken in yesterday's victory. Let him realize the folly of defying Caesar and Rome.

He glanced up at Alesia. Yesterday after his defeat, Vercingetorix had led his hopeless, weary men up the hill again to the city; while outside, the rest of the relieving army had fled like rabbits with the hounds of Hades after them. Caesar's men were too bone-weary to pursue, and besides, they had to collect the Roman dead and wounded. Not until midnight had Antony led the cavalry after the fugitives.

Yes, this victory had cost the lives of legionaries, and Critognat, he decided, would be one of those to pay for it. Let him wait with Vercassivellaunus in a dungeon in Rome until Caesar's triumph roared through the streets.

He gave the signal indicating that Critognat was to go into a special group. The other nobles would merely lose property and then be set free, for he still had to win over Gaul. He had already decided to release all his Aeduan prisoners. That act of clemency would mean that, under Eporedorix, the Aeduans would return to their loyalty. He was considering sending the Arvernians, too, back to their homes. Such an act would strengthen the hands of Gubannitio, the uncle who had opposed Vercingetorix. Besides, the Aeduans and the Arvernians were the most Romanized of the tribes.

Another noble was led forward. He fell to his knees. If Servilia could see him now, the victor, Caesar thought suddenly. Or Pompey. Or all of Rome. Only — only —

He glanced up again at Alesia. Where was Vercingetorix? Had he fallen on his sword?

Without Vercingetorix, he realized, his victory, his triumph, would not be altogether complete.

# 7

It was time to go. Vercingetorix stared at the deserted square of Alesia. Where were the high hopes, the pride, when, so long ago as it seemed now, he had stood, ten feet tall, leader of free Gaul, in front of the Council at Bibracte? Where was the exultation of two months ago when, with Comm, he had watched Caesar and his legions retreating from freed Gaul? Retreating!

His eyes were unseeing. Beside him, his black stallion, Fury, richly caparisoned, tossed its head and pawed with its foot.

"Quiet, lad," he said, returning to the present. "Just a moment, lad."

But his mind turned in on itself again. This morning, in the Council of Chieftains, he had offered his body to be delivered, dead or alive, to Caesar in return for clemency. "Surrender" was the word the envoys had brought back. No terms. No conditions. No guarantees. Surrender!

"Well then," he had cried to the Council, "let us charge out and die. Free men to the end. Free!"

Critognat had drawn his sword and flung it high. No one else had followed. They had shuffled their feet, looked at one another. At last, one had spoken.

"The men," he had said. "Starving. No fight left in them."

And no fight left in these chieftains either, Vercingetorix had realized. But he himself had a choice left. He could draw his sword now, at this moment, and fall on it. It was what a Roman would do. He was not a Roman. No, he had fought and lost. So he would face whatever was to come.

He took his helmet, the one with the golden wings flaring backward, and fixed it on his head. He mounted Fury. He paused a moment to check his accoutrements. His bronze shield, enamelled in blue in sweeping curves, was on his left arm. His gold-hilted sword was in its jewelled scabbard, his tartan cloak hanging lightly from his shoulders. He hefted the lance in his right hand and gathered the reins with his left. The sun was in his eyes as he rode along the silent streets toward the eastern gate. As he turned the black stallion down the pathway, he could see

Caesar's fortifications, still almost a mile away.

Was there a yoke and rods, as there had been for Acco, waiting for him there?

"Careful, lad," he said to Fury, as the stallion stumbled on a stone. "Easy, lad," and forced the thought out of his mind. Might not Caesar be clement? Had they not been friends once?

But not now. Face it.

He drew in deep breaths. Never had he been so conscious of the scent of each bruised herb and flower. Never had he been so alive to each call of a bird, to the warmth of the sun, to the clear outlines of the hills.

Guenome — his sons — would he ever see them again?

He put that anguish aside. Here he was at last—no, too soon— at the gap in Caesar's lines. Vercingetorix straightened his back and rode through. He was aware with the fringes of his mind of the legionaries, the lictors, the legates. But his central consciousness was concentrated on Caesar, sitting in his curule chair on the tribunal, staring at him.

Until that instant Vercingetorix had not known what he would do. Now he did.

"Fury, lad," he said with a gentle tug of his hand and a pressure of his heels.

The stallion tossed its head and whinnied. Then it responded to the signal. Caracoling, it carried Vercingetorix three times — the magic number—around the tribunal. Vercingetorix held his lance high, his head just as proudly high. After the third circle he reined in Fury, dismounted, and dropping the reins stepped in front of the stallion. Chin firm, he looked up at Caesar for an instant. To the silent watchers that instant seemed almost interminable. Then, bending, he placed his lance on the ground to his right and his shield on the left. Straightening, he undid the golden brooch at his neck and, taking off his tartan cloak, laid it, too, on the ground. Drawing his sword, he held it up high a moment, its blade gleaming in the sunlight, then put it to the right of the cloak and added the jewelled scabbard. Last of all, he lifted the golden helmet from his head, looked at it, then placed it on the ground to his left. Then, once more he faced Caesar for an

294

instant, proud and tall, yellow hair bright. Next, quietly, deliberately, he sat down on his cloak, cross-legged, folded his arms and bowed his head. Behind Caesar a legate coughed. Among the legionaries men stirred uneasily.

Caesar stared down at his friend-enemy, his mind seething. Somehow, in his moment of victory, that man down there had taken the victory away. Should he order the rods?

And make him a martyr-hero for all Gaul!

The thought seemed to be spoken to him. He compressed his lips. There was a better, a more bitter punishment: that dungeon under the Capitoline Hill — no light, no breath of fresh air, no hope.

He stood up.

"Take him away!" he said violently. "At once. Take him!"

## 8

At almost the same moment, in Vercingetorix' mansion in Gergovia, his uncle, Gubannitio, walked down the broad steps that led into the garden at the back. Guenome, he saw, was clipping late-blooming roses.

He paused to look at her. In spite of his opposition to her husband, he was quite fond of his niece-in-law — gentle, womanly, and attractive.

He coughed. She turned and saw him. She had gathered an armful of white and red roses, and that armful set off her ivory skin and the smooth blackness of her eyebrows and her hair.

"Uncle!" she exclaimed, and then, "News? Have you news?"

Gubannitio walked up to her and nodded.

"Shouted across the countryside," he said.

Her arms tightened around the roses.

"Good?" she breathed. "Or — or — "

"Beaten," he answered. "We Gauls, beaten. Totally."

Her hands flew to her cheeks, the roses scattering at her feet.

"Oh, no!" she breathed. And then in violent protest. "It can't be. I won't believe it. No! He'll still win. He must."

"The army's gone. You'll have to face it. Not a man left."

"He?" she whispered.

"He'll have to surrender, Guenome. No food left. We know that. He will have surrendered by now."

"Oh, uncle, oh!"

She had fallen into his arms, sobbing. Poor girl, he thought.

"I warned him," he said above her head. "Time and again. Now, he knows. Now he knows that no one can fight Caesar and win."

She drew back, still half-sobbing.

"Caesar! What will he do to him?"

Gubanittio looked at her. "The Romans have a saying—'Woe to the conquered.' "

She broke away from him, her eyes wild.

"I'll go to Caesar," she cried. "I'll go on my knees to him. He'll listen. I'll make him listen!"

Gubannitio was sorry that he had been right. He shook his head.

"No use, child."

"I'll go anyway. My maids! Where are they? I'll get ready. At once."

He caught her and held her. She struck at him.

"Let me go! I tell you, let me go!"

He still held her.

"Your children, Guenome," he said. "Listen to me. Your children — yours and his."

She stopped struggling. "Oh, I know, I know," she cried. "But why? Oh — why!"

At the bush beside her, a hummingbird hovered, wings a blur, drinking nectar from a rose.

# PART TWO
## 50-48 BC
# RAZOR'S EDGE

# CHAPTER I

ALMOST TWO YEARS HAD GONE BY SINCE ALESIA. By the Roman calendar it was the first day of December. In Alexandria, on the second terrace of the palace of the Ptolemies, Cleopatra, robe flung around her against the coolness of first dawn, was saying stormily to Apollodorus,

"I won't put up with it. I'll send her back to him, cut to ribbons with the whip. He'll find out who's Queen of Egypt, that bastard."

Apollodorus rubbed the sleep out of his eyes.

"Who's the bastard?" he asked cautiously. "And what's the trouble?"

"Pothinus, that's who. I wake up this morning. What do I find? A new woman sent in to be head of my maids. Glauke, that's her name. She knows that I know she's a spy for that bastard, that — that eunuch! When she crawls back to him, flogged, he'll know who's Queen."

This would have to be handled carefully.

"I wouldn't do that, my Queen," Apollodorus said.

"Why not? I have supporters."

"Consider, my Queen. Your father died a year ago. By the terms of his will, you and your half-brother were married — "

"That sneaky brat. Sucking up to Pothinus."

"And crowned as joint Pharaohs of Egypt," Apollodorus continued. "But, by your father's will, the eunuch Pothinus was appointed Chairman of a Regency Council. That Council is to rule until your brother is sixteen. He's only eleven now."

Cleopatra stamped her sandal on the flags of the floor. "I want power now. Not five years from now. Right now!"

She was vibrant, beautiful, Apollodorus thought, her eyes flashing, head up, auburn hair a tousled torrent on her shoulders.

But she must be gentled, somehow. He took a step toward her.

"I must remind you again, my Queen, that, as of this hour, Pothinus holds the army in the palm of one hand and the nobles of Egypt in the other."

Her face was still mutinous, but she was beginning to think. She turned and walked to the balustrade. He joined her. She was staring down at the Great Harbour, the ships from every port in the Mediterranean jammed into it, the cables creaking, the raucous gulls swooping over and among them. In the light of first dawn, those ships seemed a little unreal. Apollodorus leaned his elbows on the balustrade.

"Patience, my Queen," he said softly. "Who knows what will happen next year or next month or, for that matter, tomorrow?"

"I hate waiting."

"Wait for your moment," Apollodorus said. He paused. "Remember how three years ago," he went on, "when the Surena defeated and killed Crassus, you, my Queen, thought the Parthians might sweep the Romans out of Asia? Where is the Surena now? Murdered by his king. The Parthian army? Smashed last year in Syria by Gaius Cassius." He ventured to put a hesitant hand on her arm. "Those reports from Rome," he reminded her. "Trouble between Pompey the Great and Julius Caesar, they say. Suppose a Roman civil war comes? Think of the opportunities, then. I say again, 'Who knows the future, my Queen?' That's why I argue patience. Wait for your moment."

Cleopatra turned to him, a smile on her lips.

"You're good for me, old friend. Yes, I'll wait — for now."


2


In Gaul the rim of the sun was edging the eastern horizon. In Gergovia, Guenome and her uncle-in-law, Gubannitio, were watching her two sons, only a year between them, playing catch on the lawn at the back of the garden. They were handsome, sturdy lads—the elder yellow-headed like his father, the younger with Guenome's raven hair and ivory-white skin.

300

"If only their father could see them," Guenome whispered.

"The dew is still heavy," Gubannitio said. "And their feet are bare."

"Won't hurt them. They're as healthy as young bears." Then, still watching the boys, she asked, "Have you heard anything? About him, I mean?"

Gubannitio wasn't about to tell her what he'd heard. He shook his head.

"Any chance of a pardon?" she asked.

Gubannitio thought of the bitter fighting throughout Gaul after Alesia as Caesar stamped out flare after flare of revolt, the aftermath of the rising Vercingetorix had led. The Roman had become more and more ruthless. When Uxellodunum of the Cadurcans, the last town to hold out, had been forced to surrender a year ago, Caesar had had both hands of all the garrison lopped off. He shook his head again.

Guenome turned to him.

"Why not? Gaul is submissive now." She smiled a bitter smile. "When Lucter, after Uxellodunum, sought refuge with an Arvernian noble, that noble turned him over to Caesar—in chains. Caesar has nothing to fear. And he came to terms with Comm, didn't he? Comm rules an Atrebatian kingdom in Britain now. So why not my husband?"

Gubannitio, a spare, grey-haired old man, did not meet her eyes. In these past two years he had protected her from her own kinsfolk and her husband's family, since both groups were eyeing Vercingetorix' possessions greedily. But how did you tell a wife that there was no hope, that she must adapt to a life without the husband she loved, or else take another man? She was too young and lovely to do without one. But she wasn't ready yet.

The elder boy had missed a catch and was running after the ball, while the younger was yelling, "Butterfingers! Butterfingers!"

Guenome had turned to watch them.

"Already they're forgetting him," she breathed. And then, with a shrug, "Why not? Everyone else has."

"Caesar is in Cisalpine Gaul," Gubannitio said gruffly. "I'll send a courier with a letter to him."

"Oh, Uncle! Uncle!"

She had flung her arms around him and was kissing him and crying at the same time. Gaul was submissive now, Gubannitio was thinking. And this past year Caesar had been flattering the nobles, charming them. Yet there was still no hope, really. Even if he were inclined to be clement, he could not risk letting Vercingetorix return to Gaul. Yet this girl must have hope.

"There — there," he said, patting her shoulder awkwardly.

## 3

At this moment, in Massilia, Fadius was walking up the street toward Baculus' tavern. He was on his way to Cisalpine Gaul to rejoin Caesar's bodyguard, but he had found that he could spend a couple of days — and nights — with Chione en route.

At the thought of her, he quickened his pace. Because of the months of fighting since Alesia and the constant journeying in this past year, he had only managed three all-too-brief visits with her, and his last furlough had been five months ago. But he had been thinking. Why not take her to Cisalpine Gaul with him? There was peace now, and all winter to look forward to. Even when spring came Gaul would be safe. So, why not?

She would be delighted, he knew. There was a broad smile on his face as he reached Baculus' tavern and stepped through the doorway, standing still for a moment to accustom his eyes to the half-gloom. At this early hour, two slaves, he saw, were on their knees scrubbing the floor, and Baculus himself was at the back, piling the benches and moving the tables out of the way. Fadius filled his lungs.

"Anybody home?" he bellowed.

Baculus turned and saw him. "Fadius!" By the ass of Hercules, it's Fadius," he exclaimed and stumped over.

The two men embraced. Then Baculus hurried to the back, pulled out a table and a bench, and said,

"Sit down, man. Sit." He stumped over to the bar. "A cup of wine? Something to eat? Let's see, what have I got? Too early for anything hot, Fadius. Hard-boiled eggs? Bread? Salt? That do you?"

Fadius had seated himself. "Fine," he said. "Just fine." And then: "Chione?"

Baculus was carrying over the wine and food.

"In a moment," he said, setting down the food and wine. "She's in the bakery."

"Bakery?"

"I've bought it. It was next door, you'll remember. So I bought it and," he gestured, "put a passage-way through to it back there. Put Chione in charge. It's working fine. Just fine."

He was talking too much, much too much for Baculus, Fadius was thinking. Almost as if he were nervous.

"Well, I'll go and get her," Baculus said. "She'll be glad to see you. Glad."

He stumped away, swinging his game leg in a half-circle. Fadius took a thoughtful sip of wine. Something was up. But what?

He stood up as Chione came through the passage-way. She ran to him, crying, "Titus, oh, Titus!" and kissed and hugged him. Yet he felt something lacking as she drew away to look at him. Baculus stumped in, glanced at the two of them, went to the bar, and brought cups of wine for Chione and himself. The three of them sat down. Fadius had intended to burst out with his plan for Chione and Cisalpine Gaul, but something — a sort of strained atmosphere—held him back. He nibbled at an egg, looking from one to the other as they made small talk. Neither would really meet his eyes. Why? he wondered. He had expected Chione to drag him upstairs at once. Why not?

Suddenly, abruptly, Baculus slammed his cup down on the table and looked Fadius full in the face.

"You can hit me if you want," he said gruffly. "Chione and I are living together."

There was a rush of blood to Fadius' head. He half rose, hand

303

going to the hilt of his sword, seeing nothing but Baculus' face in a red haze.

"I won't hit back," he heard Baculus say, as if from a great distance.

Fadius stayed half-crouched for a long instant. Then, his hand coming away from his sword, he sank back on the bench, slowly. He heard Chione draw in a long breath and he looked at her. She was gazing at him, fear in her eyes.

"Why?" he asked hoarsely. "Why?"

It was Baculus who answered.

"The two of us working together," he said heavily. "Day after day. Not," he gestured to Chione, "that she didn't — doesn't — love you. But you're never here. A woman needs it, too, Titus. As she said, 'Feast or famine.' So then — then, finally, it just happened."

Fadius drained his cup and got up. "I'll be going," he said, and his own voice sounded strange and far away to him.

"No!" Chione exclaimed, jumping to her feet. "I want to explain, Titus — darling."

"Nothing to explain. I should have expected it. It's natural. Natural. And the two of you get along so well together, don't you? The tavern, the bakery — you've made yourself a nice nest, Chione — "

He stopped, realizing the bitterness of his words, and turned to the doorway.

"Please!" Chione cried, running after him. "Sit down with us, please. Just for a moment, anyway."

"Wish you would," Baculus said. "I'd feel better. Right now I feel like taking that sword of yours and sticking it into my gut."

"No need to," Fadius answered.

"Another cup of wine with us — at least," Chione pleaded, catching his arm. "Or — or," she glanced at Baculus, "you can come upstairs with me — you won't mind, will you?" she said to Baculus.

Baculus shook his head. "Go right ahead, Titus. We're friends here. Friends. And you had her first—looked after her—brought her here. Paid her way. No, go ahead the two of you—and give him a good screw, Chione. A real good one. The works."

304

"Come on, darling," Chione urged, pulling at him. "Come. I'm ready, darling."

Fadius disengaged his arm, gently but firmly.

"No," he said. "I'd like it. I know that. But no. I'll drink a cup of wine with you. That's all. And wish you luck, too."

They sat down again. They tried to talk, but it was difficult. Fadius was about to get up again when he remembered something.

"That Gaul I gave you," he said to Chione. "The one Caesar turned over to me after Alesia. How is he?"

Baculus shrugged. "Keeps running away," he answered. "I've flogged him time and again. Still tries to run."

"So now I have him turning the mill," Chione added. "Out in the bakery."

Fadius could visualize it, the outer rotating cylinder pinched in at the centre, and the inner core, and the endless tramp around and around, pushing the bar. He thought of Alesia and the fighting and Vercingetorix riding around Caesar's tribunal on his black stallion — and where was he now? He thought of Uxellodunum and the ten chopping-blocks and the piled-up hands, the fingers still twitching, and the stumps thrust into the vats of boiling tar before the dazed fighters for freedom were released to stumble, maimed, to their homes. Perhaps it was because he himself was suffering that he felt a twinge of pity.

"Bring that Gaul in," he said, his voice harsh.

Baculus turned and shouted to his slaves. A few moments later two of them led in the Gaul. Fadius stared at him. At Alesia he had been gaunt and starved, yet there had still been pride in his bearing. Now he stood there, head bent, back scarred by the whips, mouth hanging open, eyes blurred by a sick, glazed despair.

"What's his value?" Fadius asked roughly.

"Why?" Baculus asked.

"I'm going to free him. What's his value?"

"Free him?" Baculus asked in bewilderment. "Free him!"

"That's right." Fadius stood up, pulling a bag of coins from his belt. "I said, 'How much?'"

Chione stood up, "Not a sesterce from you, Titus. Not one.

You gave him to me. I give him back."

"I don't give a gift and ask for it back," Fadius said stubbornly. "So, how much?"

Baculus stood up, too. "I'm with Chione on this," he said. "You want to free him, he's yours. And that's it, Titus. No more arguments. He's yours."

Fadius hesitated, then he said,

"We'll all give him his freedom. Write the document, Chione. I'll make my mark. So will Baculus. And you'll sign it, too, Chione. Make sure no one picks him up. And Baculus, have that chain knocked off his ankle."

Twenty minutes later, everything done, the Gaul was brought back. Fadius spoke to him in his halting Celtic. He had to repeat before a light of comprehension appeared in the Gaul's eyes. He laughed, a sob in the laugh, and broke into a torrent of words.

"Yes," Fadius said. "Free to go home. And here," he pulled coins from his bag, "here's something to get there with."

The Gaul grabbed the coins, looked at them, and suddenly fell on his knees before Fadius, grasping his thighs with both arms, mingling sobs with broken words.

"Get up, man," Fadius said sharply. "You're a free man now. Free."

He reached down and helped him up. "You'll see he gets out of Massilia safely, won't you?" he asked Baculus, as the Gaul stood there. "I mean, he'll have the document. But you know our traders."

"I'll see to it," Baculus promised.

"Well then, I'll be off." He held out a hand. "Good luck, Baculus."

The two men clasped hands. Fadius turned to Chione, holding out his hand. Disregarding it, she rushed into his arms, raining kisses on his face, hugging him tightly, saying, "Thank you! Thank you!" over and over. Fadius began to disengage himself.

"You won't forget me, will you?" she asked, looking up into his face.

"No. I won't forget you. Well, good-bye now. Good-bye."

He got outside somehow. The sunlight was a glare in his eyes.

He stumbled over a stone into a puffed-up, pompous merchant who was coming up the street.

"Oaf," the merchant said, giving him a shove. "Drunken sot!"

It all exploded within him. Seizing the merchant by neck and bottom, he pitched him across the street. The man's slaves began to move forward. Hand on sword Fadius strode toward them. They took one look at this tall, broad-shouldered soldier and gave way. He was sorry. He wanted someone to cross his path — to oppose him — then let that man find out, let him.

People shrank away from him. As he marched on, gradually his senses returned. One couldn't blame Chione, he reflected bitterly. A woman could love you and still want security. Security! That's what all women wanted. Love took second place. That was it.

Love! When you loved you gave away a piece of yourself, he realized. And when the one you loved was taken away from you, a piece of yourself, of your inner self, was wrenched out of you — forever — and the sense of loss, the pain. Never again, he resolved fiercely. No, take them and use them. But never again give them yourself.

So, back to the army. Back to Caesar — and let no man cross his path.

## 4

In Cisalpine Gaul morning light was flooding into the solarium of a villa in the environs of Placentia and bathing Servilia and Caesar with its radiance. The two of them were enjoying a late breakfast-luncheon. Servilia glanced out at an ornamental lake. Geese, ducks, and swans were floating on it, stopping every now and then to dip down their beaks for a succulent morsel.

"Absurd that by our calendar it's the first of December," Servilia said lazily, dipping a piece of bread into a goblet of wine, "when it's really only September."

"I'll do something about that, some time," Caesar replied.

"It was *so* good last night, darling," Servilia said, glancing at him. "After so long. Was it just as good for you?"

"Wonderful!" he answered. He touched the fingers of his right hand to his lips and reached over to put the kiss on her palm. She sighed contentedly.

"I'm so happy you've taken the morning off," she said.

Caesar yawned, stretching both arms above his head. Then, he looked at her, appreciating the tousled hair done up carelessly on top of her head, and the full, pink-nippled breasts tempting him through the thin, delicate robe.

"I've been on the go—at full stretch—too long," he said. And then, since Servilia had only arrived on the previous evening and they had been much too interested in each other to spend time in talk, "What did you think of my book? On the Gallic wars, I mean?"

Servilia nibbled on an olive. "As I wrote you — the style is excellent. Superb, in fact. Such clarity. So vivid in descriptions."

"And the subject-matter?"

"Britain and Germany — the descriptions of the customs and manner of living — most interesting. The battles — " she shrugged her lovely shoulders, careless of the fact that her robe slipped down to expose her left breast—"as a woman, well, all that killing — "

"The mob in Rome likes battles — and violence."

"Did you have to massacre all those people?" She shuddered a little. "Women and children, too. I could see it too clearly, Julius."

It was Caesar's turn to shrug. "They were not Romans. Just barbarians. In war, darling, only one thing matters — to win." He paused and smiled, watching Servilia put shrimps, slices of hardboiled eggs, and lettuce on a slice of bread, and bite into it. He liked to see her eat after love-making. She enjoyed it so heartily.

"In your letters, you and Balbus," he went on, "seem most concerned about Pompey."

Servilia took a gulp of wine to wash down the bite in her mouth and said,

308

"You should be, too, Julius. The Conservatives, and Cornelia, are pushing him to the edge."

"When it comes to the point—Pompey will be a balky mule."

She leaned across the table. "That's where you're wrong, Julius. Dead wrong. Pompey enjoys his position — head of the Republic, Spain, and seven legions there. You are the only possible threat. He'd like you out of the way. Why else did he say you'd not be consul, not ever?"

Caesar looked at her sharply. "Did he really say that?"

"Reported by reliable agents to Balbus and to Curio. Curio," she added, "is worth the money you spent to buy him. Clever. And," she added with a laugh, "a different man since he married Fulvia."

"Really?"

"No longer homosexual. Or, at least, bisexual now. To come back to the point, Caesar, consider. Didn't Pompey get two legions from you on the pretext that they were to be sent against the Parthians? Where are those two legions? Not in Syria. In Italy."

"That's true." Caesar frowned. "On the other hand, darling, only the diehards want to crush me. Most of the senators desire peace. So does the middle class. Cisalpine Gaul is at its most prosperous—a whole new market in the Gaul I've pacified. It's a firm base for me."

He rose to pace around the solarium.

"But the middle class," he stopped to face her, "they don't want any disturbance. Pompey must know that."

"What if I were to tell you," Servilia said quietly, "that today perhaps even as we talk, Gaius Marcellus, the consul who married your grand-niece, Octavia, intends to propose in the Senate that you give up your provinces and disband your legions on the first day of next March."

Caesar stared at her. "The Senate won't dare!"

"The purpose is to force you to Rome, shorn of power like a sheep of wool, to be prosecuted. What would you do then, my Julius?"

Caesar's hands were clenched. "You know as well as I. I

309

haven't reached this height to abdicate my position meekly—or, like that sheep you mentioned, to stand still to have my throat cut."

She rose swiftly, her hand at her throat. "Does that mean — civil war?" Then, she came over and into his arms. "Oh, no, Julius. Not that, please. Not Roman against Roman—again."

He smiled down at her. "It won't come to that, dearest. I'll need a show of strength. I've only one legion here—so I'll alert two more. More importantly, I—no, we—will draft letters for Hirtius to take to Pompey. I'll remind him of his promise for me to stand for the consulship in absentia. I'll call to mind our long friendship. I'll point out the need for peace. You'll see. It will all work out."

She looked up at him. "Oh, Julius, I hope so."

"It will." He smiled down at her. "And now, my sweet, there's time. That is, if you want?"

She hugged him tightly. "Oh yes, darling. Yes."


# 5


As Caesar lifted Servilia in his arms, Pompey limped out to the pergola of his villa above Naples. He stood looking down at the city, rose-tinted in the sunlight. His gouty leg was almost better, and today the stomach pains which had bothered him for two years seemed to have eased.

He broke wind and felt still better. Had he taken the right course, he wondered, in agreeing to let Gaius Marcellus go ahead today?

He worked his lips in and out, thinking about it. He was contented with his position—recognized as the most important man in the Republic—and that with the blessing of the Senate. Caesar was the only wasp at the banquet, demanding to be consul again. If he were allowed the post, who knew what radical proposals he'd bring forward to upset the status quo? Besides, Cato, Domitius, Bibulus, and the Marcelli were determined to smash him. Was there anything Caesar could do?

Pompey limped over to a couch and sat down. Nothing, he

decided comfortably. Labienus had written, assuring him that, after all these years of fighting, Caesar's soldiers were ready to mutiny. The officers of the two legions he had filched from his rival agreed with that assurance. No, Caesar was a wasp shut up in a jar. If the Senate ordered him to give up his provinces, he would have no recourse except to yield.

Arranging a couple of cushions, he lay back on the couch, his eyes already closing. The Senate ought to be meeting at this moment, he reflected sleepily.

## 6

In Rome, the florid face of Gaius Marcellus, the presiding consul, was flushed with triumph. A crowd of senators was gathered around him. On the other side of the great hall next to Pompey's theatre — the burnt Senate-House had not yet been restored — only a few of the Caesar-clique were clustered around Servilia's husband, Silanus.

Marcellus glanced at Curio, the tribune. With him sat two of the tribunes-elect, Marcus Antonius and Quintus Cassius. What would Curio do this time? He had sat quiescent while a motion that Caesar be ordered to give up his provinces and disband his legions on the due date, namely the first day of March in the coming year, had been passed. Would he continue to sit still for this motion that Pompey the Great retain both his command in Italy and his proconsulship of the two Spains? Marcellus raised a hand. His voice boomed through the hall:

"I declare the motion passed."

"Veto," Antony whispered savagely to Curio. "Interpose your veto."

Curio did not move. As the senators straggled back to their seats, Marcellus, swelling with pride, lifted his hand again.

"Since the business before the Senate is now completed," he began.

Curio rose. He lifted a languid hand.

"Most noble senators," he said, "I have a motion to make, one that is very much for the good of the Republic, that is, if the

311

noble senators are really eager for peace — peace to enjoy their palaces and their villas, the peace that all Italy wants."

He paused. Marcellus' face was still flushed, but this time with apprehension. But the senators were looking at Curio. He raised his voice and, abruptly, his seeming languor left him.

"I said to you last May," he went on, "and you agreed, that what is illegal for one citizen is illegal for another, that all extraordinary commands are unconstitutional and against the interests of the rule of the Senate and, more importantly, contrary to the good of the Republic. Why should any citizen be so exalted that he is above all laws? Today, very properly, you have ordered Gaius Julius Caesar to lay down his governorships on the due date, the Kalends of next March. So why should you permit another citizen to retain two commands — two — contrary to custom and precedent?"

He looked around and dropped his voice.

"I mean no disrespect to the achievements of that great man, Gnaeus Pompeius Magnus. But why grant him what you refuse Gaius Julius Caesar? There are two men at present above the law — Pompey and Caesar. You vote to smash one, to bow down to the other. What does that contradiction mean? I'll tell you, noble senators. War! Civil war! How can we avoid it? Simple. I move that, as of this moment, the extraordinary commands and powers of *both* Gaius Julius Caesar and Gnaeus Pompeius Magnus be cancelled. Let the Senate, not those two, rule the Republic. Thus, we will be assured of peace. Thus, we will have security, not fear. There is my motion, noble senators."

"I second the motion," Antony roared.

"I refuse to put the motion," Marcellus cried.

But the senators were on their feet, shouting:

"Divide! Divide!"

With a helpless gesture, Marcellus assented. Curio stood where he was. Even he was not prepared for the rush of senators toward him. The Clerk of the Senate announced the count. Three hundred and seventy senators were massed around Curio — only twenty-two about Marcellus.

"You fools!" Cato was shouting. "You asses. You've voted

312

against both the motions you've just passed. Both of them!"

Marcellus strode to his chair. He faced the hall. He shook his fist at the senators.

"You've voted for Caesar," he cried in a choked voice. "For Caesar as tyrant. Tyrant!"

Gathering his consul's toga around him, he rushed from the hall.

"Brilliant," Antony was saying to Curio, a little later. "Absolutely brilliant."

The two of them, along with Quintus Cassius, were in the tavern of the Three Bulls at the upper end of the Subura. It was a high-class establishment which at night put on a show and had rooms at the back for the better class of prostitutes.

"It was really not too much of a gamble," Curio answered. "Last May the Senate passed the same motion, although it wasn't enforced. What the diehards forget is that most senators don't want even the chance of civil war." He finished his beaker and clapped his hands for a refill. "Today was merely another move on the chess-board," he added. "Gaius Marcellus will be back with another proposal."

"What then?" asked Quintus Cassius, a swarthy man who had to be shaved twice a day and was showing a shadow.

"Cato, Domitius, Bibulus, the Marcelli — they're all after Caesar like dogs after a bitch in heat. Their problem is to get Pompey to declare openly against Caesar."

"Caesar doesn't believe Pompey will go that far," Antony pointed out.

"Caesar is wrong," Curio said flatly. He sipped at his wine, and set down the goblet. "In ten days' time I'll be ex-tribune and you two will be tribunes. You'll need hawks' eyes." He got up, leaving his goblet half filled. "Well, friends, I must be off."

"The lady Fulvia?" Quintus Cassius suggested slyly.

"Truth in jest," Curio replied equably. "She puts ambition into a man." \

"No more boys?" Antony asked with a leer.

"Who needs boys with a woman like her?" Curio answered. With a wave of his hand he left.

"He's a changed man," Antony observed thoughtfully. "She must be quite a woman."

"You'd like to get into that, wouldn't you?" Quintus Cassius said.

Antony nodded. "But what you and I must consider, Quintus, is how to protect Caesar."

Quintus played with his goblet. "Looks like war to me," he said. "That is, unless Caesar gives in."

Antony slapped a hand down on the table. "Not Caesar," he proclaimed. "Never Caesar. He won't give in."

As he and Quintus Cassius sat in the tavern, Curio reached the tremendous palace on the Palatine that since Clodius' death had been his. Fulvia came down from the tablinum to meet him. She had already heard of his victory in the Senate.

"Wonderful!" she exclaimed, embracing him. "I'd love to have seen their faces," she added. "Cato, Domitius—they were so certain they had it in their basket."

Curio kissed her lingeringly. "Now?" he asked.

She rotated her pelvis against him for an instant, then stepped back.

"I'd like to talk first." She took his hand and led him into the Gallic salon that she had recently had done—Gallic arms, murals of villages, forests, and waterfalls with bare-breasted women and naked warriors interspersed. In the centre of the room stood a copy of the famous sculpture of a Gaul who, having just killed his wife, was holding her limp, collapsed figure by one arm while, looking back at his enemies, savage rage and pride on his face, he was thrusting his sword down into his heart.

"What do you do now?" she asked, seating herself.

Curio stood, brows knitted. "In ten days' time, as soon as I'm ex-tribune, I'm off to join Caesar."

"Why?"

"War. It's coming. I intend to be on the winning side."

"The leaders of my gangs? Shall I get in touch with them?"

Curio nodded. "There'll be work for them, when the time comes."

"And then," Fulvia said, rising, her eyes flashing, "then, I'll

314

show those bastards what a woman can do. I'll show them I haven't forgotten him — my Clodius."

"You really were in love with him, weren't you?" Curio said.

"Yes." Then, in a quick change of mood she came over to him. "But he's dead. And you," she fondled him with her hand, "you're alive. Yes, very much alive, aren't you?"

He put his arms around her fiercely, almost savagely.

"I'll make you forget," he said into her hair. "Right now. Yes, right now."

As Curio said this, in the Tullianum, below the Capitoline Hill, Vercingetorix was sitting on the stone floor, hands clasped loosely on his crossed knees. He could only dimly see the circular wall of his prison.

How often had he paced around and around the circuit of that wall? Never a ray of daylight! Never a breath of free air!

Why hadn't he fallen on his sword that last day at Alesia, he thought bitterly. Why did he not starve himself now? He had tried. His gaolers had forced food into him.

Besides, as long as one was alive, surely there might still be hope. Surely at some time Julius Caesar might think of him. After all, was it a crime to fight for freedom? And there was Guenome—and his sons—surely the gods could not be so cruel. Surely at some time he would see them again. So, up. Keep his strength.

He forced himself to rise and to pace around and around the prison, dragging his chains after him. In the villa near Placentia, Caesar lay in Servilia's arms, their legs entwined.

# CHAPTER II

A CHILL, DAMP WIND from the Adriatic was whistling through the streets and houses of Ravenna. In his governor's mansion facing on the main square, Caesar looked around at the group he had assembled on this morning of the 25th of December. Balbus, who had arrived from Rome the previous midnight, was obviously weary. There were shadows, too, under Servilia's eyes. Asinius Pollio, the ingenuous young man who had recently joined his staff, was fresh-eyed and smooth-cheeked. Hirtius, his loyal quartermaster, had lines of worry deeply etched in his cheeks and on his forehead. But Caesar concentrated on Curio.

Ever since Curio, on the expiration of his tribunate, had travelled north to join him, Caesar had been more and more impressed by the acuteness and agility of his mind.

"I'll summarize briefly," he said now, watching Curio's face. "You know about Curio's coup at the Senate meeting on the Kalends of December — three hundred and seventy votes for his proposal that both Pompey and I surrender our provinces and commands, twenty-two against.

"Meanwhile, I had sent letters to Pompey at Naples proposing friendship and a compromise."

He leaned his elbows on the conference table.

"I still could not believe that Pompey would take decisive action, not even when Curio arrived to tell me that in the Senate, on the ninth day of December, he had had to veto a proposal by the consul, Gaius Marcellus, to outlaw me; and that Marcellus, along with Cato, Domitius, and others, was off to Naples to offer Pompey command of the two legions taken from me, and a sword as a symbol of his right to levy troops against me all over Italy."

316

Caesar leaned back. "I was wrong. Balbus has brought the news that Pompey has accepted the offer, that he is starting a levy and is moving north to put troops into Rome."

"It's an open break," Balbus added. "Next will come an ultimatum for Gaius Julius Caesar to surrender all his provinces and to disband his legions at once."

"In spite of the fact," Caesar asked, "that my official term runs to the Kalends of next March and that by law I was to be allowed to run for the consulship in absentia? In spite, too, of the fact that originally I was to govern my provinces until I became consul?"

Balbus plunked a hand down on the table. "Those facts mean nothing to the diehards, or to Pompey either."

"Well, gentlemen, what is your advice?"

Curio was on his feet. "Bring in your legions from Gaul, Imperator. March on Rome."

"I agree," Hortensius said.

"No!" Servilia cried. "Not civil war! Please, Julius."

Hirtius said slowly, "I don't see what else can be done. Unless you intend to surrender, Julius?"

"And you, Pollio?" Caesar asked.

The young man flushed. "I'm not experienced enough to give advice," he replied. "I come from a small town. All I know is that the middle class of Italy wants peace."

"And their feelings are important," Caesar agreed. He stood up, and Curio sat down.

"First of all, precautions. I'm summoning into Ravenna the five cohorts of the Thirteenth stationed nearest the city. Also, I've sent word to the other five cohorts at Verona, Brixia, and Mediolanum to march here at once."

"Labienus," Hirtius began. "If he tampers with those cohorts —"

Caesar smiled. "I sent him orders a week ago to examine the defences at Novum Comum. That takes him out of the way. To continue, I also have couriers on the road to order the Eighth and Twelfth legions to march here and for the legate Gaius Fabius to move to Narbo so as to be ready to occupy the passes of the Pyrenees against Pompey's Spanish legions."

"Good!" Curio said. "Then, a march on Rome?"

Caesar shook his head. "No."

"Why not, Imperator?"

Caesar looked at Servilia. "I want peace, not war. Moreover, I want the people of Rome and Italy to realize that fact fully. So," he said, sitting down again, " — you won't like this, Curio — I intend to send a proposal to Antony for him, as tribune, to propose to the Senate that I will give up my provinces and disband my legions, if—and this is the important 'if' —they will leave me Cisalpine Gaul with two legions, or Cisalpine Gaul and Illyricum with one — and that much only until I am elected consul in absentia for the year following the coming one."

"Have you lost your senses!" Curio burst out. Then, he flushed. "I beg your pardon, Imperator."

Caesar smiled at him. "How better, Curio, can I prove to all Rome and Italy that it is not I who wants war?"

Curio's quick mind raced over the import of the words.

"I see," he said. "I see. If the Conservatives and Pompey refuse that offer, it's they, not you, who force war."

Caesar nodded.

"And, meanwhile, you gain time?"

Caesar nodded again.

"But suppose they accept your terms?"

"Then, I will abide by them."

"Even though, between the time you are elected consul and become consul you'll be open to prosecution?"

Caesar nodded once more. Curio's mind again rushed over the political situation—Pompey having shown his position, the two incoming consuls bitterly hostile to Caesar — yes, they'd force a war.

"You want those proposals of yours to Antony in Rome, when?" he asked.

"For the first meeting of the Senate in the New Year on the Kalends of January."

"You write them — I'll get them there," Curio promised.

"The Council is dismissed," Caesar said, and rose from his seat.

As he moved out the doorway, Servilia caught his arm.

"Thank you, my own," she whispered. "Thank you."

He put his arm around her waist and saw his secretary, Faberius, approaching.

"What is it?" he asked, stopping.

"A letter from Gubannitio of the Arvernians, Imperator."

Caesar took his arm away. "What's it about?"

Faberius consulted it. "Stripped to its essentials, Imperator, he asks if, for the sake of Vercingetorix' wife and children, there is any chance of clemency for Vercingetorix."

Caesar thought of a Gaul from which he might be forced to withdraw his legions.

"No," he answered.

"If that first request is refused," Faberius went on, "he begs that there be an easement of Vercingetorix' imprisonment — a villa near Rome under close guard, for example."

"I have no time to consider trivialities," Caesar told him, starting to turn away. Faberius checked him.

"Gubannitio is important to us in Gaul, Imperator," he suggested.

Caesar thought rapidly. "You've made a point, Faberius. So write him. Flatter him. Tell him how much I depend on him, how much I appreciate his unwavering loyalty — that sort of thing. Weave into the letter that I can't grant his first request but will take the second under advisement." Caesar paused an instant. "Add that I join in his concern for Vercingetorix' wife and children so that whatever he can do for them has my approval in advance. Suggest that, in view of their possible future careers, he get the lads a Roman tutor. Then, repeat my sincere appreciation, etc., etc. I suppose I'd better sign it personally, so bring it to me, Faberius. There'll be other letters to dictate shortly."

He turned to Servilia and put his arm around her again.

"You realize, darling, that in this crisis you must return to Rome with Balbus," he said.

She nodded.

"To come back here soon, I hope. Meanwhile, sweet, we must make good use of what time we have."

"First, Julius, those letters for Antony. After that — "
She smiled up at him.


## 2

On the seventh day of January, all Rome was seething with rumours and anxiety. For on the first day of the month the tribune Marcus Antonius had read to the Senate Caesar's proposals, brought from Ravenna at breakneck speed by the ex-tribune Curio. The presiding consul, Lentulus Crus, had refused to permit a vote on the proposals and the other consul, Marcellus— both of them in their first day of office—had concurred. Instead, in violent speeches, Metellus Scipio, Domitius, and Cato had attacked Caesar as a citizen who dared, actually dared, to attempt to dictate terms to his lawful government. Bibulus had popped up to move a decree that unless Gaius Julius Caesar gave up his provinces and legions by the Kalends of March, he would be declared a public enemy.

With Pompey's armed veterans thronging the streets outside, the decree was passed. Marcus Antonius interposed his veto. Since that day, there had been futile Senate meetings and intrigue after intrigue. But last evening, it was said, the diehard Conservatives had met with Pompey the Great in a villa just outside the sacred boundary of Rome. A decision, the rumour ran, had been reached. So what was to happen today? Was it to be peace or war?

That was the question that had brought the Populists, Caesar's strength, surging into the streets. It had also caused Pompey's armed veterans to mass around the Senate-Hall, even occupying its portico.

Meanwhile, in Curio's palace, Fulvia was hostess to Servilia and Balbus as they, too, awaited the result of the Senate meeting.

"It must be peace," Servilia was saying, moving closer to the brazier because outside a brisk wind was chilling the air. "When they think them over, surely the senators will accept Caesar's proposals."

"Don't count on that," said Balbus, who was sitting in a chair,

320

feet solidly planted on a mosaic of a Satyr pursuing a Bacchante. "Pompey has said that he has only to stamp his foot and legions will spring up from the soil of Italy. Domitius, Cato, Metellus Scipio, and all the others have been lobbying, telling the senators that Caesar does not dare to pull legions out of Gaul because he knows that if he does Gaul will revolt again." He clapped his hands on his knees. "They are also quoting Labienus that Caesar's troops are ready to mutiny. Stand firm, they are saying. Caesar will have to give way."

"That could mean war!" Servilia exclaimed.

"I hope it does," Fulvia put in, eyes flashing.

Balbus shrugged his shoulders. "We ought to know soon, one way or the other."

## 3

In the Senate, Calpurnius Piso, Caesar's father-in-law, had risen to demand that Caesar's proposals be discussed formally. Lentulus Crus, the presiding consul, had refused permission. Then, full of importance, Pompey's father-in-law, Metellus Scipio, got up slowly. Gathering his toga together, with practised gestures he spoke on and on, regurgitating the argument that Gaius Julius Caesar could not dictate terms and conditions to this august body, that it had been decreed that he must give up his provinces and legions by the next Kalends of March, and — "

"A decree I vetoed," Antony shouted.

"Caesar's puppet," Metellus Scipio sneered. "Whereas — "

"Come to the point, man," Cato interrupted in his harsh, grating voice.

Metellus flushed. "The point is that Gnaeus Pompeius Magnus stands ready to support any decree of this august body — "

"And I stand ready to interpose my veto," Antony roared, jumping up.

The diehards were on their feet, shouting, shaking their fists at Antony and the small Caesar-clique. Into the turmoil, Metellus Scipio shouted:

"Gnaeus Pompeius declares that it is now or never to check that degenerate, that revolutionary — "

"Caesar's toe is worth more than all of you," Antony was shouting, his face red, his right hand sawing the air, "you lily-livered bastards! If Caesar were here — "

His words were drowned out by roars of protest.

"Stop, all of you!" Cato's harsh voice boomed — and even Antony was silent. Standing in his place, high-bridged nose contemptuous, Cato looked about him slowly, deliberately.

"Words," he sneered. "Words and still more words. I'll give you action." He turned to the presiding consul. "Gaius Lentulus Crus, since Caesar's jack-in-the-box has announced that he will veto any decree against his master, I move the Ultimate Decree, namely that the consuls, the magistrates, and all ex-consuls see to it that the Republic receive no harm."

The Ultimate Decree! Last used thirteen years ago against the revolutionary Catiline!

Into the hushed silence Domitius' bull-voice roared:

"I second the motion." And then, "Divide! Divide!"

The Conservative diehards rushed towards Cato. A few senators moved toward Antony, Quintus Cassius, Curio, and Calpurnius Piso. The main mass hesitated. Lentulus Crus gave a signal, the doors crashed open—and there were Pompey's armed veterans, hands on swords, in the very doorway of the Senate-Hall.

Caesar would have to yield, most of the senators were thinking confusedly. Pompey, the greatest of generals, against him, and his own legions ready to mutiny. Slowly, with heads down, they joined the diehards.

"I declare the Ultimate Decree passed," Lentulus Crus shouted exultantly.

"I interpose my veto," Antony roared, taking a step forward.

"The Ultimate Decree is in force," Lentulus shouted back. "Martial law! Your right to veto is null and void!"

Antony strode forward a couple more steps. "The tribunician veto is sacred!" he exclaimed. "So are the persons of the tribunes! Reject the veto at your peril, Lentulus Crus!"

322

The Senate-Hall was in uproar, the senators, caught by hysteria, shouting, shaking their fists. Lentulus gave a signal. A half-dozen veterans, swords out, moved into the hall.

"Out," the centurion leading them ordered Antony. "Out."

Antony turned, face red, hand half-upraised. Curio caught him by the arm.

"Gently," he said. "Gently. We have work to do."

Antony let his hand fall. Then, followed by Quintus Cassius and Curio, chin high, eyes blazing, he marched upon the veterans. Those in the hall drew back. Those in the doorway gave way.

Antony, Quintus Cassius, and Curio strode through.

"And now what?" Antony demanded.

"To my home first," Curio told him. "Then, off to Caesar. Balbus has slave costumes for us — and post-horses ready all along the route." He clapped Antony on the shoulder. "You'll ride as you never rode before, man. We'll eat up the miles to Ravenna."

## 4

In the early afternoon of the third day out from Rome, the three men reported to Caesar in his governor's mansion. He listened, face impassive.

"The tribunician veto scorned," Curio summed up. "To the mob that veto is sacred, Imperator. Still worse, the persons of the tribunes threatened with violence — and the law is that violence to the tribunes is punishable by death. The mob will be wild, Imperator, and Fulvia's gang-leaders will keep them so."

"We'll chop the bastards, Julius," Antony exclaimed, his face inflamed, "as soon as the legions are here."

"We aren't waiting for the legions," Caesar answered quietly.

"What's that you say?" Curio demanded.

"Only five cohorts here," Antony said. "Five more on the way. Surely you're not serious."

"Look," Caesar said, "it's mid-November, in reality. Pom-

323

pey and the Conservatives plan on having all winter to raise and train troops. Let's scare them shitless, shall we?"

"By the spear of Minerva!" Antony said reverently.

"No one will dream of me acting," Caesar went on quietly. "Not with only five cohorts here and a total force of one legion. They'll be congratulating themselves down in Rome — Cato, Domitius, Bibulus, all of them. They'll be eating, drinking, sleeping, copulating, thinking they've got me. And Pompey — in his slow, massive way, he'll be drawing up lists of supplies to be got, troops to be levied, never dreaming—Now, here are my plans."

He detailed them rapidly, then paused.

"The first and most important action is to get the three of you in secret out to a lodge in the country. I have one ready."

"But why," Antony began.

"I see," Curio interrupted. "Not a word of what's happened in Rome must get out until you've acted."

"Exactly. We have two days by my reckoning before the news gets here. In that time, we cast a thunder-bolt."

# CHAPTER III

$S$ OUR WINE, GARLIC, SAUSAGES sputtering on gridirons, thick soups boiling, fish frying, onions, hams, and cheeses being sliced — the odours in this waterfront tavern of Ariminum seemed so thick, Fadius thought, that you could bite them. He and the ten veterans he commanded sat in a corner against the wall. That morning they had crossed the Rubicon, the stream that separated Caesar's province of Cisalpine Gaul from Italy. At Ariminum, a walled city and easily defensible, they were ostensibly on their way to a furlough in Rome. Similar small groups were scattered throughout the town, the whole operation being under the direction of Crastinus, a centurion of twenty years' service.

Neither Crastinus nor Fadius had any knowledge of the arrival, the previous night, of Antony, Curio, and Quintus Cassius, or of the passage in Rome of the Ultimate Decree. Their orders made them suspect that some critical move was in the offing. So now, as Fadius and his comrades washed down pea soup, garlic bread, and slices of ham with cups of cheap wine, Fadius was carefully assessing the immediate situation. In the rest of the tavern and spilling out to tables and benches on the cobblestones of the street were groups of leather-faced, gnarled-handed fishermen, grumbling as they ate and drank about the bitter wind off the Adriatic, and about the prices they got for their catch — and looking with resentment at the soldiers who could spend more than they and so got better service. Through the whole crowd scurried a trio of round-buttocked wenches, flushed by the attempt to keep up with the demands on them. Behind the counter the proprietor was bawling at the wenches and at his cooks and helpers, and shouting at a slave to light the horn lanterns. For the tenth time he glanced uneasily at the legionaries.

"A butter-ball, that one," Rullus, who was sitting across from Fadius, said appreciatively, looking at the nearest girl, a pert brunette. He clapped his hands. "Here, wench, a refill."

Soldiers tipped better than fishermen. The girl hurried over. Rullus clamped an arm around her waist and pulled her onto his knee. She giggled.

"None of that, now," the proprietor roared.

A young fisherman, who quite often bedded the girl, jumped to his feet.

"Leave that girl alone," he snarled.

"Who says so?" Rullus growled, standing up but still holding the girl. Three or four other fishermen got to their feet.

"Sit down, Rullus," Fadius snapped. He reached across the table, grabbed Rullus' arm, and yanked. "Let the wench go." And then: "That's an order."

Rullus' face was flushed, but he obeyed. The girl, uncertain, stood there.

"Run along, wench," Fadius ordered. As she tossed her head and obeyed, the fishermen sat down slowly. Fadius with a jerk of his head signalled his comrades to listen.

"Remember what we're here for," he said. "No fights. I'll knock down the first man who so much as looks crosswise."


## 2


At this moment to the north, in Ravenna, Caesar was giving a banquet for the city's notables and their wives. As he laughed and jested, not a single one of them could have guessed the tension within their host. In the morning he had sent his five cohorts under Hortensius and Hirtius marching northward, the pretext being that the Rhaetians had raided from the Alps into the Po Valley. The instructions had been to veer to the west and south, bypass Ravenna, and move to the Rubicon River. By this time those cohorts should be in position.

Meanwhile, he himself had held audiences, gone to the baths, attended a beast-hunt, met with the mayor and the councillors to discuss plans for a new gladiatorial school, and, finally, put on this banquet. All the time, he had been the charming, care-free governor; and up to this point no news of the Ultimate Decree had reached Ravenna, or, he hoped, Ariminum. Ordinary travel from Rome took at least six days, not the three Antony and his mates had used. So, if his luck held —

He leaned over to whisper an indecent jest to the mayor's wife, who was reclining on the couch next him. She giggled. On cue, Faberius came in. Caesar sat up. Faberius spoke to him. Caesar frowned, slipped gracefully off the couch, and stood. His guests looked at him.

"Dispatches," Caesar told them. "Must be answered at once." He shrugged. "The penalty of office. Please, don't let my absence spoil your enjoyment. I'll be back as soon as I can."

With a wave of his hand he left, Pollio with him. Once out of the room, it was armour on for the two of them, while Caesar listened to a travel-stained courier, just arrived from Balbus. Then it was dark cloaks, and next a swift exit through the postern door. A tradesman's cart, its driver a muffled-up legionary, was waiting in the narrow lane. Caesar and Pollio climbed into the back. The legionary took them by side streets to Ravenna's north gate. As the darkness swallowed them Caesar spoke to the driver.

"North for a quarter of an hour; then veer west and south to bypass Ravenna. Next, east to the coastal road. You know the route?"

"Yes, Imperator."

"It's dark as the inside of a horse," Caesar commented, peering out of the blackness. "Don't miss the turn-offs."

"I won't, Imperator." The legionary slapped the reins on the horse's back. "I went over the route this morning, just to make sure."

"Good." Caesar leaned against the back of the cart. "You heard the report from Balbus?" he said to Pollio.

"Yes, Imperator."

"Italy into districts for the levy. Metellus Scipio to be governor of Syria. Gaul—the Gaul I conquered—to go to Domitius Ahenobarbus. Domitius!"

Pollio did not know what to say. Caesar sat silent, thinking over his plans. The cart veered west and south in a sort of semicircle as it bypassed Ravenna. An hour later the hooves of the horse began to clip-clop on the paving-stones of the coastal road.

Caesar roused himself. The three of them had their night-vision by now. On either side marched a line of umbrella-pines. High up, the November stars were points of light. From their right came the gasping, mournful bray of a donkey. Somewhere in the distance a dog barked.

"Do you know what I'm after?" he asked Pollio, as the cart jolted over the stones.

Pollio sat up. "To defend the sacrosanctity of the tribunes," he answered, "and to assert your rights and those of your soldiers."

"True. You've missed my major objective, Pollio. What I'm really after is — peace."

"Peace!"

"Pompey, the diehards, the main mass of the senators, believe I have to yield. If I don't, they think they have months until spring to prepare. Then Pompey plans to squeeze me between his legions from Spain and the troops he'll raise in Italy. But neither he nor anyone dreams of the move I'm about to make. As Antony would say, they'll all piss their shins."

"So they'll agree to your terms?"

"Exactly — and, hence, peace."

Caesar leaned back. Young Pollio thought how fortunate he was to have been accepted as a junior officer on Caesar's staff. He'd heard of his energy, his charm, his swift decisions. Reality exceeded reports, he told himself, as the cart-wheels jolted on. And then immediately ahead were torches glinting on armour. The cart stopped. Caesar jumped out. Pollio, joints stiff, followed. Hortensius and Hirtius came forward, and saluted.

"Everything prepared," Hortensius reported.

Caesar nodded. A groom led Five-Toes forward. Caesar

glanced at the dark masses of his men on either side of the road. The stallion beside him snorted and tossed its head up and down. Instead of mounting, its master turned and walked to the bank beside the bridge over the Rubicon. He halted there, his officers gathered respectfully behind him. He stared down at the stream, a narrow ribbon of faint light flowing seaward among dried sedges.

On this bank his province. On the other, Italy. No governor was permitted to return to Italy until his term was over. If he, Caesar, crossed that stream he was, technically, in revolt against the constitutional government of the Republic. Yet what alternative had his enemies left him?

He stood there, his thoughts ranging over his career. Decades ago, when ordered by Sulla to divorce his wife, Cornelia, he had refused at the risk of his life. Cornelia, the daughter of a Popularist leader, had died years ago, but from that moment he himself had been labelled a Popularist. Then had come years of frustration, pimping for Crassus.

Meanwhile Sulla and fortune had smiled on a Pompey who, at the dictator's command, had put aside his wife and married a protégé of Sulla. Consider his luck — the command in Spain against the Popularist Sertorius, the post to sweep the pirates from the Mediterranean, and the extraordinary command in the East against Mithridates the Great. There his victories had won him enormous wealth and an overpowering reputation.

During those years he himself had had to dodge this way and that. At last, at forty-two—forty-two!—he had seen opportunity and seized it by neck and crupper. It was on his return from Spain that he found that the Conservatives had alienated Pompey as well as Crassus. From that situation he had formed what Varro called "The Three-Headed Monster".

The point was that from that moment he had marched forward and, more importantly, had discovered that the energies and abilities surging within him were real. Look what he had achieved! So why at this instant did he shrink from crossing this stream? Years ago Sulla had left his province to lead his army against the government of that day. He was no Sulla! Was it

329

because, without realizing it, he had some superstitious dread of violating the traditions and laws of the Republic?

Downstream there was a flurry of movement, a squeal of terror, and then a death-cry — some small animal seized by a weasel, probably. Republic — bah!, Caesar thought. The city mob voting mindlessly in the Assemblies; the ruling clique of nobles interested only in keeping their wealth and positions by plundering the provincials, buying off the jurors, selling positions — everything in the Republic and the Empire for sale. If Rome was to survive, someone must carve out the rotting cancers. Someone must bring in a new society, a society based on justice. And was not he the man? Yes! He could feel the power within himself. Here was the first step, the first necessary step. Force a peace — and then reform.

Caesar's chin went up. Turning from the bank, he strode back to Five-Toes, vaulted into the saddle, and waved to Hortensius.

"Bring them across," he ordered, and trotted toward the bridge. The knuckle-bones are cast, he thought—and if no news from Rome has alerted Ariminum's garrison — if my luck holds —

He rode across the bridge, Five-Toes' hooves sounding sharp and yet hollow in the darkness.


# 3


In Ariminum, the walled city that Caesar feared, it was false dawn. At the western gate of the city, except for a half-dozen on sentry duty, the guards were drowsing. Suddenly, they found the dagger-points of Caesar's veterans, led by Crastinus and Fadius, at their throats. They did not resist. The veterans flung open the gate. Then they waited, hoping that no word would get to the town's garrison.

"Where in Hades are the buggers?" Crastinus growled, staring to the west.

There was an early morning fog. Fadius got down, put an ear to the ground, and then beckoned to Crastinus.

"Horses' hooves," he said, straightening. "And the sound of boots."

"And look," Crastinus exclaimed, pointing, "standards! See? Above the fog. Caesar's here! He's here!"

Shortly afterward, when Ariminum's citizens awoke, they found gates, squares, and the main buildings occupied by Caesar's troops. The garrison, an under-strength cohort of called-up levies, had surrendered. Its commander, a Roman knight, Corius Faber, dragged from a comfortable bed, had expostulated. Caesar had smiled at him.

"You're free to stay or go, whichever you wish," he had told him.

"My cohort?"

"They will have the choice of returning to their homes or enlisting in my legions."

"You can't do this," Corius Faber had stammered. "It's against the law. You can't seize a town in Italy."

Caesar's smile had been even sweeter. "I already have," he answered.

Corius Faber opted to ride to Rome. Caesar saw to it that he was hurried away without any opportunity to estimate the number of his legionaries. At mid-morning, standing on a tribunal hastily erected on the top step of the Temple of Jupiter, he spoke to his men. They were massed before him in the town's forum, faces upturned. He told of the orders to demote him and to disband them at once, without, he cried, the rewards he had promised and which were their due. With a wave of his hand, he brought forward Antony and Quintus Cassius, dressed in slave's costumes. As the soldiers gasped in shock, taking a step forward, Caesar, using all his orator's skill, explained with dramatic gestures how these men, tribunes, sacrosanct protectors of the rights of the plebs against the insolence of the nobles, had had their inviolate veto trampled underfoot. What was even more terrible — his voice dropped in horror — they themselves had been so imperilled that only by dressing as slaves—his voice rose — had they escaped with their lives. Look at them! He flung a hand toward them. Would any Roman — would they — put up

331

with this insult, this attack by arrogant nobles on the most basic of the rights of a Roman?

There were shouts, cries of "No", a forest of waving fists. Caesar waited. Then, in a quieter tone he reminded the troops that he had doubled their pay, given them bonuses, and promised them farms when their term of service was over. But these criminals in the Senate—his voice rose again as he gestured—had determined to depose him, their commander, their friend, and still worse, he emphasized again, to deprive them of the rewards that they — through snow, through rain, through desperate battles, risking their lives over and over—had earned. Was this, he exclaimed, to be endured?

Again there were the shouts, the forest of waving fists.

"Follow me, then," Caesar cried. "Not against the Republic —oh, no! But against these criminals who have usurped power. Against these wretches who think that, at their whim, they can violate the tribunate, can treat veterans like you as if you were slaves to shrink when they wave a whip. Follow me, comrades, and by Father Jupiter himself I pledge to you rewards beyond your wildest dreams." He flung both arms wide. "Are you with me, comrades?"

The roar in answer surged above the roof-tops into the clouded sky. Caesar reached out both hands to them.

"I accept your trust, comrades. Nor will I, Caesar, fail you."

He waited for the cheering to fade. Then, with a gesture of dismissal, he stepped down from the tribunal and walked back with his officers into the temple.

"That was wonderful, Imperator," Pollio got out, stumblingly.

"I've never heard you do better, Julius," Antony agreed, tossing off his slave's cloak.

Caesar stopped and turned.

"And those were the men who, Labienus wrote, would mutiny," he said. "The diehards believed him. Fools! Their own man, the dictator Sulla, proved that any professional Roman army will follow the general who gives them pay and loot against the state."

"What do we do now?" Antony asked.

"First of all, a job for you, Antony."

"What, Imperator?"

"The other five cohorts of this legion will be nearing Ravenna. Ride to meet them, Antony. Take a hundred horsemen with you. Then sweep inland to Arretium."

"A hundred and thirty miles from Rome!" Curio exclaimed. "That will panic them, Imperator."

"Exactly," Caesar said grimly. "That's what I'm after. Panic!"

# 4

In Rome, the evening of the third day since Caesar's early-morning seizure of Ariminum, Pompey was sitting in a study of his immense palace on the Esquiline. Braziers kept off the chill. The lamps had been lit. Maps and sheets of papyrus were scattered on the tables, and two of his confidential freedman-secretaries, Theophanes and Demetrius, were helping him prepare lists of supplies to be assembled by spring: mules, wagons, horses, tunics, cloaks, weapons, artillery — all the equipment necessary for an army of ten legions.

Pompey was comfortable. His gouty leg was quiescent and the reports were that the levies were proceeding according to plan.

"The other major depots, Imperator?" Theophanes asked deferentially. "Besides Capua and Luceria, I mean?"

Pompey yawned and thought of the evening meal. He pushed back his chair.

"We've done enough for today," he decided. "After all, we have months until spring."

He got up just as his wife, Cornelia, pushed aside the curtain at the entrance. Pompey looked at her fondly.

"I'm just coming, my dear," he said.

She stepped inside. "A deputation to see you," she told him. "Cato, Favonius, Cicero, Lentulus Crus, a half-dozen others."

Pompey groaned. "Not again," he said petulantly. "I'm busy enough without listening to their maunderings. What do they want, anyway?"

Cornelia shrugged her shapely shoulders. "News of some sort, darling. I've put them in the Ephesian salon. Satisfactory?"

Pompey nodded. "Will you help me on with my toga?"

"Of course, darling."

When, a few moments later, Pompey walked into the Ephesian salon, the excited babbling stopped. Pompey greeted the senators, went over to a sofa, and sat down. He looked at the consul, Lentulus Crus.

"What's on your minds, gentlemen?" he asked.

Lentulus Crus, face flushed, eyes flashing, was too excited to stand on ceremony. Turning, he seized a travel-stained young man by the arm and thrust him forward.

"Corius Faber, commander of our garrison at Ariminum," he said in a high-pitched voice. "He's ridden night and day to get here. Tell him, Corius Faber. Tell Gnaeus Pompeius Magnus what's happened."

Pompey looked at the young man with unblinking eyes. "Well?"

"Caesar," Corius Faber gulped. "Caesar!"

Pompey leaned forward. "Caesar?" Then, "Speak up, young man."

"Ariminum — he's seized it — three days ago. I didn't have a chance. The gates were opened. First thing I knew — "

"How many men?" Pompey cut in sharply.

"Hundreds. Thousands." Corius Faber gestured vaguely. "I don't know. Swarms of them — everywhere." He looked around. "By this time, he'll be on the road to Rome."

"Ariminum!" Pompey repeated. "That's against the law. That's — "

Cato's harsh voice interrupted. "The point is, what do we do now, Gnaeus Pompeius Magnus?"

"A campaign in winter! The man's mad."

"The point is that the degenerate is in Italy. So what do we do?"

Pompey sat back, his lips working in and out. The senators began to gabble again, all at once. If they'd let him alone,

Pompey was thinking, give him a chance to estimate the situation, to make plans.

"Send envoys," Cicero was babbling. "Offer terms."

"Never," Lentulus was exclaiming.

"Get your troops moving, Pompeius," Cato was advising. "At once."

"Defend Rome," the other consul, Marcellus, was crying out. "Bring the two legions from Luceria here, Pompeius."

In the East he hadn't had this gaggle of idiots badgering him, Pompey thought. He stood up. They all turned to him.

"I'll take the proper measures," Pompey said stiffly.

"But what — what?" they almost screamed at him.

Pompey took refuge in a haughty silence. Compressing his lips, he stalked from the room.

But the next day there was a courier from Scribonius Libo who was in command in Etruria. Antony's cavalry, the courier told the consuls and Pompey, was galloping on Arretium, swarming cohorts marching behind him. He himself, Libo wrote, was abandoning all Etruria.

Caesar in Italy! Antony at Arretium. The news raced through Rome like windswept flames, and rumours, each wilder than its predecessor, leaped up to feed the fire. In Curio's palace, Fulvia, copper-red tresses flowing free, eyes flashing, faced the Clodian gang-leaders.

"Get ready," she told them. "When Caesar comes, heads will bounce on the cobblestones. Tell your men." She flung her arms wide. "Rome will be theirs to plunder. Theirs!"

A few streets away Balbus sat in Servilia's Corinthian salon.

"Civil war!" Servilia was exclaiming. She stopped her pacing to face him. "Oh, Balbus, why? Why?"

"Calm yourself, Lady."

"They say Antony is galloping here from Arretium. They say Pisaurum and Fanum have opened their gates to Julius. From Fanum a road leads straight to Rome. They say Caesar's marching on the city."

"I said, calm yourself, Lady. His moves are to force the

335

Conservatives to his terms."

Servilia sat down. "You think so?"

"I'm sure of it."

"All the shops closed," Servilia said. "The Senate hasn't met. Why, Balbus?"

"Because the diehards — and Pompey — can't make up their minds. We'll just have to wait, Lady."

They waited. All Rome waited. Each new rumour was tossed from street to street. It was said that Caesar's legions were eating up the miles, eager to plunder Rome. No, it was Antony's cavalry galloping to the city. No, both Caesar and Antony were converging on the capital. There would be massacres, the senators and knights whispered to each other — slaughter to outmatch the Marian massacres or the Sullan proscriptions. Already, it was declared, Caesar had made up his lists.

As Rome seethed like a boiling cauldron, all business was suspended. Pompey still sat silent, though the diehards kept rushing to him, demanding action. None of them knew that he had already sent two envoys to Caesar to tell him that, though his duty to the Republic came first, he was still his friend. So, let Caesar suspend his march, he suggested.

Pompey was wavering, and, besides, in the back of his mind he hoped that the envoys would slow Caesar down. Yet, he realized that he, Pompey, must do something.

As he pondered, on the fourth day after the news of Ariminum reached Rome, Labienus rode into Rome with a hundred Gallic cavalry; they were the first troops to defect from Caesar. The diehards, flocking around him, escorted him to Pompey's palace. Pompey greeted him warmly. In the Ephesian salon Labienus, his confidence restored by his reception, addressed Pompey and the diehards.

"I'm still certain that Caesar's men will mutiny," he told them. "Besides, the man's not a good general."

"How can you say that?" someone asked.

"He takes chances — reckless chances. Like now, invading Italy with one legion." Labienus snorted. "The man's a fool."

"The Gallic legions . . . " Lentulus Crus began.

Labienus waved a hand. "If he takes them from Gaul, Gaul will revolt." Labienus looked over the group. "What you gentlemen don't realize — and in his book Caesar didn't give me proper credit,"—Labienus' face was flushed—"but without me he would never have conquered Gaul."

The diehards looked at each other, somewhat incredulous.

"Explain it to them, Titus Labienus," Pompey said encouragingly.

Labienus drew himself up. "Who won his first battle for him?" he asked. "I did. Who was never defeated? Me. Caesar was beaten in Britain. He lost at Gergovia. Charging uphill!" Labienus snorted again. "Uphill! And who won his last battle for him — at Alesia? I did, I tell you." He glared around him at the group and banged his right fist into the open palm of his left hand. "If this Caesar had written the truth in that book of his, you would all have realized that compared to Pompeius Magnus here" — he flung out an arm — "he's a nothing, I tell you. A nothing."

It was what the diehards wanted to hear. They crowded around, congratulating him. It was just what Pompey loved to hear, too. He invited Labienus to dinner. Afterwards, over the winecups, they discussed the situation, one military man to another. Pompey was relaxed, comfortable.

"They want me to bring my two legions from Luceria two hundred miles south to defend Rome," he told Labienus. "But I'd be a fool to disperse my forces, wouldn't I?"

"I agree, Pompeius Magnus," Labienus answered. "Absolutely. This war will be won in the field, not in defending Rome. So what are your plans, Pompeius?"

Pompey told him. It was satisfying to find that Labienus approved. The next day, late in the afternoon, he convoked the Senate, massing, as a precaution, armed veterans outside the hall. In the meantime a new rumour had spread through the city. A courier, it was said, had reported for a fact that Antony's cavalry was galloping on Rome from Arretium — only a hundred and thirty miles away.

Antony's cavalry! The senators were hysterical. What were

337

they to do? they shouted at Pompey. What was he doing? Why weren't his legions in Rome?

Pompey sat silent, staring at the far wall. A senator, Volcatius Tullus, leaped to his feet to demand that envoys be sent to Caesar to ask for terms. Cicero supported his proposal. Pompey still sat silent. The tumult grew worse, senators shaking their fists, cursing Pompey, ordering him to take action. Finally Cato got to his feet. He stared around him until there was almost silence.

"You shriek like peacocks," Cato said in his harshest voice, "and with as much sense. Shut up, all of you." He turned to Pompey. "We've given you absolute power, Gnaeus Pompeius Magnus. It is time to hear your plans."

Pompey rose. Even as he stood up, the senators sensed a difference in him. He radiated confidence.

"My plans for the crushing of Gaius Julius Caesar are made," he said quietly. "Those plans require the evacuation of Rome."

There was a moment of open mouths and indrawn breaths. Then came uproar. Abandon Rome! What of their palaces, their families, their possessions? Pompey didn't, couldn't, mean it!

Once again Cato took charge. "Quiet," he shouted. "You're Romans — or are you? Sit down," he cried, waving his arms. "Hear Pompey's reasons, I tell you. Quiet!"

Pompey had waited, calm, impassive, until the senators were ready to listen. When he spoke again it was with the same air of authority.

"I will soon have ten legions under arms," he began.

"Ten!" the senators exclaimed. "Ten?"

Pompey nodded. "This war will be won in the field," he went on, raising his voice a little, "not by splitting my forces to defend an indefensible city." He paused an instant. "You'll soon have your palaces back," he added. "Meanwhile, I leave Rome to-night for Capua." He looked around and then spoke as if pounding in nails with a hammer. "Every senator loyal to the Republic will join me at Capua. Any senator who does not will be treated as a traitor when victory is won. Similarly, any town or city which opens its gates to Gaius Julius Caesar will be destroyed."

"The Roman mob!" a voice cried. "Who will protect us?"

"My veterans," Pompey said. He swept his toga around him. "The Senate is adjourned to meet in Capua."

He strode down the hall. Cato, Labienus, and a score of others fell in behind them. They passed out the doors into the gathering dusk. Behind them, the senators gabbled in panic-stricken groups. Some, in fear of riots, huddled all night in the Senate-House. The majority, combining their escorts of slaves and freedmen, forced their way through the dark streets, in which the Clodian gangs were already attacking Pompey's veterans, to their homes, there to decide whether to follow Pompey and, if so, how and when.

These were the points being discussed in Cicero's library between the orator, his wife Terentia, his friend Atticus, and Dolabella, the handsome, dissolute noble who had married Cicero's beloved daughter. The orator was walking nervously back and forth, talking compulsively, veering this way and that. Terentia, a tall, gaunt woman sitting rigid in a chair, finally couldn't stand it any longer.

"Make up your mind, Marcus," she said abruptly. "If you love Pompey so much, join him. If you think it is too dangerous, don't."

Cicero stopped to look at her. "It isn't so simple as that," he said indignantly. "I have to think of my reputation, my duty to the Republic."

He was interrupted by his favourite freedman, Tiro, the man who had supervised the publication of all his books and orations, walking in.

"A note from Marcus Caelius Rufus, master," he said, holding it out.

Caelius was the orator's protégé, a man he had once defended successfully against a charge of poisoning. Cicero tore open the papyrus roll, moved closer to a candelabrum, read it, and tossed it to Atticus.

"What d'you think of that?" he demanded. "Saying he's off to join Caesar because Caesar will win. Advising me to do the same, or, if not, to stay neutral."

Atticus passed the note to Dolabella. "Sound advice, I'd say,"

339

he told the orator. "About staying neutral, I mean."

"How can I?" Cicero demanded. "I, who saved the Republic—"

"Don't be a bigger ass than you are," Terentia said, getting up.

Cicero stared at her, thinking of a biting retort. But he was somewhat afraid of his wife. She was older than he, came from a better family, and, what was more important to a man who lived beyond his means, owned a good deal of property. As he hesitated, Dolabella rose, tossed Caelius' note onto a table, and turned toward the doorway.

"Where are you off to?" Cicero asked.

Dolabella paused. "To join Caesar," he said and walked out.

Cicero stared after him; the thought crossed his mind that, if Caesar did win, a son-in-law in his army would be a good thing.

"Would you like my advice, old friend?" Atticus asked.

Cicero nodded.

"I'm staying neutral, naturally. I'm a businessman. I suggest you do the same. But the Clodian gangs don't like you. So, leave Rome."

"Where to? I mean—"

"We'll go to our villa on the coast at Formiae," Terentia announced. She glanced at Tiro, whom she disliked intensely. "Get on with the packing, Tiro."

As this decision was reached, five streets over, in Servilia's Corinthian salon, a family conference was in full swing. As supporters of Caesar, Servilia and her husband, naturally, were staying in Rome. One son-in-law, Marcus Lepidus, as the son of a man who had, years ago, led a Popularist revolt in Etruria and at present was a praetor, also had nothing to fear. The other son-in-law, the bitter-faced Cassius, had announced that he was off to join Pompey.

Servilia wasn't really disturbed by this decision. She was concentrating on her son, Brutus. He was standing there, tall, high-browed, an obstinate look on his handsome, aristocratic face.

"But you can't join Pompey," she insisted. "He had your father put to death, remember? After promising him safe-conduct." She got up from the bronze-legged sofa. "Safe-conduct!"

That had been while Brutus was an infant, during the revolt led by Lepidus' father.

"When it's a question of the safety of the Republic, personal feelings no longer matter," Brutus answered stiffly.

"But Caesar isn't against the Republic, my son."

"Caesar!" Brutus exploded; he took a step forward, then stood still again, lips pressed together. His mother sensed what he wanted to say. He knew — all Rome knew — that she was Caesar's mistress. She stared at him, loving him so much, so irrationally much. She had other children and, for that matter, a son in Caesar's army. Yet this first-born of hers was the one who always pulled at her heart-strings until she could scarcely stand it. She wanted to rush to him, gather him into her arms, hug him tight.

She couldn't. Why, oh why, had she ever agreed that he be brought up by her half-brother, Cato, that man who always thought he was right and everybody else wrong? She drew in her breath, then spoke, making her voice soft.

"You have your books," she pointed out, "and your family." She took a step forward and held out her arms in appeal. "Stay neutral, my son. What do you know of war? Nothing. So wait here."

Brutus drew himself up. "I'm a Roman. A Roman can fight." He turned on his heel. "I'm off," he said, and then over his shoulder, "Good-bye, mother."

So there it was, Servilia thought, agony plucking at her. Her family divided, as she had feared. Most of all that boy, her first-born, off to something for which he wasn't prepared. Oh, Caesar, Caesar! she thought, turning away. What have you done to Rome, to Italy? Civil war! Brother against brother. Son against father — once again. And you promised!

She collapsed into a chair, staring into space.

Similar debates went on among the noble families all that night and into the next day, while in the streets the Clodian gangs fought Pompey's veterans with daggers and swords. In the morning, thanks to Terentia and Tiro, Cicero slipped out of the city. The majority of the nobles and knights were still in confusion. How were they to get their households away? Who would protect their palaces and mansions? Did they really need to leave at all, or, at least, right at once?

But in mid-afternoon a group of foam-flecked horsemen came riding into Rome. Caesar himself, they said, was plunging toward the city at the head of Gallic and German horsemen. No, they hadn't seen the cavalry. But they'd heard of their coming. Two hours away! Or at most, three!

Gallic cavalry! Long-haired barbarians! Massacres! The consul, Lentulus Crus, who was collecting carts and wagons to carry the treasury of the Republic to Capua, fled to his home to prepare for flight. Most of the senators did the same. By late afternoon and far into the night, the Appian Way for miles south of Rome was a tangle of carriages, wagons, horses, donkeys, two-wheeled carts, shouting, pushing, heavily burdened slaves, sweating senators and knights, crying children, scared wives and maids, flickering torches, whinnying horses, and barking dogs, as if the gods had seized huge cauldrons of human and animal debris and dumped them on the paving-stones. And then a bitterly cold rain poured down.

If Caesar could have seen that sight, he would have known that he had achieved panic. But Caesar was still far to the east, driving forward along the coastal road. By the Roman calendar it was the twentieth day of January.

342

# CHAPTER IV

T HREE DAYS SHORT OF TWO MONTHS LATER, at nightfall, Caesar watched the last of Pompey's transports pass out of the harbour of Brundisium in a light drizzle. His hands were clenched in tight fists. He had hoped to end this war of Roman against Roman in one bold sweep. Everything had flowed his way. All along the coast the Pompeian cohorts had either been dispersed or had joined him. His most striking success had been at Corfinium. There the whole of the army of that bitter enemy, Domitius Ahenobarbus, had been captured. Caesar had let him go free. Then he heard that Pompey was concentrating all his forces at Brundisium. That had meant that his adversary was planning to evacuate his troops to Greece.

So Caesar had driven his army by forced marches to Brundisium. He had reached that port on the ninth of March, hoping to catch his enemy there. But Pompey, he learned, had got most of his forces and the consuls across the Adriatic to Greece and was awaiting the return of his transports to put his two remaining legions on board. The envoys he sent to Pompey asking once again for a personal conference returned with a curt refusal.

Caesar had crossed the Rubicon with one legion. By this time he commanded six legions, three of them veterans marched from Gaul, the others formed from what had been Pompeian levies. He set his troops to build two causeways, one from each side of the harbour, so as to close it.

Yet Pompey had got away. As Caesar stared after the winking lanterns of the receding fleet, his disappointment was almost overwhelming. What he still could not understand was why Pompey had refused to meet with him. To abandon Italy rather than attempt to come to terms—what could his reason be? Well, he told himself, face the facts. The war must go on. So, make plans. Unclenching his fists, he turned away.

343

Had Caesar been able to see into Pompey's mind, he might have understood him. At this moment, standing on the deck of his flagship with Labienus, and looking back at the dark line that was Italy, Pompey felt a deep sense of relaxation and content. From the moment this war had started, in the back of his mind, hidden almost from himself, had lurked the thought that, were he in the East again, all would go well. Had he not won triumph after triumph there? Was he not worshipped as a god in the temples of Asia Minor? Moreover, with his fleets controlling the Adriatic and the Aegean, he would have time—time to plan, to organize, to get together massive forces. Yes, he thought, all would go well now.

At his side, Labienus stirred.

"You handled that withdrawal excellently, Gnaeus Pompeius," he said.

Pompey drew in a deep breath. "Those senators," he said, "those who wanted to stay in Italy and fight — recruits against veterans — what fools!"

"The defeat of Domitius convinced them," Labienus said. "Once we're ready we'll smash that bastard Caesar."

Pompey nodded, somewhat abstractedly. The mention of Caesar's name had brought back to him his former father-in-law's constant attempts to arrange a personal meeting. Pompey felt his gorge rise. Did that man, so much his inferior, really think that he, Pompey the Great, recognized at last as the foremost genius of all, the sole pillar that held up the Roman Republic, would allow himself to become the second man in the State, and, worse still, in the eyes of the world, hold even that position only by Caesar's grace?

"I agree with you," he said suddenly and violently, "the man's a fool."

Labienus turned to stare at him in the darkness, wondering who in the world Pompey meant. Tactfully—and Labienus was seldom tactful — he coughed, spat, and changed the subject.

"Egypt and Rhodes have warships," he said. "Ought we,

Gnaeus, to send couriers at once with orders to send those warships to us?"

Pompey roused himself. "No hurry," he answered. "Plenty of time."

<h1 style="text-align:center">3</h1>

At this moment, Cleopatra, expelled from Egypt the previous summer, was in Tyre, facing Antipater, war minister of the Jews. They were standing in a room in the third storey of the Prince of Tyre's palace, a room bathed in subdued light. Apollodorus, who had escorted Antipater in, had retired to a nearby corner, leaving the two to size up each other.

Cleopatra liked what she saw: a strongly built man with grey eyes — he was only half-Jewish, she recalled — and a thrusting beak of a nose. What attracted her most was an impression of enormous energy, held in leash at the moment.

"I assume that you know what I want," she said in Hebrew, relishing his involuntary start of surprise.

Antipater inclined his head for an instant. Then he said, "Yes, Lady," reflecting that he had heard of her proficiency in languages, but had not expected Hebrew. "An army strong enough to put you back on your throne."

Cleopatra, who had been in shadow, moved forward into the light. Again involuntarily, Antipater's nostrils flared. He had heard that the Egyptian queen was beautiful. Antipater had bedded many women and, after all, no matter how beautiful, one woman was like another. What he had not expected was a sort of emanation that seemed to make an actual physical impact. There was more than charm and beauty here, he thought somewhat confusedly. Here was an almost overwhelming personality that combined sexuality with a sense of power and — yes — an intellect. Watch yourself, he thought.

"So what have you to offer?" Cleopatra was asking. "And," she smiled, "why have you come—or rather, what do you want in return?"

Antipater had a feeling that he must plant his feet firmly, even though he was already standing. He glanced at Apollodorus.

"You may speak in front of him, without reserve," Cleopatra told him.

"Last question first," Antipater said, more gruffly than he had intended. "As a preliminary, we both know that Caesar and Pompey are two mastiffs, striving for each other's throat. So Rome, for the moment, can't interfere. And who knows the future? So, now is the time for each nation to solidify or improve its power."

"Come to the point, Antipater, War Minister of Judea."

"In Alexandria, there are thousands of Jews, jammed in the quarter known as Gamma. Other thousands are scattered through the Delta. Since you were thrust out by your enemy, Pothinus, he and the Ptolemy, your brother-husband — "

"No husband to me, that pimply-faced brat!" Cleopatra interjected violently.

Antipater spread out a palm. "That's as may be. The point is that Pothinus is turning the screws tight on the Jews of Egypt — taxes, confiscations of property, beatings, tortures, rape, and vandalism encouraged. We Jews won't allow that."

"So?"

"You have a contingent of Philistines. Another of Syrians. You hope for help from the Prince of Tyre here. Since the days of our King Solomon, we Jews have been friends with Tyre." He raised a hand as Cleopatra made as if to speak. "No, Lady, wait. What we offer is more than our influence in Tyre — a Jewish force."

"Which won't fight on your Sabbath."

"Under me, it will."

"And in return?"

"If you are back on the throne, a stop to this persecution of the Jews."

"That isn't all, is it?"

Shrewd, Antipater thought, hesitating an instant. Then, he decided that she had probably guessed the rest.

"Certain lands — Idumaea, for instance — that used to be ours," he suggested. "Egyptian, ah, influence to get them back."

"Egyptian troops, you mean, don't you?"

Antipater nodded. Cleopatra glanced at Apollodorus, who was now positioned behind Antipater. He shook his head, lifted a writing tablet, and shook his head again. He meant that this Antipater would probably ask for an agreement in writing. That would be dangerous if a copy got to the Idumaeans, or even to the Philistines or the Syrians. Neither of these last two peoples would want Jewish power extended — so one could lose the troops one had. Yet she must get Egypt back — and lop off Pothinus' head. Forced.to run for her life! Then, deposed by Pothinus' Regency Council. Was there some other way to secure this Antipater's soldiers without a written commitment?

She glanced at him, considering him. Yes, he was all male — not like the Prince of Tyre, who, though sensitive and intelligent, was mad for boys; this Antipater would know that fact, too, so no danger from jealousy. Turning, she walked out to the balcony that projected from the room. Below, one could glimpse the white crests of waves beating against the wall. Out in the hazy darkness enveloping the Aegean Sea winked a multitude of lights, a fleet of tiny boats fishing for bream, anchovies, deep-sea bass, tunnies, and dolphins. Over her shoulder, she called softly, "Would you come out here, Antipater, War Minister of Judea?"

He came out. The balcony was narrow. She smiled in the half-darkness, sensing how rigidly, in spite of his nearness, he was holding himself.

"Beautiful," she said, gesturing gracefully toward the lights. "They could be fireflies, couldn't they?"

This close, a delicate and disturbing perfume was in Antipater's nostrils, and her voice, he thought, even when using the rough Hebrew tongue, was like the faint chime of tiny silver bells. As he thought this, she rested her breasts and crossed arms on the balustrade and looked downward.

"Come closer," she said. "Lean over. See. Down there."

She had managed it so that her hip was touching him and so was her upper arm and a light caress of her left breast. She knew what she was doing to him, he thought savagely, and by the thunder of Yahweh, if —

"Perhaps those white crests are spirits," she whispered. "Restless spirits, trying to tell us something."

Antipater straightened and stepped back. She turned from the balustrade and faced him. Even in the half-darkness he could glimpse the tiny smile on her lips.

"Is there anything else you can offer, Antipater, War Minister of the Jews?" she asked, challenging him.

There was a fierce urgency in his groin. His instinct was to seize her. He held himself rigid, but to his amazement he heard himself saying huskily, "I have a certain influence with the king of the Nabataeans."

Nabataeans! Hordes of desert tribesmen!

"You have!" Cleopatra exclaimed. She moved a step nearer. Her perfume was like a mist enclosing him. "Why not have your evening meal here with me?" she breathed, and this time her voice itself was an incitement, an aphrodisiac. "We could — discuss, couldn't we?" And somehow her body was touching his, delicately.

With a low growl, deep in his throat, Antipater took her in his arms, fiercely.

Back in the corner of the room nearest the balcony, Apollodorus groaned to himself,

"Again! Yes, again."

# 4

It was exactly two weeks since Pompey had escaped from Brundisium. Outside there was a nasty winter wind and spits of rain. Servilia shivered, got up to take a robe from a chair, and flung it around her; then she came to Caesar, taking his head in her arms and pressing it against her breasts.

"Could you tell me, darling, why you're doing what you are doing?" she asked. He freed himself. "I'll tell you."

She bent to put a kiss on his bald spot, then stood up, went over to the table, poured two goblets of wine, brought them back, gave one to him, turned to pick up his robe for him, and sat beside him. He stood up, slipped on the robe, sat down again, looked at her, and said,

"I did my best to force a peace. You know that, don't you?"

She nodded, took a sip of wine, and said, "I appreciate, too, your clemency. That Domitius, for instance. Letting him go free."

Caesar took a sip from his goblet. "When I had Corfinium encircled, Domitius tried to slip away, leaving his army behind. His troops seized him and came over to me." He smiled, turning to her. "You should have seen him, Servilia, him and the nobles with him. They were sweating, lard rolling off them, and he was worst of all. Thought I'd lop off his head on the spot." He ran his fingers through his thinning hair. "Now I hear that he's put herdsmen and slaves on board warships and is making for Massilia."

"That's not honourable. However, enough of Domitius." She turned to look directly at him. "What about the war, Julius? Any chance of ending it?"

"If Pompey would only agree to meet with me. I'm puzzled, sweetheart. Why won't he?"

"You have a blind spot there, Julius. Don't you understand? You've stabbed him in his most vulnerable spot, his vanity. He won't — can't — rest until he's proved to the world that he's a better general than you. Every new success you have—all it does is to inflame the wound. If you were to approach him as a suppliant — "

"Never!" Caesar said, getting to his feet.

She looked up at him sadly. "So the war must go on—brother against brother?"

Caesar turned to look down at her. "I'll hold out an olive branch, time after time. Meantime, I must look to myself."

"Which means?"

Caesar began to walk around the room. "Consider my position," he told her as he walked. "Pompey has seven legions in Spain, five of them in the north under two fairly good generals. He controls the whole Mediterranean with his fleets. Now he'll be amassing a huge army in Macedonia and Greece. When he's

349

ready," he stopped to look at her, "he can squeeze me between his Spanish legions and his new army, either by marching a roundabout route into Italy, or by transporting that army across the Adriatic."

"So, your answer, Julius?"

"Speed," he said. He came over to sit beside her again. "I've already ordered Curio, with the cohorts I took from Domitius, to go to Sicily and seize it and then invade North Africa. Meanwhile, other cohorts are to take Sardinia. Those moves will assure wheat for Rome. I myself," he turned to look at her, "I'm off with my legions from Italy to Massilia and Spain." He smiled grimly. "Before Pompey realizes it, his Spanish army will be gone."

"Rome and Italy?"

"That's already arranged. Your son-in-law, Lepidus, will be prefect in Rome, and Mark Antony will command the garrison troops I'm leaving in all the towns of Italy." He made a brief gesture. "My clemency to the Roman leaders I've captured is already showing success. Many senators have now decided to stay in Italy. Even Cicero, for that matter, a man whose genius I want to use."

"And you've restored order in Rome." Servilia smiled. "Fulvia had her gangs all ready to riot. She must have been furious!"

"She was. But I've proved, haven't I, dearest, that I'm no Sulla? Or Marius, either?"

"Oh yes, you have, you have," she exclaimed, throwing her arms around him. "I'm proud of you, Julius. And, I see now, this war isn't your fault." She drew back, as another thought came to her. "How long are you staying in Rome?"

"Four days more."

"Four days only," she exclaimed. "Four days!"

"Speed, I told you."

"But then — then. But if you must." She nestled against him. "I love you so. Love you." Her hand went exploring under his robe. "Why, darling, he's ready. Ready!"

"By Bacchus, he is," Caesar said, gathering her to him. Her robe dropped away as she fell backward on the couch.

# 5

"Don't gawk like a man with last year's manure on his boots," Rullus said.

Fadius grinned down at the stocky Italian, "That's what I am —in Rome," he answered.

The two were on leave from the camp of Caesar's bodyguard of two thousand men, just outside the city. Fadius knew that Rullus, who had been on furlough in Rome twice, was enjoying being the guide. At the moment they were on the Field of Mars, where the Tiber, curving in a great bend, created a level area.

"What's that?" Fadius asked, pointing. "That big building over there?"

"Pompey's theatre. That one just to its left, that's the big hall he built. The Senate meets there now." Rullus gestured expansively—"Look at the swarms in those porticoes. Lots of gay girls and boys. Want to make a pick-up?"

Fadius shook his head. He turned to stare around him. Here were more crowds, vendors bawling their wares, couples strolling, and, in a cleared space, young men running, jumping, fencing, and wrestling; farther over, a few, naked in spite of the bitter February wind, were leaping into the yellow Tiber.

Fadius shook his head. "Enough to freeze their balls off," he commented.

"Come on," Rullus said, tugging at his arm. "Lots to see yet."

By afternoon Fadius' brain was a mixture of blurred impressions. There had been noise, and smells, and, most of all, people — jostling in the narrow streets between the tall tenements, women screaming at their men and men cursing back, and down below, vendors and shop-keepers shouting their wares, men and women bumping into you and swearing at you, girls grabbing hold of you, children darting in and out —

"Watch your pouch," Rullus had called above the noise, and Fadius had just been in time to stop a hand from snatching it — and had stepped into dog-droppings.

"Zeus damn it all!" he had cursed, scraping his sandal against a stone doorstep.

And then they had come to the vegetable market—artichokes, onions, leeks, melons, beans, peas, everything the market-gardens around Rome grew — and next, to the meat market. More smells, more jostling crowds, darting youngsters, yelping dogs, squalling cats; and on the counters and in the pens and stalls, carcasses of pigs, great hams, huge sides of beef hung high on arches of poles and dripping blood on the cobblestones, cages of squawking chickens and pheasants, pulled out to have their necks wrung, and carts bringing in fresh supplies.

"See the fish," Rullus said unnecessarily.

Fadius looked. Piles of dead-eyed bass, bream, bearded mullets, great slabs of tunny and dolphin, octopuses boiled pink with tentacles wrapped around them, squid, heaps of clams, mussels, everything one could think of, and behind, eviscerated and split open, reed-birds, fig-peckers, robins, song-sparrows, swallows —

"Watch out!" Rullus shouted as a voice yelled at them.

Fadius jumped out of the way of a wagon and turned to look. It was loaded with big balks of timber. Behind rattled another wagon, this one carrying huge blocks of marble, and still another piled high with bricks.

"Building," Rullus said. "Always building. And look, more carts. Meat, vegetables. You can't see it, but down there by that bridge, barges up the Tiber from Ostia are unloading. Wheat mostly. Other things, too. Linens. Big bundles of papyrus. Gems. Coloured marble from Africa. Ethiopian slaves. Name it — Rome has it."

"I've had it," Fadius said, rubbing his eyes. "Enough for today, anyway."

"Nothing doing, lad. You've got to see the Forum, I tell you. Come on."

Fadius had often tried to imagine the Forum. As he stood with Rullus on the base of a statue and stared, he was staring in wonder. Not at the crowds so much. What enthralled him were the statues, the pillars, the glittering monuments, and, straight ahead, the twin temples on the Capitoline Hill thrusting up into a blue, chill sky that was now cleared of clouds.

352

"The one on the left," Rullus said importantly, "Jupiter Capitolinus. To the right, Juno Moneta. That's where the sacred geese saved Rome when Brennus and his Gauls swept down, hundreds of years ago. And look, there to the left where that column of ships-beaks is, that's the Rostra. That's where Cicero used to spout. Our Caesar, too. And see the crowds. Pick them out, lad. Syrians, Egyptians, Jews, Greeks, Spaniards, and, over there, a clot of Germans. Any race you like—name it, it's here. Rome, the centre of the world."

Fadius gazed. "Those litters," he said, "and the sedan-chairs?"

"High-born ladies." Fadius spat. "Not for the likes of us. See? Ethiopians are all the rage these days. Eight to a litter. Now, look to the right, lad. See that tremendous palace on the Esquiline? That's Pompey's. Or was, before he scuttled."

"Oh."

"That street going up to the left, that's into the Subura. Rows of whores there. Cubicles. Girls all naked. Price for each—above her head. Any way you want it. Like to try one?"

Fadius shook his head.

"Up there is where our Caesar was born. Turn round. That's where he lives now. The Regia. Home of the chief pontiff—the high priest of Rome. See that round temple to the right? Temple of Vesta. That's where the undying flame of Rome burns. As long as it burns, Rome lives."

Fadius looked at it with a certain sense of awe.

"Up above it, that building, house of the Vestal Virgins. They tend the flame. And look up there, lad. On top of the Palatine. See the sunlight on those palaces? Each of them as big as a field— well, a small one, anyway. Marble floors. Sculptures. Gardens. Legions of slaves." Rullus spat again. "Not for us buggers. But that is where Caesar's whore lives. You know, Servilia, the one we saw in Cisalpine Gaul." He glanced at his friend. "Well, what d'you think of Rome?"

Fadius shook his head as if trying to clear it. "Sooner live on a farm."

"So would I. Come now, let's get going."

"I've had enough," Fadius objected again. "For today."

353

Rullus grabbed his arm. "Circus Maximus," he said. "You've got to see the Circus Maximus."

They jumped down from the base of the statue and shoved their way through the crowds. The Circus Maximus lay in a great trough between the Palatine and the Aventine Hills. Rullus led the way through the high-arched entrance. Fadius stared at the long spina, around which, Rullus told him, the four-horse chariots raced for seven laps to the finish-line.

There were no chariot-races today, but a couple of charioteers were trying out their steeds at starts, and a saltator with three galloping horses was practising jumping back and forth on them as they sped along. Fadius watched him, almost incredulous.

On the other side of the spina, acrobats with ropes and ladders were sharpening their skills, and there was a trainer with a dancing bear, and an elephant being put through its tricks. Fadius' gaze shifted to the immense tiers of seats on either side, empty now except for a few casual spectators.

"I've seen those seats jammed," Rullus told him with a careless wave of his hand. "The time Pompey brought in a hundred elephants for a beast hunt, and they trumpeted and cried, and the crowd all got up and shouted at him to stop it. Imagine it, lad. Tens and tens of thousands shrieking, shouting, yelling, waving their fists. It made me put my hands over my ears. Well, what d'you think of Rome now?"

"Take me a week to sort it out," Fadius answered, turning away.

"A drink, that'll fix you up." Rullus clapped his friend on the back. "Make the most of these days, Titus. You know our Caesar. We'll be off to Spain before you know it."

Spain, Fadius thought. Massilia was on the road to Spain. Would he see Chione? Did he want to see her?

"Come on, lad," Rullus ordered.

They went back outside. Along the great arches that supported the entrance to the Circus Maximus, crowds were passing and repassing.

"Everything in those arches," Rullus explained. "Shops,

354

brothels, taverns, what have you." He stopped to look after a girl, then studied the footprints left in the dust by her sandals. "'Follow me', " he spelled out laboriously. "'Follow me'. Well, we'll take care of that later." He turned into an archway. "This spot looks good, don't you think?"

It was a tavern which served soup and hunks of bread with hot sausages as well as wine. Fadius slumped down thankfully on a bench. Rullus ordered. They ate and drank, Rullus eyeing the girls as they went by. But Fadius was abstracted. A thought which had surfaced briefly in the Forum had come into his mind again. All these people, he was thinking. Men, women, children. Where would they be, a hundred years from now? Dead. And how many generations, since Rome was founded hundreds of years ago, had been born, had lived, eaten, fornicated, yelled, cursed, grown old, and died? As he himself would. So, what was the point of it all? Why all the fuss? Those people out there, he himself, Titus Fadius, were they or he any more important than the howl of a wolf in the darkness, or, better still, than an ant crawling across a pavement, or a fly on the wall?

"There's an Egyptian girl," Rullus said suddenly. He emptied his cup, flung coins on the rough table, and stood up. "I've never had an Egyptian. Meet you here? An hour from now?"

Fadius nodded. His own cup was empty. He got up, went outside, and watched Rullus catch up to the girl. She stopped. They talked an instant—price, of course, then went on together.

"Waiting for someone, big boy?" a voice said at his elbow. He looked down. A girl with liquid brown eyes looked up at him.

"I'll show you a good time," she said huskily. "A real good time."

She was nicely rounded. Why not? Fadius was thinking. Use them and forget them — that's what he'd vowed after Chione. And, even if one was no more than an ant or a fly —

"All right," he said.

Her eyes lit up. She slipped an arm through his and tugged.

"Come on, big boy," she said.

355

They were sitting in a room in the Regia, Caesar's home. He looked around at them — Servilia, Balbus, Fulvia, Antony, and Lepidus. At a desk near the wall Faberius was waiting, sheets of papyrus ready.

"So you're off in the morning, Julius," Antony said.

Caesar nodded. It was late in the evening of the sixth day of April. The wick of one of the lamps in the room was smoking. Caesar glanced at it.

"Early," he said. He leaned back in his chair. "Won't see you again until after Spain. So, we'll check." He leaned forward. "Lepidus, you're in charge of Rome. If any problem turns up, consult with Servilia and Balbus. I've assigned you enough money?"

Lepidus nodded. Caesar turned to Fulvia.

"And you, Lady Fulvia, you'll keep the peace. Understand?"

She, too, nodded. But her sleepy-lidded eyes were almost closed, and her full lips were sulky.

"If you don't," Caesar went on, watching her, "Lepidus here has orders to use troops."

She glanced sideways at him. "May I, at least, have extra wheat issued? To keep my men happy?"

Caesar considered. "Your husband, Curio, has chased Cato out of Sicily," he commented. "So extra wheat should come in soon. When it does, Balbus will look to it for you."

"Curio goes on to Africa next, doesn't he?" Antony put in.

"Yes. Antony, your job is to look after Italy. I'll need ships, too, when I get back. Two fleets — one in the Adriatic, the other in the Tyrrhenian Sea. See to it."

Antony leaned forward. "I'll need more money."

"I've advanced you plenty."

"Your troops in Italy to pay," Antony argued. "Ships to get. That'll be expensive."

Caesar considered it a moment. "I'm leaving a reserve with Balbus," he said. "If you need more, put your case to him. Faberius will keep track of it all."

"Getting money out of Balbus is like squeezing acorns out of a pig's guts," Antony grumbled. "How much did you get out of that Treasury, anyway, Julius?"

Caesar thought back to the encounter two days ago when the tribune Metellus had tried to prevent his soldiers from carrying off the state treasure left behind by the panic-stricken Pompeians. No harm in telling this group. Servilia and Balbus already knew the amount.

"Fifteen thousand pounds of gold bullion," he said quietly. "Thirty-five thousand pounds of silver. And about forty million sesterces in coins."

Antony whistled. "A few million more to me won't hurt," he suggested.

"I told you I've left a reserve. The rest is already on its way to Massilia. I need it all, Antony. My Gallic legions to pay, for one thing. For another, I plan to enlist the Gallic princes and their men. Keep them on my side. That will cost." He stood up. "Anything else?"

Fulvia was still sulking. Antony glanced at her, noting how her copper-red hair gleamed in the light of the candelabrum above her. She's a hot one, he was thinking. She'll need it — and with Curio away —

He caught Servilia smiling at him, and knew she knew what he was thinking.

"Nothing from me," he said gruffly.

"In that case," Caesar said, "Calpurnia has a collation waiting. If you ladies will go first — "

Before first light the next morning at the entrance of the atrium, Caesar said his farewells to Calpurnia. Except for the year of his consulship when he had married her for political reasons, and a couple of occasions when she had come up to Cisalpine Gaul, they had not seen each other. But he had developed a respect for this quiet-voiced, dignified woman. She wasn't a beauty. She was lean and rusty-haired. But she handled herself well. No fuss, ever.

"Take care of yourself," he said now.

She was only a couple of inches shorter than he. Her eyes were

357

grave as she looked at him. He had never taken the trouble to find out, but she admired him tremendously and was concerned about him.

"And you take care of yourself, Julius," she answered. "That cough of yours. I've put a potion in your bag. I had Charicles mix it. Be sure you take it."

"Thank you. You're a nice person," he added impulsively and, taking her by the shoulders, put a kiss on her cheek. "Good luck."

"Good luck to you," she answered as he released her. Then she watched him turn and stride out of the house. Would he be back? she wondered.

A little later, on the crest of the Janiculum Hill, Caesar had his driver stop the carriage. His mounted escort, which included Fadius and Rullus, halted. His two secretaries, sitting across from him, waited expectantly. But Caesar was looking down at Rome. Six days after ten years' absence was not enough, he was telling himself. Then, his face took on a brooding look.

Like Fadius, he was thinking of the long history of Rome, but his point of view was different. What he was considering was, first of all, the days when, seven centuries ago, there had only been stockaded peasant villages on those seven hills. Look at them now! It was a miracle, really. In the beginning, he reflected, it had been little by little. A loyal, stubborn people led by selfless, ruthless men to whom Rome came first, always. Little by little, step by persistent step — and the values had been courage, puritanical virtues, honesty, patriotism.

Those were the values to which Cato wanted Romans to return. One could never turn back the sun-dial of the years, no matter how much one wanted to. The wealth that had flooded in after the conquest of the East had swept away those values of long ago. In modern Rome it was grab, grab, grab—and all that mattered was how much you had, and no one cared how you'd got it. Anything goes — that was modern Rome.

Yet, he thought, he loved Rome—that is, the idea of Rome as ruler of the world. What other city was better fitted for that rôle?

Provided the cankers were cut out. If only a man's life were not so short.

He shifted on his seat. Time — time was so brief for one, so relentless in its pressure. He'd like to meditate now, for instance, to let his mind consider the meaning of man's presence on this earth, or whether there was any purpose for his existence, or was it all, as the Hebrew king, Solomon, had once said, vanity—in a word, nothingness. But hurry — hurry — that was his portion now. Hurry to Spain. Hurry back again. Spare Romans — because they were Romans. Barbarians? They did not matter. But Romans —

He took a last look. The thought crossed his mind that down there in that city to which dawn was coming, Vercingetorix was mouldering in prison. He had intended to do something about that. The man, after all, must be preserved to walk in his, Caesar's, triumph over Gaul; so his health was important — and now that triumph was indefinitely postponed. Perhaps, when he returned from Spain — that is, if he returned.

If he didn't return, it would not matter. But he would win, he told himself. He was Caesar. He'd win. He raised a hand to the coachman.

"Drive on," he said.

# CHAPTER V

FRUSTRATION! Caesar looked up at the massive walls of Massilia. Two months since he had left Rome and still not in Spain. For when Domitius, the enemy he had spared at Corfinium, had reached Massilia with seven warships, the city had closed its gates against the Caesarians — and Massilia sat astride the great road to Spain.

Caesar had been inspecting his siege-works. Crumpling in his hand the dispatches he had just read, he started to walk slowly back to camp, his officers following him. The sun was bright on the inland hills. The flowers of May were everywhere, and the grape-vines on those hills were in green leaf. What to do?

He paused, head down, considering the situation. He had brought three veteran legions to besiege Massilia. Since Massilia was a port and a fleet was necessary to blockade it, he had had his legionaries build twelve warships — thirty days from the moment the first tree was felled until those ships were in the Rhodanus River, ready to go. Meanwhile, he had sent the legate Gaius Fabius with six of his veteran legions across the Pyrenees into Spain, and had persuaded the Gallic nobles to lead three thousand horsemen to join Fabius.

But Massilia was a turtle with a shell that was hard to crack. One dispatch in his hand told him that Pompey was amassing huge forces in Macedonia. A second, a joint letter from Servilia and Balbus, informed him that because of his check at Massilia, Cicero had sailed to join Pompey, and the neutral senators in Rome and Italy were veering in the same direction. The third, from Fabius, said that at Ilerda in northern Spain it was a stalemate between his forces and five Pompeian legions.

He could wait no longer. His two legates here, Decimus Brutus and Gaius Trebonius, were competent generals. The three legions were enough to carry on the siege. Caesar turned to his officers.

"My tent, gentlemen," he said. "New plans."

Early the next morning, at the head of the nine hundred men of his body-guard, he was galloping toward the Pyrenees. In the early afternoon of a day in the third week of June, he was met on this side of the Sicoris River, on which Ilerda stood, by an escort headed by Fabius. As they rode across the upper wooden bridge that Fabius' troops had built, Caesar was looking this way and that, refreshing his memory about the plain which Ilerda dominated.

The plain ran from south to north on both sides of the Sicoris River until inland the foothills of the Pyrenees closed it off. Some thirty miles to the west was another river, the Cinga, which, to the south below Ilerda, curved in through low hills to join the Sicoris River. This meant, in effect, that Fabius' camp was in a sort of delta between the two rivers.

"Did you say," Caesar asked Fabius, as they crossed the Sicoris into the delta, "that your bridge downstream was swept away?"

"A storm," Fabius answered. "It's being rebuilt."

"Good." Caesar reined in his horse and looked to his left toward Ilerda. It sat on its hill on the delta side of the Sicoris, but he knew that a stone bridge linked it to the eastern bank.

"Our weakness," he said thoughtfully, "is in your two wooden bridges, Fabius. They are our only connection with Gaul — and our supplies come from Gaul."

"Another bridge?"

"Perhaps." Caesar pointed to the south. "Is that the Pompeian camp?"

Fabius nodded. It was on a hill in the delta about a third of a mile west of Ilerda.

"Their strength?"

"Five veteran legions to our six," Fadius told him. "But Afranius and Petreius have ten thousand cavalry and almost forty thousand Spanish auxiliaries."

"That many?"

361

"Yes, Imperator. A few of that forty thousand are heavy-armed troops. The most, light-armed."

"And we have only five thousand light-armed," Caesar commented thoughtfully. "Only six thousand cavalry, too. But ours are all battle-hardened. Three thousand who fought with me — three thousand Gauls who fought against us. We can make do." He paused. The plain was green with springing crops, and the low hills dotted here and there were carpeted with flowers. But Caesar was looking at the Pompeian camp and at a knoll halfway between it and Ilerda. "We can't waste time, Fabius," he went on. "I'll have to make things happen."

"How, Imperator?"

But Caesar had already turned his horse toward the Caesarian camp.


## 2


"Mars' pecker!" Rullus swore. "Look at that!"

Fadius was staring, too. He and Rullus had been leading a patrol toward Ilerda. Now, over the foothills, twenty miles away, heavy clouds, bowing toward the earth, were advancing rapidly south toward the plain. Flash after flash of lightning, both chain and fork, lit up those clouds, and crash after crash of thunder reached them, even at this distance. Although it was only late afternoon, the countryside around them had already darkened and the air was still, that deathly stillness which precedes a storm.

"See that line of white behind," Rullus said, pointing.

"Come on," Fadius ordered. "Let's get these buggers back to camp."

They started back. It was the seventh day since Caesar had arrived. In that period he had had his men build a new camp close to the Pompeian camp. Then, two days ago, he had tried to seize the knoll halfway between the Pompeians and Ilerda, hoping to cut off their communication line. He had failed. What was worse, in the ensuing battle on the slopes right under Ilerda's

362

walls, his men had been actually worsted. Caesar had retired to his camp. Now he watched with apprehension this storm from the north that was rushing down on the plain.

Fadius and Rullus had barely made it to the camp when the wind hit, tearing at the towers, the ramparts, and the tents within them. It was a short, fierce burst. Then came the rain. And what rain, cloudburst after cloudburst, as if the oceans themselves had been lifted up and dumped down. Within an hour the delta was a quagmire. So was the ground within the camp, even though it was on a low hill. Tents were beaten down into the mud. Stores were soaked. And the cloudburst kept on until near dawn. Then it settled into a steady downpour. The centurions drove the legionaries, their clothing sodden, into the rain to rescue the stores, to get their hide tents up, to dig drainage ditches, to clear the debris.

As the men cursed and fumbled in the driving rain, Caesar, in his headquarters tent, was talking to a peasant. Caesar, propraetor of Spain twelve years ago, knew Spanish.

"My crops done for," the peasant was wailing. "Smashed into the mud. Not a stalk, not a kernel left."

"What will it do to the Sicoris River?" Caesar asked.

"Over its banks already, Imperator." The peasant tore at his hair with both hands. "My cattle—they're drowning. Drowning! Can't your soldiers help? It's going higher, Imperator. Snow from the mountains melting—"

Caesar looked at Fabius. "I wonder about your bridges," he said soberly.

"Let's hope it stops soon," Fabius answered.

The rain kept on all that day and night and the next day and night. On the morning of the third day when Caesar and Fabius climbed the camp's watchtower, an ironically bright sun shone down from a new-washed sky. Neither man said a word at first as the two of them looked on flood-waters sparkling in tiny ripples to the Sicoris River and beyond. They already knew that both of Fabius' wooden bridges had been swept away and that thirty miles to the west the Cinga, too, had poured over its banks. Still worse, the stone bridge at Ilerda had held.

"It's bad, Imperator," Fabius said, shaking his head.

"Could scarcely be worse," Caesar agreed. "They," he nodded toward Ilerda, "can cross the stone bridge and forage on the other side. We, on the other hand, are isolated on this delta. No crops. No cattle. Food for man and beast will be in short supply, Fabius."

"New bridges — when the flood-waters recede?"

Caesar pointed to the flood-waters. "It'll take days for that to drain away. Afterward, for still more days the current will be too full and strong. There are three channels to the river here. So, we have to go upstream—where the current will be still fiercer." He paused. "And our reinforcements and supply convoys from Gaul," he said grimly, "have no way of getting through."

"And the Pompeians can patrol the opposite bank," Fabius added gloomily. "They can stop us from bridging, Imperator, even after the river's down."

"Exactly."

"So what do we do, Imperator?" Fabius flung out both hands. "Days. Weeks. What will we do?"

Caesar turned away, his face grim.

"Endure," he said.

At that moment, on the watchtower of the Pompeian camp, Afranius was exultant.

"We have them," he said to his grizzled second-in-command, Petreius. "Like kittens in a sack for drowning."

"It would seem so," Petreius said slowly.

Afranius was a sanguine man whose big nose dominated his face. He clapped Petreius on the back.

"No doubt about it, man." He turned to leave the tower. "I'm writing dispatches to my wife in Rome, and to Pompey. Get a swift ship ready at once, will you, there's a good fellow?"

When those dispatches reached Rome their contents spread through the city like scraps of paper blown by the wind. The neutral senators flocked to the home of Afranius on the Quirinal to congratulate his wife. In the African salon of Servilia's palace on the Palatine, she and Balbus met to discuss the news. Balbus,

364

as usual, sat on a chair, both hands planted on his knees. Servilia moved restlessly through the room, the candid eyes introspective.

"Afranius says he won a battle," she said. She picked up a statue of Venus Anadyomene done in two tones of coloured marble. "That's bad enough." She set it down on a table and turned to face her friend. "He says Julius is cut off in a delta between two rivers with no food nor forage. He says Caesar will have to surrender, or his starving troops will force him to."

"Julius has been in tight corners before this."

"But if he doesn't get out of this one," — she sank down on a sofa covered with a throw made of panther skins — "they'll lop off his head. This war — oh, how I hate it!"

"Our job," Balbus said stolidly, "is to look after Rome and Italy." He stood up. "Antony came to me today. He wants money from the reserve fund."

"Antony thinks it rains sesterces, the way he spends them," Servilia said with asperity.

"He has a point this time, Lady. With Pompey's fleets controlling the sea, ships are expensive."

"How much does he want?"

"Ten million sesterces."

"Give him half that." Servilia got up and again began to wander restlessly around the room. "Oh, Julius, Julius," she was thinking. "May you be safe!"

# 3

Meanwhile Antony was looking with disgust at the piles of reports and dispatches his secretaries had arranged on the table of his study. Paper-work! Getting up, he walked to the doorway and looked at the garden in the peristyle of his modest mansion on the Caelian Hill. Bees were buzzing around the beds of marigolds and yellow chrysanthemums, and the bower of roses was in full bloom. So were the hyacinths and irises. Antony stepped out into the hot sun, stretched his arms, and looked over the garden wall at the glittering roofs of the palaces on the Palatine.

Fulvia! he thought. And Curio in Africa! He turned back into the study.

"Answers to those that need them," he said to the two secretaries. He tossed his signet-ring on the table. "Stamp them with that. I'm going out."

An hour and a half later, freshly shaved, bathed, and perfumed, hair curled, pro-praetorian toga carefully arranged, he was drinking wine with Fulvia in an alcove off one of the gardens in the palace that had once belonged to Clodius. The scent of flowers drifted in. Close to the entrance an iridescent hummingbird was sipping nectar from a convolvulus. Just beyond it a peacock was strutting, jewelled fan outspread.

"Summer," Antony said with a wave of his goblet. "Best time of the year." He gulped his wine. "Best time for everything."

Fulvia, of course, knew why he'd come. If he thought her a tavern wench, eager for a tumble —

"Wine for Marcus Antonius," she said to the slave-girl in attendance. The girl, very conscious of this Roman's maleness, leaned close as she poured. Meanwhile Fulvia was considering Antony. Handsome. Virile, as she had sensed when she had first met him. Those two facts didn't mean too much to her. The important fact was that he held power over Italy—and Fulvia, as with Clodius and now with Curio, had a compulsive ambition.

How long could this man wield power without blundering, she wondered, watching him pinch the slave-girl's buttock and then lift the goblet to his lips. Not too long, she decided. There was no subtlety here, no sense of nuances such as Curio had. If Curio won in Africa —

"What is your estimate of Caesar's difficulties?" she asked.

Antony took the goblet from his lips. "No need to worry," he declared. He drank another gulp of wine, wiped his mouth with the back of his hand, and leaned forward. "Let's talk about you. You must be missing it."

Stupid bull! Fulvia thought.

"I manage," she said coolly.

Wanted to be coaxed, did she? Antony finished his drink, set the goblet on the citrus-wood table beside him, and leaned forward further, his gaze fixed on the full, rose-nippled breasts beneath her thin robe.

"A beautiful woman like you," he said. "I've always wanted you. You know that. Let's do something about it."

Fulvia glanced at the slave-girl. What slaves saw or heard didn't matter. All the same —

"Another refill for Marcus Antonius," she ordered.

Antony held out his goblet without taking his eyes off her.

"Let me show you," he urged. He took a deep drink from the refilled goblet, set it down, and got to his feet. "Send the girl away. Or let her stay. I'll show her — and you — something."

Fulvia was examining her painted finger-nails. "No, Antony."

Teasing him? Only one way to handle that. Antony took two steps toward her. Fulvia got to her feet swiftly.

"I said 'No'." And then, contemptuously, "You're drunk, Antony."

Antony stopped. "Never get drunk," he boasted. "Just makes me better at it." He reached for her. As his hands touched her shoulders, she slapped his face, a full swing that stung. Antony stepped back, hand going to his cheek.

"What's that for?" he asked.

Her eyes were blazing. "I told you 'No'." She gathered her robe around her. "Now get out."

"Bitch!"

"Get yourself a nice fat cow," she said. "One that suits you."

Turning, she swept out the entrance. Antony stared after her, fury boiling in him. If he ever got that bitch alone —

The slave-girl coughed delicately. Antony swung around. Well, all right! Catching her up, he carried her to the sofa and dumped her down. This one, at least, would take it.

Later, Antony sat in the fifth night haunt he had visited, with a couple of boon companions and a dozen of his personal slaves.

"Bitch!" he was mumbling to his companions. "Don't tell me

367

she hasn't someone. That red hair. Hot, I'll bet you, the bitch."
He raised his voice. "Wine!" he roared. "More wine. For everyone. D'you hear?"

"Yes, master, yes!" the owner, a Cypriot, stammered and
shouted at his slaves. As they scurried around, Antony seized the
Cypriot by the arm.

"Where's the girls?" he bellowed. "Eh? Where's the girls?"

"Right away, master. If you'll just let me go — "

"Hurry 'em up," Antony ordered. He gave the Cypriot a
shove that sent him across the floor to crash into the bar.

Two taverns back, the Cypriot had heard, this giant Roman
had smashed every bench and table into kindling-wood and had
left the proprietor with a broken arm and leg. Gathering himself
up, he scuttled behind the curtain of the tiny stage at the end of
the tavern.

"Get the girls out," he yelled at the woman with whom he
lived. "Get the curtain down."

"Make-up," the woman began.

"Get them on stage." He struck her. "Get them out."

As the woman turned to obey, the Cypriot beckoned to his
confidential slave.

"Cithaeris," he told him. "Get Cithaeris over here. Fast as you
can."

"She costs, master."

"Doesn't matter. Get her over. Tell her, ten gold pieces." He
gripped the slave's arm. "And tell her it's Mark Antony. Mark
Antony!" He turned. "Down with the curtain," he ordered his
woman.

As the curtain rolled down, Antony swung around to look. A
half-dozen girls were posed there.

"Take it off," Antony shouted. His companions joined in.
"Take it off! Take it off!"

The girls flung off their robes quickly. Naked, the girls — a
troupe from Gades in Spain — danced lewdly, bumping, grind-
ing, lowering quivering buttocks almost to the ground as they
simulated the act of sex. Antony regarded them sourly. Stage-
hands hurriedly flung down a couple of big mats on the floor of

the stage. The girls took turns, gyrating their hips, knees bent and thighs spread wide, with only their shoulders and feet touching the mats, each trying to outdo the other in movements and wanton cries.

It quickly became monotonous, one pubic exposure after another. Antony lurched to his feet.

"Not one of those cows worth a screw," he bellowed. "Here, you."

The Cypriot, who had come out to watch anxiously, turned to run. One big hand grabbed his neck and lifted him from the floor. The other seized his crotch.

"Wait, master," the Cypriot squealed as Antony swung him up high. "Wait. Cithaeris!" Antony paused. "Look, master! Look!"

Antony looked. The dancers had scuttled away. On the right side of the stage a woman stood, one hand on an indolent hip, thigh thrust forward, knee bent, hair like the gloss of a raven's wing falling over her shoulders, face ivory white, inscrutable smile, green eyes looking into the distance as if neither he nor anyone were there — and she did not care.

Almost carefully, Antony lowered the Cypriot to the floor and sat down, his eyes never leaving the woman. She took three delicate steps toward centre stage and posed again, eyes still looking into the far distance. The black mist of her robe flung around her showed and yet shadowed her, the erect, full-nippled breasts, the tiny waist, the long, rounded legs and thighs, the shaven pubic mound, and, as she turned slowly, rounded buttocks. She began to dance with long, gliding steps, again as if no one were there.

"Who did you say?" Antony asked hoarsely.

The Cypriot, no longer afraid, leered at him. "Cithaeris. From Alexandria."

She was lithe. She was graceful. The thin byssus parted and closed, revealing then concealing. The smile was still on her lips, and her eyes still looked into distance. Antony jumped to his feet.

"That one's mine," he roared. "By the phallus of Hercules, she's mine."

369

He surged across the benches and leaped onto the stage. The woman stopped dancing to face him. She was still smiling that faraway smile, and her eyes were as centreless as a rippleless, shadowed pool. With a growl, Antony caught her in his arms, swung her up as if she were a sack of feathers, jumped from the stage, and started for the exit.

"Master," the Cypriot was pleading. "Master."

Antony paused. "Throw him a bag of gold," he ordered his chief slave, and strode on, tightening his grip. Cithaeris laughed, a light, teasing tinkle of sound, and circled his bull neck with one perfumed arm. She knew about Marcus Antonius, Caesar's commander in Italy, said to be herculean in size and herculean in appetites. It was his name that had brought her, a high-priced courtesan, to this greasy tavern. She knew, too, as he carried her through the exit, that all he had in mind was gratification for a night.

But she was Cithaeris. She knew that, no matter how often or in how many ways a man had her, he would be left with a feeling that there was still a part of her he had not explored, had not mastered.

"So bull-like," she mocked as he turned down the street. "Is that all you are — a bull?"

"You'll find out," Antony said hoarsely.

4

In Spain, it was past the middle of Quintilis, the month that followed June. The floodwaters had receded, and the delta between the Sicoris and the Cinga rivers was baking under a hot sun.

But Caesar's situation was worse, not better. The Sicoris still flowed so full and strong that it was not fordable. Nor could he repair the broken bridges, not in the face of strong Pompeian forces on the opposing east bank. No word from Gaul or Italy could reach him. His legionaries were starving, and what food could be got now cost fifty times its proper price. The cavalry, by foraging in the northern foothills or using what was left of the crops in the delta, were managing to find fodder for their horses.

That fact was the only bright spot. At this moment, early in the afternoon, bodyguard behind him, he was sitting on Five-Toes, well upstream, staring across the Sicoris. On the further bank a massive convoy from Gaul — wagons full of supplies, deputations with their wives and children, camp-followers, pack-horses — was fleeing into the foothills. Their rear was protected by Gallic archers and horsemen who were holding back the Pompeian cavalry. But now three Pompeian legions had reached the scene—and he, Caesar, had to sit and watch. As he gazed, frustrated, the Pompeian cohorts charged. He saw the Gallic horsemen turn in flight, the archers cut down, a half-dozen of the wagons seized, a few groups of camp-followers caught and massacred. Grimly he waited for the Pompeians to re-form and go into the foothills after the fleeing convoy, that convoy he so desperately needed.

If he had known, that was what Petreius was urging. Afranius shook his head.

"Ravines in there," he pointed out. "Wooded gullies. Ambuscades. Why waste men?"

"It's worth it," Petreius argued. "They're disorganized. Take the whole lot."

Afranius scratched his nose. He looked across at Caesar.

"Only two legions left in our camp," he said thoughtfully. "Caesar over there is desperate. Suppose he attacks while we're up here?"

Petreius started to speak but Afranius cut him off.

"Look," he said. "That convoy can't get away. As for him," he nodded at Caesar, "he can't get away, either. All we have to do is wait. Take no risks. Just wait."

Caesar watched the Pompeian legions form up and turn to march back to camp. It wasn't what he himself would have done. For the moment that convoy was safe. If only there was some way to get it across the Sicoris.

He started to turn Five-Toes toward camp and suddenly checked his steed. Britain had flashed into his mind — and those

371

oval boats on the Tamesis—coracles, that was their name—and the convoy over there in the foothills — He swung Five-Toes around. "Upstream," he said to the military tribune with him. "We're riding upstream."

As darkness fell two nights later, a cortège of twenty pairs of coupled-together wagons, each pair carrying a dome-bottomed coracle, began to lurch upstream from Caesar's camp. Legionaries who had been in Britain had put them together rapidly from frameworks of light timber covered with wattles and hides. Twenty-two miles north of the camp, well into the foothills, the procession reached the spot Caesar had chosen.

False dawn was just breaking. As the legionaries began to off-load the coracles, Fadius and Rullus, each of whom was to command a coracle, walked to the bank of the Sicoris. The ground on which they stood was more or less level but twenty feet above the water. They looked down. Even in this light, the current was turbulent. Across the forty-foot stream was a narrow strip of beach with a low hill above it. Rullus spat.

"It'll be a bugger," Fadius said.

"You think so?" Caesar's voice said behind them.

They both turned and snapped a salute.

"It has to be done, somehow," Caesar said. He stepped forward to stare down at the current. "Our only chance, Fadius. Any suggestions?"

Fadius looked carefully up and down the stream. Then, he pointed upstream.

"Why not launch from there, Imperator?" he said. "There, where the bank is low. If we launch from here the current will carry us past that beach across from us. From up there, it might carry us just right."

Caesar clapped him on the shoulder. "Excellent, Titus Fadius," he said. "Excellent—and you'll be in the first coracle."

Should have kept my bloody mouth shut, Fadius was thinking. A few moments later, he and eight legionaries were in the first of three coracles. One of the men clutched the end of a light line to carry across if they were lucky. The rest had paddles.

372

Fadius looked downstream toward the hill. He gripped his own paddle.

"Paddle as if demons were after you," he called to his men, and then to the legionaries holding the coracle to the bank, "Let go."

An instant later the coracle was out in the stream, lurching and swinging around like a spinning top almost at the end of its gyrations. The legionaries paddled as if Fadius' demons were real. Two other coracles were launched after them. As Caesar watched, hands tightly clenched, with a final desperate lurch Fadius' coracle just managed to ground on the beach beneath the hill. Fadius jumped out to hold the coracle. The man with the line followed and began to haul across the rope attached to it. The other legionaries ran into the water to grab the second and third coracles. They unloaded, and the men in them, drawing their swords, began to climb the hill. Caesar drew in a deep breath and turned away.

"Get the engineers over here," he called to his military tribune.

To engineers and legionaries who had bridged the Rhenus River not once but twice, the Sicoris was no obstacle. Within two days the bridge was finished, and the convoy from Gaul, over six thousand souls as it turned out, was crossing it, along with enough supplies to keep Caesar's men well fed for weeks. On the next morning Caesar, scarcely believing that Afranius and Petreius were still not cognizant of what had been achieved, poured across his cavalry. The first news the Pompeian commanders had of Caesar's new bridge was when the Caesarian horsemen swept down from the hills upon their foraging parties in the plain across the Sicoris. The two commanders stared at each other.

"We should have gone in after that convoy," Petreius said. "As I wanted to, remember?"

"But who could have imagined — " Afranius began.

"Now it's Caesar, with all that battle-hardened cavalry, who's got us by the balls," Petreius interrupted, banging a fist into the palm of his other hand. "Not the other way round."

The reversal of fortune was even more damaging than Petreius had feared. As he had expected, now it was the Caesarians, with their cavalry advantage, who were able to forage freely on both sides of the Sicoris. What he had not anticipated was news that Curio had won a victory in Africa, and, even more important, that Decimus Brutus had triumphed in a naval battle off Massilia. Caesar saw to it that both successes were trumpeted throughout northern Spain. The towns which had been supporting the Pompeians changed sides. With protestations of deepest respect, they sent supplies and promises of aid to Caesar.

"He still can't beat us here," Afranius maintained. "That bridge of his is too far upstream for his legionaries to threaten us. By the time he got them up there, across, and back here again, we'd have his camp. So as long as we can prevent him from bridging the Sicoris close to Ilerda, we're safe."

Petreius nodded. But next day in the early morning he came into Afranius' tent.

"We're in trouble," he said.

Afranius put down a hunk of bread and cheese.

"What!"

"Come and see."

A few minutes later, on the watchtower of the Pompeian camp, Afranius stared northward. There, just beyond Ilerda, Caesar's legionaries were busy with picks and shovels.

"What in Mars' name — " he started to ask.

"I've been up to see," Petreius interrupted. "They're digging ditches, Afranius. From the main channel of the Sicoris to its two smaller branches. Ditches about thirty feet wide."

"To make the Sicoris fordable!" Afranius exclaimed.

"Exactly. If—no, when—he can get his legionaries across, we will be trapped in Ilerda and in our camp. We'll be starved out—in our turn."

Afranius pulled at his lower lip. "It will take that devil several days—before he can make the Sicoris fordable, I mean. So what do we do?"

"Get out before he closes the trap," Petreius said. "Retreat behind the Hiberus River."

374

The Hiberus was a big river into which the Cinga and the Sicoris rivers both emptied about thirty miles downstream.

Afranius looked around. "We can't retreat to the west or the south," he objected. "Not with the Cinga River to cross and that bastard on our backs."

"Cross over the stone bridge, over the Sicoris. Can't you see? We can get to the mouth of the Hiberus that way."

"But there's no bridge there."

"Send couriers. Tell them down there to make a bridge of boats for us. Once across the Hiberus, we're safe."

"All our stores," Afranius said dejectedly.

"Better to lose our stores than our legions," Petreius pointed out.

"All right. Let's get busy."

As the Pompeian commanders reached this decision, Caesar, after inspecting the progress of the ditching, was reading dispatches couriers had brought. They were favourable. At Massilia, Decimus Brutus had won another naval battle. From Africa, Curio reported a second victory. Even more important was the news that Gaul was loyal, and from Rome that the reports of his success in Spain had swung the neutral senators back to Caesar. A private note from Servilia, however, brought a frown to his face. It told him that Antony was travelling through southern Italy with the courtesan Cithaeris and a bevy of both sexes.

"That in itself would not matter too much," Servilia wrote, "considering Antony's reputation. But he gives receptions and banquets in the town halls with Cithaeris as his chatelaine! You know how conservative small towns are. Well, imagine the proper, respectable wives of proper, respectable town mayors and councillors forced to bow to a whore as their hostess. Just imagine the clacking tongues! And how they nag at their husbands. It's bad for you and your supporters among the middle class. Better stop it, Julius."

Caesar put down the letter, still frowning. He'd get off a sharp note to Antony, he decided. But first he'd settle with these Pompeians here.

Ten days later, on the plain to the northeast of Ilerda, sitting in his curule chair on a hastily erected tribunal, he received the surrender of Afranius and Petreius and all their forces; and he had managed it without a battle. It was a proud moment. Ten days ago he and his men had seen two Pompeian legions cross the stone bridge at Ilerda and camp on the other bank of the river. The Caesarian troops knew what this probably meant — a southward retreat down the east side of the Sicoris to the mouth of the Hiberus, and then a line of defence behind it. The job to do all over again. Caesar's men redoubled their digging, working day and night. By the following day the Sicoris was fordable for cavalry. But early in the morning of the very next day, Caesar and his troops had watched the other three Pompeian legions cross the stone bridge and the whole force, horse and infantry, turn downstream. Caesar sent his own cavalry over the Sicoris. Yet he knew and the legionaries knew that the most the cavalry could do was to harass the enemy. They could not stop the march.

Escaping! Caesar had stood, his face grim. In its main channel the Sicoris was still up to the shoulders of the infantry and the current was powerful. He was thinking bitterly that he'd have to let the Pompeians get away.

At that moment the senior centurions, led by the veteran Crastinus, came running to him with the news that the legionaries were demanding that he allow them to ford the river.

Caesar had shaken his head. "Current's too strong," he had said. "Up to your shoulders, too. We'd lose men."

"Better that than let those bloody buggers get away," Crastinus had shouted at him. The other centurions had roared assent. "We crossed the Liger, didn't we?" Crastinus had cried. "After Gergovia. Come on, Imperator!"

Caesar's face had lit up. "All right," he shouted back, "if you stupid bastards want to have a go at it, I will. Only I go first. Understand? First!"

Then, it had been a rush. As at the Liger, Caesar had put one line of cavalry upstream and another downstream to save any men who were swept off their feet. In this operation not a soldier had been lost. Then it had been a race for the main defile through the rugged hills downstream. The Caesarians had won. After-, ward, the Pompeians had been shepherded as they tried to get back to Ilerda until, cut off from water and short of food, they had given up.

All this was in Caesar's mind as he looked down at Afranius and Petreius. At this moment the future seemed as bright and fair to him as the sunlit plain around him. He had already decided to let Afranius and Petreius go where they willed, and to discharge all their troops, with permission either to return to their homes or to enlist under him. Next, with these five Pompeian legions dissolved, and his own ranks swelled, he planned to march south to take over the rest of Spain. To think, he was reflecting, that within forty days of his arrival at Ilerda he had disposed of Pompey's best army, the army on which his rival had counted! Surely his luck, Caesar's luck, was perched firmly on his shoulders.

Both armies were now assembled before him. They expected a speech, a speech of which the words, or the gist of them, would be repeated back through the ranks by those who were close enough to hear him. Caesar looked toward Italy and Rome for an instant. Yes, his words would be those of a victor — but of a clement victor. Servilia would be proud of him when, later, she heard what he had said. Gathering his proconsul's toga about him, he stood up. As he rose, throughout the massed ranks there was a silence, the hushed silence of men who, faces upturned, await the words of the master.

# CHAPTER VI

"WINE," Antony ordered.

The slave hurried to the sideboard to fill a goblet. Antony took it and drank.

"That's better," he said, and picked up Caesar's letter to reread it. The letter, a note attached to Caesar's report of his victory at Ilerda, was brief and to the point. Antony tossed it on the table, stretched, and walked to the balcony of the villa high up on Tarentum's hill where Caesar's courier had found him. Behind him, in the room from which he had just come, a dozen naked women and adolescent youths were stretched in drunken sleep after last night's orgy.

They were exhausted. Not Antony. He could throw off a night of excesses, or a dozen of them, as easily as one dropped a soiled toga. It was one of Cithaeris' charms that she shared this capacity.

At that moment she drifted in, negligée around her.

"Hi," she said, yawned prettily as Antony turned, then noticed the serious expression on his face. "What's up?" she asked.

Antony picked up Caesar's letter and tossed it to her. She read it, shrugged her shoulders, and said,

"So, I'll get my things together. Anyway," she added, over her shoulder, "it's been fun."

"What makes you think you're going anywhere?"

She turned to face him.

"Your master says to 'get rid of me'. So — " She shrugged again. Antony took three long strides and grasped her by the shoulders.

"Caesar has won," he told her. "In northern Spain. Now, he's marching south. Spain," he went on, slipping the negligée from

378

her, "is a big country and a long way off, isn't it?"

"Oh."

"So now where? On that sofa? Or the bench?"

She laughed her light, mocking laugh.

"You decide, stallion," she said.


## 2

As Antony lifted her in his arms, to the north his brother, whom he had appointed governor of Illyricum, came out of his tent and stopped, horrified. Around the island, just off the coast of his province where he had positioned his forces, the sea was dark with the ships of a Pompeian fleet. Cut off, he realized, he and his two legions. What to do? Word to his brother, somehow, he thought. But how?

While he stood there, close to panic, in North Africa Curio, Caesar's general, called his subordinate commanders into conference. The news of Caesar's victory at Ilerda had reached him a couple of days ago. Now reports had come in that the army of Juba, King of Numidia and ally of the Pompeian forces, was withdrawing. So why not sweep out of camp and win a final, decisive victory?

"Hadn't we better check those reports about Juba further?" a military tribune suggested.

"No need," Curio answered. "A patrol has confirmed it. Get the men ready," he ordered, thinking with a swelling of emotion that if he could deliver Africa, conquered, to Caesar, what a triumph!

On the afternoon of that same day, at Askelon in Palestine, Cleopatra and Antipater were discussing terms with the King of the Nabateans. The king realized as well as Antipater that, with Rome convulsed by civil war, now was the time to seize power and territory. But he was a cautious man, and Antipater and Cleopatra both knew that in their potential ally's mind was the hope of seizing the Egyptian Delta, or at least part of it. So these negotiations were sure to be long-drawn-out and tortuous.

# 3

Pompey knew nothing of these negotiations and would not have cared if he had known. On a morning three weeks after Caesar's victory at Ilerda, and some ten days since Curio had marched out for battle, he and Labienus, with reports, lists, and maps on the table, were sitting in Pompey's headquarters tent in Macedonia. It was the time of day Pompey liked best. For one thing the heat was not yet boiling on the plain. For another, the nobles in their luxurious tents — homes away from home, sodded with freshly cut green turf, hung with tapestries, filled with choice wines, gold and silver plate, and squads of slaves—were not yet stirring.

Pompey often found himself wishing that not so many of them, influenced by Afranius' boasts of certain victory over Caesar in Spain, had scurried to join him. In the meetings of what they solemnly called "The Three Hundred" — Cato, a fugitive from Sicily, had sternly pointed out that they could not term themselves "the Senate", because the Senate could meet only in Rome — they passed resolutions about how to punish those senators who had remained in Italy and, what was more annoying, about how the war should be conducted.

It was nag, nag, nag. But at this moment it was just he and Labienus, two military men making decisions. And they had just received exciting reports. In the Adriatic, fifteen cohorts of Antony's brother's two legions had surrendered and were being conveyed south to join Pompey's army. Even more welcome was the news, brought by a fast cutter from North Africa, that Curio had been killed and his army annihilated.

"Going very well, wouldn't you say?" Pompey observed.

"Couldn't be much better," Labienus agreed. He leaned back in his chair, and scratched his chin. "Strange that we've had no further word from Spain — from Afranius, I mean."

"Afranius is a good man," Pompey said comfortably. "Even if Caesar personally gets out of the trap, he's pretty well done. We shouldn't have much trouble finishing him and the rest of his legions. Not with our forces."

"I'd like to see his lopped-off head in front of me," Labienus said vindictively. "However, let's see how far our preparations are advanced." He pulled a waxed tablet to him and picked up a stylus. "With those fifteen captured cohorts," he was writing a list as he talked, "we'll have eleven legions — nine here, two in Asia Minor under your father-in-law, Metellus Scipio. Cavalry? Plenty from the client kings and princes, thanks to your reputation, Pompeius."

"And our fleet," Pompey observed. "Warships from Rhodes, Tyre, Egypt, Corcyra, and so on. How many in all, Titus?"

Labienus had picked up a list from the table. "Roughly five hundred," he answered. "Full control of the Adriatic and the eastern Mediterranean. Our stores in Dyrrachium?" He leafed over a pile of reports. "Arrows, javelins, shields, corselets — enormous stocks." He reached for another pile of papyrus sheets. "Enough wheat and other food supplies to last all winter." He leaned back in his chair. "By spring, we'll be all set, Pompeius. Ready to march from Dyrrachium up through Illyricum into Cisalpine Gaul and Italy, while your Spanish legions, Caesar or no Caesar, push through Cisalpine Gaul. A mere walk-through, Pompeius."

Pompey nodded. This was the way to make war, he was thinking. Take your time. Organize. Pile together masses of men and material. Then, roll over your opposition like a moving mountain over ants.

He clasped his hands over his comfortable belly and leaned back still further, thinking of his wife Cornelia a few miles away in a house at Thessalonica. His two sons by Mucia were with her. Perhaps he'd ride over and have dinner with them, he was thinking, and stay the night.

It was at this moment that the camp commander stepped in and saluted.

"What is it?" Pompey asked, looking up.

"Lucius Afranius, Imperator."

"Afranius? A courier?"

"In person, Imperator. Marcus Petreius with him."

"Impossible!" Pompey exclaimed, getting to his feet. Labienus rose too.

381

The commander, a knight, said stubbornly, "They're here, Imperator, requesting permission to enter."

"Bringing Caesar's head, perhaps," Labienus said, but without conviction.

Pompey's mouth, which had fallen open, snapped shut. "Show them in," he ordered.

The two men stepped in. One glance told Labienus and Pompeius that they weren't bringing Caesar's head. Afranius, a pace ahead of Petreius, was looking at the floor. Both men were travel-stained.

"What the Hades is it?" Labienus roared as they halted. Then, he bowed to Pompey. "Pardon me, Pompeius."

Pompey waved a hand. "Tell us," he said. "Come on, man."

"We came as fast as we could," Afranius began. "By boat. We drove the rowers — "

"Get to the meat of it," Labienus ordered, and again, "Pardon, Pompeius."

"Caesar," Afranius said and hesitated.

"Speak up," Pompey ordered coldly.

"Well — "

Marcus Petreius stepped forward, grey head up, grey eyes like flint.

"Caesar beat us," he said bluntly. "Your five legions — your best five — are gone, Imperator."

"Not our fault," Afranius said hurriedly. "Who could have even dreamed that Caesar — "

But Pompey had turned and was sitting down in his chair, lips pressed together. Afranius broke off what he had begun.

"And the last we heard from you, Caesar was done for," Labienus told Afranius roughly. "Trapped, you said. Soon to be forced to surrender, you said." He turned to Pompey. "I'd suggest, Pompeius, that Marcus Petreius tell us exactly what happened."

Petreius told them — the convoy, the failure to move into the hills to finish it off, Caesar's unexpected bridging of the Sicoris, the reversal of fortune, the attempt to retreat behind the Hiberus River, the undreamed-of fording of the Sicoris at Ilerda — not upstream, but just above Ilerda — the pursuit, the surrender.

When he had finished, Pompey sat as if in a trance, lips working in and out.

"I'd suggest, Imperator, that the camp commander be asked to assign these men quarters," Labienus said. "And that they be told not to speak to anyone."

Pompey roused himself. "Give the orders, Titus."

Afranius lifted his head. "I have two thousand select men of the Spanish army following me," he said eagerly. "It was a job to find boats. But I found them."

He was about to go on. Labienus interrupted.

"We'll hear about that later. Just now Gnaeus Pompeius Magnus and I wish to be alone. Correct, Imperator?"

Pompey nodded.

"A shocker," Labienus observed when they had left. He paced up and down. "A real shocker." He stopped and faced Pompey. "However, our situation is still good." Pompey looked up. "Plenty of stores," Labienus went on, frowning and thinking hard. "The East under our control. North Africa, too. Most important of all, the dominance of our fleet. Caesar can't cross the Adriatic, not with our fleets in the way. We can hold him at arm's length until we are ready."

Pompey's face had brightened. "You mean, go on as we've planned?"

Labienus pulled a hair from his nose, examined it, and let it drop.

"The veterans you've recalled to the standards need refresher drills," he said thoughtfully. "Not to mention the necessity of putting them in good physical shape. The recruits? You know as well as I, they'll have to be trained from scratch. Of our eleven legions, about five are battle-hardened. At Dyrrachium, during this fall and winter, we can make our army into a disciplined, well-trained force. Then, Pompeius, we'll be ready to attack either by sea directly across the Adriatic, or by land up through Illyricum. We'd better get on to that training right now."

Pompey rose from his chair. "Get going on it, Titus," he ordered. He frowned. "The nobles — when they hear about Spain they'll be yapping."

"Tell them to bugger off," Labienus said bluntly.

## 4

By the calendar it was the end of September. Two days ago Caesar had received the surrender of Massilia, although his enemy, Domitius Ahenobarbus, had managed to slip away on a swift boat. Caesar had also learned that in Rome his ally Lepidus had had him declared dictator. So, early this morning in the camp outside the city, he was conferring with his two generals, Trebonius and Decimus Brutus.

"You're leaving us two legions only," Trebonius, a tall fair-haired, blue-eyed man, was saying thoughtfully.

"Enough to hold Massilia and Gaul," Caesar pointed out. "I'm sending on the rest to Brundisium."

"You realize, Imperator, that the men aren't happy," said Decimus Brutus, a compact but alert man who moved as quickly as Caesar. "They expected that Massilia would be theirs to plunder like Avaricum."

"I need Massilia prosperous and well-disposed," Caesar answered. "Remember, I took away half Massilia's territory and imposed a huge indemnity. The legionaries know they're getting a bonus. Your men, Trebonius, and yours, Decimus, are to get another bonus on top of that."

"That will make them happy," Trebonius agreed. "May I tell them?"

"Yes."

"What are your plans now?" Decimus asked.

Caesar leaned forward. "The loss of Curio and his legions is bad," he pointed out. "So were our defeats in the Adriatic."

"So that's why the legions go to Brundisium," Decimus said. "To be ready if Pompeius attacks?"

Caesar at this moment wasn't ready to tell anyone his real plan. "Yes," he agreed.

As he said this Fadius was in Massilia, finding his way from the landward side towards the tavern of Baculus and Chione. The sun was hot and the townspeople, thoroughly chastened, made way deferentially for a Caesarian legionary. Fadius accepted this fact without really noticing it. He was still of two minds about

384

this visit. Southern Spain had been sun-baked and hot with a dry heat to which he wasn't accustomed. The girls had been hot, too. He had had several — swarthy-skinned, black-haired wenches, with liquid eyes that inspired one in the act of sex.

Not one had been more than casual to him, he was thinking as he turned a corner. Would he ever have a real feeling for a woman again? Or had Chione's throwing him over spoiled it for him for always?

As he asked himself this, suddenly he found himself in the street down which he had walked a year ago. He stopped, remembering, and, for an instant, agony wrenched at him, and the houses opposite seemed to tilt and sway.

He shook his head to clear it and looked up the street. There, up there, was the tavern. For a moment he was ready to turn away. Then his face firmed. He'd come this far. So, he'd face it. Chin up, he strode along the narrow street. At the entrance he hesitated again for a second. Then he stepped inside. At this hour of the morning the tavern was empty, except for a wench cleaning pots and cups behind the bar, and another slave sweeping the floor.

That slave looked up. "Not open," he grunted.

"Your master," Fadius said, squinting after the bright light outside, "I've come to see him."

"I said, 'Not open.'"

Fadius took a step forward. "Go get him," he ordered.

The slave took a second look. A legionary — and a big one. Taking his time, he stood his broom of twigs against the wall and shambled off to the stairs at the back. Fadius waited, sniffing in the smells of garlic, bread, sausages, soup, and stale beer and wine. Up above there was a curse or two, the sounds of someone dressing, a woman's voice asking a question, and then of feet stumping down the stairs. Baculus walked into the room rubbing his eyes.

"Must've had a late night, friend," Fadius said.

"Titus!" Baculus exclaimed. "Titus, by Jupiter!" and stumped over, hand outstretched. They clasped hands, then embraced. "I was hoping you'd come," Baculus went on, stepping back.

"Had almost given you up." He turned to the wench behind the bar. "Wine," he ordered, "the best." He swung his game leg over to the stairway. "Chione," he shouted up the stairs, "It's Fadius! Titus Fadius!"

There was a squeal up above and then Chione's voice calling, "Be down in a minute. Fast as I can."

What would he feel like when he saw her, Fadius was wondering, as Baculus sat him down on a bench at a table and the tavern wench put cups of wine before the two of them.

"To us," Baculus said, lifting his cup. "Long life — and success."

They drank the toast.

"How was it in Spain?" Baculus asked.

"How was it here?" Fadius countered, thinking that his friend had put on quite a few more grey hairs. "I mean, you'd be known as a Caesar veteran."

Baculus shrugged. "Tough for a bit. But a good many people owed me, one way or another. Two of the council among them. So we got by. Now, of course, business is at full tide."

"Good," Fadius said, thinking that it was taking Chione quite a while to appear. Of course, she'd want to prettify herself.

"About Spain now," Baculus prodded. "How did Caesar manage it?"

Fadius started to tell him — the storm, the crisis, the coracles.

"That's our Caesar for you!" Baculus broke in admiringly. "Now, the rest."

Fadius began again, then heard footsteps on the stairs. He interrupted himself and turned to look. Chione stepped into the room and stopped. There was a child in her arms.

A child! Fadius got to his feet stumblingly.

"Why didn't you tell me?" he said.

Baculus was grinning at him. "Wanted to see the look on your face."

"Is it — I mean, boy or girl?"

"Boy," Chione said proudly. She came forward, and lifted up the child. "See, isn't he beautiful?"

The child looked up at him gravely, blue eyes unwinking. It

386

had a mop of curly hair, Fadius realized.

"Two teeth already," Baculus said proudly, coming over. "Healthy as a pig."

"Never cries," Chione said just as proudly. "Not this baby. Here, take him."

"No," Fadius said, stepping back.

"No, take him," Chione ordered, following him and thrusting the child at him.

Perforce, Fadius took him, holding him gingerly.

"That's your Uncle Titus," Chione said to the child. "Smile, baby. A smile for Uncle Titus."

Fadius stared down at the infant. It was still looking up at him, gravely. But suddenly the child's chubby hand found one of his thumbs and closed around it firmly.

"He likes you," Chione cried, clapping her hands. "He likes you."

That little hand clasping his thumb. So trusting. It was the strangest feeling. He looked at Chione. Baculus had put an arm around her. For the first time he really saw her. Her face was chubbier. She was, in fact, chubbier all over. Looking at the two of them, their happiness so evident, and this child, their child, in his arms, suddenly his remnants of bitterness left him. This wasn't the Chione he'd lost, the laughingly tender and wanton girl. This was a mother — and she and Baculus a family. He cleared his throat.

"I'm glad for you," he said gruffly. "Glad for both of you."

"Oh no!" Chione exclaimed, stepping forward. "He's wetting you."

"Doesn't matter," Fadius said, just as gruffly. He fended off Chione. "Let me hold him." He sat down on the bench, the child still grasping his thumb tightly. "Wine. Can he have a drop of wine? Off my finger?"

Baculus laughed. "Mixes well with mother's milk, eh, Chione?"

She laughed happily and sat down beside him.

"Just a drop," she said. "Here, I'll wipe off your finger, first."

As she wiped off his finger and dried it, he was thinking,

387

'Cured. Freed. Now, if I should happen to meet a girl, a real girl — '

With a grin on his face he dipped a finger in his wine and held it to the child's mouth. It opened. The infant sucked on it eagerly. 'Yes,' he told himself, 'released at last. Free.'

5

"So it's still hurry, hurry, hurry," Servilia said, watching Caesar walk up and down with quick, nervous steps. He stopped.

"Yes. So much to do. Stores to collect. Ships to get. That mutiny of the Ninth at Placentia held me up. Don't really blame the beggars. They'd marched all the way from Brundisium to Spain — and then been told to march all the way back."

"You beheaded twelve, you said?"

Caesar nodded. "The ringleaders. I couldn't let it go. There are times when one has to be ruthless. Never out of anger, Servilia dear. From policy, carefully thought out."

They were in Caesar's villa on the right bank of the Tiber, and by the calendar it was the end of November. Servilia stirred on the sofa.

"What is your real plan, Julius?" She made a tiny gesture with her hand. "I know you've said your troops and ships are to defend Italy against a Pompeian invasion. That isn't the real reason for the concentration at Brundisium, is it?"

Caesar considered her gravely. "I'll tell you, darling. Lock it inside, will you? Not even to Balbus. Promise?"

"Of course, Julius."

Caesar sat down on a stool opposite her. "Spain was a success," he said. "Curio a disaster. By the way, how did Fulvia take the news? Of his death, I mean?"

"Calmly. She wasn't involved emotionally as she was with Clodius. Watch her, though, Julius. Ambition rides her."

"I'll remember that. To resume. Again on the debit side, Antony's brother got himself and fifteen cohorts captured, and Dolabella, Cicero's son-in-law, lost his Adriatic fleet to the

Pompeians. My Tyrrhenian war-fleet didn't fare much better."
Caesar paused. "All the same, I'm going to invade Greece."

Servilia jumped to her feet. "What!" Then, "You mustn't,
Julius. There's a huge Pompeian fleet waiting in the Adriatic to
gobble you." She came over to him. "Tell me you don't mean
it."

Caesar stood up, put an arm around her waist, led her back to
the sofa and sat beside her, arm still around her. "Look, my
sweet," he said. "My agents report that Pompey is moving along
the great road toward Dyrrachium in his usual leisurely fashion.
He thinks he has all winter to get ready, just as he thought last
year when I shocked him and everybody else out of their sandals
by crossing the Rubicon. Now I'll shock him again. Capture
Dyrrachium and all his stores, eh?"

"But the risk, Julius. The risk."

"Antony's getting the transports collected."

Servilia freed herself. "You're keeping him on? After Cithaeris
— and him defying your orders?"

"If Curio were alive . . . " Caesar shrugged a shoulder. "Antony is the best man I have left. And he's loyal."

Servilia examined her rings. "Cithaeris? What about her?"

"Antony's got rid of his travelling brothel. On my written
order. I've made it clear, too, that now he has to stick to business.
No more of the mistakes he's made. Cithaeris?" He shrugged
again. "I'll decide when I meet Antony."

"You wouldn't be thinking, you bastard — "

"Too busy," Caesar cut in quickly. "Far too busy. Consider,
Servilia," he went on persuasively turning to look at her. "As
dictator I'm holding the elections here for next year's consuls."

"With yourself as one of the candidates. That's clever, Julius."

"Of course. Then I'll preside over the festival of Jupiter of the
Latins. Also — and I haven't told you this yet — I'm planning a
bill to provide for debtors to repay their debts, not in today's
inflated values, but in terms of pre-war prices."

"Good!" Servilia said, sitting up. "That will please the middle
class." She looked at him, eyes alive. "Why not have the interest
already paid on debts deducted from the principal?"

Caesar got up from the sofa, paced a step, then stopped.

"Excellent! You've given me another idea. Why not set the interest rate at five per cent instead of twelve?"

She nodded vigorously. "Yes. I agree." She looked up at him. "We *are* a team, aren't we?"

"I always get ideas, talking things over with you," Caesar said fondly. He walked over to her, smiling. "Now, darling, since we're through talking — "

She got up. "No time," she said. "Not with that dinner of Calpurnia's coming — "

"We'll make time," he said, taking her in his arms and replacing her on the sofa gently but firmly.

"With all the Spanish women you've had," she said, resisting him. "At Massilia, too — "

"Not one woman since I had you last," Caesar sat up. "Not one. I hadn't realized it. Not one!"

"I don't believe it."

"It's true." Caesar glanced down ruefully. "He's forgotten how, by the looks of it. The hurry, the rush — "

"I'll take care of that," Servilia said. "Not one, you said. Oh yes, I'll take care of that." She bent over him.


# 6


"Too risky, Julius," Antony expostulated. "I know it's my fault. Putting my brother in command and risking Dolabella's fleet, as well as sending in the Tyrrhenian ships for a second attempt to save my brother. But look at the facts, Julius. Transports for only half your army. Only twelve warships. Down at Corcyra, Bibulus — and how he hates you — with one hundred and ten warships—quinqueremes, quadriremes, and triremes. You'll be massacred."

They were in Brundisium's citadel, which overlooked the harbour. Caesar was sitting, Antony standing. Caesar glanced up at his cousin.

"What was done is done," he said. "Forget it." He tapped the sheet of papyrus on the table behind which he sat. "This report

says that Bibulus has his ships in harbour more or less disman-
tled, and that his rowers are drinking in the taverns. He thinks
nothing will happen until spring. So, now's the time to cross."

"If a storm comes up? Tomorrow's the fourth day of
January."

"But really only the end of November," Caesar waved a hand
toward the Adriatic. "Tonight, the sea's calm. Tomorrow, with
luck, the calm will last."

"I still say it's mad," Antony repeated stubbornly.

Caesar got up. "I'm going. Your job will be to get the rest
across. I'll be depending on you, Antony. No more mistakes."

"You can be certain of that," Antony assured him fervently.

"That's settled, then. Now, this Cithaeris — let's see her."

Antony went to the doorway and called. She took her time.
Antony, as nervous as a skittish colt seeing a bridle for the first
time, waited, then said,

"Venus damn her! I'll go get her."

"Give her time," Caesar said, thinking with some amusement
that this was most unusual for Antony.

They waited. At last they heard steps outside. Cithaeris
walked in. She was in the same sort of outfit as when Antony had
first seen her, a thin mist of black byssus around her, black hair
flowing over her shoulders. She took three steps into the room
and posed, careless hand on out-thrust hip, chin up, centreless
eyes staring into the distance. No one, except Caesar, could have
guessed that within herself she was willing this Caesar, this
master of Antony, to be attracted to her. Yes, if she could ensnare
him —

Caesar had not got up. He was leaning back in his chair, a smile
on his lips, assessing her. Antony was sweating.

"I agree. She's quite something," Caesar said, speaking as if
she were a prize mare to be considered.

She did not react. She simply stood, still staring into the
distance. Antony turned to Caesar eagerly.

"Then — " he began.

"It occurs to me," Caesar went on deliberately, "that Fulvia is
again a widow."

He saw Antony's head jerk. Cithaeris took a couple of gliding steps, bringing her closer to Caesar, and half turned to show herself in profile. Caesar felt a stirring in his groin, noting the thrusting breast, the smooth, round buttock, and the way her inaccessible eyes still gazed into the distance. Yes, he could understand why she fascinated Antony. Besides, she was here and Fulvia was in Rome.

"No objection to you keeping her here," he said, observing the relieved exhalation of Antony's breath, "provided you do your job." He got up. "Well, lots to do before morning, Antony."

Dismissed as if of no account by this Caesar, Cithaeris thought in fury. Examined as if she were a — a thing. She turned and glided to the doorway.

"See you later," Antony called after her.

She paused in the doorway. "Don't be too sure," she said over her shoulder and laughed her light, mocking laugh. "No, don't be too sure."

She went out.

"Quite a girl," Caesar commented, looking after her.

"Yes, isn't she?"

"As I said, let's get to work."

At least he still had her, Antony thought. Then, dismissing her from his mind, like Caesar he turned to the list of things to be done before tomorrow's embarkation.


# 7


Sitting huddled on the foredeck of Caesar's flagship, Fadius was staring out at the grey Adriatic. Grey clouds like floating billows hung above the huge array of transports, feeble lights winking. The sight made Fadius think of the other time he'd been on board ship, on the way to Britain. Could that be only five and a half years ago? He'd seen so much, experienced so much, since then.

Near him a soldier retched. The same stink of vomit, Fadius thought. Only Uncle Thermus had been with him then. Uncle Thermus! It wasn't length of time that mattered, Fadius told himself. A month that dragged could seem like a year. On the other hand a moment could be an hour — or a day — or a year.

As he thought this, on the poop Caesar was standing with the young Asinius Pollio. Caesar, too, was staring out at the wintry waters of the Adriatic. He knew that this was the greatest risk he had ever knowingly taken. If he were caught out here by Bibulus' war-fleet, it would be the end of him. Worse still, it would be the end of his army. He glanced at the transports. Aboard were fiteeen thousand infantry, carrying only light baggage, and five hundred horses with their riders. Had he been right in committing them, men who trusted him, men who were, in effect, his comrades, to a danger such as this?

Well, he had cast the knucklebones. Wait now until one saw the luck of the throw. The sea at least was still reasonably calm and the wind favourable. So, no use worrying.

Turning, he sat down on a seat made of heavy rope coiled in tiers, and let his mind wander. Cithaeris, he thought. It was amusing to see how she baffled Antony. He felt again a stirring in his groin. If he came across her again, he told himself, offering herself when she was no longer Antony's leavings, he'd teach her. That aura of inaccessibility, the aura that bewildered Antony, he'd strip that from her — and enjoy doing it. A one-night stand, of course, as compared to Servilia.

A tender smile curved his lips as he remembered Servilia. What was the last thing she had begged of him?

"Brutus," she had pleaded. "If — no, when you defeat Pompey, will you make sure our Brutus is safe?"

He had assured her he would.

"Promise," she had cried. "Promise me, Julius. By the love between us, promise."

He had promised.

"A signal," Pollio was crying in his ear. "A signal, Imperator."

"What is it?" Caesar asked.

"A patrol boat, Imperator," Pollio said, pointing south. "It has escaped our warships. It's scudding south, to Corcyra."

Bibulus! Caesar thought. If he catches us now!

But then Pollio swung round. "Imperator, look!" he was crying exultantly. "Look!"

Caesar looked. Straight ahead, rising out of light mist, was a ridge of mountains. The peaks of Epirus! Greece! The knucklebones had turned up Venus, the highest throw. Caesar's mind raced ahead.

"As soon as we land, I'm marching north," he said. "Your job, Pollio, is to get the transports as fast as we offload on their way back to Brundisium. Understand?"

"Yes, Imperator."

In Corcyra, Bibulus was enjoying a leisurely dinner with a couple of his sub-admirals. In the midst of it, an aide brought in the captain of the patrol-boat. He told his news.

Bibulus gasped. Then, he roared,

"Not in winter. You're crazy, man."

"With my own eyes," the captain, a bluff mariner with no respect for landsmen, said and added, "Imperator," as an afterthought. "Hundreds of ships."

Bibulus rolled his heavy belly off the dinner couch and stood up.

"Get the rowers out of the taverns," he bawled to his sub-admirals. "Get our fleet out and after the bastard, Neptune damn him."

It took a couple of hours and more to get the fleet on its way. Then there were fifteen miles and more to row to Caesar's landing-place. By that time, Caesar's troops were on their way to the first important town northward on the coast, Oricum. Behind him Pollio completed the offloading of the spare weapons, war-chest and other stores, sending back each convoy of transports as soon as they were cleared. That last group, however, was late in leaving. As Pollio watched anxiously the evening breeze off the land wafted them westward into the gathering dusk. He heaved a sigh of relief, not knowing that just beyond his view the breeze had failed.

That last group of transports got out oars. They were still labouring toward Brundisium when Bibulus' warships fell upon them. The crews had no way to resist. They surrendered.

"Orders, Imperator?" Bibulus' second-in-command asked.

"How many?"

"Thirty ships, Imperator. Maybe one or two more or less."

"Take fire from our galleys and burn them."

"Shall I transfer the crews to our ships? We could use them."

The veins on Bibulus' neck stood out. "Burn them, too."

"Burn them!"

"Let everyone who so much as lifts a thumb to aid Caesar learn what fate awaits him!" Bibulus exploded. "Burn them, I said."

Back on shore, an aide plucked at Pollio's arm.

"Look, Legate," he was babbling. "Look."

Pollio looked. Out at sea on the horizon a gout of flame was spouting up, then another, and still another, until the whole sky seemed aflame. Pollio stood transfixed. But he did not know the full extent of the horror until late in the night a small boat grounded on the beach. When Pollio and his staff hurried down to it, he found the captain of one of the transports. In the light of the horn lanterns his eyes were red-rimmed, his hair burnt, and his face scorched. With him were three other men in the same condition, and in the bottom of the boat, scarcely breathing, a sailor looking like a charred piece of meat.

"What happened?" Pollio wanted to know.

The captain, who had stumbled out onto the beach, stared at him, weaving slightly.

"You Romans! We'd surrendered, hadn't we? But no!" The captain, a Graeco-Illyrian, made a violent gesture. " 'Burn the boat,' they said. We went to get off. They drove us back. 'Toss them into the fire,' they were shouting, 'every last son of a she-goat!' " He spat. "Romans!"

"You — how did you — "

"Rushed them. Got this boat off and into the water somehow. They shot at us. Shot at us! If I ever get a Roman in my hands—"

"How many ships burned?" Pollio interrupted.

"All of those in that last lot. And who's going to pay?" the captain burst out. "All those ships. All those men. Their women — their children — "

Pollio had turned away. How was he going to explain to Caesar, he was thinking. Thirty transports lost.

As Caesar drove northward along the rugged coast toward Dyrrachium, Pompey's army was moving at a leisurely pace along
the great inland road toward the same destination. Pompey
himself was riding in a carriage chatting with Domitius, who had
joined him after his escape from Massilia. Labienus was mounted
on a roan, his favourite steed, a little way ahead. A chill wind was
blowing, and snow had sprinkled the tops of the hills and mountains.

Pompey, wrapped in a thick cloak, was comfortable in mind
and body. He had sent his wife and his younger son to winter on
the island of Lesbos. The elder lad, Gnaeus, had a command in
the Pompeian fleet, and the reports on his conduct were excellent. Pompey knew that his column of march, thanks both to the
heavy baggage and artillery, and to the carts and wagons carrying tapestries, swansdown pillows, rugs, costly foods, and rare
wines for the noble senators, stretched for more than twenty
miles. In front and behind at intervals between the transport
trudged the legions.

The whole column, Labienus had observed sourly — and
especially the nobles and their cortèges of slaves and possessions
— was like a portable picnic. Except for Cato. Cato insisted on
marching with the legions.

"Ride if you like," he had said to his nephew, Brutus. "Our
ancestors marched with their men."

The legionaries stank. But Brutus stubbornly kept pace with
his uncle, in spite of the smells, his aching calves and thighs, as he
limped along — and the blisters. Stoic aphorisms said that what
happened to the body was unimportant, so Brutus tried to
dismiss the thought that maybe those Stoic philosophers had
never known blisters, or smells, or aching bones.

Back in his carriage Pompey pulled the rug higher over his
knees and relaxed into a gentle doze. He was awakened by
Labienus stopping the carriage and opening the leather curtains
to shake his arm.

"What's the matter?" Pompey asked, rubbing his eyes.

"Vibullius Rufus," Labienus answered. "Used to be your chief of engineers. Captured by Caesar in Italy and again in Spain. Remember? He's here."

"Here?" Pompey said, struggling to comprehend. "Why?"

Labienus leaned in the window, looking at Domitius and lowering his voice.

"Better keep this between the three of us. He says Caesar, now that he's been elected consul, sent him to offer peace."

"Never!" Domitius exploded.

Labienus leaned in further. "Not the important thing," he said, lowering his voice still more. "He says Caesar's landed! With an army!"

"What!" Domitius exclaimed.

"Says he already has Oricum. Says he's marching on Dyrrachium."

"I don't believe him. It's not possible."

"Here he is," Labienus turned. "Get in, Vibullius. Tell them."

Vibullius, who had ridden day and night since landing, told them. Domitius, after one or two violent exclamations, gradually took it in. He looked at Pompey. So did Labienus. But Pompey, as seemed to happen to him now when crisis struck, sat as if in a trance, or as if his mind were a complete blank.

"Where was Bibulus?" Domitius exclaimed. "That Zeus-damned horse's ass."

"Sitting in Corcyra," Vibullius answered. "It's winter, you know."

"The point is, Pompeius, that we have to move — and fast," Labienus said. "Get to Dyrrachium before Caesar. Or we're done for."

Pompey seemed to snap out of his trance. "Forced marches," he said decisively. "Day and night. Get the men moving, Titus Labienus. And Domitius," he turned to him, "get back to the nobles. Tell them to get a move on. Whoever or whatever can't keep up is to be left behind. Move, Domitius."

When, a week later, Caesar, having captured all the towns along the coast, came in sight of Dyrrachium, he was appalled by what he saw. There, on the opposite bank of the Apsus River,

397

barring his way, was the entrenched camp of Pompey. With only half his army, all Caesar could do was encamp on his side of the river. When Antony brought the rest of the army across, he told himself, he would move. Until then — wait.

# CHAPTER VII

IT WAS MID-FEBRUARY BY THE SEASONS. In the sun-room of her villa in Askelon, a sun-room which faced both east and west, Cleopatra looked at Antipater as he paced about.

"What flea's biting at you now?" she asked.

Antipater glanced toward Jerusalem. Last evening there had been a spectacular thunderstorm over the Judean hills. This morning a chill wind from the northwest was driving scudding clouds across the sky, and, if one looked the other way, the Aegean waves were white-capped.

"That agent Julius Caesar sent," he said. "You know, the one to whom our high-priest gave his blessing."

"The one who tried to persuade you Jews to begin a revolt so as to hold Pompey's two legions in Asia Minor?" Cleopatra, who was reclining on a lounge, shrugged. "We aren't about to do that, are we? Now that we're getting an army together against Pothinus?"

Antipater stopped his restless pacing. "I was just thinking — suppose this Julius Caesar wins?"

Cleopatra said negligently, "The latest reports are that this Caesar is cooped up in Epirus in Greece." She sat up gracefully. "Pothinus has sent warships — and troops even — to Pompey. That shows who he thinks will win."

"The chances of war are incalculable," Antipater answered stubbornly. He spread his hands. "Of course, we Jews are not going to start a revolt against Pompey. Wouldn't hurt, though, to keep this agent of Caesar sort of on the hook, would it? Have him over for dinner, for instance. Flatter him."

Cleopatra considered the point briefly. Antipater was a satisfactory lover. Over the months she had learned to trust his judgment and ability — the way, for example, he had man-

399

oeuvred the Nabatean king into sending horsemen with nothing as bait but promises, which could be broken.

"As long as we keep on collecting stores and men for our spring campaign," she said, "and don't let anything interfere, not anything, I have no objection. Have him to dinner."

Antipater smiled at her. "It's just, as they say, an anchor to windward," he told her. "This Caesar—my information is that he wins." He came over and looked down at her.

"Are you — could you be — in the mood?"

"Why not?" she said, smiling up at him, and gratified by the sudden, eager light of passion in the grey eyes. It was good to know that, although he constantly strove to be his own man, he always succumbed. She lay back on the sofa. As he dropped to his knees on the floor beside her, she allowed his hands to explore her, at first tentatively, then more demandingly. Men! One could always manage them.

## 2

Across the Aegean in Epirus the same sort of chill wind was blowing, only this one came from the northeast. In the headquarters tent of his camp on the north bank of the river Apsus, Pompey was listening with half an ear to the interminable list of stores and supplies his quartermaster was reading to him. The major part of his mind was reflecting that everything was going very well indeed. His supplies came in by boat from Dyrrachium, so his men were well fed. By contrast, he knew that in the camp across from him, Caesar's men had lately been reduced to bread made from roots mixed with milk and ground into a paste. Moreover, although Bibulus had died from pneumonia, the Pompeian fleets still controlled the Adriatic, so that no troops and no supplies could slip through from Italy to his rival.

Pompey yawned, reflecting that Labienus was rapidly caning the army into shape. In the spring his father-in-law, Metellus Scipio, was to bring over the two legions from Asia Minor; then would be the time to cut Caesar off from all supplies from inland Greece. His former father-in-law, Pompey thought somewhat viciously, would discover that getting half his army across was not a coup but a tumble into a pit. He probably would not even have to fight a battle. Instead, he would just wait for surrender. That pit was one that Caesar couldn't climb out of; he'd surrender or starve.

## 3

Caesar had reached a somewhat similar conclusion. On the evening of the same day he stood on the beach of a tiny cove, gazing westward toward Italy. Behind him were Pollio and two aides. To his right, Fadius and three legionaries waited. On his left was the burly master of the fishing-boat that lay in front of them, its prow drawn up on the sandy gravel. Two and a half months since he'd landed, Caesar was thinking. No sign of Antony and the rest of his army.

He looked at the burly Greek sailor.

"Ready to go?" he asked.

The sailor nodded. Behind Caesar, Pollio spoke:

"I beg of you, Imperator — "

Caesar cut him off with a flick of his arm.

"Someone has to stick a goad up Antony's behind," he said. "Give this man his money, Pollio. The half he gets before we start."

"Keep it," the boat-master said. "It's a rough night out there. If I don't get back, give it to my woman."

"May I speak, Imperator?" Fadius asked diffidently.

Caesar glanced at him. "If you're afraid — "

"It's not that, Imperator, if you'll pardon me," Fadius interrupted. "I've listened. You've said a small boat can run the blockade to Brundisium where a big one can't. Agreed. But, Imperator, if you're lost, the whole army's lost. That's what bothers me."

"No one but those here know I'm going," Caesar said quietly. "So the Pompeians won't be watching for me. I can't, won't, stick here, Fadius, stalemated."

"As I've said a dozen times, Imperator," Pollio began from behind him, "the risk — "

"Haven't you heard of Caesar's luck?" Caesar answered with a laugh. He turned to the boat. "Let's go, Captain."

The Greek drew his heavy brows together. "As long as you understand it's a bad night out there," he said. "Good for running the blockade." He moved to the waiting sailboat. It had a crew of six, already in position. The Greek stepped to the steering oar at the stern. "Choppy seas, veering winds," he went on as Caesar got in. "We may not make it."

"You carry Caesar," Caesar answered, settling himself.

"Pull, boys," the boat-master said. As Fadius and the three legionaries pushed at the prow, the crew pulled at the oars. The boat floated free, bobbing up and down. Fadius and his three comrades splashed into the water and rolled in over the sides. The rowers got the prow around and headed it out. Two of the crew ran up the sail. The wind, off the land for the moment, filled it. As the boat began to swim outward over the comparatively calm water of the cove, Fadius looked back. The single lantern on shore was a feeble, flickering light. In front of him Caesar was staring straight ahead. Brundisium, he was thinking. The rest of my legions.

Caesar felt the motion of the boat change. They were out of the cove. A promontory to the south still gave some protection, but the boat was dancing now. And then they were in the open Adriatic, and the waves were high and choppy—and suddenly a gust of wind from the southwest hit them.

"The sail!" the boat-master shouted. "Drop it!"

He was too late. The boat heeled over and veered. A wave caught them broadside and abruptly everyone was knee-deep in water.

"Pull!" the boat-master roared to the four rowers as he struggled with the steering oar, and to Caesar, Fadius, and the three legionaries he yelled, "Bail for your lives! Bail!"

They bailed with their helmets. Somehow the boat-master got the blunt prow head on to the next wave. They crested it. The sail was in ribbons. Then, abruptly, a gust and a wave, too, from the northwest this time, hit the boat and swung it around. It wallowed in the trough.

"Pull," the boat-master called. "Back to shore. Pull."

"No," Caesar shouted, trying to stand and falling to his knees in the water in the boat. "No. Keep on."

The boat-master paid no attention. Somehow he got the craft around before the next wave, the wave that would have swamped them, reached the boat. Even after they had turned around, it was still dicey until they reached the shelter of the cove. As the keel grated on the beach, the boat-master and his crew jumped out to drag the boat farther up on the sand and gravel. Caesar, lips pressed together, stepped out. Fadius and the legionaries followed. Pollio and the two aides had run down to meet their commander.

"Are you all right, Imperator?" Pollio cried. Then, "You're soaked, Imperator. Dry clothes. At once."

Caesar paid no attention. He turned to the boat-master, who was drawing the back of his hand across his forehead.

"I ordered you to go on," he said coldly. "So why did you turn back?"

The burly Greek dropped his hand and looked him straight in the eyes.

"My boat," he said. "My crew. I wasn't about to lose both. Not for any crazy Roman bugger."

It was a long time since anyone had called him a bugger to his face. Caesar suppressed a smile. He turned to Pollio.

"Pay him," he said.

The Greek made a violent chopping motion with his right hand.

"Won't take it," he said. "Not a drachma."

"Why?" Caesar asked.

"Our bargain was for me to get you to Brundisium. I didn't. So, not a drach."

He was about to turn away. Caesar took him by the arm.

403

"Would you mind coming over here for a moment?" he asked.

The Greek allowed himself to be led a few steps up the beach. Caesar spoke in a low voice.

"If I gave a message for the commander in Brundisium," he said, "would you take it across? When the sea's favourable? For the same price, of course?"

The Greek considered for a moment. He nodded.

Caesar thrust out a hand. "It's a bargain then?"

The Greek looked him in the face. "Bargain," he said, clasping the hand, and added, "Imperator."


# 4


"Great balls of Pan!" Antony exclaimed, "we'll end up at the top of the Adriatic."

"If you want to smash your ships against those rocks," the master of his flagship said, with a wave of his hand toward the coast of Epirus, "give the word!"

It was a wild March gale before which Antony's ship and the transports scudded. When they had set out it had been a strong south wind, one that had enabled them to outspeed the Pompeian war-fleet off Brundisium. Abruptly that wind had risen to almost hurricane-force. They had already passed Oricum. Now they were approaching Apollonia, the port in which they were supposed to land, and the shipmaster had announced that with this gale it was impossible to turn in.

Antony stared around at his fleet. In those transports were three veteran legions and one of recruits, not to mention eight hundred cavalry. Somehow he had to get them to Caesar. One sentence in the message he had received had stung.

"If Cithaeris has drained all the juice out of you," Caesar had written, "turn your command over to Fufius Calenus."

So Antony had sent Cithaeris off to the villa in Tarentum. He had dispatched Gabinius, the barrel-trunked man under whom, years ago, he had served in Palestine and Alexandria, north with fifteen cohorts. That move had two objectives — first and more important, to draw squadrons of Pompeian ships up the Adriatic coast, and second, to march around the top of the sea and move south through Illyricum. Then, at the first favourable wind Antony had loaded the troops on board.

"Apollonia," the shipmaster said, with a wave toward the shore.

Antony glanced at the white houses rising up the hill above the harbour, and whistled tunelessly. Soon they would be passing the opposing camps of Pompey and Caesar on the Apsus River south of the harbour of Dyrrachium; and Caesar would be watching.

Caesar, alerted by smoke signals, was indeed watching. Face impassive, he saw Antony's transports scurrying by. The gale that drove them was so strong that he and his aides had had to shelter on a ledge on the side of a rocky hill. And there, he noted, in the harbour of Dyrrachium, Rhodian war-galleys were rowing out in pursuit. They had no chance of catching up with Antony, he told himself. Though where Antony and the legions he so desperately needed would end up was an unanswered question.

And then, just as the Rhodian war-fleet, oars at double-quick beat, cleared the harbour of Dyrrachium, Caesar exclaimed, "Oh God!" As abruptly as if Neptune had waved his trident, the gale had dropped to a dead calm. Antony's transports, just nicely beyond Dyrrachium, were losing way. Across the river Apsus Caesar could hear cheering from the Pompeians. The Rhodian galleys were driving forward. If they caught Antony's transports, it would be a massacre, like wolves against sheep. Those legions — lost!

Caesar would have prayed to the gods, had he believed in them. He stood tight-lipped. On board his flagship, Antony bawled to his ship-master. "Signal 'out oars'," he shouted, knowing that the order was futile. The lumbering transports had neither sufficient oars nor the build to out-race the swift Rhodian triremes and quadriremes. "Turn in to land."

405

"No place to land," the ship-master retorted. "Not here."

"All right. We'll fight. Signal the transports. Soldiers on deck."

"With those brazen beaks ramming into us broadside? Better pray to Aeolus."

"Aeolus?"

"King of the winds." The ship-master nodded to a sailor who was on his knees, arms outstretched to the scudding clouds, high above in the sky.

Antony looked back at the brazen-beaked warships. Soon they would be on them. The gods meant nothing to Antony, except as convenient curse-words. But in this case—In great strides he seized the praying sailor and carried him to the side of ship. He lifted him high, kicking and screaming, in the air.

"A wind, Aeolus," he shouted. "Give us a wind. Look, a sacrifice!"

He tossed the sailor into the sea.

"You're crazy, man," the shipmaster bawled, picking up a rope to throw to the sailor. "Crazy!" Then, he stopped. There was a sudden blast of wind, then another.

"A ram to Aeolus," the shipmaster cried. "A vow, Aeolus. A vow."

"Ram?" Antony said. He stretched out his hands, palms upward. "A hecatomb of bulls, Aeolus. I vow it. Give us a wind."

As he spoke the gale hit the transports again, full force. They staggered, started, and once again drove northward in full flight, leaving the Rhodians rowing stubbornly behind them. On shore Caesar let out a long breath. "Caesar's luck," he said softly; and then to an aide, "Cavalry patrols. Have them ford the Apsus upstream and ride north. Find out what happens to those transports and report back. Get moving."

Though Caesar did not know it, his luck was still sailing with the transports. As the sun dropped toward the west, the wind began to drop too. At the moment Antony's fleet was scudding past Lissus, a port held by the Pompeians.

"What now?" Antony asked his shipmaster. The shipmaster, a bearded Illyrian, put one finger on a nostril and blew to clear the other one. He wiped off the snot and flung it on the deck.

"That headland up there," he said. "See? Just beyond is the harbour of Nymphaeum. It opens to the south. We could sail right into it. Mind you, with this wind, we'd hit the beach hard. A few ships wrecked, maybe." He moistened a finger and held it up. "The wind's dropping still more, I'd judge."

Antony glanced back at the Rhodian galleys, still in grim pursuit. "We'll risk it," he decided. "Send the signal."

The transports turned in. Suddenly, as the first ships passed between the harbour's sheltering arms, the wind ceased completely. The transports hit the shore with no more than a gentle shock. As each vessel beached, the legionaries spilled over the sides, waded ashore, and, under the vine-rods of the bawling centurions, formed into centuries. They were led to the nearest hill to throw up a camp.

"Two transports missing, Legate," an aide told Antony. "That's all."

"A bloody miracle," Antony, who was overseeing the rapid digging of the trench and the building of the rampart, said almost reverentially. He squinted out to sea at the Rhodian war-galleys, now approaching the harbour. "We'll be ready for those carrion-eaters when they get here."

The miracle wasn't over. As the lean triremes and quadriremes headed, close to shore, for the harbour, just as abruptly as before, the gale drove down again. Not from the south this time. From the southwest. The western headland protected Antony's transports, but the foremost war-galleys were caught broadside. The shore was too close to escape. Antony watched as decked warship after warship was hurled onto the rocks.

"Get men over there," Antony ordered his aides. "Save as many as you can. Make them prisoners." And then: "Sixteen of them," he went on. "Sixteen. Another bloody miracle," he added, almost awed. He raised his arms. "Not one hecatomb of bulls, Aeolus. Two. Do you hear me? — Two, if I get a messenger to Caesar — safe."

Six days later, Antony led his men out of a camp south of Lissus to meet Caesar's advancing army. He and Caesar, broad

407

smiles on their faces, rode up to each other, clasped hands, then, dismounting, embraced.

"I got them here, Julius," Antony said as they stepped back from each other.

"And Pompey waiting down there," Caesar gestured toward the southwest, "to ambush you."

"I know, Julius. That's why I camped here to wait for you."

"When I saw your ships scudding by and then the calm and the Rhodian warships almost upon you," Caesar said, "I thought my luck had deserted me."

"I was scared shitless. And then the wind again." Antony rubbed at his nose. "I've almost come to believe in the gods, Julius."

"The important thing is that you're here. Now, Antony, I'll make things happen."

"For instance?"

Caesar glanced at the legionaries. Many from both contingents had broken ranks and were greeting old friends.

"I have my whole army now," he said. "Pompey's left his camp. So have I. I'm going to sweep in suddenly, and seize the neck of land that connects Dyrrachium to the mainland. Then, we'll see if Pompey will fight."

Pompey did not accept battle. Instead, he moved his camp to a rocky hill halfway down the Gulf of Dyrrachium. Let Caesar hold the neck of land that connected Dyrrachium to the mainland if he wanted to, was his thinking. Dyrrachium itself was too strongly fortified for any assault, especially as the Pompeian ships controlled the sea and the gulf.

It was soon stalemate again. Caesar convoked an assembly of his legates, aides, and centurions. A large map of the Gulf of Dyrrachium was pinned on a board.

"Remember Alesia," Caesar began. He paused and looked around. "Yes, remember Alesia and what you and your men achieved with pick and shovel. That was what sealed the fate of Gaul and the Gauls. Picks and shovels."

He waited as his audience absorbed his words; then, picking up a pointer and turning to the map, he went on,

408

"A line of redoubts and trenches from this point on the Gulf just north of Pompey's camp in a semicircle," he traced it on the map, "to here."

The "here" was the gulf to the south of Pompey's camp.

"The Pompeians can still get supplies by sea," a centurion said, stating the obvious.

"I know," Caesar answered, turning to him. "But if we blockade the Pompeians from the land side, first of all we'll prevent their cavalry from cutting off our supply convoys. Secondly, we'll limit that cavalry in their foraging for fodder. We'll dam or divert every stream, too. Make them short of water. Lastly, you and everyone here can understand the effect on Greece — on the whole East — when they hear that Pompey the Great is hemmed in by a force two-thirds the size of his own."

There was a murmur of assent.

"So, picks and shovels," Caesar ordered. "Tell your men — hard work but remember Alesia. Picks and shovels."

# 5

Defeat! Caesar looked around him, not believing it. His veterans were running away! Running even though *he* had been leading them!

For once, Caesar completely lost his coolness in a crisis. He rushed among his men, shouting at them to turn around, snatching at them, roaring at them to face the Pompeians. It was no use. They were trampling each other in their unthinking, crazy fear. And there was the eagle-bearer of the Ninth, running too, eyes glazed. Caesar caught at the shaft of the eagle.

"Turn around, Galba," he shouted, wrenching wildly at the eagle-pole. "Face the enemy, you bastard."

The man dropped the eagle. All he knew was that here was a man preventing him from saving his life. He pulled out his sword and raised it. Another sword flashed, cutting off the eagle-bearer's arm at the shoulder. As the man staggered back, clapping his left hand over the spouting blood, Caesar turned. It was Fadius who had saved him.

"No use, Imperator," Fadius said steadily. "You can't stop it. Not now."

The light of reason returned to Caesar's eyes.

"I'll take the eagle," Fadius said, holding out his left hand. "Best get out of this, Imperator. Back to high ground. Have Antony bring reserves from the redoubts."

"Thank you, Titus Fadius," Caesar said quietly, passing the eagle to him. "You're right. Back. Organize a defence."

As Caesar reached high ground and began to summon reserve troops, Pompey, on the terrain below, had his trumpeters blow the signal for his troops to halt and re-form. Labienus rode up to him, blunt face flushed, eyes gleaming.

"Victory!" he cried. He waved an arm at Caesar's broken ranks, scrambling up the hill. "After them, Pompeius."

"It's uphill," Pompey said, doubt in his voice.

Labienus looked, beginning to hesitate in his mind.

"That wood to the right," Pompey went on, pointing. "If we were ambushed from there — "

Labienus scratched himself, considering.

"Perhaps you're right," he conceded. "We've won two battles. Breached Caesar's lines. Shattered his best troops."

"So why risk a check now? He can't get away, not with us on his heels. If he does, where can he go? No ships. Morale low."

Labienus grunted. "You're right, Gnaeus Pompeius. As always."

Pompey breathed out a long breath of relief. After his unwonted exertions, what he desired most was a good meal and a rest.

"Will you see to the guards and the outposts?" he asked. "The dead and wounded, too? And lead the legions back?"

"Gladly," Labienus answered. Then: "Could I deal with the prisoners we took?"

"Whatever you wish," Pompey answered.

He turned to ride along the line of his legions, now re-formed. They cheered him tumultuously, shouting, "Imperator! Imperator!"

410

He was still Pompey the Great, Pompey told himself, lifting his arm to acknowledge the cheers. That Caesar who had thought to challenge him — he knew now. Pompey the Ever-Victorious!

## 6

Two hours later, Caesar stood on a hill looking down on the scene of his defeat. Behind him, the hills were green under the breath of late May. In front, beyond the level ground below, the waters of the Gulf of Dyracchium were sparkling, mirror-calm, in the light of the low-dropping sun.

The moment was meant for quiet reflection on the beauty, the peace, the immutability of the changing yet eternal seasons. But in Caesar's mind was a swift consideration of the fact that if he had been in Pompey's mantle, by this time he, Caesar, and his army would have been destroyed. Why, he wondered briefly, had Pompey halted his victorious legions? The fact was that he had. Equally briefly Caesar reviewed the events which had produced this moment. For weeks on end his men had laboured until they had built a line of redoubts and entrenchments almost seventeen miles long. In spite of fierce onslaughts by the Pompeians, the blockade had held firm, and it had begun to have the effects he had predicted. The towns of Central Greece, for instance, had started to come over to him.

Then, in one day — there was a rush of blood to his head — in one day his plans had been shattered. He controlled himself. Two errors on his own part, he admitted with a sour bitterness in his mouth. He had had two lines of ramparts and ditches down there, six hundred feet apart, leading to the beach south of Pompey's camp. A cross-wall had been started to prevent an assault between them from the sea. He had not seen to it that that cross-wall was completed. The first error.

The second was that when two Gallic chieftains had been proved to have embezzled the pay for the cavalry, he hadn't lopped off their heads. He had merely ordered them to pay back

411

the funds. So they had deserted to Pompey. He deduced now that it was they who had divulged to Pompey and Labienus the lack of that cross-wall. So, this morning at first light, an attack by land and sea had come. The whole of that part of his lines had been captured. Had it not been for Antony hurrying down with troops from the high ground, the defeat would have been complete. As it was, when he himself had arrived from his camp to the north, he had found that Pompey had built an encampment close to the breach in the Caesarian entrenchments.

But then — he shifted his gaze from the breached lines and Pompey's new camp to a former camp directly below him. His own men had used that camp and abandoned it when no longer needed. Later, Pompey had occupied that same camp for a while and had, in turn, left it. Early this afternoon, he had seen Pompey sending a single legion into that abandoned camp.

There was a wood near it. He, Caesar, had seen his chance. Collecting a force of over three legions, and using the wood, he had suddenly assaulted it.

It should have worked, he told himself now. He himself had led the left wing. The legionaries had battered their way in. But the right wing had lost their way among additions made by Pompey. Suddenly there were five Pompeian legions upon them. Then, panic. Except, again, for Antony, the beggars would still be running — and if Pompey had charged, the whole army, scattered over those sixteen miles, his army, would have been swallowed up as if they were so many gobbets of meat. As it was, nearly a thousand legionaries had been killed.

So much for analysis, Caesar told himself. He glanced back at his legates, grouped sombrely behind him. They knew better than to interrupt him. Now, for options.

Risk a battle? Too few men, and their morale was poor. So, get out — fast. Almost four months of work gone down the sewer, he thought bitterly. But, get out. March inland?

He'd have to. Couriers at once, he realized, to the legion and a half in detachments in Central Greece. A courier also to the two legions he had dispatched into Thessaly to intercept the two

412

Pompeian legions marching under Metellus Scipio, Pompey's father-in-law, through Macedonia toward Dyrrachium. First of all, though, get away from here — if he could. When Fortune's wheel is at its nadir, he told himself with a sour smile, it can't go any way but up.

He turned and waved to his legates. They gathered around him.

"We retreat," he said abruptly.

"Must we?"

That was Antony.

"Lucky if we can, with Pompey in pursuit. Then, we march inland."

Someone else cleared his throat and spoke hesitantly:

"If we march inland, doesn't that mean that the Pompeians could transport their army to Italy and seize it?"

That was young Pollio.

"They could," Caesar told him. "But Pompey would have to abandon Scipio, his father-in-law. I don't think he will. Now, for your job, Pollio. Collect the wounded and the baggage. At nightfall, remember, set out. On the dot. The Ninth will march with you."

Pollio saluted. "Understood, Imperator."

"Antony."

"Yes, Imperator."

"You and the other legates get all our men collected here. An hour after midnight lead them out stealthily, except for two legions and the cavalry."

"Those two legions?" Antony asked.

"I will bring them myself. At first light. Drive the men, Antony. We must not, I repeat, must not, let Pompey catch us on the march."

"Yes, Imperator."

At that moment, in front of Pompey's camp Brutus was standing amid a group of nobles. They were watching the Caesarian prisoners from the day's two battles being lined up, hands tied behind their backs.

Brutus was wondering somewhat vaguely what Labienus intended to do with them. By this time he had experienced battle. Not in actual personal combat. Because he had always been awkward in physical co-ordination, he had been put on staff as an aide. Yet the whole thing had produced revulsion in him. Not that he lacked courage; but the groans, the shrieks, the blood, the stench, the sweat, the fear one smelled, the brutal, animal-like reality, were not like what one read about battles.

He glanced at his uncle, Cato. It was Cato, really, who kept him going—Cato and the belief that he, Brutus, was in this war for an ideal—the Roman Republic and freedom. Though sometimes one wondered. His fellow-nobles, like Domitius, quarrelled about precedence, lived in luxury, discussed endlessly what properties and positions they would have when Caesar was killed, that sort of thing. His uncle did not live lavishly. Yet even he was always wrangling about constitutional technicalities.

Labienus was coming out. Brutus turned to look at him. A select group, the Celts who had followed him to Rome, was behind him. Two of them carried a squared-oak chopping-block. They set it down in front of the line of prisoners, over a hundred in all. Two other Celts, big-limbed, fair men, stepped forward with axes. What was going to happen?

Brutus did not have too long to wait. Labienus walked along the line of prisoners, stopping here and there to speak to this or that one. Only when Labienus neared the end of the line closest to him could Brutus hear that he was mocking and sneering at those who had chosen to follow Caesar rather than himself. When he had finished, he returned to the chopping-block, faced the prisoners, and boomed out:

"These men shall know—every man who follows Caesar shall hear — the fate that waits for traitors to the Republic."

He raised his hand. Four of the Celts seized the first of the bound Caesarians, dragged him struggling to the chopping-block, forced him to the ground, head on the block. An axe flashed down. The head bounced on the ground. The Celts dragged the body aside, its neck spouting blood. Four other Celts had the next shrieking prisoner ready. The next head bounced — and then another.

A Stoic must not show emotion. As the blood gushed and the heap of twitching bodies mounted, Brutus stood motionless, feeling somewhat faint, but controlling himself. At his side his uncle Cato spoke in his harsh voice:

"A waste, Labienus, of good fighting material."

Labienus did not reply. Nostrils dilated, eyes with a glint of red in them, he watched. This was his triumph, his revenge. Two or three files over from Cato, Domitius said loudly,

"When Caesar's head bounces there I'll be happy. Not before."

# CHAPTER VIII

I T WAS WEEKS after Caesar's defeat at Dyrrachium. A summer sun was baking Greece and the Aegean Sea. In her camp some thirty miles north of the northeasternmost mouth of the Nile, Cleopatra was storming at Antipater.

"Why don't we attack?" she was saying. She glanced from the open doorway of her tent across the deep-gorged rivulet flowing down to the sea at the camp of Pothinus. "Why sit here like a turtle in its shell?" She stamped her sandal. "I'm ordering you, Antipater. Attack."

"And I won't, Lady," Antipater said equably. He, too, glanced across the rivulet. "The core of that army is the Roman force Gabinius left in Alexandria. Their general, Achillas, is competent."

"A cockadoodle," Cleopatra said. "Struts like a peacock."

"But competent."

"When, then? Tell me."

"When the Nabataean horsemen get here." He glanced at Cleopatra. "When I'm sure we'll win."

"But now that Pompey's beaten Caesar — when Pompey gets here, our chance —"

"Look, Lady," Antipater interrupted. "After Pompey finishes Caesar, he still must reoccupy Italy. Not to mention the three Gauls and Spain. We have months and to spare, Lady."

"I get so tired, waiting," Cleopatra said, pouting.

"I know." Antipater took her arm gently. "We'll win, I promise. Now," he turned her to the tent, "let's relax, shall we?"

As he led Cleopatra into the tent, far to the East, in a garden of her palace on the Palatine, Servilia was wandering about restlessly. She touched a yellow daffodil, and noted that the jonquils were almost ready to bloom.

Her mind could not concentrate on such trivia. She stopped, her eyes unseeing, her ears not hearing the robins calling to one another. Where was Caesar now? There had been nothing since the news of his defeat at Dyrrachium, news that had put Rome and all Italy in turmoil. A recent rumour had reported that he had moved inland in Greece. So, where was he? What would happen to him if he were beaten?

She knew. Death. Yet, if he should win — and that seemed impossible now — what would happen to Brutus, her son — and perhaps his?

War! she thought as she thought so often, what folly!

She wanted to wring her hands. She must not. She was Servilia. She was giving a dinner shortly, she remembered, just as if Mars' hand were not clamped around her heart. Things to do. She turned to leave the garden, her face composed, head high. Ah, let them both be safe! she was crying wordlessly.

As she left the garden, in Thessaly Caesar had just come out from the main gate of his camp, his aides behind him. He glanced first to the east, at the ridge where Pompey's camp sat quiet. So, what to do?

He looked across the plain to the west. The sun was dropping toward the mountains. He reflected that today was by the calendar the eighth of August. He and his army had sat here for days. As he had expected, Pompey had followed him and was now, with Metellus Scipio's two legions joined to his own nine, at full strength. Yet, though he had over twice the numbers of the Caesarians, he had refused to fight. Each day he, Caesar, had let out his men and arranged them in battle formation. Each day, too, Pompey had let out his men. But he had drawn up his line on the ridge close under the protection of the ramparts of his camp, so that no engagement was possible.

Sound strategy, Caesar admitted to himself ruefully. Why risk a battle when he had Caesar's army confined like a buzzing bee in a round-bellied jar? Let Caesar march and countermarch his men in Central Greece until his money and supplies ran out.

What he, Caesar, had to have was a battle. At the moment the morale of his troops was high. When the first town he reached in

417

Thessaly had closed its gates against him, he had assaulted and captured it within three hours, then given it over to his legionaries for rape and plunder. The other towns, like Pharsalus, just south of his camp, had hurried to come over to him. Besides, the wheat in the fields on the plain was ripe, so he had supplies for the time being; and, in addition, ever since his veterans had heard how Labienus had killed their comrades who had been taken prisoner at Dyrrachium, they had been eager for revenge.

But what would happen if supplies ran short; or, more importantly, since it was imminent, when he could no longer pay his troops? He was still a bee buzzing in a jar with the top sealed. A battle was essential; and there were reports that the nobles were assailing Pompey violently for not fighting. So what to do?

Caesar paced slowly back and forth, hands behind his back, considering. He reached a decision, then he summoned his legates.

"Tomorrow we march," he said.

"Where to, Imperator?" Antony asked.

Caesar had the map ready. "Here, to Scotussa," he said. "It outflanks Pompey's camp. Perhaps—just perhaps—a chance for a battle will come."

"If it doesn't?"

Caesar shrugged. "We move again. Sooner or later those nobles may get so tired of it all they'll force Pompey into action." He rolled up the map. "Let's hope for that, gentlemen."


2


Late that same afternoon, in a marquee set up in Pompey's camp by Domitius, a group of nobles were banqueting. The couches and tables stood on fresh-cut turf. Tapestries concealed the walls. Newly gathered flowers rested in baskets. Course after course was brought in on gold and silver dishes. Behind the couches slaves leaned over to keep the goblets filled with Samian wine.

In the place of honour Pompey was reclining, a garland on his

418

head. Beside him was his father-in-law, Metellus Scipio, whom Pompey had appointed co-commander. Next to him was Labienus.

As the candelabra were lit and the dessert was carried in — apples, dates, pastry in varying shapes filled with jellies — and Rhodian wine was poured, Pompey could hear snatches of conversation. Serious drinking was now beginning and, while the cool breeze of evening flowed in through the open front of the marquee, voices rose louder. At one table there was an argument about who was to have which of the palaces of the rebels when they returned to Italy. Close to Pompey, Domitius and Lentulus Spinther were continuing a dispute about which one was to become Pontifex Maximus when Caesar, who held the post, was killed. Metellus Scipio, who was also eager to be high priest, leaned forward to interpose his claim. Soon, Pompey knew, Scipio would be turning to him for his support.

Pompey shifted his position, sick of it all. Down in the main body of the marquee Brutus, too, shifted on his couch. In spite of himself it was being forced upon him that these nobles, the long-time rulers of Rome, cared more for possessions and position than for the Republic. He wished that his uncle Cato were here to tell him that the Republic was all in all, no matter what its supporters were like. But Cato had been left in command at Dyrrachium.

The arguments grew more violent. A voice boomed out, "After Caesar is killed." From a couch near Brutus, Favonius, the imitator of Cato, suddenly stood up.

"Listen to me," he shouted. "Listen." The volume of noise grew less as the nobles, wine-cups in hand, turned to look at Favonius. "There's a country saying," Favonius barked, "first, kill your wild boar; then gut him and divide the pieces." He looked around and snorted. "You — all of you — talking what you'll have when Caesar is dead. Caesar is still alive."

Domitius jumped to his feet. "So, why don't we fight?" he called to Pompey. "Why don't we smash the bastard?"

Pompey pursed his lips, working them in and out. At the back of the marquee a drunken voice called,

"I'll tell you why. Yes, I'll tell you. Because Gnaeus Pompeius Magnus likes to have the nobles of Rome in his saddlebags."

Pompey had realized that this sort of thing was being said. But never so openly as this. He flushed. He was certain that his strategy was sound. On the other hand, even Labienus had said yesterday, "We can beat him any time, Pompeius. Any time."

So, why not?

Pompeius got off his couch deliberately and stood up.

"My battle-plan is already made," he said. "We fight tomorrow."

Tomorrow! For an instant the nobles were hushed, then suddenly they were all on their feet, cheering, shouting, clinking goblets together. Tomorrow! Victory! Then home to their palaces. Home! Pompey raised a hand. They turned to him, abruptly silent, approving.

"The battle-cry is 'Hercules, Ever-Victorious'," Pompey said strongly.

"I'll drink to that!" a voice cried out, high, almost hysterical.

"Yes — yes — Hercules, Ever-Victorious," a hundred voices shouted in unison, goblets raised.

3

It was first light of the next day. The hide tents had been struck. The troops were lining up, preparing to march. As Caesar stood watching them, Volusenus, prefect of his cavalry, galloped in, halted, and cried,

"They're marching out, Imperator!" He waved his arm wildly. "Moving down into the plain. Pompey's army!"

Caesar's chin jerked up. "You're certain?"

Volusenus slipped from his horse and ran over. "I'm certain, Imperator."

Caesar turned to an aide. "Quick! Bring me my scarlet mantle."

Two hours later, his legates and aides around him on a knoll, he sat on Five-Toes and watched the battle-lines form. Pompey,

420

he saw, had rested his right wing on the bank of the Enipeus River, so that it could not be turned. His centre and left extended over the trampled wheat into the plain. Beyond that left wing, massed in bedecked squadrons, was his seven thousand cavalry. Behind them were the archers and the slingers.

He looked at his own army. Like Pompey's it was in three massed lines, except that, since he had only twenty-two thousand legionaries to face Pompey's forty-seven thousand, his three lines were thinner. But they were almost all veterans.

Caesar drew in deep breaths of the clear, scented air of morning. Here all the weeks and months since his crossing of the Rubicon were narrowed down to the hour about to come. Never, he thought, had the sky seemed more blue, the morning sun more like a god. Never, either, had the rose-pink and white of the oleanders along that river seemed more brilliant in colour, or the song of the larks above them so piercingly sweet. Never, for that matter, had the standards and the spear-points above the ranks glinted and sparkled so brightly. Was it because the instant of decision was upon them all? Was it because the vampires of death and agony were hovering?

"Remember, Marcus Brutus is to be taken alive. Alive! Tell your men that again," he told his legates.

No one said anything. Caesar examined his lines once more. They were ready now. He had already given his men the regular exhortation and the battle-cry: "Venus, All-Conquering". That battle-cry had made his men grin and shout cheerful obscenities.

It was good to see their spirits so high. His gaze shifted for the dozenth time to Pompey's battle-formation. He could see his rival's scarlet mantle behind his left wing. His battle-plan was equally obvious. Caesar had only a thousand horsemen, Pompey seven thousand; though, while Caesar's was made up of war-hardened Gauls and Germans, Pompey's cavalry, except for a few squadrons of nobles, consisted of tribal contingents from Macedonia, Thrace, and Asia Minor. Pompey's plan clearly was to sweep Caesar's cavalry from the field and then have the victorious cavalry swing to attack the rear of Caesar's right wing. So, how to meet that danger?

The answer seemed to leap into his mind. He waved his legates to come closer. "Antony, Calvinus, Sulla," he said to the three whom he had put in command of, respectively, his right, centre, and left, "pick me six cohorts from my third line. Move them quietly—quietly, mind you—to the edge of our right wing and have them squat down, out of sight. I will take command of them. Get going."

As they rode off, Caesar turned to Volusenus, his cavalry commander. "Listen carefully," he said. "Charge at the signal. You'll be driven back — weight of numbers. But withdraw in good order. In good order, I repeat, and to your right. Understand?"

"Yes, Imperator."

"Then, watch for the moment. When it comes — charge in."

Volusenus saluted and rode off. Caesar watched the six cohorts moving to his right. When they were hidden in position, he said to the rest of the legates,

"To your posts, gentlemen. When my trumpet sounds, charge. And good luck!"

They, too, rode off. A small bodyguard around him, Caesar cantered Five-Toes to his six cohorts and summoned the centurions to him. He explained what they were to do and added,

"One other thing. Tell your men not to hurl their javelins. Use them as spears. Understand? As spears."

He rode back to the knoll, took one last look around him, and raised his hand. The trumpet shrilled. The bugles and the warhorns answered. The Caesarian lines charged forward. But the Pompeian lines did not. Caesar looked at them, puzzled. The space between the two battle lines was just enough for each line to charge and hurl their javelins. Why did Pompey's men stand still? Was it because a good many were recruits? Or didn't he trust the two legions he had filched from Caesar? Or was he hoping that Caesar's men would be out of breath?

Caesar's men were veterans. Halfway across they halted to get their second wind. When they charged again a wild whoop went up from them. They hurled their javelins. The Pompeians hurled theirs. Then there was the unforgettable rasp of thousands of swords pulled from their scabbards. The two lines met. Into the clean, clear air rose the clang of meeting shields, of swords clashing on swords, and, mingled with those sounds, shouts, groans, and shrieks. The future of Rome and himself was boiled down to this fierce hour, Caesar thought again.

Yet the battle would not be decided there. To Caesar's right the Pompeian and Caesarian cavalry had met in battle-shock. Volusenus' first charge had flung back the foremost enemy squadrons. But the masses behind rallied and charged. As Caesar watched, the cavalry battle became a seemingly confused tangle of wheeling, charging units. Yet Volusenus, though his horsemen were being forced back, was keeping control and withdrawing gradually to the right.

Caesar looked at the infantry. The two lines still struggled like two lovers intertwined. But then he saw the second Pompeian line going in. Caesar had his trumpeter blow two notes. His second line moved into action. As they charged, he observed that the cavalry battle was almost over. He cantered Five-Toes to his concealed fourth line and waited.

Behind his left wing Pompey, riding a roan, was also watching the battle closely. So far, he noted with satisfaction, his infantry was holding. He glanced back at the cavalry engagement. Caesar's horsemen were being forced off the field. Good, he told himself, the plan was working. Victory—soon. He'd have to let them lop off Caesar's head, he reflected. Regrettable. Because of Julia, he thought with a touch of nostalgic sentiment, he would have preferred to spare her father's life. But the nobles wouldn't have it any other way.

"Imperator," an aide said, pointing. "Our legions are giving way."

That line had to hold until his cavalry swept around Caesar's right flank.

"Send in the third line," he ordered. As it charged in and stopped the retreat, Pompey rode to his left and then pulled up. His cavalry had re-formed. Now, with exultant yells they were sweeping around Caesar's right flank. Pompey gripped his bridle-reins tightly. Now into the rear of that right flank — and victory!

But what was that?

The "that" was a line of cohorts rising, it seemed, from nowhere to meet the cavalry. As Pompey sat frozen to his saddle, he saw his horsemen pulling up in confusion as the cohorts charged. Those cohorts were spearing men and horses. Once again it was being proved that cavalry could not meet the onslaught of disciplined heavy-armed infantry. Pompey gripped his bridle-reins more tightly. They could still withdraw and re-form.

At that instant, Caesar's cavalry struck their left flank. Death from the front. Now death on their flank. The Asia Minor contingent was the first to wheel its horses around. In what seemed like an instant, the others followed. Pompey groaned and did not know it. His cavalry, the cavalry he had believed to have won the battle, was galloping in panic toward the horizon. And there was Caesar's fourth line, cutting down the Pompeian archers and slingers whom the cavalry had protected, and swinging in to attack Pompey's left wing. There was a roaring in Pompey's ears.

"Beaten!" that roaring cried. "Beaten."

He did not know it, but in that instant he turned his horse around and galloped toward his camp, his mind frozen, his eyes staring.

Caesar did not see him ride away. He had turned to look at the infantry battle. His two lines were holding the three Pompeian lines, but only just. Now was the moment.

His trumpeter blew three high notes. With a hoarse shout Caesar's fresh third line charged. At the same moment his fourth line completed their onslaught upon the Pompeian left wing.

That wing broke. Then, as Caesar's third line hit them, the whole Pompeian front dissolved. Caesar's veterans were too experienced to allow either resistance or escape. They pounced on the broken enemy like panthers, slicing, slaying, pursuing. As Caesar's legionaries cut down the fleeing Pompeian infantry, Caesar's cavalry, bursting through, was wreaking havoc farther afield on the panic-driven nobles. Thus, a mile from the battle-field, a unit of German cavalry caught up with the fleeing Domitius. A spear-thrust tumbled him to the ground. He rolled over, his gilded helmet and armour glinting in the sun.

"Gold!" he shouted to the spears above him. "A hundred pounds. A thousand."

It was the gold-inlaid armour that fascinated the Germans. The spears thrust downward. Five minutes later, his body stripped, the lifeless eyes of the owner of a hundred thousand Italian acres and of tens of thousands of cows, calves, and bulls stared upward at the noon sky.

Caesar's cavalry continued their ruthless pursuit. Behind them the Pompeian infantry was still being slaughtered, as Caesar's infantry ignored their exhaustion in their determination to finish the job. The main mass was fleeing from the merciless swords toward the camp that, full of confidence, they had left that morning.

In that camp Pompey had been sitting in his tent, bowed forward, in a sort of stupor. The sounds of uproar aroused him. He sat upright and stared around. His tent! How had he got here? Why was nobody else here? Just what, exactly, had happened? Suddenly he recalled the banquet last night. A battle! There was to be a battle today. That was why he was wearing armour. He must get out to his men. A battle! He stood up.

It was at that moment that, frozen in horror, he remembered. His cavalry — running. Beaten.

What had he done then? There was a confused recollection of turning his horse, of wanting a chance to rest, to think, to plan in quiet. Then, nothing.

He sank down on his chair. If he had left in the midst of a battle — the unforgivable sin —

The shouting outside was louder. What did that mean? He must get up, go out, find out. After a moment, he thought. He'd take a moment to rest, to think —

Suddenly there were men in the tent, hands tugging at him.

"Quick, Imperator," a voice was saying. "They're getting into your camp."

"Into my camp!" he said stupidly. "Who?"

"Caesar's men. Come, Imperator."

He let the two aides lead him outside and put him on his horse, his eyes blinking in the bright sunlight. The aides had collected a score and a half of horsemen. As they started toward the rear gate

Pompey came further awake. He pulled up his horse.

"Back," he said hoarsely, trying to turn his steed. "We must defend the camp."

"Too late," one of the aides said, catching the reins and turning the horse back again. "The camp's lost. Lost, Imperator."

Pompey gave up. As he and his escort galloped through the rear gate, behind them the last resistance collapsed. The remains of Pompey's army fled out the rear and side gates, and toward the ridge of hills to the seaward side of the camp, hoping to escape, somehow. With them were Labienus and Metellus Scipio. On the second hill, they and the senior centurions got the fugitives halted.

"Reorganize into centuries and cohorts," Labienus said to a hastily convoked Council of War. "Then, we'll retreat to Larissa." He paused, added, "We'll have time. Caesar's men will be plundering our camp."

But Caesar and his legates had persuaded the legionaries to finish the job, and end the war here and now. Dusk was approaching when, with four legions, Caesar overtook the retreating Pompeians. They took refuge on a hill, washed at the foot by the Enipeus River. When below them they saw Caesar's indefatigable troops cutting off the water supply, the beaten men gave up. A group of centurions came to Labienus.

"We're surrendering," their spokesman said.

Labienus burst into curses. The centurions turned their backs on him. Labienus broke off in mid-curse.

"What now?" Metellus Scipio asked. "Surrender?"

"Never!" Labienus exclaimed with a violent chop of his arm. "Not to Caesar!"

"What then?" Afranius, the general who had been beaten in Spain, inquired, somewhat timidly.

"I have my Celtic horsemen. They know their fate if they're captured; they're the ones who cut off Caesarian heads at Dyrrachium. And the back side of this hill is unguarded."

An hour later he, Scipio, and Afranius were riding westward, their objective the Pompeian fleet at Corcyra. In Labienus' mind was a jumble of thoughts. If Pompeius, that pricked pig's bladder, had not run from the battle—if Caesar had not tricked them with that fourth line — if — if —

He, Labienus, would still prevail over Caesar, he told himself strongly. They still had a navy — and an army in Africa. He clapped a hand on his thigh. Yes, Africa.

# 4

As Labienus continued to ride westward, Caesar came out of the tent which had hastily been put up for him. He yawned and stretched, then drew in lungfuls of fresh air. It was well past midnight. Around him, wrapped in cloaks and sleeping on the ground, were huddled shapes as far as his vision could reach.

His men. And what men! Battle until noon, then pursuit, then the storming of Pompey's camp. Yet when he had called upon them to cut off the retreat of the rest of the defeated army, they had responded. Did any general ever lead better troops?

He did not think so. He turned to look up the hill where the Pompeian fugitives were huddled. He had arranged that they were to surrender in the morning, the terms being that the Pompeians were either to enlist in his army or be demobilized. In the tent behind him he had been working with his aides and with Hirtius, his quartermaster. The reports were that about fifteen thousand Pompeians had been either killed or wounded. Yet, incredibly, he himself had lost only two hundred legionaries and thirty-six centurions killed. Among those centurions, he remembered, was the grizzled veteran, Crastinus. He'd have an individual funeral pyre for him, he decided.

Up there on that hill were, according to the envoys of surrender, roughly twenty-four thousand Pompeians. The rest of Pompey's army would be scattered far and wide.

So he, Caesar, had won, completely. Why, then, was he depressed?

He looked around him again. In the west a crescent moon rode low. In the hills the tiny Athena owls were calling to one another. Somewhere near him a cricket was chirping. So peaceful. Yet, for him, so much to do. Patrols had told him Pompey had ridden to Larissa, that town to the north and east of the battlefield. He must catch up with Pompey, not to kill him but to offer him friendship. It was the diehards who had used Pompey as a tool. Then, there were all the immediate arrangements to make; and he was so weary — so very, very weary. The let-down, he supposed. From somewhere he must summon reserves of strength.

With a long sigh he turned back to the lighted tent. Brutus had not been found yet, he remembered. He'd put Antony on to it in the morning — and morning would soon be here. He bent his head to enter the tent.

## 5

By nightfall of the day after the battle, Caesar had established his headquarters in the town hall of Larissa. Pompey had eluded him. The word was that he had sailed from the mouth of the Peneius to Amphipolis, a hundred and eighty miles to the east. Meanwhile, the enormous amount of plunder from Pompey's camp had been apportioned among the victorious legions. New legions were being formed from those Pompeians who had decided to enlist.

Caesar had already arranged for forces to occupy southern Greece, the Peloponnesus as the Greeks called it. At the moment he was telling Antony that his task would be to lead the main mass of the army back to Italy.

"And don't let Cithaeris distract you too much when you get there," he added.

Antony grinned just as Fadius stepped into the hall and saluted. Caesar leaped to his feet.

"Brutus?" he asked.

"Here, Imperator," Fadius answered and stepped aside. Brutus walked into the hall, a bandage around his head, and halted.

Caesar vaulted the table, ran down the hall, and seized Brutus' hands.

"You're wounded!" he exclaimed.

Brutus wrenched his hands away. "Your prisoner, Gaius Julius Caesar," he said stiffly.

"Not prisoner — guest," Caesar said warmly, and to Fadius, "Bring a physician."

"It's nothing," Brutus said, but staggered a little before he recovered. "Tumbled from my horse," Brutus went on, self-accusingly. "Hit my head on a stone. When I came to, all the fighting was over." He put up his chin. "Tried to make it to the camp — our camp."

Caesar had brought over a chair. "Sit down, lad," he ordered.

Brutus did not want to. But it had been a heavy fall and he was still dizzy — no food, no drink — and his head was aching, fit to split.

"Thank you," Caesar said to Fadius, who had come in with a Greek physician from the town, and then to the physician, "Do a thorough job," and to Antony, "I'll talk to you afterwards."

The physician did a careful examination.

"Nothing too serious," he said finally. "A bath — food — bed-rest, those are the best curatives."

Two hours later, bathed and perfumed, clean tunic and loose dinner robe on, Brutus reclined with Caesar on a couch in the house that Caesar had commandeered. Before them was a cold collation — greens, shrimps, sliced breast of pheasant, hard-boiled eggs with dates, apples and sweets to follow. The wine was quite a decent local one.

Brutus was confused. With him was his mother's lover, the man Cato had trained him to hate. Yet who could have been more kindly, more charming? He could not help noticing either how abstemiously Caesar ate and drank. When one compared him to the nobles in Pompey's camp a couple of nights ago, or when one considered the treatment of the Pompeian prisoners as compared to Labienus and his lopping off of heads . . .

"I love the Roman Republic as much as you," Caesar was saying. "Only its institutions need to be reformed."

Brutus' head was still aching, a dull ache. He strove to bring his thoughts into focus.

"For instance?" he said stiffly.

Caesar picked up a fig and nibbled at it. "You're a philosopher," he said. "You'll remember Heracleitus: 'No one can step into the same river twice'. In other words, ceaseless change is the law for all life. The basic principles of the Republic are sound—government by its citizens and freedom under law. But should there be, Marcus Junius Brutus, a small privileged class—multimillionaires one might call them, with every possible luxury according to their whim — and on the other side tens of thousands living on the dole?"

"No," Brutus agreed.

Caesar took a small sip of wine. "And should that small privileged class rule the Republic with two allied objectives—to keep their power, and to use that power so as to add to their possessions?"

"No."

"Should the provincials be robbed? Should the middle class of Italy founder in billows of debt?"

Brutus raised himself on one elbow. "You intend to cancel all debts?" he asked sharply.

Caesar smiled and shook his head. "A man who works hard to get money or property, honestly, I repeat 'honestly', that man is entitled to keep what he has achieved. One of the greatest of fallacies is, as some Greek Utopians have proclaimed, that all men are born equal in ability. No, the superior man will inevitably be superior in one way or another. Nor should he or anyone have to pay for the living of those who don't or won't work. I've shown, I think, the need for reform. I also think I know what to do."

"For example?" Brutus' voice was still sharp.

Caesar nibbled at a bite of cold pheasant. He leaned closer.

"Stop the plundering of the provinces for one thing. Lower the interest rate for another. For a third get the thousands on the dole working."

"How? There is no free land in Italy."

Caesar glanced at him. "Overseas colonies," he said. "Such as the Gracchi proposed, three-quarters of a century ago. The major point, Brutus, is to offer people work. If they won't work," Caesar shrugged, "they won't eat."

Brutus sank back on the cushions. It seemed logical. He raised his head again.

"How will you get all this done? By the vote of the Senate and the Assemblies?"

Caesar shrugged again. "Too late for that," he said. "A dictatorship. At first, anyway."

Brutus was sitting up. "What will that do to freedom?" he asked, his face flushed.

"If by freedom you mean the freedom of the privileged few to rob, to plunder, to use their money to escape the courts, none of that will hold. But if, Brutus, you mean, as I think you do, freedom under law with due respect to the rights of others and with the freedom to think and say what one likes, that freedom will remain." Caesar smiled wryly. "Did I ever take any action inimical to the poet Catullus when he lampooned me?"

Brutus still sat, thinking. Caesar laid a hand gently on his arm.

"I'll need your advice, Marcus Junius Brutus, when I begin my reforms."

"*My* advice!"

"Is not your family one of the very oldest in the Republic? Does not everyone know that you are in love with freedom? If you will be willing to advise me — Brutus — will you?"

His head was still aching and he felt completely confused.

Caesar went on softly, persuasively, "You're free to go wherever you will, Marcus Brutus. Dare I hope that you will return to Italy?"

Brutus knew by now that he was no soldier.

"Perhaps I will," Brutus said slowly. "Perhaps I will."

An hour later, when Brutus was asleep, Caesar summoned his swiftest courier. He reread the note he had written to Servilia:

"Your son is safe. He is with me now. Soon he will be back with you. My love, as always. Yours, Julius."

He rolled up the note, tied a cord about it, dropped a blob of melted wax on the knot, and pressed his signet-ring on the wax.

"There," he said, handing the roll to the courier. "And here," he picked up another, "written orders for every officer, every official, to speed your way."

"Any other dispatches, Imperator?" the courier said.

"Only this one. As fast as you can, Racilius." He dipped into a bag and pulled out a handful of gold coins. "Don't spare horses, or ships. To the Lady Servilia. Understand?"

The courier saluted. Caesar watched as he hurried down the hall. She'd know soon how much he loved her, he was thinking. Her son — and perhaps, his — safe!

But now —

With a sigh, he reached over to pull a pile of papers to him.

# CHAPTER IX

THE DEFEATED DRINK FROM A BITTER CUP. After his flight Pompey's first stopping-place was in Macedonia at Amphipolis. There the ex-consul Lentulus and the King of Galatia joined him. With their help he collected a few ships and issued a call to all Roman citizens in Greece to take up arms for the Republic, a call that had no effect.

Then he heard that Caesar with his cavalry was galloping to Amphipolis. Hastily weighing anchor, he sailed east to Mytilene, the capital of Lesbos, to take his wife, Cornelia, and his younger son, Sextus, on board. His wife seemed to restore his confidence. Was he not still Pompey the Great? Were there not temples in Asia Minor in which he was worshipped as a god? So why not raise a new army?

The King of Galatia went off to his realm to gather troops. Envoys departed to the cities of Asia Minor. They returned. Smyrna, Ephesus, Lampsacus, all the cities had locked their gates against him; and Caesar was already leading legions toward the Hellespont.

"Why not Syria, then?" Lentulus asked, seeing Pompey slumped back in a chair, shoulders hunched.

Pompey looked up. "Syria?"

"We have garrison troops there," Lentulus pointed out. "Its capital, Antioch, is full of supplies and money. There's Rhodes, too, near by, and Cyprus."

"We'll go to Cyprus," Pompey decided, in one of the fits of energy which these days alternated with bouts of lethargic despair.

From Paphos in Cyprus he sent Lentulus to Rhodes and an envoy, his son's tutor, a persuasive Greek orator, to Antioch. While he awaited their return, he learned that the allied warships

433

from Alexandria, Rhodes, Tyre, and all the Aegean islands and cities, had deserted the Pompeian fleet.

"Rats scurrying to their hidey-holes," Cornelia commented.

Pompey did not answer. He himself had collected close to fifty vessels of varying types. But what had happened to those nobles who had escaped from the battle, and to his stores at Dyrrachium?

A couple of days later, from merchant ships reaching Cyprus, he learned that Cato had evacuated Dyrrachium. Some of the stores had reached Corcyra. But tons of wheat, hundreds of jars of wine, tremendous stocks of war-engines, javelins, arrows, and other arms had been either left behind or looted or burnt. Thirty merchant vessels, too, had had the torch put to them. Then a Council of War had been held at Corcyra.

What had they said about him? Pompey wondered. He did not dare to ask. Instead, he was told that a number of senators, including Cicero, had returned to Italy, but that the main mass of the irreconcilables, led by Labienus, Metellus Scipio, and Cato, had fled to North Africa with a hundred Roman warships and the garrison troops from Greece.

Pompey was pondering this news on the deck of his flagship when both Lentulus and the envoy to Antioch returned. Rhodes would not receive him, he was told. Neither would Antioch. He who had once been fêted — no, worshipped — in Rhodes and Antioch! Pompey turned and stumbled blindly to a chair set up under an awning on the foredeck. He sank into it. He looked so old, so—so beaten, Cornelia thought. In a swift movement, she came over to kneel beside him.

"It will be all right," she said. Putting an arm around his shoulders she gave them a quick squeeze. "All right."

"What are we to do now, Pompeius?" Lentulus asked.

Cornelia looked up. "Why not sail to North Africa?" she asked. "At once?"

How could he face Labienus? Or any of the others? He who had run away from the battle! Pompey shook his head violently.

"Why not?" Lentulus asked.

"Not unless I have an army," Pompey said, not looking up.

Lentulus, a man with a certain amount of sensitivity, understood. He paced the deck a moment or two, thinking; then he stopped and said,

"Egypt!"

Pompey looked up, "Egypt?"

"There's a civil war," Lentulus explained. "Rhodes was full of it. Two armies, thirty miles north of Egypt. One led by Cleopatra, one of the Flute-Player's heirs. The other by the eunuch minister — what's his name? Oh yes, Pothinus — for the boy Ptolemy."

Pompey slumped down in his chair again. "What of it?"

Lentulus took a step toward him. "The real value of that army, Pothinus' army, lies in the soldiers Gabinius left in Egypt years ago. Most of those soldiers served under you, did they not, Gnaeus Pompeius Magnus?"

Pompey was abruptly on his feet, his eyes bright, alive. "They won't have forgotten me, either." He struck his hands together. "Besides, I have a copy of the Flute-Player's will. He asked Rome to assure the carrying out of his last testament. I'll go there as Rome."

"We have no troops," Cornelia objected.

Pompey turned to her. Once again he was Pompey the Great, decisive, in command.

"Troops?" he said. "We'll arm slaves. Give them their freedom. Make the merchants of Cyprus agree. Make them give donations, too." He clapped his hands together again. "See to it, Lentulus. At once."

An army, ready-made, Pompey was thinking. Then, I can sail to North Africa. Or fight in Egypt. Whichever I choose. I can do it. I can still do it.


2


Six mornings later, the two opposing armies of Cleopatra and Pothinus watched the approach of Pompey's little armada with two thousand armed slaves on board. The sun was bright on the

435

sails, hulls, and oars. It was the twenty-eighth of September, Pompey's birthday and the date when, thirteen years before this, he had celebrated his conquest of the East by the most magnificent triumph Rome had ever seen. By the Egyptian calendar reckoning it was over two months earlier; so the day was already hot, and in Egypt itself the inundation from the Nile covered the land.

"I wonder why he's coming?" Cleopatra said, as she looked at the ships.

Antipater shrugged. Both camps knew of Caesar's victory and that Pompey was fleeing from him. "Looking for help, my Queen," Antipater said.

Cleopatra, too, shrugged. "Nobody helps a loser. Now, if it were Caesar out there —"

At the tone of her voice, Antipater glanced at her sharply. The tiny smile he had learned to distrust was curving her full, sensual lips. Well, Caesar was a long way off, he told himself, and turned to look again at Pompey's vessels, now coming about to anchor.

Across the gorge Pothinus, Achillas, and Theodotus, the boy Ptolemy's tutor, had also been watching the approaching ships. "With those ships," Pothinus was saying, "if he made a deal with that bitch over there," he gestured at Cleopatra's camp, "he could land troops in our rear."

"No legionaries," Achillas, the flamboyant, confident leader of the Gabinians and the whole army, said contemptuously. "Freed slaves, that's all he's got."

"They've anchored," Theodotus pointed out. "Look, they're sending a boat to us."

"We're agreed, then, on what action we should take," Pothinus said. "But who?"

"The centurion Septimius," Achillas told him. "His Alexandrine whore has expensive tastes. If you have a bag of gold handy, Pothinus."

"I have."

They watched the boat come closer.

On board the flagship Cornelia, Pompey, and Pompey's son Sextus, watched it, too. In it was Pompey's envoy, the ex-consul

Lentulus. How would he be received? The beach was three hundred yards away, but they could see and hear the boat ground. Lentulus, a tiny figure now, stepped out. He rearranged his toga, then walked forward to a group that advanced to meet him.

"No swords out," young Sextus breathed.

"They seem to be embracing," Cornelia added, straining her eyes.

"See, they're leading him to that pavilion, father," said Sextus.

Pompey let out his breath. "It's going to be all right, I do believe," he said.

They waited. A half-hour later, they saw a group emerge from the pavilion, come down to a pinnace, and step into it. The pinnace was rowed toward them, the half-dozen oars on either side flashing brightly in the sun as they dipped, rose, and dipped again.

"I don't see Lentulus," Pompey observed, peering at the boat as it came closer.

"I don't either," young Sextus agreed.

"There's half a dozen men," Cornelia said. "All in armour. But no Lentulus."

"How's my armour?" Pompey asked. "And my cloak?"

Pompey had put on his best armour, with a general's crest on the gilded helmet.

"Perfect," his wife said. "Let me just straighten that fold." She stepped back. "Just perfect."

At that moment, the boat hove to under Pompey's flagship, and a voice shouted in passable Latin,

"Hail, Gnaeus Pompeius Magnus."

Pompey stepped to the rail to look down. A gorgeously armoured man was standing in the boat, balancing himself carefully as it bobbed against the larger vessel. He saluted.

"Achillas, Commander-in-Chief of the army of Egypt," he said. "Ptolemaios Dionysos, Pharaoh of Egypt, sends his greetings, Gnaeus Pompeius Magnus. He begs you to come to him on shore."

"Greetings, Achillas, Commander-in-Chief of the army of Egypt," Pompey answered stiffly. "Where is my envoy Gnaeus Lentulus Crus, ex-consul?"

"Drinking the cup of friendship with the Ptolemy and his advisers," Achillas answered. He made a wide gesture and almost overbalanced. "They wait to welcome you, O Conqueror of the East," he went on, when he had recovered his footing. "So if you will step into this pinnace — "

He gestured again.

"Don't go!" Cornelia hissed abruptly.

Pompey stood silent, chewing at his nether lip. Another soldier in the boat, the crest of a centurion on his helmet, stood up and saluted.

"You won't remember me, Mighty Conqueror," he called. "But I served under you years and years ago, that year when you swept the pirates from the seas like chaff before a mighty wind."

Pompey took a step forward. "You did?" The centurion saluted again.

"Titus Septimius, Imperator," he said. "At your command, Imperator. All of us Romans there on shore are waiting to salute you, Imperator. Could I, could any of them, ever forget that triumph of thirteen years ago? I marched in that triumph, Imperator."

So they remembered him, those old veterans of his. Pompey's face was flushed, his eyes alight. He straightened his shoulders, remembering — the cheering crowds, the wagons of loot, the captives — and himself in his triumphal chariot, a strong young god in the morning of the world.

"I'll go," he decided.

"Don't!" Cornelia cried, falling at his knees and clasping them. "Please. Don't."

"Your soldiers wait to welcome you, Imperator," Septimus called.

An army to lead, just as he had hoped. Veterans who had not forgotten him. Freeing himself gently from Cornelia, Pompey walked to the rope ladder which had been lowered, and got on it. Hands reached up from the boat to steady him, and two of his

438

bodyguard followed. As Cornelia watched from the rail, Achillas and Septimius helped him down the ladder and to a seat well forward in the pinnace. Sextus edged along the rail to stand beside her. As the boat pulled away, they saw Pompey take off his helmet, run his hand through his greying hair, and turn to Achillas beside him. The two men seemed to be talking with animation. Cornelia let out her breath.

"It seems to be all right, after all," she said.

"Look," young Sextus cried. "Look!"

Cornelia looked. "No!" she screamed. "Oh, no!"

Behind Pompey a man had stood up, sword in hand.

As Cornelia cried again, "No—No!" the sword flashed in the sunlight. The figure of Pompey slumped forward.

"They've cut off his head," Sextus whispered. "His head!"

But his stepmother had fallen in a faint to the deck.

On shore, in front of Cleopatra's pavilion, Antipater remarked drily,

"Well, that settles that problem, doesn't it?"

Cleopatra had watched, incurious. "Didn't you say," she said, "that this Caesar, the one you said could not win, was in close pursuit of that corpse out there?"

Antipater glanced at her even more sharply than before. One could never be quite sure what was going on in that proudly poised head — but, this time, he thought he knew.

"I did," he answered.

Out on the dead Pompey's flagship, Cornelia got to her feet. She brushed away her maids. She looked at the beach once. She turned away.

"Sextus," she said.

"Yes?"

"Up anchors. Away to North Africa. Give the orders, Sextus Pompeius."

# 3

Three days later Caesar stood on the foredeck of his flagship, staring ahead at the wavering line which ought to be the coastline of Egypt. There was a controlled excitement within him. When he had heard that Pompey had sailed from Cyprus, he had deduced that his defeated rival was making for Egypt. So he had hurriedly collected twelve decked warships, ten of them Rhodian, and enough transports to carry two veteran legions. Then he had set out for Alexandria.

"How much farther?" he asked his admiral, Euphranor, a Rhodian.

Euphranor pointed. "That column — see? No, a shade to the left. That's the Pharos."

The Pharos! Caesar thought. One of the seven wonders of the world. Four storeys — almost five hundred feet in height. He stared at the Pharos, at this distance a slim pillar shimmering in the heat.

"I've seen its beam twenty-seven miles out to sea," Euphranor added. "Or farther."

The Pharos, the beckoning finger to the greatest city in the world.

"How much longer?" Caesar asked.

"Three hours," Euphranor replied. "Or more." He gestured. "Those transports, they slow us down."

Caesar knew that he ought to be dictating dispatches. But ahead of him was Alexandria, a city he had never seen, the city built by his boyhood hero, Alexander the Great. He reviewed swiftly in his mind the arrangements made in the seven weeks since his victory. Asia Minor had been occupied by two legions, and Greece had been cleared of the enemy. The fact that the irreconcilables were gathering in North Africa did not worry him. They would be a miserable remnant at best. Meanwhile Antony, Brutus with him, had conveyed his army back to Italy, leaving only the garrison troops in Greece and Macedonia, the two ex-Pompeian legions in Asia Minor, and the two veteran legions with Caesar.

Those two veteran legions, he remembered, had been reduced by battles and sickness to a total of only three thousand, two hundred legionaries. There were auxiliaries, of course, and some eight hundred cavalry on board. Still, it was a small force with which to be approaching the greatest city — over a million souls — in the known Roman world.

Caesar dismissed the twinge of caution. In Asia Minor, all the cities had fawned on him, the victor. Alexandria would be in the same mood. Now, if he found Pompey here, met him as a friend, reassured him, put an end to this deadly struggle of Roman against Roman —

"You can make out the island of the Pharos now," Euphranor said, interrupting his thoughts. "See, it lies broadside to us. The lighthouse is on its eastern tip."

"And a pier with arches, almost a mile long, joins the island of the Pharos to the mainland," Caesar added. He smiled at the look on Euphranor's face. "I've studied the plan of Alexandria a thousand times, friend," he said, as he mopped the sweat from his face.

He turned back to stare ahead again, an almost uncontrollable, boyish eagerness rising in him. Alexander the Great's body lay in a crystal tomb in Alexandria. To look upon the face of that mighty conqueror! To see the "mother" and the "daughter" libraries! Between them, he knew, they held a copy of every known book in the world. And beyond Alexandria — yes, beyond Alexandria — the fabled pyramids, thousands of years old when Rome was but a huddle of thatched huts on the Palatine Hill. Oh yes — Egypt!

By this time his flagship was nearing the great lighthouse. Caesar knew that the pier which linked it with the mainland made two harbours. The one to the west was called in Greek "Eunostos", which meant "Safe Return". The eastern one, which they were approaching, was known as "the Great Harbour". Part way along the eastern promontory, which stretched out a finger to the lighthouse, was the palace of the Ptolemies with its own small harbour as an adjunct to the Great Harbour.

His flagship was furrowing through the entrance to the Great

Harbour. Caesar glanced briefly at the palace rising to his left, terrace on terrace, and then, just as briefly, at the palm-studded avenues behind the Great Harbour. He knew the plan of the city as laid out by Alexander the Great's architects almost three hundred years ago, rectangular and built of stone, lying between the coastline and a long, shallow freshwater lake. But his attention was directed to the Egyptian war-fleet, fifty decked quinquiremes and quadriremes anchored in the Great Harbour. They appeared unmanned — but were they?

"Signal our warships to halt and man for action," he told Euphranor. "Have the transports lay to just outside."

Euphranor gave the signals. Then he pointed.

"See, Imperator. A pinnace from the Royal Harbour. Flying the royal colours."

"Ah," Caesar said. He turned to Fadius, the centurion in charge of his small bodyguard. "Bring your men closer," he ordered. Then, to an aide, "Bring me my consul's toga, and range my lictors behind me."

He waited. The pinnace reached the flagship and hove to. A herald stood up.

"Pothinus, Chief Minister of the Ptolemy. He brings greetings to Gaius Julius Caesar, consul of the Roman Republic."

No mention of Pompey, Caesar thought. He nodded to his chief lictor. The man stepped forward.

"Gaius Julius Caesar, Imperator, consul of the Roman Republic, acknowledges the greetings. He invites Pothinus, Chief Minister of the Ptolemy, to come on board."

"Safe-conduct?" the herald queried.

"Under safe-conduct," the lictor answered.

A rope ladder was lowered. Laboriously, helped from below and aided, at a nod from Caesar, by two of the bodyguard, Pothinus made it to the deck. As he gathered himself together Caesar estimated him — the unwieldy body, the bejewelled fingers and toes, the heavy eyebrows, and, most of all, the shrewd, cunning eyes. Then, he glanced at the others—a Roman centurion, a Greek professor, and several courtiers — who were following Pothinus. His gaze returned to Pothinus. This was the man to watch.

442

"Ptolemaios Neos Dionysos?" he asked, being careful to give the boy's exact title.

"The divine Ptolemy is in bed, ill," Pothinus answered in Greek. He wiped sweat from his forehead. "We have heard of your great victory, Gaius Julius Caesar," he went on, "and we congratulate you. But the Ptolemy has asked me to inquire why the Consul of the Roman Republic has honoured us with his presence," — his gaze shifted to the transports — "and with an armed force."

Still nothing about Pompey. Well he, Caesar, could be indirect, too.

"By the will of the late Ptolemy," he answered, also using Greek, "Egypt was placed under the protection of the Roman Republic. Moreover, the Republic was asked to ensure that the terms of that will were enforced." He paused for an instant. "By those terms," he continued, speaking slowly and deliberately, "two persons, the Princess Cleopatra and the boy Ptolemaios Neos Dionysos, were to be co-heirs and share the throne. But now those two lead armies against each other. Rome cannot permit this violation."

Pothinus' face flushed red. But his voice was still smooth.

"With all due respect to the Roman Republic," he replied, "Egypt can — and will — settle her own problems." He bowed and straightened. "There is no need for the Consul of the Republic to land his troops. If recuperation is needed, you may encamp them outside the walls to the west of the city."

"There is, furthermore," Caesar went on as if Pothinus had not spoken, "the question of the monies — enormous sums — owed by the late Ptolemy to Rome, and, as it happens, to myself."

An enigmatic smile appeared on Pothinus' face. He beckoned behind him. A centurion came forward with a sack. What in Hades was this? Caesar wondered.

"We offer Gaius Julius Caesar a gift greater than any monies Egypt may owe him," Pothinus said. He signalled again. "Behold!"

The centurion up-ended the sack. Out rolled a head, bounced on the deck planks once, twice, thrice, then came to rest at

443

Caesar's feet. Up at him stared the eyes of Pompey, once called "the Great". Caesar heard the involuntary movements and indrawn breaths of his lictors, his aides, his bodyguard. Euphranor choked out an expletive. Caesar himself stood motionless, staring down. Part of his mind told him instantly that this was the best thing that could have happened — Pompey dead but no blood on his, Caesar's, hands. The rest of him was filled by a mounting fury. Pompey had been a Roman, a great Roman. How had these men of a lesser breed dared — actually dared —

He lifted his eyes. He looked at Pothinus.

"Who did this?" he asked so coldly that Pothinus recoiled. Caesar took a step forward. His voice rose a notch. "Who dared? Tell me. Who dared?"

"Safe-conduct," Pothinus babbled. "The word of a Roman. Safe-conduct."

"Who dared?" Caesar's eyes were blazing. Reaching forward, he seized Pothinus by the back of his neck and, for all his weight, shook him almost as a terrier shakes a rat. "Tell me."

"Him!" Pothinus cried, pointing to the centurion. "Him. The man with the sack, Titus Septimius."

Caesar tossed Pothinus away to reel back to the rail, all his chins and bellies jiggling.

"Seize him," he said, pointing to Septimius. "That block, over there."

The lictors seized Septimius. "What the God-damned . . . " he screamed, struggling. "Hell, not *me*!" And then, as he was dragged to the block, "He ordered it." He was pointing at Pothinus. "Him. A bag of gold. Him."

Caesar looked at Pothinus.

"Safe-conduct," he was babbling again, hand at his neck. "Word of a Roman. Safe-conduct."

Safe-conduct once given could not be revoked. Caesar turned away. The lictors were forcing the neck of Septimius, who was still screaming, across the block. An axe flashed, cutting him off in mid-scream. Septimius' head, spraying blood, rolled over to the scuppers. Caesar looked at Pothinus again.

"My troops are landing," he said in savage, measured words. "We will march through Alexandria, fasces in front. So will your

444

people realize that the real ruler here is not you, but Rome. Now," he made a violent gesture, "off with you. Before I forget I promised safe-conduct."

Pothinus almost stumbled off the ladder in his eagerness to get away. Behind him Caesar bent to pick up Pompey's head. He looked at the face a long instant, tenderly.

"Rest in peace, old friend," he said.


# 4


Five weeks later, a small boat, rowed by four Nubians whose tongues had been cut out in their youth, was hugging the shore of the delta. Inland the peasants, worrying about the lowest inundation on record, slept in their mud-brick villages. Ahead the beam of the Pharos flashed out to sea. To its left an illumination in the sky marked Alexandria and its brilliantly lit pleasure resort, Canopus.

"You're gambling your life, Lady," Apollodorus, who was steering, grumbled. "It's still not too late to turn back."

Cleopatra, wrapped in a dark cloak, was leaning over the bow of the boat, watching a creamy line slip away in the darkness on either side of the keel.

"And let Pothinus and my pip-squeak of a brother manoeuvre this Julius Caesar into doing what they want?" she said over her shoulder.

"Think of the guardships at the harbour entrance, Lady. And the sentries at the palace. Better turn back. Wait on events."

"Wait!" Cleopatra said in an intense voice. She turned to face him. "I can no longer pay my troops. My army is dissolving, except for Antipater and his Jews."

"Antipater won't like you slipping away — and he will know by now that you've gone."

"But not where I'm going. Can't you see, Apollodorus? My only hope is to win this Julius Caesar to my side."

"Riots against him in Alexandria — or so we've heard, Lady. Suppose this Roman — "

"This Caesar always wins, doesn't he? Even though everybody—and you, too—thought Pompey would defeat him." She paused and went on almost as if to herself. "And now this man, this one man, rules the world. Power. He has the power."

"What makes you think you can influence him, Lady? Ruthless, we're told. Greedy for money and—"

"I have confidence in me," Cleopatra said, sitting up proudly.

He knew what she meant. He was past the stage of jealousy, or so Apollodorus told himself. Yet it was always a fresh stab to realize—

He cut off the thought. "Then pray to the gods, Lady, that we get there safely." He pointed. "There's Canopus. Next the guardships at the entrance by the Pharos. Soon, Lady, soon, we'll either reach this Caesar, or bob, headless corpses, in the Great Harbour."

At this moment, in the audience hall on the second floor of the palace of the Ptolemies, Caesar was completing a discussion with Pothinus. Five weeks ago, still in a fury at the murder of Pompey, he had landed his troops and marched through the streets of Alexandria with his lictors carrying the fasces in front of him as if entering a conquered city. He had not anticipated the rage of the Alexandrians. This city had never seen a conqueror since Alexander the Great had founded it. Its citizens had gathered in yelling, stone-throwing mobs. The Graeco-Macedonian garrison had even ventured an attack.

The Roman legionaries had put a swift and bloody end to that attack. But the temper of the great city of over a million souls had been so hostile that Caesar had promptly occupied a defensible area—the palace itself, with the Ptolemy and his court in it as hostages, the theatre next to it, the parks surrounding both, and, farther inland, curving around the Great Harbour, the Museum with its zoological gardens and the grounds and buildings of the so-called "Mother Library". He had also sent orders to his legate in Asia Minor to ship him another legion, and to Cleopatra and Achillas to disband their rival armies.

Yet well over a score of his men had been stabbed in the taverns or brothels of Alexandria, and one or two had had a knife slipped into them on the streets in broad daylight.

446

"No more of these killings," he was saying sternly to Pothinus. "Or someone will suffer for it."

Pothinus knew that Caesar knew that Pothinus had agents out stirring up the populace. He twisted his thick lips into an oily smile.

"I will see to it," he said. "Yet it seems to me, Gaius Julius Caesar, Consul of the Roman Republic, that you must have much more important affairs in Rome than the small problems of us Egyptians."

It was true that Caesar was anxious to return to Rome as soon as possible. On the other hand, control of Egypt was vital to Roman mastery in the East. He remembered that as early as seventeen years ago Crassus and he had made an abortive attempt to get permission to take over the country.

"Collect the money Egypt owes the Republic and me, then," he said sharply. He looked at Pothinus, disliking the eunuch intensely. With only two under-strength legions, and that trouble-maker Achillas leading at least twenty thousand men, many of them Roman-trained, he needed to walk carefully. "Also," he went on still more sharply, "those orders I sent for your general, Achillas, and Queen Cleopatra to disband their armies have not been obeyed."

"Let Queen Cleopatra obey first. After that — " Pothinus spread his hands wide. "Trust me, Gaius Julius Caesar, Consul of the Roman Republic. Leave at once, if you wish." He paused, then went on, the hint of a leer on his lips. "As I understand it, in Alexandria your health is none too good. Perhaps, in the climate of Rome — "

He paused again, delicately. Caesar knew what the leer meant. He, Caesar, had tried an Alexandrian woman, then two together, then three. Failure. Nothing. In a palace and a city such as this, the story had spread almost instantaneously, it seemed, and snickeringly. Caesar's cheeks flushed in spite of himself. He had been sitting in his curule chair. He got to his feet.

"Collect the money," he said in his iciest voice. "And be sure of this, Pothinus, Chief Minister of the Ptolemy. I will not leave until I get it and until I have settled this dispute between the

447

Ptolemy and Queen Cleopatra."

He turned on his heel. Pothinus bowed to his back, mockingly, and waddled away to the side door which led to those parts of the palace left by Caesar to the Ptolemy and his court. Caesar looked toward the room behind the audience hall. In it his secretaries were waiting. He turned and walked out to the second-floor terrace. This part of the palace, fronting on the Royal Harbour, had been cleared of Egyptians and occupied by his own aides, officers, and guards. From the terrace, he could see the lights flickering on the ships in the Great Harbour—and to his right the brilliant beam of the Pharos. To the left, when he looked that way, there were the clusters of lamps on the Canopic Avenue and the broad street which at the Soma crossed it at right angles.

There at the Soma he had gazed on the lineaments of Alexander the Great, sitting on a throne within his crystal tomb. Did Alexander's spirit hover there, he wondered now. Did he ever return to gaze on the marvels his architects had wrought, the broad streets, the blazing lights on that avenue which led to the Canopic Gate to the east and the Canopus itself, those lights which some Greek poet, he couldn't remember his name at the moment, had called "the Sun in small change"?

His eyes slid over to the Museum. Fascinating things there, too. That model of an engine propelled by steam, for instance, working parts of copper, invented by a Greek called Hero some two hundred years ago. Could something be made from that to speed up the slow communication by sail or oars? Or of the Egyptian calendar, so much more accurate than the Roman?

So much that could be done, if human life—his life—were not so brief. Caesar drew in a long breath and shifted his glance to the Pharos. Somewhere in that direction was Rome. As soon as he had seized the palace, he had sent a courier to Rome to tell of Pompey's death and also to carry orders to Antony and Balbus to have him, Caesar, appointed Dictator of the Republic for the first day of the coming year. Antony was to be his Master-of-Horse. There had also been a letter to Servilia in answer to her outpouring of gratitude for the safe return of her son, Brutus. In her letter

448

she had told him that, on receipt of the news of his victory at Pharsalus, the Roman mob had torn down the statues of Pompey and set up statues of him, Caesar, the victor.

"You will return to the plaudits of all Rome, my Julius," she had written. "Those senators who stayed neutral will be the foremost to bow at your feet."

So he was now sole master of the Republic and its empire. Yet what if he were impotent, he to whom a woman's arms had always been the supreme reward for achievement?

It wasn't possible, he told himself, staring unseeingly at the bright beam of the Pharos. Not at his age. Not at fifty-four. It was simply because he had been at full stretch, both mental and physical — defeat at Dyrrachium, regrouping, victory at Pharsalus, the pursuit of Pompey, all the multifarious problems, for that matter, that the victory had imposed on him.

Yet these Egyptian women — the nagging memory returned. Beautiful, skilled, eagerly subservient, yet nothing, absolutely nothing —

If one were impotent, what use to stand on the apex of power?

He thrust away the fear. When he met Servilia again, then, perhaps — no, certainly . . .

He heard a challenge down below and peered. A small boat was being beached at the landward end of the pier of the Royal Harbour. A man was getting out, and four other men — Nubians by the look of them — carrying a long, rolled-up bundle, were following him. Caesar saw Fadius, who was in charge down there, step forward. The first man out of the boat was arguing, gesticulating, with Fadius.

Caesar lost interest. Fadius would look after the matter, whatever it was. With a last glance toward Rome, he walked back, somewhat wearily, to the room where his secretaries were waiting. There was the question of Pompey's head, he recalled as he entered the room. He was having it embalmed. Was it wise to return it to Rome for cremation or not? Well, back to work.

A quarter of an hour later, already deep into dictation, he heard a knock at the entrance.

"Who is it?" he called in irritation.

449

"The centurion Titus Fadius."

"Come in, man." He looked at Fadius as he entered and saluted. "What's the trouble?"

"A rug, Imperator. The Greek in charge says it once belonged to Alexander the Great. It's a gift, he says, from the King of the Nabataeans."

The Nabataeans, Caesar thought, sitting back. They controlled, he remembered, one of the principal trade routes to Babylon —and Alexander had died in Babylon. Besides, the Nabataeans could be important allies.

"I'll take a look at it," he decided.

Getting up, he walked into the brightly lit audience hall. The rug, still rolled up, was on the mosaic of the floor. On each side of it stood two Nubians in loincloths. In front, facing Caesar, was a middle-aged, balding Greek, forehead furrowed. Around him, the Nubians, and the rug, Fadius had stationed a half-dozen guards, swords drawn.

"This the rug?" Caesar asked.

The Greek, bowing, began to talk, gesticulating. Caesar interrupted him. It was the name, Alexander the Great, which had brought him out.

"Yes, yes, I've heard," he said impatiently. "Unroll it. Come on, man."

The Greek spoke to the Nubians. Rapidly, working from both sides, they unrolled the rug. In the centre lay a woman, wrapped in a cloak.

"Well!" Caesar said.

The Greek looked at him. Fadius, sword out, stepped between him and Caesar. In one fluid movement, the woman was on her feet. The Greek stepped to one side, Fadius following him, keeping close watch. The woman tossed back her hair—flowing to below her waist, Caesar noted, rich, vital, glossy auburn hair —straightened the circlet on her head so that a golden cobra, the insignia of Egyptian royalty, faced Caesar. She stood there, proudly erect, challenging him.

Caesar had already guessed, but he asked,

"And who are you?"

"Cleopatra, Queen of Egypt," she answered, and let the cloak drop to her feet. A gossamer-thin robe, rosy-pink, clung to her body. Caesar looked, seeing proud, erect breasts, set wide apart and thrusting upward, a slim waist, rounded hips and thighs, rounded yet firm, almost boyish, graceful legs, shapely high-arched feet.

Over and beyond that, one sensed the emanation of a sexuality that was delicate—dainty, he thought, might be the word—and yet was compelling in its impact. Caesar felt the old, the almost forgotten, stirring in his loins.

"And why have you come, Cleopatra, Queen of Egypt?" he asked.

"To put myself under your protection, Gaius Julius Caesar, Consul of the Republic of Rome."

Part of his mind noted that she spoke perfect Latin with no trace of an accent.

"Leave us," he said, not taking his eyes from Cleopatra. "All of you."

Fadius barked an order. His soldiers ushered out the Nubians and the Greek, and neither Cleopatra nor Caesar noted the Greek's backward glance as he left.

"Any other reason why you have come, Cleopatra, Queen of Egypt?" Caesar asked softly.

She put up her chin a little, letting her eyes—hazel with flecks of green, he noted — look directly into his.

"Is that not something for you to discover, Gaius Julius Caesar?" she said.

Impotent! Caesar thought. Not any longer! No!

With a laugh that blended joy and exultation, he stepped forward, swept her up, and, careless of his secretaries, carried her through that room and the next and into his bedroom. Behind him his secretaries quietly gathered their papers and tiptoed away.

# 5

Cleopatra in Caesar's arms all night! The news flashed through the palace. In his section of the wide-ranging buildings Pothinus summoned Theodotus, the tutor of Ptolemy. After a brief discussion, the two hurried into the Ptolemy's room. The Ptolemy was lying at ease among cushions while three Egyptian women and two curly-headed youths practised the intricacies of Alexandrine sexual sport for his delectation, and a third youth served the Ptolemy.

"Out," Pothinus hissed at them. "Out, you whores, you sons of she-goats." He aimed a kick at the nearest bottom, missed, and almost overbalanced. But they all hurried away. The Ptolemy sat up, very much annoyed.

"Bursting in like this!" he exclaimed. "How dare you!"

"Cleopatra!" Theodotus said.

"That bitch. What about her?"

"She's here."

"Here!" The Ptolemy got up. "In the palace? You can't mean that."

"She's here," Pothinus told him. "In Caesar's bed."

"Caesar's bed! Did he screw her? I mean, you said — "

"He screwed her thoroughly," Pothinus answered brutally. "Again and again. For all I know, he's screwing her right now."

"Whore — bitch!" the Ptolemy yelled. He followed with a string of curses and obscenities. Then he quieted down. "By all the demons of the underworld, how did she get here?" He pointed a finger at Pothinus. "Those guard-ships of yours—you said — "

"Heads will bounce," Pothinus answered. "But she's here. That's the fact. The other fact is that, obviously, she's pleased this Caesar."

"She-goat!" the Ptolemy cried. "Bitch in heat! Oh, I could—I could—if I could get my hands on her, the things I'd do. Slice off her breasts, the whore. Stick a knife up her vagina—oh—oh—"

He fell back among the cushions in a tantrum, kicking, screaming, mouthing obscenities. Pothinus and Theodotus let him wear himself out. Then, when he quietened, rubbing the froth from his mouth and sweat from his face, Pothinus held out a sheet of papyrus and a pen.

"Sign this," he said.

The Ptolemy took it. "What is it?"

"An order to Achillas to march the army here."

"To attack?" the Ptolemy asked, signing.

"Of course," Pothinus answered. He rolled up the sheet, tied a string around it, melted a blob of wax in a nearby lamp to put on the knot, then ordered, "Now put your seal on it."

"When do we join Achillas?" the Ptolemy asked, pressing his signet ring into the wax.

"We don't," Theodotus told him.

"Don't?"

"We stay here," Pothinus explained. "Pretend we trust this Caesar. All the while our agents stir up the Alexandrians to join Achillas."

"We'll make this Caesar wish he'd never come here," Theodotus added.

The Ptolemy gave the sealed order to Pothinus. "Promise me one thing."

"What?"

"When we get Cleopatra, you'll turn her over to me."

Pothinus grinned at him. "Gladly."

As Pothinus planned his moves, Cleopatra and Caesar half sat, half reclined on piled cushions in Caesar's bedroom. Bread, wine, and a bowl of figs, dates, and grapes were on a low marble table within easy reach. Caesar was about to put a piece of bread dipped in wine into his mouth when Cleopatra, who was lying on her side next to the wall, reached across him for a date. As she carried it to her lips, he paused. After so many years and so many women, the lovely line of breast, insink of waist, and swelling, rounded hip could still stop his breath.

Impotent? he thought exultantly, putting the bread in his mouth and chewing on it. Toss away that fear. Never had he been more virile, more subtle in the mastering of his partner. At first she had tried to control the love-making. Natural, he supposed now, for this girl-woman who was also a queen, accustomed to dictating to the men she favoured. He had soon shattered that attempt, shuddering her into orgasm after orgasm. He watched her start to eat the date. There was something explicitly sensuous in the way she looked at him, savouring the date, then licking her fingers one by one. Well, if—

"Pass me a napkin," she said.

"Say 'please'," he answered lightly, teasing her.

Her face was mutinous for an instant. Then she smiled. "Please." She took the napkin and, sitting up, began to wipe her fingers. What a picture, he thought, the rich auburn hair falling below her waist, the pink-nippled breasts peeking through at him.

"When are you going to kill them?" she asked, tossing the napkin aside.

"Them?" Caesar asked, frowning.

She looked at him. "Pothinus and Theodotus, of course. By this time, they'll know I've been in your bed."

"Do you mind?"

She laughed, a rich, bubbling laugh. "Of course not. I want them to know." Her face was serious. "By this time, they will be making plots. So you must kill them at once. My brother, too."

"Your husband, I understood."

"As if I'd ever let that pimply-faced brat touch me."

"Why not, shall we say, a reconciliation?"

Cleopatra sat up straighter.

"I won't share Egypt with anyone. Certainly not with him. So have him strangled, Gaius Julius Caesar. Like my father had my elder sister, Berenice, his own daughter mind you, strangled when she tried for the throne."

"What about your younger sister — Arsinöe is her name, I believe?" Caesar asked, testing her.

Cleopatra considered, frowning prettily. "She'd like to be queen. Perhaps it would be better to have her put out of the way, too."

Little savage, Caesar thought. He clasped his hands behind his head.

454

"I'm not having any of them killed."

"What!" she exclaimed, turning to face him.

"Not even Pothinus and Theodotus," Caesar said, stretching. "Not just now, anyway."

She jumped to her feet. "You fool!" she cried, her face contorted with fury. "Worse than a fool, an ass." She stamped her foot, forgetting she had no sandal on. She hopped around on one foot for an instant, "Isis damn it."

Caesar was on his feet, too. "Sit down, Cleopatra," he ordered.

"I won't! I won't!"

He caught her by her upper arms. She tried to break free to strike at him. His grip was too firm. "You're hurting me," she gasped.

Any other man would have let go, would have said he was sorry, would have commiserated with her. This Caesar did not. All he did was to repeat, "Sit down." She looked up into his eyes, those eyes which had been so warm, so tender, so loving. They were stern, icy. She sank back among the cushions.

"Never tell me, Cleopatra, Queen of Egypt," he said, looking down at her, "what to do. Never call me 'fool' either. Think it if you like. Don't say it."

She had not enthralled this man, she thought, looking up at him, not altogether, at least. But she would. Give her time. Oh yes, she would. Meantime —

"Very well," she said, lowering her eyelashes. "I'll remember."

Caesar's face softened. He was recalling that this girl-woman was about the same age as his own daughter, Julia, when he had married her off to Pompey. It was a thought which had crossed his mind in one of the interludes during the night — and, he recognized now, it had seemed to add zest. A degenerate thought, perhaps, but a fact. He sat down on the cushions beside Cleopatra.

"Listen to me, my dear," he said. "I know as well as you that force rules all human affairs. It may be the force of a superior personality or intelligence, or even of a superior talent for in-

455

trigue. In the final issue, however, it comes down to physical force—or the threat of it. For instance, in the case of my enemies in Rome, I tried to use reason. They would have none of it. So, I had to use physical force — violence, if you like. Yet to use physical violence is a sign of weakness."

In spite of herself, Cleopatra was intrigued by that last statement.

"I don't quite know what you mean," she said, looking at him.

"At times the human psyche responds to reasonableness, my dear," Caesar clasped his hands behind his head again and leaned back. "It also responds to justice and to clemency — yes, clemency. When I defeat Romans, that's my policy. Clemency."

Cleopatra sat up again, eyes flashing. "Reasonableness! Justice! Clemency! Do you know what those words, those policies, mean to Pothinus, to Theodotus, to all Alexandrians, all Egyptians for that matter? Weakness, Gaius Julius Caesar. Just weakness! Expect daggers in your back, Gaius Julius Caesar. Appeal to reason! Hah!"

Caesar smiled up at her. "If anyone uses violence against me, he — or they — will get violence back — and more than they bargained for."

"Why not before they start?"

Caesar sat up again. "What if I were to point out to you that I am using your brother—and Pothinus and Theodotus, too—as pawns?"

"Pawns?"

"As long as I hold them here, the Alexandrians may be furious, yet my decrees will be issued in the name of your brother, the Ptolemy — and now of you, too — their legitimate rulers. See?"

"If Achillas and his army — "

"If Achillas marches, it will be a revolt."

This man was more subtle and complex than she had thought. All the more reason, therefore —

She turned to him. "Why waste our time arguing?" she whispered. "Especially, if he" — her exploring fingers found him —

456

"why, yes, he can be. Marvellous!"

Caesar's arms went around her. His lips found her nipples to kiss them, caress them, give them little nips. Such lovely breasts, he was thinking, firm, rounded —

"Let me," she was saying breathlessly. She freed herself. "No, lie back. I know what he'd like. Let me."

Half sitting, Caesar watched the shining hair go lower and lower, felt the lips and mouth caressing until they found him. Oh yes, that was it. He put a hand gently on her head and thrust upward a little. She continued to caress him expertly, delightfully.

"There," she said, "he's ready."

Before he could realize it, she was crouching on the bed, hips raised up, face pressed to the cushions but turned, eyes heavy-lidded, warm, full lips parted to look at him. In an instant, Caesar was on his knees. He looked down at himself. Potent! So potent!

Taking her hips in his hands, he thrust forward gently, ever so gently. Her eyes closed. She moaned softly and moved her hips back to him.

## 6

On that same morning, in Rome, Servilia sat in Brutus' library. He was behind a table, an unrolled book in his hand, which he was pretending to read. Ever since his return she had tried to reach him, but had failed. When she had told him that Caesar had written, hoping to use his, Brutus', advice when he came back to Rome, there had been a brief spark of interest. Then he had gone back to his book.

She looked at him, loving him so much, so very much. She felt certain that she knew the reason for his remoteness. Should she try a desperate gamble? She drew in a deep breath. A late fly, a big one, was buzzing around Brutus' head. He slapped at it.

"I have a certain influence with Caesar," she said. "I, too, will use it for the good of the Republic."

He grunted and unrolled another sheet of the book. That

action made up her mind for her. She stood up.

"I'm Caesar's mistress," she said, her chin up. "You know it. All Rome knows it. But not while your father was alive."

She saw his head jerk up. Yes, that was it.

"Not while your father, Marcus Junius Brutus, was alive," she repeated, not caring about the lie. "You're his son. Understand? His son."

He had jumped to his feet. "Will you swear to that?" he asked, his voice hoarse.

"By all the gods," she answered, thinking in the back of her mind that quite likely it was true. "By any oath you ask."

Not Caesar's bastard, as he had heard people hint, and as Uncle Cato had once said bluntly was probable. No. But Marcus Junius Brutus in reality as well as by name. He came out from behind the table, looking at his mother.

"If that's really true," he began.

She put her chin up a fraction of an inch. "I've said I'll swear to it, haven't I? Yes, Marcus Junius Brutus, you are the descendant of that Marcus Junius Brutus who, centuries ago, gave freedom to the Republic. Be proud of your name, my son."

At last he could love this grey-eyed, dignified woman he had always wanted to love. Caesar's mistress? What did that matter? In Rome every noble matron had a lover — or two — or three.

"Mother!" he exclaimed, and opened his arms. She ran into them. They hugged each other, tightly.

"My son!" she was sobbing. "My son!" And did not know that by her equivocation this morning she had bought a dagger for the future.


## 7


The villa at Tibur in which Antony had installed Cithaeris, since it was on the face of a cliff, was built from the top downward. On this same morning, Antony plunged down its steps. On the third level below the upper entrance he found her. She was having her nipples rouged and her toenails painted. She looked up as he entered.

"What brings you here from Rome?" she asked negligently.

He stared at her, feeling that he could never quite comprehend this woman. Before Caesar at Brundisium, she had been everything a man could want a woman to be. But since his return from Greece with the victorious legions, she had not seemed to care whether she pleased him or not.

"A letter from Caesar," he said.

Caesar — that man who had looked her over as if she were a mare and then dismissed her. Cithaeris looked pointedly past Antony. Just outside was a terrace with splashing fountains. At a still lower level were the gardens—paths, flowers, tall cypresses, and above them a blue but somewhat chill early November sky.

"Bring me a cloak," she said to the girl who was putting rouge on her left nipple. At the same time she gave the command, she was thinking that she was getting somewhat bored with Antony. That Dolabella, now, Cicero's son-in-law — he was handsome, and he seemed to be gaining in power; he could be had.

"I'm moving into Pompey's palace," Antony blurted.

Pompey's palace! That huge one on the keel of the Esquiline. Cithaeris said, "Wait," to the slave-girl and looked at Antony, her eyes focussing for once.

"Pompey's palace?" she asked.

"I'm to rule Rome and Italy until Caesar gets back," Antony told her, grinning. "So Pompey's palace it is. He doesn't need it any more."

Ruler of Rome! Pompey's palace! To think she'd been considering tossing this man overboard!

"Out, all of you," she ordered her maids. They scurried away. "Off with your clothes, stallion," she said, tossing her negligée aside. "We ought to celebrate, ought we not, my stallion?"

Yet even as, a little later, she mounted him, Antony, lying on his back, was preoccupied. He was savouring in his mind the overtures Fulvia, Curio's widow, had made to him last evening, after the news of his accession to power was out. That red-haired bitch, he thought. After him, now that he was important. He'd take her, then toss her aside.

And did not know that when these thoughts reached fruition he would find himself a bull caught in a net.

# 8

In Alexandria it was early afternoon of that same day. Caesar was standing on the second-floor terrace, looking out at the ships in both of the harbours. Within him was a complete relaxation and a great contentment, along with a feeling that if he were asked to move even the pyramids, he could do it.

Rome? He glanced out to sea. Beyond the Pharos were white-caps on the waves. At the moment Rome seemed very far away. Antony, Balbus, and Servilia between them could manage it and Italy. As for the remnants of the Pompeians in Africa, they were like a clump of ripened dandelion heads. A single puff would blow them away. So, he could stay here in Egypt, savour its atmosphere and its wonders as long as he liked. Savour this girl-queen, too, this wonderful, wonderful woman, one who had had the courage to risk what he himself, Caesar, would have risked in her situation — the thought of his attempt to sail single-handed, so to speak, to Brundisium crossed his mind flickeringly — and in whom he had found not only a primitive savagery and a passionate sexuality, but also, he sensed, a quick intelligence and a tremendous ambition. What a team the two of them could make!

The thought brought Servilia to his mind. A wave of tender-ness flooded through him. They had been — were — a team. Servilia was more mature, far wiser, and, he realized, loved him with her whole being. Be realistic, he told himself. Recognize this Cleopatra as an interlude, and, likewise, as a person who intended to use him to advance her own ambitions. She would never know, he thought, that in his turn he would be using her to reach his own objectives.

As if thinking about Cleopatra had summoned her, at that moment she came through the audience-hall to stand beside him. She had on a sky-blue cloak. With a happy sigh she leaned in against him. He put an arm around her.

"I feel so wonderful," she said, resting her head against his shoulder.

460

"I've sent a ship to bring your maids and clothes here," he said.

"Oh, thank you."

"I have news for you, too."

She lifted her head. "Oh? What?"

"Pothinus has sent an order to Achillas to march his army here."

She pulled away against his restraining arm to look up at him. "How do you know that?"

Caesar smiled down at her. "Did you think, Queen of Egypt, that in five weeks I would not find agents to keep me informed?"

"Who?" she demanded.

Caesar shook his head. She tended to forget, she reminded herself, how complex this man was.

"Actually," Caesar went on, "I will execute Pothinus — and Theodotus — when the right time comes. But for a reason, Cleopatra, you will not understand."

"Why, then?"

"Because they murdered Pompey."

She really pulled away from him this time. "But he was your enemy!"

"He was also a friend — and a Roman."

"Roman — what has that to do with it?"

His face was stern. "Egypt must learn — the world must learn — that no one, except a Roman, can kill a Roman and not pay the penalty."

She stared at him. He meant it, she realized, really meant it. Add another wrinkle to his complexity. She relaxed.

"Very well, as long as you kill them," she said. And then, with a swift change of subject: "Have you seen Alexander the Great? His mummy, I mean."

He nodded. She looked straight at him.

"Do you know what I've been thinking?"

He shook his head.

Her face was vivid, alive. "Why should not you, Gaius Julius Caesar, out-Alexander Alexander the Great? March where he marched — and farther?"

461

It was a day-dream he'd once had. Could it be more than a dream?

"With the might of Rome behind you, and you its master," she pressed on. "Use Egypt, my Egypt, as a base. So, why not?"

His imagination was already vaulting further. Settle affairs in Rome first. Destroy the Pompeian remnants in North Africa. Then, turn on the Parthians, the Parthians who had defeated Crassus and captured the eagles of Roman legions. That far, already, he could see as possible.

The eagle look was on his face. She recognized it. How to capture this man, make him hers, she was asking herself. She had achieved part of it this morning. But he was too intelligent to be caught and held by sexuality. And he had ambition—and power, the power she craved.

The answer leaped into her mind. A son by him! A son!

With a little laugh, she came into his arms.

"Must you work this afternoon?"

"Yes," Caesar said, feeling heat in his groin as she delicately but definitely rubbed her pelvis against him.

"He's getting ready," she whispered. "I can soon make him more ready if you want. Remember?"

Why not? Caesar thought abruptly. This was interlude, was it not?

He swung her up into his arms. She twined her arms tight around his neck. He turned to carry her to his bed. And did not guess to what future this impulse was to lead him—and Rome.

# EDITOR'S NOTE

Readers eager to follow the dramatic events of Caesar's career will be glad to know that the narrative continues in a second book, *The Bloodied Toga*, now being completed by Dr. W. G. Hardy for publication in 1979.

## EDITOR'S NOTE

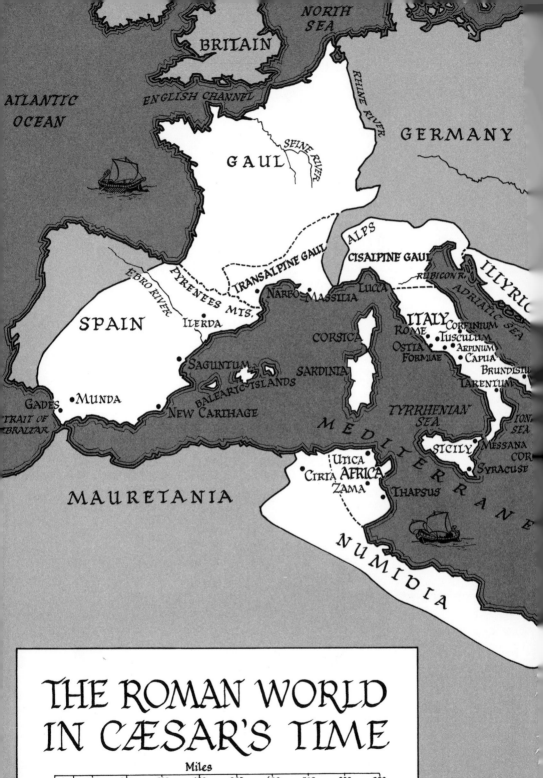

ATLANTIC
OCEAN

NORTH
SEA

BRITAIN

ENGLISH CHANNEL

GERMANY

RHINE RIVER

GAUL

SEINE RIVER

ALPS

TRANSALPINE GAUL

CISALPINE GAUL

ILLYRIC

RUBICON R.

ADRIATIC SEA

EBRO RIVER

PYRENEES MTS.

LUCCA

NARBO

MASSILIA

SPAIN

ILERDA

ITALY

ROME

CORFINIUM

TUSCULUM

OSTIA

ARPINUM

SAGUNTUM

CORSICA

FORMIAE

CAPUA

BRUNDISIUM

SARDINIA

TARENTUM

BALEARIC ISLANDS

GADES

MUNDA

TYRRHENIAN
SEA

ION-
SEA

STRAIT OF
GIBRALTAR

NEW CARTHAGE

SICILY

MESSANA

COR

MEDITERRANE

SYRACUSE

MAURETANIA

UTICA

AFRICA

CIRTA

ZAMA

THAPSUS

NUMIDIA

# THE ROMAN WORLD
# IN CÆSAR'S TIME

Miles

| 0 | 50 | 100 | 200 | 300 | 400 | 500 | 600 | 700 | 800 | 900 |

Kilometers

| 0 | 50 | 100 | 200 | 300 | 400 | 500 | 600 | 700 |